Echoes
of Revolt

Echoes of Revolt:
THE MASSES

1911-1917

Edited by William L. O'Neill

Introduction by Irving Howe

Afterword by Max Eastman

ELEPHANT PAPERBACKS
Ivan R. Dee, Inc., Publisher, Chicago

To Max Eastman

First ELEPHANT PAPERBACK edition published 1989 by Ivan R. Dee, Inc., 1332 North Halsted Street, Chicago 60622. Manufactured in the United States of America.

Library of Congress Cataloging-in-Publication Data
Echoes of Revolt.
    Fiction, art, etc., selected from The Masses.
    Reprint. Originally published: Chicago: Quadrangle Books, 1966.
    Bibliography: p.
    1. Socialism. 2. Socialism in literature. 3. Journalism, Socialist. 4. Socialism and art. 5. Social problems. I. O'Neill, William L. II. Masses (New York, N.Y.)
HX73.E27   1989   335'.3   89-12001
ISBN 0-929587-15-4

To *The Masses*—
With Love and Envy
IRVING HOWE

I
T IS HARD, THESE DAYS, FOR A SOCIALIST WRITER AND EDITOR TO AVOID SOME FEELINGS OF ENVY—TOGETHER, of course, with a large affection—as he looks back upon the life and times of *The Masses*. This delightful magazine draws one back into a happier or at least more innocent world of an earlier American radicalism, in which native moral indignation and European political thought, a flare of cultural exuberance and some sharp-teethed criticism of our social arrangements all came together. And all thrived together. It was a brief joining of political and cultural energies, and in a few years it would come to an end. In a few years, as our culture became more slick and sophisticated, as our dominant politics slid into a devious Wilsonian idealism, and as our radicalism took a disastrous plunge into a peculiarly sterile form of communism, the spirit of *The Masses* would be dead. Then and later, lots of bleary ideologues would come to mourn it, perhaps on the principle that the job of a mourner is to deny that the dead were ever quick.

For a brief time, roughly between 1912 and 1918, *The Masses* became the rallying center—as sometimes also a combination of circus, nursery, and boxing ring—for almost everything that was then alive and irreverent in American culture. In its pages you could find brilliant artists and cartoonists, like John Sloan, Stuart Davis, and Art Young; one of the best journalists in our history, John Reed, a writer full of an indignation against American injustice that was itself utterly American; a shrewd and caustic propagandist like Max Eastman; some gifted writers of fiction, like Sherwood Anderson; and one of the few serious theoretical minds American socialism has produced, William English Walling. All joined in a rumpus of revolt, tearing to shreds the genteel tradition that had been dominant in American culture, poking fun at moral prudishness and literary timidity, mocking the deceits of bourgeois individualism, and preaching a peculiarly uncomplicated version of the class struggle.

There has never been, and probably never will again be, another radical magazine in the U. S. quite like *The Masses,* with its slapdash gathering of energy, youth, hope. Not the *Liberator,* which succeeded *The Masses* but soon took a hand in stirring up the infantile disorders of communism; not the *New Masses* of the thirties, which did corral a good many talented people but exploited them cynically in behalf of Stalinism; not the *Politics* of Dwight Macdonald, in the forties a brilliant magazine but run as a one-man show vulnerable to the eccentricities of that one man; and not, I'm sorry to say, *Dissent,* which in its concern for political reconsideration and its entrapment in the consequences of socialist defeat, looks and sometimes is pretty gloomy by comparison. Nor (to push things a little further) did *The*

Masses succumb to the generational paranoia or the urge to self-righteousness which afflicts the journals of the "New Left" in our day.

Only one magazine in recent cultural history might be said to have exerted an influence or played a role at all comparable to that of *The Masses,* even though in style and tone it was radically different. During the late thirties *Partisan Review* brought together anti-Stalinist Marxism and *avant-garde* culture with a boldness that for a time made it a significant innovating force. It was a much more serious magazine than *The Masses,* and it published literary and intellectual work that seems likely to be of more lasting value than anything *The Masses* offered. But in the years of fascism and Stalinism a left-wing magazine could not possibly aspire to the gaiety of *The Masses,* to say nothing of its innocence. Both *The Masses* and *Partisan Review* did, however, succeed in accomplishing what every magazine expounding a point of view hopes to accomplish: they affected the intellectual temper of their day.

I have spoken of the innocence of *The Masses,* and that seems an inescapable word. For the brimming young men who edited *The Masses* fifty years ago came to their rebellion fresh and unstained, without earlier experiences in frustration and defeat. "The broad purpose of *The Masses,*" wrote John Reed,

is a social one: to everlastingly attack old systems, old morals, old prejudices—the whole weight of outworn thought that dead men have saddled upon us—and to set up new ones in their places. Standing on the common sidewalk, we intend to lunge at spectres—with a rapier rather than a broad-axe, with frankness rather than innuendo. We intend to be arrogant, impertinent, in bad taste, but not vulgar. We will be bound by no one creed or theory of social reform, but will express them all, providing they be radical . . .

The very rhythms of Reed's prose echo the defiance of nineteenth-century American writers, and his words share in our characteristic—our utterly innocent—assumption that the past can simply be eradicated by decision. *The Masses'* editors had not yet fully experienced the decay of European social democracy into a group of stultified party machines. They did not have behind them the agonies and betrayals of Stalinism. Except for Walling, who sensed that politics might not be quite so simple as Reed supposed or Eastman tried to suppose, and who also recognized that the modern state, no matter who ran it, could become an inhumane and ominous power, the writers for *The Masses* usually felt secure in the assumption that they were riding high on the wave of progress and that all would be well, the good society within reach, if only "we" took over the government. They could not anticipate—why should they have?—the traumas of totalitarianism. They did not suppose that American society might reach the strange impasse of "solving" certain of its grosser economic problems while simultaneously throwing up a great many new social and psychological troubles for which no easy solutions seemed immediately at hand. For in socialism they had found a faith militant, not yet flecked by doubt or creased by complication.

Lucky devils, happy comrades! They heard the stirring voice of Eugene Debs, that most compassionate of American voices since Lincoln, and they knew it rang with truth. The old society was dying; the workers grew stronger each day, more self-confident and bound into links of solidarity; revolt crowded the horizon; and socialism was an outcome virtually ordained. I exaggerate a little, of course, since no one can live for any length of time in a state of such unqualified assurance, and the editors of *The Masses,* being men of intelligence, also had their moments of uncertainty. But if I do exaggerate it is to underscore the difference between the radicalism of then and now, at least as it strikes someone caught up with the problems of the "now." Listen to the voice of a *Masses* contributor, the poet Arturo Giovannitti:

The Masses is the recording secretary of the Revolution in the making. It is NOT meant as a foray of unruly truant children trying to sneak into the orchards of literature and art. It is an earnest and living thing, a battle call, a shout of defiance . . .

Sometimes, to be sure. the contributors to *The Masses* did resemble a foray of unruly children trying to sneak into the orchards of literature and art—but what was so dreadful about that? Were not the orchards also for them? By and large, however, they did not think in terms of a conflict between politics and culture, since they could not have imagined, let alone be subjected to, the kind of coarse party dictation that would characterize the Stalinist period. They were the kind of craftsmen who would have contemptuously dismissed any effort by agents of any party to control their work. Nor were they much troubled, as yet, by the problem of "success," which would become so difficult for later generations of writers and artists. They were in the happy situation of being free both from the burden of overwhelming defeat and the temptations of overwhelming success.

I do not wish to imply that *The Masses* people were any the less intelligent than later generations of American intellectuals. What I would stress is that they shared in the sentiments of their age, its characteristic lilt and bravado, quite as we share in the characteristic droop of our age. They regarded themselves as soldiers in an irregular army, which would triumph through the power of truth, the power of beauty, the power of laughter. We can no more fault them for what may now seem their innocence than we should be faulted for what may seem our preoccupation with intellectual doubt and complication.

One of the most attractive sides of *The Masses* tradition was the feeling its writers had toward worldly power. They were not, by and large, tempted to settle into comfort. They did not subject themselves to ideological rites of purification, as many left-wing intellectuals did in the thirties. They did not fret the way younger radicals of the sixties do, from fear of selling or copping out. They felt they had a strong grip on the future and thereby on themselves, and this gave them an easy and quite admirable sense of ease as to their own probity.

For behind them still throbbed the tradition of nineteenth-century American radicalism, the unambiguous nay-saying of Thoreau and the Abolitionists. This tradition implied that the individual person was still able to square off against the authority of the state; it signified a stance—one could not quite speak of it as a politics—of individual defiance and rectitude, little concerned because little involved with the complexities of society. The radicalism of nineteenth-century New England had been a radicalism of individual declaration far more than of collective action; and while Eastman and his friends were indeed connected with a movement, the Socialist party of Debs, in essential spirit they were intellectual freebooters, more concerned with speaking out than speaking to. They swore by Marx, but behind them could still be heard the voices of Thoreau and Wendell Phillips—and it was a good thing.

Except for an occasional piece by Eastman or Walling, not much of the political writing in *The Masses* has worn well over the years. Some of it, I must confess, strikes me as tiresome in its sloganized simplicity. Hard thought, theoretical reflection, and above all the effort to think against the grain of one's predispositions, so that one may discover the weakness of one's views—these were not the characteristics of *The Masses* any more than they were of Debsian socialism.

Now, from the vantage point of distance, one can see the faults in their work. John Reed was a splendid journalist, a master at evoking the aura of a bitter strike, the harshness of a mill town. But does not his Paterson strike reportage also bear the seeds of that somewhat decadent journalism—febrile, fuzzy, insinuating, exploitative—which would reach perfection of a kind during the Popular Front years and later become absorbed into the high-powered and well-paying American newspapers and magazines? Reed could hardly have foreseen all this; he was caught up with literary impulses he could not quite understand or control, and later, in his ultimate doubt or disenchantment with Bolshevism, he paid heavily for his ingenuousness. Eastman was a brilliant polemicist, but he too could not long preserve the innocence of *The Masses*—no one could have. He found that he had to start asking questions of himself, and once you begin doing that you can never be sure the answers will please you. Thus Eastman began his astonishing political career, for a time dropping into the dogmatism of early American communism, then moving, in the late twenties, to the honor and courage of being the first left-wing anti-Stalinist intellectual in this country, and finally becoming a convert to the conservatism of *The Readers Digest*.

[7]

Once you start thinking in such a way that you pose to yourself the questions that your most formidable opponent might, it becomes impossible to sustain the tone of the early *Masses*. Uncertainty breaks the rhythm of laughter; abandoning set convictions ends the security of self-assurance. The innocence of *The Masses* cannot be recaptured, and we should not want it if it could. Perhaps in the future we American radicals, even while retaining our inescapable commitment to problematic thought, may also regain something of the gaiety and confidence of *The Masses*.

Still, as one looks back across the shambles of the intervening decades, it is hard not to envy them: the fierce young Reed making his prose into a lyric of revolt, the handsome young Eastman mediating among a raucus of opinions, the cherubic Art Young drawing his revolutionary cartoons with the other-worldly aplomb of a Bronson Alcott. History cannot be recalled, but in this instance at least, nostalgia seems a part of realism. For who among us, if enabled by some feat of imagination, would not change places with the men of *The Masses* in their days of glory?

Contents

II. THE FREEDOM TO EXPRESS

III. THE CLASS STRUGGLE

IV. MORAL ISSUES

V. WARS IN GENERAL AND THE WAR IN PARTICULAR

The Policy of *The Masses*: An Editor's Reflections
BY MAX EASTMAN   301

Echoes
of Revolt

THE absurdity of defining magazines as "big" or "little" in terms of their circulation becomes obvious when we look back to the periodicals of an earlier generation. So-called "big" magazines like the *World's Work* and the *Woman's Home Companion,* great when the century was young, have vanished without a trace or a tear, while their tiny sisters like *Poetry* and the *Little Review* (the latter for many years now extinct) continue to engage our attention. But of all the "little" magazines which still exercise an influence, few compare with the legendary old *Masses,* the Greenwich Village literary and political journal which flourished briefly in the early 1900's. Although its circulation was never large, it was very big indeed in importance and excitement, and it rang bells worth hearing today.

The Masses was founded in 1911 by Piet Vlag, a bearded Dutchman more interested in cooperatives than in either art or the social revolution. But its real history began late in 1912 when Max Eastman was elected editor. Among the original artists and writers who maintained the magazine during its fitful first year and a half were John Sloan, Art Young, Charles and Alice Beach Winter, Maurice Becker, Louis Untermeyer, Mary Heaton Vorse, Ellis O. Jones, Horatio Winslow, and Inez Hayes Gillmore. In August this group notified Eastman of his appointment by sending him a telegram which read: *You are elected editor of The Masses. No pay.* Thus, in what was to be its characteristically abrupt and off-hand manner, *The Masses* entered a new phase, a phase which was to make it one of the most remarkable ventures in the history of American journalism.

Eastman possessed gifts which made it possible for him to succeed where Vlag and several other editors had failed. Aside from his more strictly editorial talents, he was tall and strikingly handsome, so much so that one admirer, on meeting him for the first time, noted that "he is very much like Apollo must have been both in appearance and in temper. In him you have wisdom without timidity, strength without insolence, and beauty without vanity." More to the point, Eastman had strength of character, tenacity, great charm, a gift for oratory, clarity and grace of literary style, intellectual flexibility, and considerable organizational powers. All of these qualities were to prove indispensable in dealing with the multitude of problems which were to afflict the magazine, not least of which was to be *The Masses* group itself.

The artists and writers who contributed regularly to *The Masses* and who, theoretically at least, shared in its management, were a talented, contentious, colorful lot. Although factions were constantly forming and dissolving, the group was fundamentally divided along functional and ideological lines. The artists and the writers were frequently at odds. The artists professed to resent the fact that the only paid employees were writers; the writers, for their part, were sometimes envious of the artists who, especially at first, received more public attention. A more serious conflict was the perennial art versus propaganda question, which proved a source of countless policy quarrels. Everyone was agreed that *The Masses* should simultaneously promote both art and the social revolution, but when it came to the specifics of executing this principle almost every poem, drawing, or article was in some respect found wanting. In general, the artists tended to favor an art-for-art's-sake policy while the writers were more militantly socialistic.

It was Eastman's task to reconcile the warring factions, synthesize their points of view, deal with a great number of financial and other details, and somehow in the midst of all this produce a magazine modeled on the European satirical journals that was at once both revolutionary and artistic. In a showdown, he could usually count on the support of the key members of the group. The two leading spirits among the artists were Art Young and John Sloan. Young was a great cartoonist who had come to socialism slowly and painfully and was a more fervent socialist for the effort. Although his amiability and generosity made this portly, older man easily the best-loved figure in the group, he could show his teeth when the basic revolutionary quality of the magazine was threatened. Sloan, on the other hand, though also a devoted socialist, represented the interests of the less articulate artists who pressed for greater aesthetic freedom and a purer devotion to art. Periodically, they would revolt against the editorial practice of putting captions under their pictures—an act of desecration they considered the ultimate in left-wing philistinism. Yet in a pinch Eastman could reconcile the divergent views of both artists and marshal their support on his behalf.

In addition to Young and Sloan, Eastman had the backing of John Reed and Louis Untermeyer —and soon also that of Floyd Dell. Dell came to New York from Chicago, where he had edited the Literary Supplement of the *Chicago Evening Post*. An important figure in the Chicago literary renaissance, young Dell relieved Eastman of most of the routine editorial chores and infused *The Masses* with his own passion for a socialist culture. With Dell handling the routine matters and soothing the ruffled feathers of the various outraged factionalists, Eastman was freed to concentrate on policy matters and on the crucial task of raising funds to keep the magazine going. Financial deficits, the permanent economic condition of all unsponsored little magazines, consumed much of Eastman's time, for he had constantly to be on the move, speaking, cajoling, and wheedling groups and individuals for contributions. Although the magazine was a cooperative venture with a fairly wide readership on the liberal left—its average circulation was roughly twelve thousand copies, each of which passed through many hands—the bulk of its survival money was provided by private donors. Among them were the lawyer Samuel Untermeyer, the copper king Adolph Lewisohn, Amos Pinchot, and E. W. Scripps. Few of the editors appreciated the irony of this situation, although Untermeyer believed, apparently half seriously, that the money came from wealthy clubwomen eager to protect themselves against the day of revolution.

The Masses' unique character was shaped at its monthly editorial meetings. Here editors, contributors, friends, and the merely curious attempted to set policy as well as accept or reject manuscripts and drawings. Eastman made the final decisions when agreement could not be reached, but the monthly meetings had a great deal to do with forming the nature and spirit of the group. Written pieces were read aloud, either to applause or catcalls. Comments were frequent, rude, and to the point. Writers and artists struggled for space, and everyone joined in the free-for-alls which erupted from time to time. Eastman mediated when he could and dictated when he had to. Some of his solutions were most ingenious. On one occasion Stuart Davis produced a drawing of two ugly girls intended as a protest against both commercialized glamor and *The Masses'* tendency towards sentimentalized drawings set off by biting captions. Two editors threatened to resign if it was printed in the magazine. Eastman met the challenge by putting Davis' picture on the cover instead of inside the magazine; the two editors' faces were saved, and with Sloan's caption, "Gee Mag, think of us on a magazine cover," Davis' drawing became one of *The Masses'* most memorable covers.

What emerged from this pulling and hauling was a magazine of great vigor and wit. It stood, as Floyd Dell was later to write, for "fun, truth, beauty, realism, freedom, peace, feminism, revolution." Eastman pressed constantly for the greatest possible latitude of taste and politics. He tried to publish anything of interest that did not compromise *The Masses'* revolutionary socialist character. In practice this meant that most contributors on the left were eligible, though Eastman and many of the editors were hostile to anarchism—a feeling reciprocated by the anarchists. Neither the direct-actionists like Emma Goldman nor the more dilettantish philosophical anarchists like Hutchins Hapgood cared much for either Eastman or his magazine.

While *The Masses* took its politics very seriously indeed, it was not for its political theory, propaganda, or reporting that it is best remembered, despite its excellent forays into these fields. A radical, working-class magazine which few workers read would not have had the impact of *The Masses*. The magazine was the most important organ of what Henry F. May, in his book *The End of American Innocence*, has called the Rebellion—the wholesale assault of the younger artists and intellectuals against the American moral and cultural Establishment. For the group which formed around *The Masses* helped to break down the unifying assumptions on which American life then rested and opened the way for revolutionary changes in taste, habits, and morals which have since become a permanent feature of modern life. The movement's names are many—the Revolt against Formalism, the Revolt against the Genteel Tradition, America's Coming of Age—all signifying that the radical intellectuals who came to maturity before the First World War were dissatisfied with the Victorian world of their fathers and yearned for a new world of passion, variety, and freedom. Most of all they wanted freedom: free verse, free art, free love, free milk for babies. Their political radicalism was a corollary of their artistic radicalism. Just as the artists wanted to be free of the academy and the writers of the genteel *Atlantic Monthly,* both groups wanted all men to be free of the crushing drabness and insecurities of industrial society. At bottom they were utopian socialists who hoped for a good society that owed more to William Morris and H. G. Wells than to Karl Marx.

The Masses attracted the men and women of the Rebellion even under Vlag, but when Eastman took over and eliminated its piously reformist overtones, the magazine reached its full stature. Contributions flowed in from the best and brightest minds in America. Besides its open editorial policies, *The Masses* offered, thanks especially to John Sloan, a handsome setting for artists who could see their drawings excellently reproduced on big pages. The captions over which so many battles took place were usually short and pungent, in contrast to the extensive dialogue ornamenting commercial magazine illustrations of the day. *The Masses'* format was exceptionally good, and if it had no money for its contributors, it gave them the pleasure of seeing their best work beautifully produced. Floyd Dell has recently pointed out that there were good reasons for this policy. Artists like to get paid, he said, and "if you can't pay artists, you give their pictures a good display—or you don't get any more pictures from them."

No one can fully appreciate the visual impact of *The Masses* who has not seen an actual copy, for the total effect produced by its size, quality, and composition was far greater than the sum of its parts. The selections in this volume, however, give some idea of the richness and variety of its materials. *The Masses* not only had room for Sherwood Anderson and Carl Sandburg, but militant atheists and pious Christian Socialists as well were thrown together in its pages. It had, as Granville Hicks put it, "the seriousness of strong convictions and the gaiety of great hopes."

Despite the polyglot mixture of ideas and styles, a few themes found expression over and over again in the pages of *The Masses*. Its editors had fairly conservative literary tastes. Floyd Dell put it plainly in a letter to Arthur Davison Ficke when he said: "I believe *The Masses* has the opinion of itself that it cannot be shocked: I know better. And you know that poor old Floyd, with his classical standards still fluttering in the cyclone of modernism, is very capable of it. . . . I do not understand the new ideas about form." One found neither Ezra Pound nor James Joyce in *The Masses*. Amy Lowell was about as *avant garde* as the magazine ever got, and the editors were not above printing curiously awkward material like Sarah Cleghorn's "Comrade Jesus" when it suited their purpose. Some of the fiction was extraordinarily good. Several of Anderson's best *Winesburg* stories appeared in *The Masses,* and John Reed and Floyd Dell, to name only two others, wrote interesting and effective tales for the magazine. Despite their sometimes shocking themes, most of the stories were simple and realistic in style.

The fine drawings which first made *The Masses* famous were also largely realistic. John Sloan, Boardman Robinson, George Bellows, and the other artists created strong, dramatic pictures which put *The Masses* far ahead of any other contemporary magazine. Yet, however effective this style was for cartoons and political sketches—indeed, perhaps no better has ever been devised—as art it hardly represented the crest of the new wave, as represented in such little magazines of the twenties as *Broom* and *Secession* and in the Armory Show of 1913.

The Masses was, as a matter of course, strongly anti-clerical. It liked drawings which pointed up the hypocrisy of Christians, and enjoyed comparing the effete mendacity of modern churchmen with the brawny radicalism of what its editors imagined to be the historical Jesus. Hence, Art Young's cover showing a wall poster with the head of Christ labeled "Comrade Jesus, He stirreth up the Masses," which, predictably, outraged the orthodox. Similarly, prostitutes were depicted as the innocent victims of capitalist greed and brutality, and their essential good-heartedness and generosity were contrasted with the soulless bestiality of their bourgeois creators.

In these ways *The Masses* showed the influence of Greenwich Village, for it was not only a national magazine for the radical intelligentsia but also a local institution reflecting some of the idiosyncrasies of the pre-war Village. Life in Greenwich Village has been written about so extensively that it hardly requires further description. Yet, the colorful antics and bohemian extravagances which so impressed contemporaries, and still dominate many recent accounts, ought not to obscure the fact that the Village was in many respects a genuine community. Some writers have argued that the Rebellion was centered in Greenwich Village simply because it was a cheap and convenient place to live. Economy did have something to do with it in the beginning, but the gathering together of a large group of writers, artists, radical intellectuals, and social workers in one small part of a great city took place in obedience to laws other than those of the marketplace.

Irving Howe, in his biography of Sherwood Anderson, has observed that young writers coming from the small towns of America to the city in search of freedom invariably band together for comfort and fraternity. They end by creating bohemias in the urban wilderness "in the image of those ideal communities for which they had yearned during their original town loneliness." There is abundant evidence to support this thesis, for over and over again in New Orleans, Chicago, and San Francisco the pattern repeated itself. The Village was larger and more durable than other bohemias partly because the others were way stations while New York was the end of the line, and partly because the Village developed a number of institutions which gave cohesion to its scattered cliques. Besides *The Masses,* life in the Village was enriched by the Liberal Club where Villagers gathered to debate among themselves and with outsiders, and which with Polly Holladay's restaurant downstairs formed a community center where dinners, plays, poetry readings, debates, meetings, and parties took place. The Provincetown Players absorbed a large amount of the Village's energy for several years. Other, less stable institutions included various residences, perhaps most prominently Mabel Dodge's famous salon, the only one, as Max Eastman remarked, "ever established by pure will power."

Caroline Ware, who made an intensive study of the social and cultural life of Greenwich Village, stressed the differences between the Village during *The Masses* years and the Village of the 1920's and thirties. Although her work was done in the 1930's, this sophisticated social scientist believes that it is possible to determine the significant differences between the Villagers of the pre-World War I period and the postwar Villagers. The older generation, she argues, was made up of unusually able people with deep political and social interests who developed a reasonably stable and well-integrated community life. They maintained high standards of their own which went hand-in-hand with a warm, tolerant, and creative atmosphere. The postwar Village, on the other hand, was broken up physically by high-cost housing and the intrusion of rapid-transit facilities. The old Villagers, including the teachers and social workers who were the backbone of the community, moved out and a new element with more money and neuroses moved in. The institutions which the old Village had developed were not replaced, and the Rebellion gave way to mere rebelliousness, a change marked, as Miss Ware puts it, by "the disappearance of smoking as an issue, the spread of drinking, and the passing on from free love to homosexuality. . . ."

Caroline Ware's conclusions are supported by the memoirs of the Villagers who nearly all agreed that the Village of *The Masses* years was a small and intimate place. Susan Glaspell, a novelist whose husband, George Cram Cook, founded the Provincetown Players, recalled in *The Road to the Temple* that "you had credit at the little store on the corner, and the coal man too would hang it up if the check hadn't come. I never knew simpler, kinder, or more real people than I have known in Greenwich Village." Mabel Dodge's memories were less genial. "Everybody had a little knowledge or at least a fore-knowledge of all the others," she recalled, "and generally it was rather negative, outré or unsympathetic."

While it was possible for Single-Taxers, Socialists, Anarchists, Syndicalists, and mere Progressives to co-exist more or less happily in the Village, there were certain norms which it was thought tasteless to ignore. Few subjects acquired more significance in those years than sex. Free love was, of course, the ideal, but it was not expected that many would be able to meet its strict demands. The important thing was to recognize the desirability of free love in principle, even if it was beyond you in practice. The shining example of free union at *The Masses* was provided for three years by Floyd Dell. When Dell's informal relationship dissolved, he fell in love again, this time marrying, and proclaimed the superiority of marriage as an institution, insisting that he had always believed in it. Some of his friends and followers were dismayed. It was, Joseph Freeman wrote, "almost as if William Z. Foster had come out openly in favor of private profit. It meant practically the sexual counterrevolution."

In practice free love was not very different from bourgeois love, except that it had the effect of strengthening the position of young women. The feminist thrust had a lot to do with these peculiar sexual standards, which amounted at times to role reversal. Men, especially bohemians, had always been free to philander, but their women paid the price. Free love was supposed to put women on an equal basis with men, since a free relationship of equals would be more durable and satisfying than either a quick, tawdry affair or a traditional marriage with all its grey, authoritarian overtones. In many ways, however, the man was at a disadvantage for, as Hutchins Hapgood noted, "the woman was in full possession of what the man used to regard as his 'rights' and the men, even the most advanced of them, suffered from the woman's full assumption of his old privileges." Some of the most "advanced" men, finding it difficult to accept the new sexual order, came to believe that the whole idea was a mistake. Dell soon decided that this kind of feminism was fundamentally anti-masculine. By encouraging feminism in hopes of form-ing women who would be better companions and playmates, he felt men were really hastening the day when women would be able largely to do without them.

While such themes were frequently expressed in *The Masses* and were important in the formation of the magazine's personality, they were always subordinate to its primary interests—politics and culture. The magazine's history under Eastman can be divided roughly into three periods. The first two years through 1914 were devoted to fun and the class struggle. During this time *The Masses* published brilliant articles on the Paterson silk strike, the Ludlow Massacre, and other campaigns in the class war. The sense of impending revolution pervades all of this material, which now seems to have been written in anticipation of a cosmic event which never occurred and in blessed unawareness of the one that did.

With the opening of the Great War *The Masses* entered its second period. This consisted of the magazine's strenuous effort to adjust to the international collapse of the socialist movement and the com-pletely new environment of a world at war. Most American socialists were initially opposed to participa-tion in the war, but there were degrees of sympathy for the Allies, hatred of the Germans, and confidence in Woodrow Wilson which divided them. As time went on these divisions became sharper, and in 1916 *The Masses* group began to dissolve and reconstitute itself. The long-standing quarrel between art and propaganda finally came to a head, and there were resignations which threatened to destroy the magazine altogether. Appalled by the steadily deteriorating political atmosphere which only increased their escapist tendencies, the bohemian artist faction led by John Sloan, after an unsuccessful attempt to take over the magazine, finally resigned. Boardman Robinson and some of the other veterans stayed on, and the loss of Sloan, Glen Coleman, and Maurice Becker was somewhat repaired by the acquisition of such new artists as Robert Minor and Arthur B. Davies, who helped *The Masses* maintain its high standards.

As America came closer to actual entry into the European war, *The Masses,* like the Left generally, was convulsed over the question of proper strategy. Since most of the editors had been against American support for either the Allies or the Central Powers from the very beginning, they sided with the Socialist party which went down the line for neutrality. The most serious defection as a result of this policy was that of William English Walling. Walling had not only contributed a monthly column to *The Masses* called "The World Wide Battleline" but was one of the leading intellectuals in the Socialist party. The wounds caused by the intraparty struggle over American entry were never healed. Years later Eastman observed bitterly of Walling that he "was so far ahead of his time in those days that hardly anybody noticed him, and he has fallen so far behind now as to be practically invisible. That is one of the peculiar results of a patriotic psychosis masquerading in the dress of a War for Democracy."

The elimination of the more bohemian artists and the pro-war socialists, far from weakening *The Masses,* actually improved it. The remaining editors, strengthened by the addition of new talent and united in their hatred of the Nation in Arms, now brought the magazine to its highest creative pitch. It became, as Eastman was later to write, "a kind of spearhead for the native American resistance to our intervention in the European war." Despite a reduction in size and in the quality of its paper, *The Masses* flamed with rebellion and in the few months of its third phase—total resistance to total war—achieved an uncommon brilliance. In bold defiance of the tightening censorship net and the mounting hysteria of a nation infatuated with belligerency, *The Masses* showed what a few sane men in a world gone mad could do. Its last issues were not simply magnificent attacks on the war hysteria that prevented Wagner from being performed in public and cast the Debs, Goldmans, and pacifists of all persuasions into prison, but represented no less than the last, glorious swan song of the innocent Rebellion. Floyd Dell later wrote that "the 'renaissance' that had been predicted in 1911, that had begun in 1912, was still—fantastically!—going on. The war did not stop it. The war only made it bloom more intensely. And *The Masses* became, against that war background, a thing of more vivid beauty. Pictures and poetry poured in—as if this were the last spark of civilization left in America. And with an incredible joyousness, the spirit of man laughed and sang in its pages."

Soon this lone voice was stilled and the Rebellion was over. In August 1917 *The Masses* lost its mailing privileges, and a few months later the last issue appeared while five of its editors were indicted under the infamous Espionage Act. The two *Masses* trials were drawn out, inconclusive, and controversial. Both ended with hung juries, and the most militant anti-war radicals accused the indicted editors of compromising their position in order to avoid conviction, while for their part the editors insisted they had taken the strongest line possible. Moreover, the Russian Revolution confused the issue even more, with some leftists concluding that the Bolshevik uprising changed the character of the war, making it, at least in part, a fight for the preservation of the social revolution. On these grounds Dell obediently reported for induction when his draft number came up; he served for ten days until it was discovered that he was still under indictment for obstructing the war effort, and he was discharged.

In March 1918, when preparations for the second *Masses* trial were still under way, the group brought out the first issue of the *Liberator.* The *Liberator* resembled *The Masses* in that it had a similar format and much the same personnel. But it differed in a number of important ways. It was entirely owned by Eastman and his sister, and contributors were paid for their work. This gave Eastman greater editorial control than he had previously enjoyed. While the war lasted, the *Liberator* was more circumspect than *The Masses* had been. For this reason John Reed sorrowfully resigned later in the year, although he respected Eastman's belief that it was vital to keep the *Liberator* alive in order to say even a part of what needed to be said. In a few more years the personnel and policies began to change also. Eastman himself resigned and went to Russia in 1922; various editorial combinations, including Joseph Freeman, Mike Gold, Claude McKay, for a brief time Floyd Dell, Robert Minor, and others, maintained the quality of the magazine. But eventually the funds gave out, and in 1924 the magazine was turned over to the Communist party which merged it with two other party publications. The peculiar spirit of Rebellion which had nourished *The Masses* was dead. As Freeman put it: "The tense romantic mood about the social revolution which had animated them [the *Masses* group] from 1912 to 1921 had collapsed."

But in its short life *The Masses* achieved a number of things which make it worth reading today. Not the least valuable of its achievements was joy. The excitement of working on the magazine detailed in the memoirs of its contributors was translated into drawings, poems, sketches, stories, and satirical pieces that are still a pleasure to read. Even taken out of context and stripped of the timeliness which made them more exciting for contemporaries, these items still have the power to move us. They also tell us something about the spirit of their times that we can learn almost nowhere else. Aside from its value as a part of the historical record and as a source of pleasure, however, *The Masses* remains important for the role it played as an agency in the first stirrings of the Revolution in Morals.

We have become more aware in recent years that the dramatic changes in custom and behavior which marked the 1920's were made possible by the altered climate established in the Progressive Era. The short skirts of the Jazz Age seemed less radical when measured against the near nudity of Isadora Duncan, while the Charleston and the Black Bottom evolved from the Bunny Hug and the Tango of an earlier decade. In the same fashion, the overt sexuality of the twenties came after the mood of lofty, romantic, idealistic sensuality with which *The Masses* attacked Victorian taboos. Every Main Street had its rebels who were inspired by *The Masses* and its fellows to live more freely and passionately than their fathers.

Finally, and most importantly, *The Masses* is perhaps the best example in American history of a nearly successful synthesis of poetry and propaganda, politics and art. For *The Masses,* beauty and the revolution were the same thing, or rather parts of the same thing. The Revolution was beautiful and beauty was revolutionary. In practice it was a constant struggle to maintain a balance between the two, and both Eastman and Dell constantly sought finer expressions of revolutionary art. Eastman was more deeply committed to politics than Dell, who was always drawn to literature for its own sake. But Dell devoted more thought to the problem of combining the two and believed that *The Masses* could be the instrument that would inspire a genuinely revolutionary literature.

It is striking proof of the capability of the editors, and of their devotion, that the last issues which came out at the peak of the war hysteria and under the shadow of government suppression offer some of the best examples of art as propaganda. While the ingredients which made the *Masses* experiment so satisfying can hardly be duplicated, the magazine remains a stirring example of what can be accomplished given strong and sensitive editorial direction, a large, talented group of contributors, and a climate of opinion in which anything seems possible. America has traveled a long road since 1917, and *The Masses* continues to remind us what we have lost along the way.

AN UNDERTAKING of this sort inevitably requires the talent and assistance of many people. I am indebted first of all to Quadrangle Books, and especially to Ivan Dee, for the energy, enthusiasm, and skill which have turned an idea into a reality.

For advice and encouragement I am grateful to Professor Lewis Feuer of the University of California, who first brought my attention to the usefulness of an anthology of *The Masses,* to Professor Henry May of the University of California, to Professor Milton Cantor of the University of Massachusetts, and to Professor Joseph Slater of Colgate University.

Floyd Dell's pungent criticism of my introduction was helpful, and while he disagrees with much of what we say about *The Masses,* this volume is in part a tribute to him, for if *The Masses* was great he helped make it so.

Most of all I owe an unrepayable debt to Max Eastman. Without him *The Masses* would not have flowered and this collection would have been impossible. For his thoughtful assistance, patience, courtesy, and great good nature I feel far more gratitude than I can ever put into words. Max Eastman needs no tribute from me; his life and his work are monument enough. But it is my hope that this book will serve as a reminder of what he has contributed to American thought and culture.

Finally, a word of thanks to all those men and women, living and dead, whose wit and genius are here recorded.

WILLIAM L. O'NEILL

A SELECTED BIBLIOGRAPHY

Daniel Aaron, *Writers on the Left,* New York: Harcourt, Brace & World, 1961.

Van Wyck Brooks, *John Sloan: A Painter's Life,* New York: E. P. Dutton, 1955.

Allen Churchill, *The Improper Bohemians,* New York: E. P. Dutton, 1959.

Floyd Dell, *Homecoming,* New York: Farrar & Rinehart, 1933.

————, *Intellectual Vagabondage,* New York: George H. Doran, 1962.

Max Eastman, *Art and the Life of Action,* New York: Alfred A. Knopf, 1934.

————, *Enjoyment of Living,* New York: Harper & Bros., 1948.

————, *Heroes I Have Known,* New York: Simon & Schuster, 1942.

————, *Love and Revolution: My Journey Through an Epoch,* New York: Random House, 1964.

————, *Venture,* New York: Albert & Charles Boni, 1927.

Joseph Freeman, *An American Testament,* New York: Farrar & Rinehart, 1936.

Susan Glaspell, *The Road to the Temple,* New York: Frederick Stokes, 1927.

Emma Goldman, *Living My Life,* New York: Alfred A. Knopf, 1931.

Hutchins Hapgood, *A Victorian in the Modern World,* New York: Harcourt, Brace, 1939.

Granville Hicks, *John Reed: The Making of a Revolutionary,* New York: Macmillan, 1936.

Irving Howe, *Sherwood Anderson,* New York: William Sloane, 1951.

Mabel Dodge Luhan, *Movers and Shakers,* New York: Harcourt, Brace, 1936.

Henry F. May, *The End of American Innocence,* New York: Alfred A. Knopf, 1959.

Albert Parry, *Garrets and Pretenders,* New York: Dover, 1960.

George T. Tanselle, *Faun at the Barricades: The Life and Work of Floyd Dell.* Unpublished Ph.D. dissertation, Northwestern University, 1959.

Louis Untermeyer, *From Another World,* New York: Harcourt, Brace, 1939.

Mary Heaton Vorse, *A Footnote to Folly,* New York: Farrar & Rinehart, 1935.

Caroline Ware, *Greenwich Village, 1920-1930,* Boston: Houghton Mifflin, 1935.

Art Young, *Art Young: His Life and Times,* New York: Sheridan House, 1939.

I
Matters
of Policy

THE MASSES' revolutionary eclecticism was not easily defined. Everyone connected with the magazine happily spent endless hours wondering exactly what they stood for, and what offerings were consistent with their principles. For the editors these were more than academic questions, but the basic policy statement which Eastman wrote in his first editorial was adhered to more or less faithfully throughout the life of the magazine. As the items in this section indicate, there were several crucial differences between *The Masses* and other periodicals on the left. For one thing it was, as the masthead boldly declared, "A revolutionary and not a reform magazine." This statement alone excluded most American socialists, who were closer to the progressives of their time than to the ardent radicals of *The Masses*.

An allied distinction was *The Masses'* support of the sexual revolution which similarly repelled conservative socialists like Paul Douglas. If in retrospect Douglas' use of the word "nastiness" to describe what the magazine was encouraging hardly seems appropriate, it surely reflected the feelings of most Americans who thought themselves radical. It took substantially less daring to attack the profit system than the marriage system. In no other area was *The Masses* more ahead of its time than in its treatment of sex. The mere fact that they found Comstockery absurd suggested the distance between the editors and most of their contemporaries, for to see what was absurd about something so delicate and fraught with anxious consequences as sexual censorship required a point of view light years removed from the moral earnestness of the Progressive Era. Most feminists, reformers, and orthodox socialists wanted to eliminate not only prostitution but dance halls, cheap romances, and anything else which lowered the sexual threshold. A magazine which held that sex of itself was a good thing, and which regarded the nude human body as the most beautiful product of the material universe, clearly had nothing to say to them.

The Masses' viewpoint antagonized not only those politically to the right but also the hard left as well. *The Masses* may have seen the social revolution and the sexual revolution as inseparable, but real revolutionists like the Wobblies and the Anarchists did not. The connection between undraped females and the good society remained obscure to them, and even avowed enemies of marriage and the family like Emma Goldman had no room in their austere philosophies for the playfulness and sheer good spirits of *The Masses*. The essential prudishness underneath the formal libertarianism of the revolutionary left foreshadowed what would happen when professional revolutionaries actually came to power. The kind of mentality which views sex as just another biological function to be rationalized and efficiently administered is more likely to create a Ministry of Sex than to unleash the creative energies of the human libido.

Another important distinction between *The Masses* and the other left periodicals was a special delicacy of perception and fineness of balance which is so rare as to be almost non-existent in the annals of political journalism. It was equaled in its own time only by the *New Republic,* but *The Masses* was more faithful to its insights than the *NR*, as a comparison of their respective wartime issues demonstrates. (On this point, see Christopher Lasch's splendid chapter on the *New Republic* and the war in his book, *The New Radicalism in America.*) William English Walling's "Class Struggle Within the Working Class" not only suggests how good the prewar Walling could be, but exemplifies the analytic deftness which *The Masses* at its best called up. For instance, everyone who looked to the labor movement for leadership often was disappointed, and a variety of explanations were advanced to explain why the trade unions were so reluctant to perform their historic mission. But Walling was almost alone in seeing that much of the confusion came from the inability of labor's friends to see that the ownership of an "exceptional training or education acts precisely like the ownership of capital." Walling's point was not only true and acute but remains even today crucial to any appreciation of the dynamics of the modern American labor movement.

Equally impressive was *The Masses'* surefootedness among a welter of clashing tendencies, tactics, and ideologies. That the glorious revolution did not come to pass in America was hardly *The Masses'* fault, for it did its utmost to steer a course between the two extremes of hopeless utopianism and crass expediency which flanked the currents of radical change. It was aware of the pedestrian inadequacies of the Socialist party, yet at the same time it realized that no other practical vehicle for the revolution existed in America. It appreciated the nobility of the anarchist vision, but it did not sentimentalize or linger over doctrines which bore little relationship to the real world in which revolutions were won or lost.

We can see now that the failure of *The Masses* was not a failure of tactics or strategy on its editors' part but resulted from the larger failure of the revolutionary ideal itself. If one believed that a social revolution was both possible and desirable, then the atmosphere which *The Masses* encouraged became a necessary condition of the good society. There was, however, no way of knowing in 1917 that the revolution in America was going to be technological rather than social. Today the controversies between possibilists and impossibilists, dual and single unionists, anarchists and social democrats seem trivial and unreal. Yet if the social revolution had been accomplished, the answers to these questions would have shaped the world in which we live.

Thus, for all its gaiety *The Masses* took serious questions seriously. Its editors were not frivolous bohemians, as later critics have sometimes charged, but men and women who were responsibly involved with what they thought were the most urgent matters confronting society. They were betrayed, not by their spirits or whimsical inclinations, but by History which destroyed their frame of reference and made the objects of their concern seem fanciful and unreal.

Editing a Radical Magazine

[*From time to time the editors made formal policy statements which indicated the kinds of problems they were most conscious of, as well the goals they were attempting to achieve.*]

MAX EASTMAN
Editorial Notice

We plan a radical change of policy for THE MASSES, and we appeal to our subscribers and contributors to help us put it through. We appeal to everybody who reads this notice to consider the proposition it makes, and co-operate with us if he can.

We are going to make THE MASSES a *popular* Socialist magazine—a magazine of pictures and lively writing.

Humorous, serious, illustrative and decorative pictures of a stimulating kind. There are no magazines in America which measure up in radical art and freedom of expression to the foreign

satirical journals. We think we can produce one, and we have on our staff eight of the best known artists and illustrators in the country ready to contribute to it their most individual work. Their names appear upon the opposite page, and you are at liberty to write to them in regard to their interest in this venture. We shall produce with the best technique the best magazine pictures at command in New York.

But we go beyond this. For with that pictorial policy we combine a literary policy equally radical and definite. We are a Socialist magazine. We shall print every month a page of illustrated editorials reflecting life as a whole from a Socialist standpoint, besides Horatio Winslow's page on "The Way You Look at It." In our contributed columns we shall incline towards literature of especial interest to Socialists, but we shall be hospitable to free and spirited expressions of every kind—in fiction, satire, poetry and essay. Only we shall no longer compete in any degree with the more heavy and academic reviews. We shall tune our reading matter up to the key of our pictures as fast as we can.

Observe that we do not enter the field of any Socialist or other magazine now published, or to be published. We shall have no further part in the factional disputes within the Socialist Party; we are opposed to the dogmatic spirit which creates and sustains these disputes. Our appeal will be to the masses, both Socialist and non-Socialist, with entertainment, education, and the livelier kinds of propaganda. —December 1912

Editorial Note

[*This statement came in the middle of an editorial note in the second issue produced under Eastman's direction. It was suggested by John Reed, but its phrasing was Eastman's. Thereafter it appeared on the masthead of each issue.*]

A revolutionary and not a reform magazine; a magazine with no dividends to pay; a free magazine; frank, arrogant, impertinent, searching for the true causes; a magazine directed against rigidity and dogma wherever it is found; printing what is too naked or true for a moneymaking press; a magazine whose final policy is to do as it pleases and conciliate nobody, not even its readers—there is room for this publication in America.

—January 1913

MAX EASTMAN
Currency

The first question of editorial policy that rose in my mind after we launched this magazine, was the question whether I should know everything or not. From the time Moses published the Ten Commandments it has been the custom of all editors to know everything. It used to be the custom of a whole lot of people to know everything—prophets, saints, doctors, astrologers, philosophers, midwives, medicine men—it was quite a common profession. But since the world began to enlarge (and mankind dwindle) about the time of Copernicus or Francis Bacon, this custom has died out. Everybody has gone in for a specialty. And the only people that can still be relied upon to know everything are editors.

Now it seemed to me that this fact offered an opportunity both to distinguish oneself and to save labor—two well-nigh universal objects of

desire. And so, after deliberating the matter with my confreres, I decided that I would endeavor to maintain a little editorial ignorance.

This, in the face of all precedent and public expectation, has proven difficult, requiring constant vigilance, but I believe I have so far succeeded. And I attribute my success mainly to the fact that I did not undertake too much, I did not try to make my ignorance cover too large an area. I decided at the outset that about one topic would be all an editor could maintain an absolutely virgin mind upon, and this topic should be an easy one—easy, that is, to insulate oneself against.

I chose the topic of Currency. It is a topic about which a Socialist editor would naturally learn little through experience or actual contact. And it is also a topic about which one can read whatever may fall under his eyes without danger of any accidental understanding. Upon this propitious subject-matter, therefore, relying on the assistance of my friends, I have established the first authentic example of editorial ignorance—little enough in itself, but an innovation which I believe will grow and expand until some day it covers the earth with its fruits of candor and clear thinking.

—August 1913

MAX EASTMAN
Editorial Policy

[*With three years experience under his belt, Eastman again addressed himself to the problems of making policy for a magazine like* The Masses.]

There is a limit to one's desire to be "understood." One desires to have his mood felt. But points of misunderstanding arise between THE MASSES and some of its readers, which hinder a possible concord of feeling. For instance, a correspondent objects to our "tone of perpetual protest and rebellion."

"Isn't there anything all right?" he asks. "For Heaven's sake show us a pretty woodland scene or tell us a happy story. Life isn't all sweat and struggle."

Well—we would be glad to publish happy stories and woodland scenery in THE MASSES if we had plenty of room, and money to pay for them. As it is, we do not pretend to reflect the whole of life. We do not imagine THE MASSES to be the only thing you read in a month. It is a part of what you read, a part of life reflected, a part of American journalism, and—if we may explain—a very definite part.

It is the part that doesn't pay.

Now, if you would remember this—remember that nobody was ever paid a cent for any paragraph or picture that appeared in THE MASSES— you would begin to enter the mood of understanding it. Artists and writers, like human beings, want to live and have a good time occasionally, and for that reason they do not automatically give away what they can sell for a fair price. Indeed there is no reason for giving things to THE MASSES, which would attain a wider circulation in a magazine that paid for them. THE MASSES exists to publish what commercial magazines will not pay for, and will not publish. It cannot, therefore, cover the whole range of what has value in current literature and art. It tends to cover the range of what has value without having commercial value.

Woodland scenery (with nymphs) is worth several hundred dollars a yard, and optimistic stories retail in New York at five cents a word. *Life* buys cupids by the pound. Those things are "economic goods." They are staples. Pictures of girls in bathing suits with their skin slippery from the water, are standard coin in the magazine realm. And we do not deny that all these things are a part of the routine enjoyment of life; we feel that they are adequately advertised and distributed by the commercial magazines. Our function is supplementary. We come around afterwards, and offer you the goods whose value is too peculiar, or too new, or too subtle, or too high, or too naked, or too displeasing to the ruling class, to make its way financially in competition with slippery girls in tights, and tinted cupids, and happy stories of love.

And if you don't want these supplementary goods that we offer at all—why, don't subscribe! None of us are depending on you—we get our living elsewhere.

Mr. R. M. Little, the general secretary of the Society for Organizing Charity in Philadelphia, is one who doesn't want our wares, and he writes us a perfectly acceptable letter about it.

Dear Sirs:

I write to utter a protest against the blasphemous articles published in THE MASSES for September. I have never read coarser and lower toned articles than the ones "To Billy Sunday" by Carl Sandberg, and "Heavenly Discourse" by Charles Erskine Scott Wood. Such articles make your paper too indecent and outrageous to touch. *Cancel my subscription at once.* Very truly,

R. M. LITTLE,
General Secretary.

We like a letter like that. It doesn't leave any points in dispute. It doesn't give us that troubled feeling so many letters do, that we have failed to convey our message to someone who might have received it. And then also we are relieved to think that Mr. Little will not be troubled either—as maybe he was before. He will simply never look at us again. That is one of the great superiorities of writing over talking. If you talk out loud, everybody within range of your voice is compelled to hear you, but when you write, you can be perfectly sure that no one who is not really attracted to what you say, will read you through to the end.

On August 23rd there came to our desk two of these letters which leave no doubt or troubled feeling in their wake. I quote the essential paragraph of each.

Just read some of THE MASSES, it should be spelled *Asses*—Foul and filthy—Why don't you cut it out?— Good men and women should fight everything that emphasizes vileness—you cannot find inspiration in a sewer nor can you touch filth, physically or mentally without being contaminated. K. C. G.

I have bought and watched THE MASSES since it began. It is like a ray of light when one who loves his kind becomes discouraged. I often wish I were rich, so that I could give money to it. However, the years have taught me that simply to get the word into print to a few thousands is all money can do for propaganda. C. A. W.

Those two letters are typical of our correspondence. It is full of that violent contrast which assured the editors that they are publishing something.

Here are two more communications of the summer:

Dear Sirs:

Congratulations to you artists! You are publishing the only drawings comparable in truth and vividness of line to the famous satirical magazines of France and Germany. Your letter-press is mostly pure tommyrot. Your editor has few wise words to say: But here's luck to the first magazine of art in America!

Yours,
Emery Stoughton.

Dear Sir:

I oil up my little typewriter for the purpose of registering a gentle kick. In the name of all that's unholy where does the art editor get the junk he uses for cover designs and distributes thru the otherwise immaculate pages of THE MASSES? "Otherwise immaculate" is not written with irony, sarcasm or double meaning. The written matter in THE MASSES is a model of lucid concise English and gives pleasure to and cultivates the tastes of the readers. On the other hand I repeat, what in God's name do the illustrations mean? They turn the stomach. For example, in the July number you print a crude drawing showing three ships on an inky ocean. The title was "Munitions of War for Europe" or something to that effect. What is illustrated that needs illustration in this sketch? It might just as well have been entitled "Bibles for China" so little does it illustrate the title given. Meaningless sketches, however, can be endured, but meaningless sketches combined with gruesomeness and repulsiveness insult both the eye and the intelligence and give just cause for protest.

Hoping you are the same, Yours truly,
CHANNING S. BARKER.

All those letters leave us happy.

But there is another kind of letter we receive, which makes us think there is something the matter with language, or something the matter with pencils and paper. We want to call the writer up on the telephone, and make an appointment for a companionable parley on the question of life's values. Here is a man who lives in Bethesda, Maryland (whatever that is), and he writes a letter that almost makes us cry.

Editor Masses,
    Dear Friend:
I am in receipt of postal card asking for sub to THE MASSES. I am sorry I cannot comply with your request. I did subscribe from one of your agents in March, more out of sympathy for his economic condition, but as for appreciating THE MASSES I must frankly confess I don't. You may mean well all right, but THE MASSES is too crude for me, I am some crude myself but your paper is too much for me. Perhaps I don't catch the ideas right that are attempted in some of your cartoons. One I remember entitled "putting the best foot (or leg) forward," I failed to get the sense of it, other than one of sensual brutality. I may be wrong. Another I remember, a big fat fellow and something about decency was repulsive. The really good thing was that strike-breaking cartoon. Anyhow THE MASSES of the people are crude and brutish enough without having to be pandered to by such crude stuff as we find in THE MASSES. I do not think it of you yourself, Mr. Editor. I believe you are refined and artistic and maybe you think it necessary to produce such a magazine as THE MASSES. But is it? You will please excuse me but I cannot push THE MASSES.
    Yours Fraternally,
        H. HENDERSON.
Bethesda, Md., Aug. 7th, '15.

Now what can you say to a man who gently avers that he believes you are "refined and artistic," after all the crude and repulsive horrors you have inflicted on him, and seems really sorry you did it, because he would like to give you a dollar just out of the kindness of his soul, if you could only be a little more decent! A letter like that is unsettling.

Here is another of the same kind from Riverside, California:

Dear Sir:
Your postal card asking me to secure a friend as a subscriber to THE MASSES has been forwarded to me here.

After reading an article in one of your last numbers purporting to be dialogue between God and Jesus Christ, I can not refrain from entering my protest against a spirit which to me is blasphemous. Is it a necessary part of your propaganda to cause many of your readers pain in handling religious feelings thus? Many of us who are Christians can stand for the Church being made a target of abuse but we feel that the line should be drawn somewhere.

I should like on my return to New York in the fall to drop in your office some time and have a word or two with Mr. Eastman or some of your members of the staff and state my standpoint as a subscriber.

I do not write this for publication at all—simply for your information. That article left a bad taste in my mouth: so I am not answering your postal request to find another subscriber with enthusiasm. You say in it "the magazine is more yours than ours"—hence I take this liberty of making my sentiment known.

Keep hammering away at the failure of us who profess faith in the Lord Jesus Christ—we need it: we must never think we are following his ideals as closely as smug complacency suggests. But please do not serve up in your columns more of such articles as that to which I have referred, which alienate without benefiting—and which are in bad taste, I firmly believe.

Such a letter one can hardly answer at all, so remote is its view-point, and yet so warm its good will. It is as if a being from some other planetary system should write in, asking why we assume that every heavy thing drops to the earth. We wonder how this being who lives under the Lord Jesus as an anthropomorphic God, ever wandered into the orbit of THE MASSES—and yet, now that he is there, we would like to hold his interest and faith, for he evidently has a little faith in us.

And perhaps there is some ground for it. We believe in Jesus. We believe that he lived and died laboring and fighting, in a noble atmosphere of disreputability, for the welfare and liberty of man. To us his memory is the memory of a hero, and perhaps a good deal of our indignation against the Church, rises from that. We are indignant, not only because the Church is reactionary, but because the Church betrayed Jesus. The Church took Christ's name and then sold out to the ruling classes. The Church is Judas. And to us that little immaculate ikon that sits at the right hand of the image of God in Heaven, is a part of the whole traitorous procedure. Whoever puts Jesus up there dodges him down here—that has been our experience. Look into your mind and find out whether it *is* Jesus of Nazareth that you want to defend against satire, or a certain paste-and-water conception of him which assuredly needs your defense.

To us a dialogue that ridicules, with exquisite art, this translated Christ and denatured gospel of a church that justifies exploitation and comforts with sanctimonious emotions those whose pockets profit by it—such a dialogue expresses the very sharpness of our reverence for the memory of Jesus.

It happens indeed that these dialogues are written by a man who is, to a greater extent than we are, and perhaps even than our correspondent, a spiritual follower of Jesus—a man of sublime imagination and gentle good works, who is not afraid to call himself an anarchist, who is not afraid to confess in the face of respectability that he *really* believes a few of the things that Jesus taught.

C. E. S. Wood is now risking his reputation as expert counsel to the corporations in Portland that can pay him money, in order to go down to Los Angeles and defend the forlorn hope of two of the reviled and persecuted, Schmidt and Kaplan, who will be put on trial for their lives this fall. We wonder if our correspondent in Riverside is gearing his Jesus up with the current reality any better than that.

And while we are in the pleasant business of appreciating C. E. S. Wood, let us say that humor in an absolute idealist is like water on a mountain peak, and we hope the Heavenly Dialogues may prosper along with the defense of the prophets.

This discussion was to have ended there, but one more coincidence adds itself on October 4th. I dined last night with Frederic C. Howe, the Single Taxer, Immigration Commissioner, author of optimistic books about realizing democracy. We discussed THE MASSES. "That Heavenly Discourse," he said, "was about the best thing you've ever had in there. That was great."

This morning I find on my desk the following letter from Vida D. Scudder, the Professor of Literature at Wellesley College, who is also noted for books about realizing democracy:

Wellesley, Mass., Oct. 4, 1915.
Editors of THE MASSES,
  Gentlemen: You sent me an appeal for subscribers. Slowly and lazily I had just reached the point of getting you one when I received the *Heavenly Dialogue* in your last month's issue. You will get no subscribers through me. I am not afraid of blasphemy, as I do not think the eternal verities are ever injured by it, and

I like and approve sharp, clever attacks on all that is false and conventional in religion. But the smart and cheap vulgarity of that thing was too much for me. It is a pity.
  I have read few remarks about the war that struck home to me as did those by Max Eastman in the same number.
  Whenever THE MASSES comes I instantly pounce upon it lest it be seen by my innocent relatives. I read it in private, tear it into small pieces, and put it into the waste basket at once. I wish it could manage to avoid offensiveness with no sacrifice of its trenchant quality, and I think it could, perfectly well, if the editors chose to do so. If this were merely a personal opinion I should not be sufficiently impertinent or courageous to write it to you, but I hear the same feeling expressed over and over by straight radicals who like part of what you do so much that they are all the more exasperated by the way in which you cheapen yourselves and limit your appeal.
      Fraternally and cordially,
              VIDA D. SCUDDER.

Now about a large majority of matters Fred Howe and Vida D. Scudder would hold the same opinion. They are both free and clear-minded radicals. I am disposed to think this is a difference of personal environment. Miss Scudder is in a suburb of Boston: Fred Howe is on Ellis Island. Now that Heavenly Dialogue ridiculed the petty God and Jesus of churchdom, and their "holy matrimony" that suspends its sanctitude for the purpose of war, and it did this with the wit of everyday conversation. And I suppose it is natural to think that the writer of such a dialogue merely lacks reverence altogether, unless your own everyday conversation contains greater gods and sanctitudes. And everyday conversation in the cultured circles of New England does not often contain the greater gods. They dwell only in the minds of the few people there like Miss Scudder herself.
                              —December 1915

PAUL H. DOUGLAS
Letter to the Editor

[*Aside from the fact that this subscriber later became a distinguished United States Senator, his criticism indicates how unappealing* The Masses' *brand of radicalism was to more sober-minded socialists.*]

HORRIBLE EXAMPLE

As one who thoroughly believes in the mission of the Socialist press, I wish to protest at your inclusion of the *New Review* with THE MASSES. The *New Review* was performing valuable service; it was fearless, yet decent. Joined to THE MASSES it is lost in the welter of sex literature and illustrations that fill your columns. Like you, I believe the profit system to be vicious, but I do not see how the co-operative commonwealth is being furthered by the nastiness that you encourage.

Do not fall into the mistake of labeling as prudes all those who object to your methods. We are simply those who do not believe that the proper way to attract a man's attention is to pander to his passions. That is why we object to you and

Hearst. An examination of your files is enough to turn the stomach of the healthiest.

As to your actual ideas, you are, I fear, merely sentimentalists in revolt. The poses that you assume may be indigenous to Greenwich Village, but they can only repel everyone who is seriously at work. You are furnishing conservatives with much excellent material, for you are a horrible example of "how not to do it."

PAUL H. DOUGLAS.

Cambridge, Mass.

—November 1916

The Masses and the Press

[The Masses *was almost continuously embroiled in controversy, but its running battle with the Associated Press was to prove particularly important. It did much to establish the magazine's reputation, while at the same time demonstrating the lengths to which the editors were prepared to go in defense of its freedom and flavor.*]

FLOYD DELL
Indicted for Criminal Libel

Our readers will wish to know these facts:

Last summer, after a number of publications, including *Collier's Weekly* and *The Independent,* had delicately intimated that the Associated Press gave the country no fair amount of the struggle between labor and capital in West Virginia, THE MASSES decided to look into the case. It decided that if this thing were true, it ought to be stated without delicacy.

The result was a paragraph explicitly and warmly charging the Associated Press with having suppressed and colored the news of that strike in favor of the employers. Accompanying the paragraph was a cartoon presenting the same charge in a graphic form.

Upon the basis of this cartoon and paragraph, William Rand, an attorney for the Associated Press, brought John Doe proceedings against THE MASSES in the Municipal Court of New York. Justice Breen dismissed the case.

Rand then went to the District Attorney. And the District Attorney considered the case serious

enough to receive the attention of the Grand Jury. He secured an indictment of two editors of THE MASSES for criminal libel. Max Eastman and Arthur Young were arraigned on December 13, pleaded not guilty, and were each released on $1,000 bail. The date for the trial is not set. The penalty for criminal libel may be one year in prison, or $500 fine, or both.

We do not invite your solicitude over the fate of these two editors of THE MASSES. But we do invite you to arouse yourselves against any attempt to put down by force of legal procedure the few free and independent critics of the Associated Press. The hope of democratic civilization lies in the dissemination of true knowledge, and every man must be free to keep vigilance over the sources of knowledge. The Associated Press boasts of supplying news to one-half the population of this country. And if that boast is true, or if it remotely approximates the truth, then a criticism of the Associated Press is a criticism of the very heart of the hope of progress for mankind in America. And if the Associated Press proves powerful enough— as it may, for it is the biggest political force we have—to silence such criticism, we may as well forget all about the New Haven Railroad, and the Telephone Trust, and the Standard Oil Trust, and the Steel Trust, and the Money Trust, and every other problem of combination that confronts us, for they are little or nothing by comparison with a sovereign control of true knowledge.

In our effort to secure a just decision of this case and the principles involved in it, we expect the

Drawn by Art Young, December 1912

The Freedom of the Press

[Art Young had that singular contempt for the pretensions of the press which only long and intimate association produces. As a professional cartoonist he knew whereof he drew, and the scorn he lavished on the A.P. was only part, as this drawing indicated, of the utter distaste he felt for the brothel economics of the industry as a whole.]

support of every man and woman who believes in democratic civilization and the freedom of the press.

If you control or influence any avenue of publicity in the country, go out and help us get the case before the public. And if you know any other way to contribute to a legal struggle, do not pause or postpone it. The issue is not ours, it is yours.

The defense is in the hands of Gilbert E. Roe, 55 Liberty street, New York, a former law partner of Senator La Follette and a distinguished fighter against Privilege.   —January 1914

The Associated Press

We print below a defense of the Associated Press which appeared in the New York Times of March 7, and a reply to that editorial by Mr.

Amos Pinchot. This reply was sent to the Times, but was not printed there. It appeared later in the columns of the New York Sun. We offer our readers the choice between the two views of the Associated Press and its activities.

THE TIMES EDITORIAL

The men who centuries ago fought and won the great fight for freedom of speech and of the press were stout and worthy champions of the liberties of the people. Nowadays those who bawl loudest for freedom of speech are persons who make or wish to make the unworthiest use of the privilege. When men or women inciting mobs to riot and pillage come into collision with the police we always hear much prating about freedom of speech.

The freedom of speech and of the press found defenders of the "free press protest meeting" held in Cooper Union Thursday evening, under the management of the Liberal Club. Mr. Lincoln Steffens was there and spoke. There were feminists and suffragists. But Mr. Amos E. Pinchot was the star of the evening. The meeting was called as a measure of protest against the Federal indictment for criminal libel that has been found against Max Eastman and Art Young, the editor and the cartoonist of a Socialist publication, THE MASSES. These men published in their paper a cartoon representing Mr. Frank B. Noyes, President of The Associated Press, as poisoning the waters of public opinion by causing to be sent out false and distorted news to the newspapers served by that organization. This cartoon was examined by a Federal Grand Jury, adjudged to be libelous, and an indictment for criminal libel was brought. Mr. Amos E. Pinchot insisted that a protest should be made against the use of the Federal District Attorney's office for the muzzling of those who criticised The Associated Press monopoly. In a matter of criminal libel the office of the public prosecutor can be "used" only when the prosecutor finds a case for submission to the Grand Jury, and the Grand Jury in its finding represents not the prosecutor but the people. Mr. Pinchot should understand that this is not an Associated Press suit; it is a Government suit, an action brought by the people to punish the lawless.

The speakers at the Cooper Union meeting, and others besides, insist that there should be an investigation of The Associated Press. The indictment of Eastman and Young makes certain that an investigation will be had, a thorough, searching, and perfectly impartial investigation. The Socialists who perpetrated the libel will have every opportunity in the world to show that Mr. Noyes does in fact poison the news, mislead the public, and pervert its notions of current affairs. If The Associated Press has guilty secrets they will get full publicity. What more can be asked by the volunteer defenders of the press against an odious monopoly? The surface appearance of the transaction is that The Associated Press has courted an investigation of the most far-reaching kind.

Mr. Pinchot is a careless man. He made this statement:

"I have had a long acquaintance with The Associated Press. I am perfectly willing to stand behind the charge made by Eastman and Young that The Associated Press does color and distort the news, that it is not impartial, and that it is a monopolistic corporation, not only in constraint of news but in constraint of truth."

It is not necessary to say that Mr. Pinchot does not know what he is talking about and to apply unpleasant epithets to him and to his utterance. He is confuted and made ridiculous by the facts of the case. The condition he describes is impossible, it could not arise and continue in The Associated Press. This is made clear by an admirable statement of the matter which we take from the editorial columns of The Springfield Republican. Referring to the charge that The Associated Press has power to color the news, and so determine "in what form and to what extent the news of the world shall be given from day to day to the average citizen," The Republican says:

"But The Republican knows from actual ex-

Drawn by Art Young, July 1913

Poisoned at the Source

[*This cartoon, showing the Associated Press poisoning the reservoir of news, triggered the controversy described by these selections.*]

[35]

perience and from many years' study of the daily press of the United States that the worst abuses of news publication are perpetrated by the reporters of individual newspapers in their local field or by the special correspondents directly serving them at a distance. The more papers a reporter or a correspondent serves—papers with interests and sympathies far from uniform—the closer he approximates usually to impartial presentation of facts. And that is precisely the position of the news-gathering representatives of The Associated Press."

Anybody but a Socialist champion of freedom of the press would find this statement convincing. All sorts of newspapers are served by The Associated Press—Republican, Democratic, Bull Moose, Independent, pro-Bryan, anti-Bryan, some that insist that the corporations are too much abused, and others insisting that they are not abused enough—in short, newspapers representing every shade of opinion. Now, if Mr. Noyes should attempt to

Drawn by Art Young, April 1914

The A.P. and *The Masses* Editors

If there has been a feebleness of expression, a tremulous note, throughout the literature and pictures in THE MASSES the last eight months, our readers must remember that during this time we have been haunted by a dreadful nightmare. "Beware!" says the presiding spirit of 894 American newspapers, clanking with medals and honorable tributes from all the crowned heads of Europe and most of Asia. "Beware!" (In deep sepulchral tones) "The Jail!"

[*As this cartoon indicates, Young found it difficult to take the A.P. suit seriously.*]

use his dyestuffs on the news served to all these papers there would be a deafening uproar and tumult all over the country. The Associated Press would be split into fragments and the views openly expressed of its management would make the cartoon of THE MASSES look like an expression of confidence and esteem. If there were a church press association and the management should serve purely Methodist news or Dutch Reformed news to the subscribers, the case would be an exact parallel to that alleged by THE MASSES and declared by Mr. Pinchot on knowledge to exist. Mr. Pinchot has no such knowledge. He bears false witness and foolishly butts his head against a rough stone wall. If the assailants of The Associated Press would now and then find something true to say about it, if they would base their arguments on some other structure than one built up of glaring falsehoods and owlish stupidities, their antics would be more interesting.

MR. PINCHOT'S REPLY

To the Editor of the Sun—Sir: The subjoined letter in reply to an editorial article in defense of the Associated Press and in condemnation of its critics was sent to the New York Times on March 7, but has not been made public by that newspaper:

To-day's Times publishes an editorial over a column long defending the Associated Press as to the indictments against the editors of THE MASSES and attacking myself and others who "insist that there should be an investigation of the Associated Press."

The Times says that the Associated Press could not possibly color the news, because it serves all kinds of newspapers—"Republican, Democratic, Bull Moose, Independent, etc."—so that if it was not impartial "there would be a deafening uproar and tumult all over the country." I do not think that this is either an impressive argument or a fair statement of the case.

As a matter of fact there has been a tumult of protest against Associated Press news coloring throughout the country. And with this protest newspaper owners who are members of the Associated Press and dependent upon it for their information are in many instances heartily sympathetic. Within the last month I have talked with a number of editors of newspapers that are members of the Associated Press. They assured me that the charges of suppression and misrepresentation made by THE MASSES are well within the truth. They, each of them, expressed the sincere hope that there would be a searching investigation which would result in a change of policy.

These gentlemen, however, are not free to state their opinion of the Associated Press openly, either in their papers or otherwise. For, under the by-laws of the Associated Press, they would at once be subject to fines or other discipline. Moreover, Section I of Article II provides that the corporation shall have the right to expel a member "for any conduct on his part, or on the part of any one in his employ or connected with his newspaper, which in its absolute discretion it shall deem of such a character as to be prejudicial to the interest and welfare of the corporation and its members, or to justify such expulsion. The action of the members of the corporation in such regard shall be final and there shall be no right of appeal or review of such action."

The Sun to-day reprints an editorial from the Peoria Star, which describes how membership in the Associated Press is restricted. It says: "Membership is restricted in each city, and no new member can be taken in except by consent of every member in the city belonging to the trust. In some places membership is held at an exorbitant figure running up into hundreds of thousands of dollars. * * * It can readily be seen that this is the worst possible monopoly, because the newspapers belonging to it are obliged to print what the management desires, and they are prohibited from criticising any of its acts."

When, in addition to this, we note that the ultimate control of the Associated Press does not lie in the vote of the newspapers belonging to it but in its bond ownership we realize that partiality and news coloring can be indulged in by the Associated Press, even though, as the Times says, all sorts of newspapers are served by it.

No newspaper can itself gather all its news. It must depend on some news agency for its information. The Associated Press is the only great news-providing agency that serves morning newspapers. To the morning newspapers it is more important than the railroads are to industrial organizations. For, while railroads merely transport the product of industry, the Associated Press both gathers and transports the material of which newspapers are made.

The Associated Press is certainly a monopoly. It is a monopoly controlling the distribution of a vital necessity of civilization, controlling the price at which this necessity shall be sold; and it goes still further than other trusts in monopolistic

Drawn by Art Young, February 1916

Madam, You Dropped Something

[*The A.P. ingloriously withdrew from the field of battle by quietly dropping its suit. Young, however, was not prepared to let it off so easily.*]

power, for it exercises an absolute discrimination as to whom its products shall be sold to.

The Times editorial, in denouncing those who hold that the District Attorney's office shall not be used by the Associated Press, seems to me to be inclined to cover up the real issue. It does not mention that two criminal indictments were brought against Eastman and Young for publishing the same editorial and cartoon.

In the first indictment the figure depicted as poisoning the reservoir of public news and labelled "The Associated Press" is alleged to refer, as in fact it was meant to refer, to the Associated Press, a corporation. In a trial under such an indictment there would naturally be admitted the broadest evidence upon the questions whether the Associated Press colors news and exercises a monopolistic control over the distribution of information to the public. In a trial upon such an indictment a searching investigation into the policy and organization of the Associated Press, its attitude toward labor and capital, its control by bond ownership, etc., would be inevitable.

But it seems that the Associated Press is unwilling to appear in court as a complainant in such a trial. For, just thirty-three days after Eastman and Young were indicted and admitted to $1,000 bail each, Mr. Noyes again complained to the District Attorney, and they were again indicted. This time, however, the figure in the cartoon labelled "The Associated Press" is alleged to be a picture of Mr. Noyes, and the charge in this indictment is not that the Associated Press is libelled, but that Mr. Noyes personally is libelled. The Assistant District Attorney in charge of the case now expresses his intention of dismissing the first indictment, and only trying Eastman and Young on the second. He contends that upon the trial of the second indictment evidence in regard to suppression and coloring of news by the Associated Press shall be inadmissible, and the trial shall be limited to the narrow question as to whether Mr. Noyes and the dignity of the people of the County of New York were injured by the publication of this cartoon.

It would seem as if this was an unfortunate change of ground, because it is much more important for the public to discover whether the Associated Press is guilty of news coloring and monopolistic practices than whether Mr. Noyes and the public have been harmed by the publication of Art Young's picture.

I sincerely hope that all this agitation, the indictments of Eastman and Young, the mass meeting of protest, the discussions and recriminations in the papers and, finally, the approaching trial in the criminal courts, will have some beneficial and constructive outcome. It is perfectly clear to those who have thought of the question calmly that this outcome must inevitably be along legislative lines. The nature of the Associated Press, its control over the distribution of news and the size and scope of its operations demand that it shall be considered a common carrier in the sense that railroads are common carriers. Its service must be open to all those who can pay for it, its control known and all of its operations conducted with the fullest publicity.

The initial and necessary step in this programme is an investigation which will go deeply into the very important questions involved. Many people have hoped that in the trial of Eastman and Young such an investigation could be secured.

I hope that in spite of the by-laws of the Associated Press, which I realize would, under ordinary circumstances, prohibit your publishing what I have written, you may decide that the present situation would justify you in doing so.

AMOS PINCHOT.

New York, March 9.

—April 1914

Drawn by Art Young, April 1916

April Fool

[By way of adding insult to injury, Young closed his war with the A.P. by reproducing the original cartoon with a few little changes.]

The Masses and the Censor

[*Since* The Masses *was the boldest journal of its time, it frequently ran afoul of the censor. By successfully maintaining its attitude of gay defiance and by constantly pressing against the outer limits of community tolerance, it substantially increased the editorial freedom of all periodicals.*]

GERTRUDE MARVIN
Anthony and the Devil

[*Despite its brevity, this is probably the most revealing interview with Anthony Comstock ever held.*]

Anthony Comstock was seated at a table piled with letters and papers, the annex of a huge roll-top desk completely buried under evidences of his notoriety.

He seemed like a harmless old gentleman. He had white hair, mild blue eyes behind spectacles, bushy white side whiskers, a shaven pink chin peeking out between, and a gentle, almost furtive manner. But when I asked him what he thought about teaching sex-hygiene in the schools, he assumed immediately the dignity of the Secretary of the Society for the Suppression of Vice.

"For 42 years of public life," he began, "if I live until March, I have been fighting in the defence of the moral purity of the childhood of the nation. My work has brought me in contact with many parents and teachers of the young and even more with the boys and girls."

He believed, he said, that it was the parents' place to instruct their children in all these matters which pertain to the higher spiritual nature.

"The heart of every child is a chamber of imagery, memory's storehouse, a commissary department of the soul, where all the good and evil influences are stored up for future requisition, not only by the child, but by the Devil also. There is nothing the Devil likes better than to bring a pure young mind to turning on vile, pernicious thoughts. When a link is formed from the reproductive faculties of the mind and imagination to the sensual nature, one might as well throw a loop around the child's neck and hand the other end of it to the Devil. And no one thing is contributing more to the Devil's Kingdom than these attempts to popularize indecencies, on the ground of warning children."

Asked about "Damaged Goods," Mr. Comstock said that he had not seen the play, and that he heartily disapproved of it.

"Remember this," said Mr. Comstock earnestly, " 'Be not deceived, God is not mocked, for whatsoever a man soweth, that will he also reap.' The Devil is always waiting for a chance to corrupt a pure mind."

"You believe in a real personal Devil?"

"Most emphatically I do! Don't you?"

"No, sir."

"I'm sorry for you," he said sadly. A pause, and then he became emphatic again.

"A man can't be in my business for 40 years without knowing positively that there is a personal Devil sitting in a real Hell tempting young and innocent children to look at obscene pictures and books. If you had seen, as I have, children who were tempted into looking just for an instant at a vile picture, and then for the rest of their lives were never able to wipe the memory of that picture from their minds, you would know, as I do, that it was the Devil who was responsible for it.

"Certainly I believe in the Devil."

Through the office window I could see the solid granite columns of the post office building. The sight steadied me, and thanking Mr. Comstock for the interview, I hurried out into the wholesome mud of Park Row.   —February 1914

Are We Indecent?

[*Unlike the other forms of retaliation against* The Masses, *which resembled badges of honor more than real blows, the decision of the firm operating the newsstands in the New York Subway System to drop the magazine markedly reduced its circulation.* The Masses *made strenuous but unsuccessful efforts to force the company to reverse its position, as this story indicates.*]

The opportunity to present the Ward & Gow censorship of THE MASSES before the Thompson Legislative Committee came to us rather as a surprise. August Belmont, director and former president of the subway company, had been questioned by the committee on the terms of subway's contract with Ward & Gow, as a matter of public importance.

Drawn by Robert Minor, October–November 1915

O Wicked Flesh

[*This rendering of Anthony Comstock, Secretary of the New York Society for the Prevention of Vice and the nation's most conspicuous censor, as a sadistic pygmy typified* The Masses' *attitude toward moral censorship. Robert Minor was at this time probably the country's most famous newspaper cartoonist.*]

It seemed to us that the way Ward & Gow made use of their privilege was no less a matter of public interest; and we were glad to find that the chairman of the committee, Senator Thompson, agreed with us. A hearing was held on June 28.

August Belmont was the first witness, and was given an interesting ten minutes. Max Eastman asked if he could put some questions to Mr. Belmont. The first questions dealt with the terms of the Ward & Gow contract.

"Is there anything in the terms of that contract," asked Mr. Eastman, "which allows Ward & Gow to exercise a censorship as to what magazines they will sell on the subway?"

A. "I don't recall."

Q. "Would you mind giving me your personal opinion as to whether you think they have a right to exclude magazines from the subway stands because they don't like them?"

A. "I wouldn't express an opinion as to that, a personal opinion."

Q. "Mr. Belmont, is Ward & Gow's function there a public service, in your opinion?"

A. "They conduct newsstands under the same privileges as any newsstand, I presume."

Q. "Well, is the function of any newsstand public service?"

A. "I don't quite understand the purport of it. A public service—they are newsstands, they conduct a newsstand like any other newsstand. I don't know what you mean. Do you mean that they have a moral obligation to the public? Is that what you mean? I am more interested in their legal obligations than I am in their moral obligations. I believe if they are of public service, they have some legal obligations that they have not if they are not of public service. I can't help you on that."

Q. "Mr. Belmont, the Interborough Company is of public service, is it not?"

A. "Oh, yes."

Q. "Well, does not the relation between the Interborough Company and Ward & Gow entail the conclusion that they also are a public service?"

A. "I could not express anything but an opinion on that subject."

Q. "That is exactly what I want you to express. It would help a lot if you would express an opinion."

A. "Why?"

Q. "Because your opinion is very important."

A. "I don't see that it is. My private opinion does not seem to be pertinent here on a question

of that kind. You are asking me about the actual relations between the two, and so far as Ward & Gow is involved as a public servant, I think it is. As to its contract with the Interborough, I can't give you an opinion."

Q. "May I ask you if you *have* an opinion about it?"

A. "As to whether an objectionable publication should be sold there or not?"

Q. "Yes."

A. "Yes, I think if there was any legal method of preventing an objectionable publication from being sold on a stand it ought to be done."

Q. "Will you tell me whether you have an opinion as to whether Ward & Gow is a public service?"

A. "I can't give you that either, it would be worthless."

Mr. Eastman: "Don't you think, Senator Thompson, that Mr. Belmont's opinion would be pertinent to the question of whether a law on this subject would be proper or not?"

Senator Thompson: "I should think so, very much so."

Mr. Eastman: "Won't you give us your opinion, Mr. Belmont?"

Mr. Belmont: "I don't think you want my opinion on a subject like that. You would have to make that very specific."

Mr. Eastman: "Senator Thompson, will you please make my question specific? I don't seem to know how."

Senator Thompson: ". . . He wants to know if in your opinion the sale of these magazines on the newsstands of the Interborough is a public service, that is, a service that they are bound to give to the public; it is in the nature of a monopoly, and he also wants an opinion as to whether, if it is not now under the jurisdiction of the public service, it should be?"

Mr. Belmont: "Yes, it is."

The witness was excused, and Mr. Eastman proceeded to lay a complaint against the firm of Ward & Gow for excluding THE MASSES from the subway newsstands. His statement is printed on page five of this issue. The grounds of exclusion having been the "blasphemous and indecent" character of THE MASSES, he asked a number of representative citizens to testify as to their opinion of the magazine. The first of these witnesses was Professor John Dewey, of Columbia University. Mr. Dewey said:

"I have been a fairly regular reader of THE

Drawn by Art Young, April 1915

[*In true radical-bohemian fashion, The Masses gloried in the slams it received from "respectable" quarters. Columbia University's cancellation of its subscription was a matter of special pride for its editors; it officially marked the magazine's arrival as a recognized enemy of capitalist culture.*]

MASSES, and I have never seen anything which I regarded as either indecent or blasphemous."

Q. "Do you think that Ward & Gow have a moral right to exclude THE MASSES from the subway stands?"

A. "It is my personal opinion that it is very unfortunate that any private business corporation should have it in its power to determine in any way the trend and set of thought and ideas that should percolate to the community. That is to my mind the most serious feature of the present case —the exercise of a censorship by a business organization."

Senator Thompson: "Is it a power that ought to reside anywhere except in the Legislature?"

A. "My own judgment is that it should reside simply in the Legislature and in the decisions of the courts pursuant to the acts of Legislature. I think otherwise we might find that certain business interests might object to any propaganda and exercise their power to cut it off."

Lincoln Steffens was then called to the stand. He told how he had gone, at the request of THE MASSES, to see an official of the Ward & Gow Company, to see if it were not possible to persuade Ward & Gow not to exercise censorship over THE MASSES, and to put it back on their stands. "The purpose of that move from my point of view," he

[42]

said, "was to see if we could not get them to see the point about free speech and free press, without making a fight."

"Some of the men on THE MASSES wanted to make a fight and I am against fighting except when it is necessary. However, I went down to see Mr. Atkinson and he received me and asked me curtly what my business was and I said it was to ask him to raise the embargo upon THE MASSES, and he said, 'That cannot be done.' I asked him if he would give me a hearing and he said, 'Yes.' So I went inside and sat down at his desk with him and I said, 'Mr. Atkinson, I used to be what they call a muckraker, had access to magazines which gave me a certain power and I abused it. I used that power to blame men, to express more or less my feelings against men, individuals, and I know now that men are not at fault, and I said, 'Now, here comes THE MASSES, a lot of young men. They have talent and their publication amounts to power.' I said, 'They abuse their power as they are bound to do, as all men in power abuse power.' I said, 'Then come Ward & Gow and they have a privilege from a privileged concern, which gives them the power to say what publications shall be presented in a certain way to the public and which shall not, so of course Ward & Gow abuse their power. This usually means fighting. Men can't express themselves, can't get together and can't have any understanding among themselves, and so they go to War as they do in Europe.' He said, 'Well, why not make THE MASSES stop publishing what they are publishing all the time?' I said, 'That is not the way to begin. They are young men and they think these things and feel these things, let them express themselves. We don't want them repressed.' . . .

"Well, the result of the interview was that Mr. Atkinson said that it was a new point of view to him and he said he would take it up with Mr. Ward and would try to persuade Mr. Ward. So he went to see Mr. Ward and he told me a week later that they could not move Mr. Ward. Then I got his permission to make my appeal to Mr. Ward and I went and saw him, and Mr. Ward was hard. He was very explicit. He said that he had excluded THE MASSES from the stands because it had offended his religious sense. 'Now,' he said, 'I have a right on any grounds to exclude anything. I have two hundred applications for publications for space on my stands and I can't receive them all, so I have to exclude some, and I exclude some because there is not space, but in the case of THE

MASSES I exclude it because it offends my religious sense.' Then I said, 'Mr. Ward, you are acting as a censor and you are deliberately taking over the responsibility for everything that is on your stands.' He said, 'I am willing to do that; THE MASSES shall not go back on my stand. It is mine, it is my private property, I rent and control it, it is mine. Now,' he said, 'I won't say it never will go back on the stand, because if they become decent and produce a publication like the *Atlantic,* then I will let it back upon the stand.'

"The whole point was that he was acting as a censor and that is very clear.

"It seems to me," Mr. Steffens said, "that it is one more entering wedge by which not only Ward & Gow, but all of what we now call the interests, are closing in on the press and all of us who write for the press, to keep us from saying the things that will improve conditions in the United States."

The Rev. Percy Stickney Grant, pastor of the Church of the Ascension, took the stand, and said:

"I do not think THE MASSES should be excluded from the subway stands. I do not think it is indecent or blasphemous." He had felt that the publication of the "Ballad," which was the cause of its exclusion, was a matter of bad taste or of editorial inattention, "or it might have been carrying out the theory of THE MASSES, which after all is the theory of giving to the proletariat the widest expression of their beliefs, carrying that expression to an extreme. And yet," he said, "I think that theory cannot be carried to such an extreme as to make it wise to put that publication under the ban on any stand. . . . I am too accustomed," he said, "to free expression by workingmen and their sympathizers on religious subjects, to be personally disturbed."

Asked if he read THE MASSES regularly, he replied:

"It is one of the papers that I look forward to with great pleasure. I feel that the sympathy and intelligence of the writers of THE MASSES, and their expert knowledge of social and industrial conditions, make a reader confident of the reality of what he gets in THE MASSES. That is a great relief today, to a reader of periodicals."

Abraham Cahan, editor of the Jewish *Daily Forward,* being put on the stand, said that he had been brought up in Russia, and was used to the idea of magazines being suppressed because they were good, because they told the truth. "To me," he said, "it is a Russian affair all the way through. It almost makes me homesick."

Rose Pastor Stokes testified that she had been familiar with the story of Jesus as related in the "Ballad" printed in THE MASSES. It was an old Jewish legend, which she had never regarded as irreverent.

The Rev. Edward A. Saunderson, formerly pastor of the Church of the Pilgrims in Brooklyn, and now connected with the Good Will industries in the same city, testified that he did not regard THE MASSES as blasphemous. "I am too familiar," he said, "with the Bible itself, to feel at all shocked by any of the conceptions either of God or Christ that have been published there. I feel that as far as blasphemy is concerned, conceptions of God which you can take out of the Old and New Testaments are far more of a calumny against God than anything I have ever seen in THE MASSES."

Amos Pinchot testified to his belief that the exclusion of THE MASSES was an infringement of the right of free expression. He said: "History has

Drawn by Art Young, May 1916

The Latest

Arrested for Criminal Libel by the Associated Press—

Expelled from Columbia University Library and Book Store—

Ejected from the Subway and Elevated Stands of New York—

Suppressed by the Magazine Distributing Company in Boston—

Quashed by the United News Co. of Philadelphia—

Kicked Out of Canada by the Government—

shown pretty plainly that all of these movements to guard people from ideas are unsound; and that the only safe, conservative thing to do is to let the ideas loose in the community. If they are bad ideas, they will be destroyed by the good ideas that are in the world; if they are sound ideas, they will maintain their position in the world, and grow in strength.

"Now," he said, "I have seen THE MASSES on tables of girls' boarding schools. It is on my table. I never miss a copy; my children read it. I give it to my little girl, because the art features of it are very, very fine, I think. I like to have them read it; I like to have them get away from the idea of prudery and secret things, and come right out in the open. I like to have my children talk to me; I hope they always will, as frankly as THE MASSES talks to the public, and I regard it as a very, very valuable publication.

"I agree with Senator Thompson and Mr. Moss, that the great danger to this country is in the control of ideas, for ideas are the source of everything. Any man that controls ideas, controls the world, and if there is one single principle that is absolutely vital to society, more vital than any kind of physical freedom, it is mental freedom, for that is the basis of all freedom."

Senator Thompson: "The question of what is decent and what is indecent is one that is very hard to pass upon."

A. "Personally, I have never seen anything that I considered indecent in THE MASSES."

—September 1916

Some Recent Workings of the Censorship

In the past six months six radical periodicals have been suppressed by the Post Office Department without the formality of a trial and without possibility of redress: *Revolt,* of New York; *Alarm,* of Chicago; *The Blast,* of San Francisco; *Voluntad* (Spanish); *Volni Listy* (Bohemian); and *Regeneracion* (English-Spanish). All of these papers, except the last one, were denied the privileges of the mails on the grounds that the Post Office Department "did not like the tone of the paper." *Regeneracion,* as will be remembered, was handled more crudely: the Federal Department of Justice confiscated its presses on the ground that an article which it published, advising the Mexican people not to trust the Carranza government, was "treason." And at the same time

two of its editors, the Magon brothers, were beaten into insensibility by detectives, and the entire editorial board was indicted.

The Post Office examination and censorship of mail is strictly illegal. Several times the Post Office has asked Congress to grant it definite rights in this matter, and Congress has refused. Cases which have been carried up to the United States Supreme Court have been decided on the legal merits of the particular case—the Supreme Court has refused to pass on the principle of the Post Office censorship.

This method of suppressing publications without trial was begun during the administration of Theodore Roosevelt, when *La Questione Soziale,* of Paterson, N. J., was so forbidden to publish or circulate.

We bring these instances of lawless tyranny to the attention of our readers, to further prove that the governing class of the United States has not the slightest respect for that "law and order" which it professes to uphold against "dangerous revolutionists" like us.

Passing from philosophy and economics to art and literature, we catch a glimpse of the reason why America is so hopelessly inferior in artistic and philosophical expression to the rest of the world.

We find in the literary section of the Boston *Transcript* a notice to the effect that "the Committee on Suppression of Cincinnati and New York" has instituted proceedings to suppress Theodore Dreiser's great novel, "The Genius," on the grounds of "immorality."

We also happen to know that "The Rainbow," by D. H. Lawrence, one of the finest novels ever written in the English language, has been barred from publication here—after appearing in England—by the threat of the Society for the Suppression of Vice—on the grounds of "obscenity."

Then there are "Hagar Revelly" and "Homo Sapiens" and an infinite number of other books. Likewise the publishers of translations of Russian literature have been warned against introducing here some of the greatest books of all time—which are freely available to the public of every other country of the world, including China.

In the theatre we have a recent example in the outrageous censorship of the Russian Ballet in New York, and the stupid suppression of serious plays in Boston, Philadelphia and Chicago; while undisturbed, the silly and lascivious burlesque show, musical comedy and vaudeville act go on.

Drawn by George Bellows, June 1915

Exposed at Last! The Nude Is Repulsive to This Man

[*Bellows, who drew this caricature of Anthony Comstock, was a key figure in* The Masses *group.*]

The moral is, of course: "As long as you are vulgar you are safe."

And we have with us always what the *Little Review* calls "the most perfect system of Birth Control for genius and art ever devised—The National Board of Censorship."

But the latest activity of our national pruriency is in the realm of painting. Jerome Blum, a painter of reputation, returned from China this spring, bringing with him a little collection of Chinese and Japanese paintings. Among them was a book containing eight original paintings on silk by one of the ancient Chinese masters, and a Japanese scroll of exquisite workmanship.

The Customs Appraiser of the Port of Chicago declared these two works obscene, saying "they would arouse the passions of an ordinary man."

Upon this evidence the Collector of the Port ordered them to be destroyed, informing Mr. Blum that he had laid himself open to thousands of dollars in fines and five years imprisonment. Mr. Blum offered to paint out the objectionable parts, to return them to China, or to present them to some museum. But the Customs official's decree was: "Art or no Art, all paintings of the kind are to be burned." So the two paintings were destroyed!

No one of the slightest education need be told that all Art—and all religion—arose from the desire of humanity to recreate for the hearts of men the mystery of the creation and reproduction of life. The Art of the Orient is almost solely concerned with these subjects. And not only that; the steeple of every village church in the United States, the form of the cross on its altar, the shape of a bishop's hat—are all "obscene" phallic symbols.

We wonder how the Customs officials of the Port of Chicago can bear to go around carrying the shameful male organs of generation. But perhaps, after all, they haven't any. —October 1916

Sumner vs. Forel

[*John Sumner, who replaced Anthony Comstock after the latter's death, did not follow up on the one-man raid described in this note. It indicates, however, the kind of routine hazards to which the staff was exposed.*]

You may have heard that John S. Sumner, the successor of Anthony Comstock, paid a visit to our office recently, confiscated all the September numbers of THE MASSES on hand, and arrested our circulation manager, Merrill Rogers. The reason was that we had advertised and sold "The Sexual Question," by August Forel—a book recognized as one of the great authoritative works on the subject of sex. The case will be fought to a finish in the courts. In the meantime it is interesting to have a personal statement from John S. Sumner, made to one of our editors, explaining his animus against the Forel book. He says: "It advocates sodomy"! Our readers have our word for it that it does, of course, nothing of the sort. If our recommendations had any weight with the authorities, we should suggest that some of our prominent vice experts be detained for observation in Bellevue; their minds really do not seem to us to be normal. For the time being, however, they dictate what you shall buy and read. —November 1916

The Masses and the Left

[*True to the tradition of radical magazines,* The Masses *devoted much time to establishing its position in relation to other elements on the left. The following selections, mostly on the lighter side, indicate how it went about doing this.*]

MAX EASTMAN
One of the Ism-ists

Yesterday coming into the subway I was greeted, or rather seized by, a large acquaintance of mine —one of those voluble and vivacious sisters who make a quiet man feel like a corpse.

"O, Comrade Eastman," she exploded, "I'm so glad to see you! I was just *wanting* to talk to a party member! I——"

"Are you a party member?" I said. "Then I can't talk to you. I'm sorry. I don't talk to party members. It isn't safe."

"Why? What's the matter? You're not a Syndicalist, are you?"

"O, no!—no! no! no!"

"Direct Actionist?"

"O, my, no!"

"Sabotist?"

"O, my God!"

"Well, what *are* you then—a Laborist?—Industrialist?—Anarchist?"

"I'm sure I don't know."

"A Syndicalist, you know, is a Possibilist Anarchist, just as a Socialist is a Possibilist Utopist, but a Syndicalist is an Impossibilist Socialist. The truth is, a Syndicalist is an Antistatist, whereas a Socialist is a Statist and Political Actionist, only an Antimilitarist and Pacifist. I'm a Collectivist Revisionist myself. Now, it's a funny thing, but my brother claims to be a Hervéist, and says he's a Possibilistical Sabotist, but at the same time an Extremist Communist and Political Actionist. I don't think that's a possible thing, do you?"

"I thought he was a Chiropodist," I said.

"Well—what's that got to do with it? I'm talking about what he *believes in!*"

"Oh, I see what you mean. He *practices* chiropody, but he *believes in* political action?"

"I guess you're joking."

"I think so—a little."

"Well—I'm serious. I think things are getting awfully complicated these days. Sometimes I feel as if I just couldn't tell what I *do* believe in! I feel like throwing over the whole business and going about my work."

"Yes—that's a good idea," I said. "When you get that idea carried out, I'd like to talk to you. I'm sorry I must leave you now."

"O, are you going?"

"Yes—I'm a Get-offist. That is, I'm going to get off at this station."   —March 1913

MAX EASTMAN
The Anarchist Almanac

I call it by that name, because the choice by its editors of the name "Revolutionary"—as though that were an exclusive possession of those who look to the abolition of the state—smacks to my mind of a little Bohemian priggishness. I do this also because the word *revolution* is for me defined and consecrated to the uses of science. And its meaning, as so defined, has little to do with programs of the future constitution of society. As to what may issue when the working classes win to power, those who enjoy speculation have every reason to speculate—but the concern of the revolutionary is that the working classes should win.

However, the crowing is mostly on the covers, and you will find within the almanac a quantity of matter for joy and meditation. I am, for my part, confirmed in one or two tentative opinions concerning the philosophy of Anarchism by reading it —confirmed at least to the point of putting the opinions where my Anarchist friends can read them.

Anarchism has always seemed to me to hark back to "literary" times, whereas we live in the times of science. And what I feel in this almanac, again, is a strong literary infatuation, a love of the flavor of ideas of revolt, rather than a concentrated interest either in an end to be achieved, or in ideas as working hypotheses for its achievement. There is small satisfaction for the spirit of experimental science—which is the only new thing among us all—in these pages. And there is a good deal of rather undiscriminating hurrah. At least so it seems to me.

I would not traduce some of the quotations, like this from James Russell Lowell, by naming them literature:

> "They are slaves who fear to speak
> For the fallen and the weak;
> They are slaves who will not choose
> Hatred, scoffing and abuse——"

But still I do think there is an undue predominance of what we used to call "English" throughout this almanac. I emerged upon that back cover with so little additional knowledge, and so few ideas indicating definite action in the complex of our own life, that I was not altogether sorry to see THE MASSES omitted from the "revolutionary" publications listed there. It gave me a kind of corroboration, and at the same time an opportunity to say all the mean things I could think of about Anarchism without appearing to have started the argument.

The state of mind propagated by Anarchists as such, besides being literary, is negative and therefore uncompelling. Anarchists do, to be sure, along with all other revolutionists, radiate that brotherly-rebellious spirit which promotes the hope of industrial democracy. But in so far as they are distinguished from the rest, they are distinguished by a negation. *Anarchy* is a privative word. It is a word that merely denies. When you grasp it, there is nothing in your hand. And the spirit of man will never be kindled to high endeavor by such a word, no matter how negative the actual thing he has to do. He will act with a creative vision when he acts to a great end.

[47]

It is this weakness, I think, that drives the editor to quote so much from men and women who would not touch the philosophy of Anarchism, and from others who have touched and rejected it. And it is this, too, that has driven the Anarchists so joyfully to the banner of the I. W. W. That organization, with its strike program, its plans of an industrial organization of society, gives them a chance for affirmation. And in so doing, perhaps little as they suspect this, it brings them nearer to co-operation with their ancient enemies but potential friends, the Socialists. Of that the future can judge.

—March 1914

WILLIAM ENGLISH WALLING
Class Struggle Within the Working Class

We are beginning to realize that the forces of conservatism are composed as largely of the owners of "jobs" as of the owners of capital. The literature of Socialism and Unionism has shown the change for several years. Debs has repeatedly said that the older unions have their basis in the desire of their members to protect themselves and their jobs against the great mass of workers, and the I. W. W. declares that "the day of the skilled worker has passed." In proportion as the unskilled workers and machine operatives attempt, in industry after industry, to improve their lot, they find that these owners of jobs oppose them almost as bitterly as the capitalists do. The owners of jobs do not want to be thrown out of work for the benefit of another group of workers. And they want nothing to do with a unionism which preaches that the best labor union policy is to sacrifice the immediate present for the Socialist future that lies (we confess it) a few years ahead.

For many years revolutionary unionists and Socialists have realized the conservative position taken by the "aristocracy of labor," both in politics and labor union matters, but they have not always realized that this may be a *permanent and fundamental* characteristic of all skilled labor, although Debs has said that only electric locomotives, in replacing the steam engineer by a motorman, would teach the engineer the lesson of Socialism and Industrialism—which means that the skilled worker could only learn this lesson by ceasing to be a skilled worker (steam engineer) and becoming a machine operative (motorman).

We Socialists have been led on by an ultra-optimistic faith that all employees *ought naturally to act together when guided by an enlightened self-interest.* This older Socialist and labor union view, which we may call "Laborism," based all its hopes on the possibility of the common action of all employees, and so blinded its followers for a while to the true bearing of the most obvious facts, even when they saw those facts and admitted them. Now comes Industrialism and points to the lesson of recent experience, which teaches that the ownership of a privileged position, due to an exceptional education or training, acts precisely like the ownership of capital.

The new revolutionary labor union movement has been called "Industrial Socialism," and represented as an extension of political Socialism into the field of labor union action. It has also been viewed as an extension of labor union action from the every-day struggle about wages into the field of revolutionary Socialism. But no combination of Socialism and labor unionism, however revolutionary, can account for it. It has incorporated many Socialist and labor union principles and methods, but at the same time it marks a complete and revolutionary departure. For, as a matter of fact, it is based not upon all working people, including the aristocracy of labor, but upon all working people, excluding the aristocracy of labor. The skilled workers are invited to come in, of course, as they can be of no little use in times of strike, but like capitalists asked into the Socialist party, they are invited to take back seats—and it is not expected in either case that many will accept the invitation. In this respect revolutionary unionism differs absolutely from the political movement (the older Socialism) or the economic movement (the old labor unionism), which represent skilled and unskilled labor alike, but *as a matter of fact* give the skilled workers, though they are so much weaker in numbers, a weight equal to or greater than that of the unskilled.

The new unionism for the first time introduces democracy into the labor movement; for the organization of the skilled and unskilled into a single industrial union means that everything is placed absolutely in the hands of the unskilled majority. And as democracy is taken seriously by the workers, this means the gradual annihilation of all the advantages of the skilled, which explains sufficiently why they refuse every invitation to affiliate with the new organization. Our Socialist philosophy teaches us that most of us would be equally backward if we were skilled workers, but it also teaches us that it is idle to expect them to do anything else.

Until the new organization was formed the only hope of unskilled labor to win strikes lay in securing the cooperation of the skilled. And many industrialists still hope that the skilled may be persuaded or forced to cooperate with their unions. But they now begin to realize that where this is impossible they must proceed without the skilled and *if necessary* even *against* them. In this case we shall have a labor union movement directed in part against the unions of certain groups of skilled workers.

Similarly Karl Marx and his successors hoped to make up their revolutionary political majority only with the aid of both the skilled and unskilled workingmen. But if the skilled manual laborers either form anti-revolutionary Labor Parties of the British or Australian type, or come into the Socialist Party as an anti-revolutionary element, the Marxists will have to make good the loss elsewhere, as by recruiting among the brain-workers and professional classes. In this case we shall have a Socialist movement directed against the political organizations the skilled workers control.

I have used the expressions "skilled" and "unskilled" because these are the terms employed by Socialists and labor unionists. But this classification of the workers is insufficient and does not allow the whole situation to be seen. Both the terms were handed down to us from the days of the craftsmen and craft unions, when all the rest of the workers were either apprentices, helpers, or common laborers such as porters, dockers, hod-carriers, ditch-diggers, etc. But ever since railways and steamships began to bring the factory system into its present dominating position a middle group of workers, chiefly factory and mill employees, has been growing in importance until it overshadows both the extremes. The majority of these *machine operatives* are not exactly skilled, because it requires a very short time to learn their work. Neither are they common laborers, because they become gradually more and more specialized with time. It is not mere muscle that is required, but speed, accuracy, endurance and reliability. As these qualities are all *gradually* acquired, this kind of "skill," if we continue to use that word, does not divide the workers into any hard and fast groups.

In times of strike the machine operatives in factory, mill, and mine are not so easily replaced by workers from other industries as entirely unskilled

or common laborers would be. When the *unskilled* are unionized they cannot hope to win their strikes, as a rule, without the aid either of other unions or of the government—as we saw in the recent dock strike in Great Britain. When *operatives* are thoroughly organized they can win even against the opposition of the skilled workers, as at Lawrence, and the only way the employer can hope to beat them is to arouse the whole capitalist class by the fear of lawlessness, disorder, or rebellion, and then to call on the government and courts to take his side and suppress the strike.

Politically the *unskilled* are exceedingly weak. It is different with the *operatives,* who must be influential in many localities—until the central government or higher courts interfere. As the unskilled workers and operatives, satisfied that they will be opposed by the aristocracy of labor until the very day of the great change is at hand, cannot hope to become a national majority alone, they will have

Drawn by Art Young, July 1917

"Of course, even anarchists have to get together and decide on certain laws and rules of procedure, do they not?"

"Oh, yes, certainly—but you see we don't abide by our decisions."

[*This drawing was based on a famous exchange between Floyd Dell (though Young's portly straight man bears no physical resemblance to Dell) and Hippolyte Havel, a famous Village figure who also worked on* Mother Earth. *The incident began at one of the monthly editorial meetings, when a vote was taken on whether or not to include a particular poem. This provoked Havel to cry out: "Bourgeois! Voting! Voting on poetry! Poetry is something from the soul. You can't vote on poetry." Dell then asked Havel how anarchists handled such problems.*]

[49]

to seek for other allies until this day arrives— and they will find them in those elements of the salaried and professional classes which every- where make up a large and revolutionary element of the Socialist parties.

They will need this aid not only politically, but also in strikes and in the final revolution. For in order to win strikes they will have to win a part of the public, enough somewhat to check govern- mental interference. And to do this they will have to wage their war not against the employers of one industry, but against the united employers and capitalists of all industries. For wages must be increased at the expense of profits—which evi- dently spells class war. Otherwise increases of wages are only an illusion and not real, every rise of wages being accompanied by a more than cor- responding rise of prices—as in the British sea- men's and railway men's strikes and the coal strike in this country. And this raises the cost of living not only for the union workers themselves, but also for their natural allies, who, having less opportu- nity to strike, have less means than the manual workers of increasing their incomes. These allies are naturally alienated by this, and cannot be won back until the workers' struggle for higher *money* wages is accompanied by an equally vigorous and successful struggle for higher *real* wages, *i. e.*, for higher wages and lower prices all along the line. Until this policy is followed, the capitalists, by making concessions to skilled labor and by turning the rest of the unionized manual workers and intel- lectual workers against one another, will be able to prevent either economic or political advance of the masses.

Industrialism as a movement of non-privileged labor, *i. e.*, of unskilled labor *and* machine opera- tives, will ally itself not with privileged labor, but with the non-privileged *of all classes,* and Social- ism will do the same thing. The class struggle will continue, but with a new alignment. On the one side will be all the non-privileged, the low paid manual and brain workers, whether employed by capitalists or governments, the small farmers who do their own labor and expect to continue to do it. On the other hand will be not only the capitalists,

but also the majority of those possessing an excep- tional skill, an exceptional education, or a favored position of any kind. It will no longer be a strug- gle between Capital and Labor, even though the larger number of capitalists may still be on the one side and the larger number of laborers on the other.

This will mean a complete revolution both in Socialism and labor unionism. Marx wanted a clear line of demarcation between those classes which, acting on the customary selfish motives, would defend existing institutions and the existing society, and those which would stand for Socialism, and for reasons of enlightened selfishness be ready to make the sacrifices necessary to bring it about. The division between rich and poor, privileged and non-privileged, Marx felt, was not sufficiently sharp for the purpose of agitation and education. He therefore selected the clash of interest between employer and employee as his dividing principle.

It seems possible now that the theories of half a century may have to be abandoned. The masses are coming to understand that they will never be able to rely, either in elections or in strikes, on the support of all classes of workingmen, and certainly not on that of the aristocracy of labor. The larger number of manual employees will evidently hold together, but a very considerable minority will al- most certainly continue for many years, and prob- ably until the next revolution approaches, to act with the ruling and exploiting class.

The whole philosophy that has hitherto under- lain Socialism, together with its political and labor union tactics, is being completely revolutionized, then, by the fact that the owner of the job has become the enemy, as much as the owner of capital or the employer of labor. But the reinvigorated political and labor union movement that has arisen in conscious opposition to this aristocracy of labor, is preserving every practical and revolutionary Marxian principle. There can be little question that with these changes we are entering into a new epoch, or that the struggles that lie immedi- ately before us will entirely eclipse those of the past—in magnitude, intensity, and significance for the revolution that is to come.   —January 1913

II
The Freedom to Express

THE generous proportions of *The Masses* allowed it to print a wealth of material that would never have appeared in a smaller or more single-minded journal. The editors never hesitated to print what amused them and scorned the grubby point of view which insisted that everything published must in some way advance the day of revolution. But they also believed that the society they were building had to be fun as well as moral. It was hardly an accident that three of Eastman's book titles began with the word "enjoyment," for he and his friends had not become revolutionaries in order to usher in an age of cheerless conformity. Thus every joke and cartoon, however irrelevant it seemed to the walking delegates and agitators who were getting their skulls cracked on picket lines, was a reminder that bread and justice were not enough. If their distance from the social battle prevented the editors from entering fully into the proletarian consciousness, which it was their purpose to crystallize and interpret, it made possible the detachment essential to their special function.

Another remarkable feature of *The Masses* was the easy relationship which the editors enjoyed with the cultural *avant garde*. Unlike purely literary journals on the order of *Poetry* or the *Little Review*, *The Masses* was not determinedly in pursuit of the new. The editors read Keats and Shelley and Whitman as well as Amy Lowell, and they printed any kind of poetry which took their fancy. Most of the writers thought themselves poets (as some of them, in fact, actually were) but they were entirely unself-conscious about their literary tastes. This kind of confidence seems so foreign to our experience that it warrants special attention.

What the editors did not like they ignored, and what they did like they published without explanation or apology. The critical position which insists that only one mode of expression is valid or legitimate and attacks all others would have offended the editors' deepest instincts. Men like Louis Untermeyer and Max Eastman maintain this perspective and give us some sense of what it was like before the critical wars began to rage in earnest. This is not to say that *The Masses* did not have likes and dislikes, but its emphasis was always on cultural diversity and it admitted a broad range of literary forms and traditions. The editors took their poetry, like their politics, seriously, but they did not elevate cultural fashions into absolute standards.

This same tolerance and lack of pretension characterized the painters as well as the writers. John Sloan did not care much for cubism, although he had helped arrange the Armory Show which made cubism notorious. Neither did he feel obliged to call down the wrath of heaven upon this impious new school of painting, and his good-natured comment in this section reflected a confidence in his own worth which modern artists might well envy.

The Masses' fiction was probably its most advanced feature. It is not clear why this should have been so. One possibility is that few of the editors cared about short stories, which gave Eastman and Floyd Dell a freer hand in selecting them. It was Dell, himself a deft short story writer (as his own story, "The Beating," demonstrates), who secured the *Winesburg* stories. The general excellence of *The Masses'* fiction owed a good deal to his discerning eye. Some of the stories, like those of James Hopper, were clearly selected for their shock value, while others were more purely propagandistic in intent. But the overall standard was remarkably high and reflected a stronger and surer editorial hand than was present in those fields where reader interest was greater and controversy more frequent.

Its art work first brought *The Masses* to public attention, and for years the writers worked in the shadow cast by such great names in American painting as George Bellows and John Sloan. While this was hardly fair to the writers (who in any case came into their own later), the great reputation which the magazine enjoyed in the art world was entirely deserved. Artistically *The Masses* came along at just the right time, for the strong, vigorous, earthy mode then at its zenith was well adapted to the requirements of a journal which proposed to use art as a weapon in the class struggle. There was nothing vulgar or coercive about this process. It bore little relationship to what was later to be called Socialist Realism or to the self-consciously Proletarian Art of the 1930's. It just happened that artists like John Sloan had both a deep commitment to social justice and a style of painting that was perfectly suited to a direct expression of their concern.

Of course *The Masses* profited from the work of artists who were not stylistically aligned with The Eight or the "Ash Can" School. Since the editors were interested in art for its own sake, they could enjoy the delicate work of Arthur B. Davies as well as the bold caricatures of Art Young. Hugo Gellert's gay covers contributed nothing to the social struggle, but they were light and amusing and attractively offset the stern, uncompromising work of Robert Minor. *The Masses* believed in art, but it did not make a religion of it. It offered little to those who believed that art and life were unrelated, though, neither did it accept the premises of the Village wag who wrote:

> They draw fat women for *The Masses,*
> Denuded, fat, ungainly lasses—
> How does that help the working classes?

No part of *The Masses* was more idiosyncratic than its book and drama reviews, which, as with its fiction, largely reflected the personal tastes of Floyd Dell. Dell brought to *The Masses* not only a substantial reputation as a critic in his own right but also an exceptionally broad acquaintance with contemporary literature. He seems to have read everything that appeared in English, and he had an instinct for European works that were useful and relevant to young Americans. Many first learned of psychoanalysis from Dell, for he was equally at home with serious and polemical writings. While he lacked the advantages of a formal education, he had compensated for it by digesting huge amounts of nineteenth-century literature; what he didn't know about Abelard and Aquinas was balanced by what he did know about Emerson and Carlyle. His very modernity was to prove a disadvantage in later years, for he had entered almost too fully into the spirit of his time. When it gave way to the drastically different circumstances of the postwar period, he barely made the transition. Some of his best work (notably *Intellectual Vagabondage*) was done after the war, but spiritually Dell was a product of the radical optimism of the high Progressive Era and was never entirely at home outside of it.

Dell's total identification with his own time was immensely useful to *The Masses.* He had some help from people like Louis Untermeyer and especially Charles W. Wood, but he bore the biggest load himself. Wood did most of the drama reviews and was an immensely likeable and freewheeling critic. His maiden effort began, "The purpose of this new department in *The Masses* is to provide me with free tickets to New York theaters." He went on to declare that he was not himself a dramatic critic, adding: "But then the New York shows are a long way from being drama." This was a far cry from George Jean Nathan, but it was acute, funny, and a healthy counterpart to the seriousness with which *The Masses* habitually treated literature. Here again is that special *Masses'* style with its peculiar mixture of flippancy and seriousness, art and politics. There are magazines today which are more successful in any given area than *The Masses,* but none with its unique flavor and texture. Now the cultural lines are drawn more rigidly, and our best magazines, rather than being joyously committed, are humorlessly "engaged"—a word and a frame of mind which *The Masses* would have found very strange indeed.

Just for Fun

[*Many of the items printed in* The Masses *were intended to express nothing more than their creators' sense of fun. This was particularly true of the drawings which were often collaborative efforts, with one of the editors conceiving the idea and then persuading an artist to execute it. In other cases the artists, and especially the extraordinarily imaginative John Sloan, were entirely responsible for the finished product.*]

ROBERT CARLTON BROWN
The Ingenuity of Yvette

[*Brown was a facile and productive writer who resigned in sympathy with the seceding artists in 1916.*]

The world had plunged into being. Earthquakes, cataclysms and all the spasms of space had rumbled and roared through their courses. Then came quiet—conscious, deadly quiet, perfect but for the incessant chatter of the race of simians with which the earth was peopled—a rare old species of chimpanzee which took to the trees in fright and shivered and waited, their teeth clicking, until the time when the kingdom over which they were to rule should be perfect.

Time rolled on, as time will. The earth passed safely through the colic days, its rugged surface gradually took form and began to cool. The ancient race of chimpanzees, unacclimated, moved steadily toward the equator in a frantic endeavor to keep warm. Some were left behind in the migrations, and thus at length the world was populated.

Then came one, little Eva by name, who put up what back hair she had, and changed her name to Yvette, eons before the world possessed stage heroines called Gwendolyn and cash girls named Dorothea.

Yvette looked round with the calculating eye of a new woman, sized up the limitations of the little old world and forthwith decided to be the Mrs. Pankhurst of her day. Remember that this was in the good old times when fellow simians addressed each other of mornings with, "Is my vertebræ on straight?" and "How is your evolution?"

Yvette had a passion for progress; she had been favored by birth with a fairer skin than her family and she despised her parents for their hairiness; also, having no fear of cataclysms, which were not

Drawn by Art Young, May 1913

" 'I gorry, I'm tired!"

"There you go! YOU'RE tired! Here I be a-standin' over a hot stove all day, an' you wurkin' in a nice cool sewer!"

so stylish then as in the times of her ancestors, she could find no excuse for living in a tree. To Yvette it was vulgar, and she spent most of her time on the ground, practicing to walk exclusively on her hind legs and experimenting with new modes of speech. The simian vocal box was to her mind despicable, and the habit of walking on four legs, old-fashioned and offensive. She was the new order of things, and suffered both the censure and the abuse of her day.

"Forward hussy!" exclaimed the neighbors as she tilted about on tip-toes and picked fig leaves, which attracted her from infancy.

"What will we do with our little Eva?" said her father.

"The Lord only knows; I only hope she doesn't come to some bad end," responded his trial-marriage wife, for that was in the halcyon Nat Goodwin days.

But Yvette had no patience with her family, and in answer to their scoldings she would always say, "Prithee, leave me alone, you will yet have cause to be proud of me—who am y-clept Yvette."

Yvette was quite too self-sufficient to seriously consider her parents. She was no idle ape. She originated the study of eugenics, and though there were few among her friends advanced enough to see what great good she was going to do the world, Yvette did not despair.

There was among her acquaintances a friendly boa constrictor with whom she was wont to discuss her plans for world progress.

Balboa, this serpent, held high sociological ideals and loved to exploit them to his simple but sincere lady-friend. In close confab they foresaw together equal suffrage, trust annihilation, and the solution of the liquor problem, which subjects were then far in the dim future.

"Ah, Balboa," pined Yvette one day as she sat beneath the apple tree about which her coily friend continually twined, "if I could only find a noble knyght, yonge and freissche, one who would a loyal housbondes meke, then we could properly propagate the race." She spoke partly in the poetic tongue which Chaucer later adopted. It was new in those days and considered quite an innovation.

"I know the piece of protoplasm for you," answered Balboa in the vulgar tongue of that archaic day. "Great stuff! Adam's his name. If you an' him get hitched an' settle down to life on the installment furniture plan it'll be nothin' but brussels sprouts and camembert for life. He's quite a

superior organism, parts his hair in the middle with his front feet. Believe me, he's the boy for you! You're always kickin' about the limitations of simian speech. Why, Adam's got a vocal box that would make a harmonica jealous. Possibly you might arrange together to—well, I think I could fix it so you could meet him some night. Would you like to have me bring him around?"

"Pray do," responded Yvette, which is the first reference to bridge whist in history.

The wily serpent, out of a lofty interest in eugenics, brought the two most perfect creatures of the day together and introduced them with grave formality, as Luther Burbank would present a pomegranate to a cauliflower for the good of posterity.

"Much obliged to meet you," said Adam, who was very uncouth, standing with difficulty on his hind legs while giving one of his fore-paws to the lady. But his voice was perfect in range and his hair was neatly parted.

"And you are y-clept Adam," breathed Yvette.

"It's easy to see she's dead gone on him," snickered the serpent.

"That's my handle, Miss," replied Adam, a little put to it because of her quaint, archaic phrase.

"Prithee sit thee down on yon bramble bush and we will hold converse," breathed Yvette, who had the temperament and wasn't at all practical.

Adam said he preferred standing, and was immediately sorry for having committed himself, because he found it difficult to stand on his hind feet, and Yvette frowned if he even rested a fore-paw on a rock.

"What do you know about eugenics?" asked Yvette with much naiveté, the serpent having modestly withdrawn.

"I don't know him, but I think I seen his sister last night," replied Adam impromptu.

"I mean, don't you think our race is shamefully degraded? Don't you feel that by applying scientific principles and——"

"I get you—I get you," answered Adam slyly, though he didn't understand a word of it.

"What are your notions on race suicide?" asked Yvette pensively.

"I don't know how anybody could think of suicide at all, when they look into those lamps of yours," which shows that Adam was the original Hibernian.

"Methinks you'll do. You show signs that I've hoped to see in posterity," remarked Yvette.

"I don't care anything about posterity, but I'd

STUART DAVIS 1913

Drawn by Stuart Davis, June 1913

"Gee Mag, Think of Us Being on a Magazine Cover"

[*Davis, whose work grew increasingly abstract, became one of America's outstanding painters. At the time this drawing appeared he was a protégé of John Sloan. He left the staff during the great artists' revolt in 1916. This was the cover of the June 1913 issue.*]

[57]

like to be shuffled into the pack along with you. Will you marry me?" said Adam, with what would seem a little precipitation if his crude times were not taken into consideration. Remember, this was even before the stone age, and love-making was just an ordinary Robert W. Chambers affair.

"But my family, they would never allow it; mother wants to keep me at home to help wash up the cocoanut shells after dinner," said Yvette sadly.

"Then we'll elope!" he spoke with primitive emphasis.

The notion fitted in nicely with Yvette's advanced theories, and because she had never even heard of an elopement she sympathized heartily with the movement.

So they took the serpent into their confidence and he told them of a garden where they could live happily and alone.

Yvette ran home to get her vanity box, which consisted of little more than a bit of red chalk and some ground rice. In ten minutes the pair was palpitating on the edge of the home-thicket waiting for Balboa to say that the coast was clear.

Drawn by John Sloan, February 1914

Mid-Ocean

"Are there enough lifeboats for all the passengers?"
"No."
"Are there life preservers for everybody?"
"No."
"Well, hasn't anything been done in preparation for shipwreck?"
"Well, the band has learned to play 'Nearer, My God, to Thee' in the dark."

The friendly serpent soon glided up to them and remarked, "It's all fixed. Make a neat getaway and good luck and long life to you! It's a day's journey to the garden, and in case you get hungry here's something for lunch." He slipped an apple into Yvette's hand.

Next day the happy bridal party entered the Garden of Edam, and there they lived happily for many a day, unbothered.

At length Yvette presented Adam with a babe. Together they marvelled at the fine fair skin of the youngster and at his lusty cry, so un-simian, almost human.

Yvette never allowed her babe to crawl, but taught him to stand upright from the first.

"Isn't it a pretty thing!" she would dotingly say to Adam. "We will call it our man-child and it shall be first of the tribe to be known as Men."

"I wanted to call him Esau," pleaded Adam, pitifully, his lower lip trembling.

"No! Never! See what a vast improvement he is on us! He has no barbarous coat of fur. As scientists, as inventors, we have the right to name this new species a new name. We will call him Man, and when he grows up he shall stay in the Garden of Edam, and never know to his shame from what common stock he sprang."

"Oh, well, have it your own way," said Adam. "The kid may be all right for a scientific experiment, but I hoped all along for a nice little buffalo rug of a boy we could have called Esau."

"You're not worthy the name of scientist!" cried Yvette, putting down the fig leaf nighty she was darning. "You've done your Darwinian duty; be of good cheer, our names will go down to posterity for this creation of ours, linked together for all time."
—May 1913

LOUIS UNTERMEYER
A Horrible Example

These Times, by Louis Untermeyer. $1.25 net. (Henry Holt & Co.)

This volume, sent originally for review, has been lying around my desk for a couple of months and causing me no little concern. For I find it difficult to appraise it properly. I have taken the book up a dozen times, read most of the poems and put it down with the proverbial mingled emotions. It is, I may as well state at the outset, a pernicious and poisonous volume. And yet there is something about it that I like. It may be the strange choice of subjects, or the sheer physical exuberance of the author, or the neat punctuation that appeals to me; I am not sure. There is, I cannot deny it, a certain personal quality, a familiar flavor that intrigues me; an occasional note that, somehow, touches an echoing chord in my coarse and commercial nature. There are moments when I am actually charmed by the ease and fluency of the man's writing. But this unaccountable weakness shall not affect my critical attitude toward what, I repeat, is a most subversive and damnable piece of work. To particularize:

I turn to page 68 and under the promising caption of "Portrait of an American," I note that the first four lines run:

> "He slobbers over sentimental plays
>   And sniffles over sentimental songs.
> He tells you often how he sadly longs
>   For the ideals of the dear, old days."

This, aside from all considerations of how the classic sonnet has been debased into a string of vulgar colloquialisms, is not only a bad poem, it is a malicious libel. It is the sort of thing one might expect from a person who had been influenced by the reading of such anarchist-making publications as "Mother Earth" and the Congressional Record. The American, as recent events so eloquently prove, is anything but a sentimental person and, instead of longing for "the ideals of the dear, old days," he is imbued with a revolutionary ardor, a lust for democracy so generous and progressive that he is ready to ram it down the throat of anyone that doesn't happen to possess it; more than that, he is even willing to sacrifice what little he has of it in order to force it on some one else. Mr. Untermeyer's verses take no account of these practical and sacrificial passions. But I pass to other and even more condemnable exhibits.

On page 113 I find what is supposed to be a child's poem, "concerning God," that begins:

> "Well, God does nothing all day long
>   But He sits and sits in His chair."

Such a cool and casual interpretation of the deity could not, I am sure, have originated in the mind of a child. So I am forced to the unpleasant conclusion that Mr. Untermeyer himself planned this irreligious conceit. My conviction is strengthened by a study of the author's other poems that reveal, all too plainly, a lamentable lack of reverence and no decent fear of things that should be kept respectably sacred. True, his intimacy with God is not quite so patronizing and brash as it was in "Challenge," but it still stands in need of

Drawn by Art Young, November 1914

"No thank you. There's a lot of trouble coming, and I'll be blamed for it."

the services of a proofreader and a few clergymen. But if he trifles less with the Eternal, he bandies words with matters that are less infinite but even more powerful. For instance, I find on page 77 the following portrait of a Supreme Court Judge:

> "How well this figure represents the Law—
>   This pose of neuter justice, sterile cant;
> This Roman Emperor with the iron jaw,
>   Wrapped in the black silk of a maiden-aunt."

To pat God on the shoulder is bad enough, but to insult so venerable a lawgiver as Judge ——! . . . I cannot contemplate the consequences without a shudder.

Similarly reprehensible are the author's views on such grave topics as life, prison reform, selling jewelry, the hereafter and piano-playing. The talk of the queer couple in "Cell Mates" and the absurd feminism of "Eve Speaks" is only one shade less grotesque than Mr. Untermeyer's own impertinences in "On the Palisades" or his over-athletic "Swimmers" with its concluding flippancy:

> "Life, an adventure perilous and gay;
>   And Death, a long and vivid holiday."

But still more serious than these defects is the author's penchant for the lewd and libidinous. I find the word *"body"* fourteen times in the first hundred pages, *"barbaric"* seventeen times, *"love"* (without reference to anything legal or spiritual) twenty-one times, and the words *"passion"* and *"passionate,"* thirty-two times! In fact, in one poem entitled, innocently enough, "To A Weeping Willow," I find—But nothing can be gained by enlarging this shameful catalog.

Altogether, I do not hesitate to pronounce this one of the most noxious and notorious books of the season. In spite of a few readable lines and a half-dozen whimsicalities which may please the unwary, I strongly advise against the purchase of "These Times." It is incomprehensible that so reputable a firm as Messrs. Henry Holt & Co. should have printed the affair. It is by turns violent, valueless and vicious. And yet, in spite of everything there is something about this volume that I like. Something that makes me turn to it again and again. I cannot explain it.

—October 1917

Drawn by John Sloan, July 1913

The Return from Toil

Fiction

[The Masses *printed many short stories, most of which could not at the time have appeared anywhere else. The following stories are not necessarily the best, but they are representative of the kind of work which the editors believed it was their duty to encourage.*]

JAMES HOPPER
The Job

[*Although Hopper never became well known and eventually dropped out of sight, he was regarded at the time as a highly promising short-story writer.*]

We were yet "new ones," Gray and I, and we thought that we were seeing Paris. We had been spending the late hours up on the Montmartre, in red windmills and cabarets of death, when we came upon a place which, we decided, might well close the evening's entertainment.

In a vacant lot, between two high buildings towering black, was a booth of painted cardboard and wood. Flanking the entrance like statues, were two men in red and gold livery, each holding in his right hand a roaring torch. Between them, his lined face very yellow in the light, another man stood, clad in evening dress.

His apparel was very correct—which means that he was all black with three exceptions: his white gloves, his sepulchral bosom, and a livid line upon the top of his head, impeccably drawn, from which his bluish hair fell off to the right and the left in pomaded rigidity. A collapsed opera hat was upon his hip, a monocle in the convulsed arcade of his right eye; we felt that he also must be perfumed.

At regular intervals, standing there with his heels together, his bust tilted slightly forward, he delivered, without a movement, without a gesture, in a manner frigid and disdainful, the following speech:

"Mesdames et Messieurs: We have here, within, the marvel of the Universe—or rather, should I say, the marvel of this little old ball which you, with a certain fatuity, insist upon calling The Universe. When I say 'marvel,' mesdames et messieurs, I mean none of these puerile and ridiculous objects which you, in your childhood, have been trained to consider marvelous. Inside of our little

barraque, you will find no Eiffel tower, nor Bridge of Brooklyn, nor Colosseus. No, mesdames et messieurs, you will not find that. The marvel that we present to you is not material and gross; it is scientific and psychologic. The marvel we present to you consists of men. It consists of two men. These men are savages. Incidentally, for those who are patriotically inclined (patriotism, ladies and gentlemen, among the superstitious is one of those which I admit as, after all, eminently respectable), I will add that these savages are the latest acquisitions, down on the shores of the Ougandi, to the citizenship of the French Republic. Like all savages, they are very ugly and very black. But that which marks them apart from other savages who are very ugly and very black, and which makes them the marvel which I promise to you, is the matter of their diet. These savages, ladies and gentlemen, eat rats. And the rats that they eat, ladies and gentlemen, are alive. If you do not believe me, enter and view. They eat the rats, and the rats are alive. The proof of this is that, while being eaten, the rats squeal. Also, they bleed."

We entered—moved by a curiosity neither scientific, psychologic nor patriotic. The place was small; some twenty spectators were standing, while others were on the one bench, forward. Among these, and right before us, were a little shopkeeper, and his wife with a beflowered bonnet, side by side like rotund little pumpkins. Up on the stage, seated on stools, were two extravagant beings. Their faces were smudged with soot; and black tights, carelessly wrinkled till they looked very little like the skin they were meant to represent, were their only clothing. Curtain rings were through their nostrils, wigs of black wool upon their heads, and upon the wigs were crushed stovepipe hats. They sat there motionless in the flare of the gasoline torches, in postures meant to be rigid but which were creased with weariness.

A violin, a cornet, a bass-drum and cymbals suddenly struck up a violently rhythmed cacophony, and the two "savages," springing up like automata, began to dance. They stamped, bounded, shouted, slapped their thighs, made hideous grimaces. One was a big, deep-chested man, with the torso of a wrestler; the other was thin, with rounded shoulders and caved-in ribs; in spite of the smudge upon his face, his nose showed long and sharp, and this long, sharp nose, motionless and frigid, reserving its character, its dignity, as it were, above the mad trepidation of the body, in the midst of the convulsions of the visage, somehow was very sad.

The music quickened its precipitate beat; they gyrated clumsily, sprang up into the air, contorted themselves, howled like dogs. Suddenly, from a table behind them they picked up each a cage— one of these cages in which rats are caught alive. Holding them with outclutched fingers, they whirred them in circles at the end of their arms, their frenzy, consciously worked up and partly real by now, rising the while. Then, in unison, they snapped open the steel doors and pulled out, each, by its long tail, a great gutter rat.

And then—we turned our faces away. We could not look. And the fat little shop-keeper's wife capsized upon the bench, and hid her pudgy face between her pudgy arms, oblivious of the damage to the beflowered bonnet. But the husband, very stiff, his hands upon his knees, looked on with eyes round as an owl's.

Two street gamins near us kept us apprised of the progress of the performance. They were continuing a discussion.

"But I tell you that they *are* savages."

"Allons!—do skins of savages wrinkle like that —like accordeons? They are black tights. They're savages from Batignoles!"

"But they eat the rats."

"That is a trick."

"No—they eat—look at that one's teeth—see?"

"It's a trick. They slide them under the tights."

"But I tell you they are eating! Hear them squeal?"

"Yes, they squeal—tonnère de Dieu, that is true! they are eating the rats!"

"And look at the blood."

"Br-r-r—that is true; they eat the rats."

"And they are alive."

"They are alive!"

"And they are not savages."

"They are not savages, and they eat the rats."

"Alive!"

"Tonnère!"

The music stopped abruptly, as if it had struck a wall. We looked up. The "savages" were again upon their stools, motionless, except that they oscillated from side to side unconsciously, as if dizzy.

We went out. The night was very black and a cold wind had sprung up, but somehow we could not bear the thought of walls. We strolled to and fro up on the hill, taking big gulps of frigid air, which came from the East, where, we knew, there were mountains, and pines, and we looked down upon the city, glowing dully beneath a sky low and opaque like a cupola of lead. And within us there was the same torment, for when Gray said, hesitatingly, "Let's go back, what do you say, down there, to the barraque, to see them come out?' he said what I wished to say.

So we went back. They were still there—the man in full-dress and the torch-bearers—but they were all shivering miserably. He said his speech once more, in precisely the same detached and contemptuous manner, but this time he followed, within, the little band of midnight derelicts he had persuaded. The torch-bearers disappeared behind him, and we were alone in the street, unconsciously hugging the wall as if planning evil.

The madly rhythmic music came attenuated to our ears, and also a stamping and clogging and hoarse cries. This ceased after a time; the door opened and the spectators trooped out. We watched the side door. It opened, and through a pool of light splashed down from the near gas lamp, the spieler passed, a threadbare cape over his full-dress, a cap upon his head (the collapsible opera hat evidently was stage property). Then came the musicians and the torch men.

Another moment passed, long to us, hiding there in the dark. The door went open again—and a man burst out.

"It's the big one," whispered Gray.

It was the big "savage." He fairly ran by us, his face purple—and we saw him go down the street with great strides and dive head first into the luminous rectangle made by the open door of a drinking shop.

After a while, the door opened once more—but very softly, and the second "savage," the thin one with round shoulders, shuffled slowly into the light. His hands, in the pockets of his thin jacket, drew it tight over his caved-in ribs; his neck was bent, chin forward, with a mournful stork-like expression, and in the smudge of his visage, only partly cleaned, his long sad nose shone very white.

He stood there a moment, uncertain—and suddenly we saw that he was not alone. From the darkness across the street a little girl had emerged; she now stood before him—a little girl of misery, clad in tatters. A shawl was upon her head; it descended down both sides of the face, but far back, enough to let us see her profile—and this profile, wizened and pinched, was the man's.

"Oh, here you are, la p'tite," he said, hoarsely.

She looked up at him, sharply, like a little squirrel. "What luck to-day?" she asked.

"Better," he said. "Yesterday, I couldn't—I couldn't. But to-day, I did—several times, I did. I made one franc."

She seized his hand, feverishly. "Vite," she said, "quick, père, let's eat; quick, let's eat; there is a bouillon over there"—she pointed down the street—"I smelled the soup of it all to-day. Let's eat."

But at these words a weakness seemed to seize him—and, as if dissolving, he crumbled down upon the curb, and sat there, both his hands sunk into the hollow of his stomach, his long nose almost touching his knees.

"Oh, père," she cried, impatiently; "come on now, quick now!"

"Yes, ma petite fille; yes, ma petite fille," he said at length; "yes—you go—here it is, the franc." He fumbled in his pocket. "Take it and go—do what you want to do—but do not talk—say no word to me about it. Go—I'll wait for you here—till you have finished."

She took the money, eagerly, ran a few steps down the street then came back. "Père, come with me; you must eat," she said.

"Go!" he cried, hoarsely. "Go!" he bellowed, in sudden rage. His hand rose above her, hovered —but when it came down it lit gently upon her shoulder. "Go, little girl," he said. His voice rose again, threatening. "But say not a word to me about it! Don't say that word!" he screamed.

She flitted off into the darkness. And he, on the curb, doubled up, his hands sunk into the pit of his stomach, trembled long with convulsive disgust. Finally, he seemed to master himself; he passed his hand, limply, over his forehead—it must have been wet with a cold perspiration.

"Quel métier," he muttered, whimsically; "tonnère de Dieu—what a job!"   —March 1913

FLOYD DELL
The Beating

[*Dell became a successful novelist after his first novel,* Moon-Calf, *made the best-seller lists in 1920. His only previously published fiction consisted of short stories like this one.*]

A sixteen year old girl sat on the bed undressing. It was in one of the two upstairs dormitories in the Training School for Girls, otherwise the Girls'

Reform School. The room held a double row of hastily made beds. Across the wooden headboard of each bed was stretched a piece of clothesline, on which hung a towel and a nightgown. Beside each bed was a white-painted washstand. On the whitewashed wall at one end of the room, hanging from a nail, was a little framed motto: "God Is Love." High up in the thin whitewashed partition behind the bed on which the girl was sitting was a little window, barred against the other dormitory. In the opposite wall were a number of similar windows, barred against the world. In the fourth wall was the door, which was now locked.

Minnie was getting ready to be whipped. She was undressing slowly, because she knew she had about half an hour. They had not yet whipped Jeanette, and Jeanette had been the first over the high picket fence in the break for liberty the night before. Minnie had followed, and so she would be whipped afterward. Minnie, who understood little of the ways of Miss Hampton and Miss Carter, and those other people who "ran" the Reform School, could understand that. She would have resented being whipped first. Besides, she wanted to hear how Jeanette would take her beating.

Jeanette had sworn to her that she would "never let them devils lay a hand on her again"; she would kill herself first, she said. Minnie did not take that very seriously. She knew Jeanette was in for a beating all right, and a good hard one. But there was one funny thing. Jeanette had had one beating in the month she had been there, and the girls said that "They"—meaning Miss Hampton and Miss Carter—couldn't get a whimper out of her. They had taken turns, and beaten her until they were tired, but she wouldn't make a sound. Well, they would see that she hollered this time!

Minnie would be able to hear it all—and perhaps even see, for there was that window in the partition right above her bed. The first day Jeanette had been there, a girl named Anna had been beaten in the other dormitory, and she and Jeanette had hidden here to listen. Jeanette had seen this window, and climbd up on the headboard of the bed to get to it. She had "gone up there like a cat," and caught hold of the bars of the window, and looked through. Minnie was not so tall as Jeanette, but she might see too if she was careful.

Minnie smiled, remembering how Jeanette had acted that time. She had turned—like the heroine in a show Minnie had seen—and told what was happening on the other side of the partition. She did that for a while, and then jumped down—anyhow. It was lucky she lit on the bed. She didn't care what she did, it seemed like. She just seemed to go crazy.

The way she had raged around that dormitory frightened Minnie now to think of it. She had beat on the walls with her fists, and kicked at the beds, and flung herself on the floor and rolled and writhed, screaming and kicking.

They had put her in the "strong room," which existed for just such cases. She could kick and scream there all she wanted to—she would get tired of it after a while.

The thought of all these things agitated Minnie as she undressed. It made her fumble as she unbuttoned her dress in the back, and it made her pull one of her shoe strings into a hard knot. She sat there jerking at it savagely and stupidly, drawing it tighter and tighter. She cursed, in a vicious monosyllable; and then, her nervous tension seeming to find relief in this, all her excitement flooding this channel, there poured out a stream of vile words. A stranger to her kind, hearing her, would have felt her words like a blow in the face. They would have seemed to him horribly and unthinkably foul. But she did not have any idea of that. She had learned those words when she was fourteen years old, at the box factory, and they had seemed "smart" to her then. She knew they were considered "bad," and she did not let Miss Carter or Miss Hampton catch her saying them. But it made her feel good to do it, and so now she spat them out, a putrescent stream. Then her unconscious lips smiled sweetly, as she caught the right end of the string and pulled the knot loose.

She went on undressing, faster now, for she could hear sounds in the other room. They were dragging out the bed from the wall, so that someone could stand at each corner and hold the girl who was being whipped. Minnie kicked off the last of the soiled and ragged underclothing furnished her by the state, and reached up for her coarse nightgown.

She had very little of that physical charm of adolescence in which a mother might take pleasure. Her chest was narrow, and her breasts, with their pale nipples, were barely rounded out on her bosom; she sat ungracefully, her back bent, her feet twisted under the edge of the bed—an undernourished, undeveloped little woman-child.

As she sat there she bit her under-lip a little. It was a trick she had caught from Jeanette, who

always did it when she was thinking. Minnie's thoughts were half-defined, and intermixed with vivid memories that flowed through her mind in an uneasy stream.

She thought of the night before, when she had tried to run away. She hadn't much wanted to try —she didn't believe they would succeed—but she had to go with her chum. She knew all the time it would only end in a beating. But she had been beaten at home often enough to know what a beating was. She didn't care much.

She had shown Jeanette her back and legs, on which, at that time, the marks of her last beating still faintly remained—little purple bruises. She was rather amused at the way Jeanette took it: she turned white. Jeanette said she had never been beaten in all her life. "Just you wait," Minnie told her, "you will be." And Jeanette had been. But she hadn't made a sound. It was game of her, all right.

There were a lot of queer things about Jeanette. The time they had waited to hear Anna get whipped Jeanette had stretched herself out languorously on the coverlet. Lying there, Jeanette had asked, "Why do they call us delinquent?" Minnie had said, "It means bad, doesn't it?" And then Jeanette had laughed and said: "No, I know what it means. It means that we came along too late. I ought to have lived a thousand years ago. . . . I'll bet they wouldn't have put me in a stockade and learned me to sew and cook and scrub. . . . Sew and cook and scrub! . . . I wonder if I'll ever get what I want?"

And when Minnie asked, "What do you want?" she said: "What every girl wants—to wear nice clothes, and talk to men—and make love."

Minnie thought she meant the "red light district," but found out that she was mistaken. Jeanette had never heard of it. She had lived seventeen years in a little country town, and did not know what prostitution meant. Minnie explained. Jeanette was disgusted.

"Well," Minnie said, "you needn't try to make out that you're so good. How about those drummers?" And Jeanette flushed and said: "Oh, that was different." Jeanette had told her about the things she had been sent to the Reform School for; when she talked of them, a light came into her eyes. Jeanette was a queer girl. She thought that such things were beautiful. . . . Jeanette was queer.

Minnie did not understand. Minnie was not "queer." She would have made, under other circumstances, a dutiful wife for the same reasons

Drawn by John Sloan, August 1914

that now made her an inmate of a Reform School. She had never been other than passive and acquiescent. She had never wanted to be "bad"—and wouldn't have been, if they had only let her alone. But the boys at the box factory and the tablet factory, who took her to the parks and nickel theaters, were insistent. She had never encouraged them; she had been merely apprehensively submissive. There was nothing beautiful about that.

Minnie meant to be "good" when she got out, so as not to run the risk of being sent back to this place again. But Jeanette wasn't going to be

"good" she said; and she wasn't going to come back here, either. Minnie couldn't understand what she meant. She only remembered that right after that they had had a quarrel. Jeanette had a curious set of circumlocutions, which she used instead of the simple and vulgar terms which served Minnie's needs in these discussions. Jeanette had objected with a sudden fierceness to Minnie's terminology. Minnie's lips moved unconsciously as she rehearsed what they had said to each other.

A sound came from the other dormitory, and Minnie jumped up and came over close to the par-

[65]

tition. There was a noise of scuffling—and she knew they were dragging in Jeanette to be whipped.

Minnie jumped up on the bed. She seized hold of the top of the headboard, and drew herself up. She made an ineffectual clutch for the sill of the little window high above, missed and fell, scraping her knee against the sharp edge of a panel in the headboard. She rose, panting, and seized hold again. More carefully this time, she drew herself up, supporting one foot on the tiny eighth-of-an-inch panel edge on which she had scraped her knee. She reached up, biting her lower lip cruelly, and caught the sill of the window with her fingers' ends. She steadied herself, pulled herself up once more, and in a moment was safely clutching the bars of the window, while her feet rested on the top of the headboard.

She was sorry she was not so tall as Jeanette. She could not see through the window while standing on the headboard. But she *must* have a glimpse. So she pulled herself up by main strength, and rested with a forearm flat on the sill while the other hand gripped a bar in the window. Hanging there, her body hunched awkwardly against the wall, her neck craned uncomfortably, she gazed through into the other dormitory. The scuffling had ceased, and there was Jeanette lying on her face on the bed, with one of the "goody-goods"—meaning the girls, who were going to be let out soon, and who curried favor with "Them" rather than be kept longer—at each corner of the bed. Each "goody-good" held an arm or a leg, held it tightly with both hands, while the girl lay a limp, exhausted thing on the sheets, panting audibly. Only her nightgown, which should have been slipped up to her shoulders, was not on her body at all. Minnie saw with a thrill, before she slipped down the wall and rested her feet again on the top of the headboard, that it was lying scattered all over the floor, in shreds and threads.

Minnie was sitting on the edge of the bed, listening dully to the regular sound of blows from the other side of the partition. She had grown tired of hanging there, and had climbed down. She had not been able to see very much, after all. She could see Miss Hampton and Miss Carter, as they stood between her and the low window, and she could see first Miss Carter for a while and then Miss Hampton stoop as she brought down the piece of hose on Jeanette's bare back and legs. But she could not see Jeanette, and could not tell whether she flinched and writhed or not. Certainly

she did keep silent. The "goody-goods" said nothing, and there was no sound, except the hysterical laugh of Miss Carter and the cold tones of Miss Hampton, and the dull impact of the hose against the girl's flesh.

Minnie had been disappointed. She hardly realized it, but she had been expecting some spectacular action on the part of Jeanette. And here was Jeanette merely lying still and letting them beat her. Minnie listened. There was a little pause in the thud, thud, thud, and then it commenced again. Miss Carter was doing it now. Miss Carter struck more quickly, and with less strength; sometimes her blows went wild. . . .

Suddenly Minnie realized what was happening; it flashed on her mind like a vision. She had seen the thing, and had been unmoved, because she had not realized it. But now the mere sound of it had somehow brought realization. First she felt—with a keenness greater than she had ever felt it in her own body—the pain of those blows on Jeanette's flesh; and more than that—a sensation she had never experienced—the humiliation of them. She felt the pain, the shame, and wanted to cry out; and then she felt with a shock the violent mastery which Jeanette had put upon herself to keep from crying out. The realization shook her from head to foot. She drew her breath heavily, and her heart labored painfully in her breast. As she listened, time seemed to have commenced to run more slowly, so that the blows fell at a longer interval. She waited for each blow, she braced herself in imagination to meet it; she felt it fall, and suffered the exquisite torture of the fire that ate fiercely into the flesh, burned red-hot for an unendurable moment, and then died slowly down. She caught her breath, braced herself anew for the next blow, suffered its pangs; and the next, and the next, and the next.

Her wide open eyes saw, as though no partition were there, the quivering body on the bed; her mind, more appreciative than it had ever been of the emotions of another, viewed the struggle with pain, the terrible struggle for silence, that was fought and won ten times in every minute—won and almost lost, renewed and won again, endlessly.

Minnie put her fingers in her ears, but she heard her heart keeping time to the blows, and took them out again. There was a little pause, and Minnie gasped with relief; but the blows commenced again, more steady than before; Miss Hampton was taking her turn again. Minnie began desperately counting them; but she stopped at ten, and again put her fingers in her ears for a moment. Then she began to walk up and down the aisle, between the beds, lingering as she neared the window through which the sounds came. Twice she went back and forth, walking and running, and then she flung herself sobbing on the bed. But in a moment she was up again, and transformed. She rushed down the aisle, striking blindly both ways with her clenched hands, wounding them on the wood and iron of the bedsteads.

At the other end of the room she saw the little sign, "God Is Love." She stopped short. Trembling uncontrollably all through her body, she threw back her head, and uttered a hoarse, agonized cry. As she did so, the sounds in the other room ceased. There was silence for a whole minute, and then the key turned in the lock, and the door of the dormitory opened.   —August 1914

SHERWOOD ANDERSON
Hands

[*Anderson had been discovered by Dell, who published some of the best* Winesburg, Ohio *stories in* The Masses. *This didn't make Anderson any richer (he later estimated that all of the* Winesburg *stories together brought him less than $100 when first published), but the critical reputation these stories brought him paved the way for the collection which made him famous.*]

"Oh, you Wing Biddlebaum! Comb your hair! It's falling into your eyes!"

Wing Biddlebaum, a fat, little old man, had been walking nervously up and down the half decayed veranda of a small frame house that stood near the edge of a ravine. He could see, across a long field that had been seeded for clover, but that had produced only a dense crop of yellow mustard weeds, the public highway. Along this road a wagon filled with berry pickers was returning from the fields. The berry pickers, youths and maidens, laughed and shouted boisterously. A boy, clad in a blue shirt, leaped from the wagon and attempted to drag after him one of the girls, who screamed and protested shrilly. A boy, clad in a blue shirt, leaped from the wagon and attempted to drag after him one of the girls, who screamed and protested shrilly.

As he watched them, the plump little hands of the old man fiddled unconsciously about his bare, white forehead as though arranging a mass of tangled locks on that bald crown. Then, as the berry pickers saw him, that thin girlish voice came mockingly across the field. Wing Biddlebaum stopped, with a frightened look, and put down his hands helplessly.

When the wagon had passed on, he went across the field through the tall mustard weeds, and climbing a rail fence, peered anxiously along the road to the town. He was hoping that young George Willard would come and spend the evening with him. For a moment he stood on the fence, unconsciously rubbing his hands together and looking up the road; and then, fear overcoming him, he ran back to the house and commenced to walk again on the half decayed veranda.

Among all the people of Winesburg, but one had come close to this man; for Wing Biddlebaum, forever frightened and beset by a ghostly band of doubts, did not think of himself as in any way a part of the life of the town in which he had lived for the last twenty years. But with George Willard, son of Tom Willard, the proprietor of the new Willard House, he had formed something like a friendship. George Willard was reporter on the Winesburg Democrat, and sometimes in the evening walked out along the highway to Wing Biddlebaum's house.

In George Willard's presence, Wing Biddlebaum, who for twenty years had been the town mystery, lost something of his timidity and his shadowy personality, submerged in a sea of doubts, came forth to look at the world. With the young reporter at his side he ventured, in the light of day, into Main street or strode up and down on the rickety front porch of his own house talking excitedly. The voice that had been low and trembling became shrill and loud. The bent figure straightened. With a kind of wriggle like a fish returned to the brook by the fisherman, Biddlebaum the silent began to talk, striving to put into words the ideas that had been accumulated by his mind during long years of silence.

Wing Biddlebaum talked much with his hands. The slender expressive fingers, forever active, forever striving to conceal themselves in Wing's pockets or behind his back, came forth and became the piston rods of his machinery of expression.

The story of Wing Biddlebaum is a story of hands. Their restless activity, like unto the beating of the wings of an imprisoned bird, had given him his name. Some obscure poet of the town had thought of it. The hands alarmed their owner. He wanted to keep them hidden away and looked with amazement at the quiet, inexpressive hands of other men who walked beside him in the fields or passed driving sleepy teams on country roads.

When he talked to George Willard, Wing Biddlebaum closed his fists and beat with them upon a table or on the walls of his house. The action made him more comfortable. If the desire to talk came to him when the two were walking in the fields, he sought out a stump or the top board of a fence and with his hands pounding busily talked with renewed ease.

The story of Wing Biddlebaum's hands is worth a book in itself. Sympathetically set forth it would tap strange, beautiful qualities in obscure men. It is a job for a poet. In Winesburg the hands had attracted attention merely because of their activity. With them Wing Biddlebaum had picked as high as a hundred and forty quarts of strawberries in a day. They became his distinguishing feature, the source of his fame. Also they made more grotesque an already grotesque and elusive individuality. Winesburg was proud of the hands of Wing Biddlebaum in the same spirit in which it was proud of Banker White's new stone house and Wesley Moyer's bay stallion, "Tony Tip," that had won the "two-fifteen" trot at the fall races in Cleveland.

As for George Willard, he had many times wanted to ask about the hands. At times an almost overwhelming curiosity had taken hold of him. He felt that there must be a reason for their strange activity and their inclination to keep hidden away, and only a growing respect for Wing Biddlebaum kept him from blurting out the question that was often in his mind.

Once he had been on the point of asking. The two were walking in the fields on a summer afternoon and had stopped to sit upon a grassy bank. All afternoon Wing Biddlebaum had been as one inspired. By a fence he had stopped and, beating like a giant woodpecker upon the top board, had shouted at George Willard, condemning his tendency to be too much influenced by the people about him. "You are destroying yourself," he cried. "You have the inclination to be alone and to dream and you are afraid of dreams. You want to be like others in town here. You hear them talk and you try to imitate them."

On the grassy bank Wing Biddlebaum had tried again to drive his point home. His voice became soft and reminiscent and with a sigh of contentment he launched into a long, rambling talk, speaking as one lost in a dream.

Out of the dream Wing Biddlebaum made a picture for George Willard. In the picture men lived again in a kind of pastoral golden age. Across a green open country came clean limbed young men, some afoot, some mounted upon horses. In crowds the young men came to gather about the feet of an old man who sat beneath a tree in a tiny garden and who talked to them.

Wing Biddlebaum became wholly inspired. For once he forgot the hands. Slowly they stole forth and lay upon George Willard's shoulders. Something new and bold came into the voice that talked. "You must try to forget all you have learned," said the old man. "You must begin to dream. From this time on you must begin to shut your ears to the roaring of the voices."

Pausing in his speech, Wing Biddlebaum looked long and earnestly at George Willard. His eyes glowed. Again he raised the hands to caress the boy, and then a look of horror swept over his face.

With a convulsive movement of his body, Wing Biddlebaum sprang to his feet and thrust his hands deep into his trousers pockets. Tears came to his eyes. "I must be getting along home. I can't talk any more with you," he said nervously.

Without looking back, the old man had hurried down the hillside and across a long meadow, leaving George Willard perplexed and frightened upon the grassy slope. With a shiver of dread, the boy arose and went along the road towards town. "I will not ask him about the hands," he thought, touched by the memory of the terror he had seen in the man's eyes. "There is something wrong, but I don't want to know what it is. His hands have something to do with his fear of me and of everyone."

And George Willard was right. Let us look briefly into the story of the hands. Perhaps our talking of them will arouse the poet who will tell the hidden wonder story of the influence for which the hands were but fluttering pennants of promise.

In his youth Wing Biddlebaum had been a school teacher in a town in Pennsylvania. He was not then known as Wing Biddlebaum, but went by the less euphonic name of Adolf Myers. As Adolf Myers he was much loved by the boys of his school.

Adolf Myers was meant by nature to be a teacher of youth. He was one of those rare, little understood men who ruled by a power so gentle that it passes as a kind of lovable weakness. In his feeling for the boys under his charge he was not unlike the finer sort of women in their love of men.

And yet that is but crudely stated. It wants the poet there. With the boys of his school he had walked in the evening or had sat talking until dusk upon the schoolhouse steps lost in a kind of dream.

Here and there went his hands, caressing shoulders of the boys, playing about the tousled heads. As he talked his voice became soft and musical. There was a caress in that also. In a way the voice and the hands, the stroking of the shoulders and the touching of the hair was a part of the schoolmaster's effort to carry a dream into the young men's minds. By the caress that was in his fingers he expressed himself. He was one of those men in whom sex is diffused, not centralized. Under the caress of his hands, doubt and disbelief went out of the minds of the boys and they also began to dream.

And then the tragedy. A half-witted boy of the school became enamored of the young master. In his bed at night he imagined unspeakable things and in the morning went forth to tell his dreams as facts. Strange, hideous accusations fell from his loose-hung lips. Through the Pennsylvania town went a shiver. Hidden, shadowy doubts that had been in men's minds concerning Adolf Myers were galvanized into beliefs.

The tragedy did not linger. Trembling lads were jerked out of bed and questioned. "He put his arms about me," said one. "His fingers were always playing in my hair," said another.

One afternoon a man of the town, Henry Bradford, who kept a saloon, came to the schoolhouse door. Calling Adolf Myers into the schoolyard, he began to beat him with his fists. As his hard knuckles beat down into the frightened face of the schoolmaster his wrath became more and more terrible. Screaming with dismay, the children ran here and there like disturbed insects. "I'll teach you to put your hands on my boy, you beast," roared the saloon keeper, who, tired of beating the master, had begun to kick him about the yard.

Adolf Myers was driven from the Pennsylvania town in the night. With lanterns in their hands a dozen men came to the door of the house where he lived alone and commanded that he dress and come forth. It was raining and one of the men had a rope in his hands. They had intended to hang the schoolmaster, but something in his figure, so small, white and pitiful, touched their hearts and they let him escape. As he ran away into the darkness they repented of their weakness and ran after him, swearing and throwing sticks and great balls of soft mud at the figure that screamed and ran faster and faster into the darkness.

For twenty years Adolf Myers lived alone in Winesburg. He was but forty, but looked sixty-five. The name of Biddlebaum he got from a box of goods seen at a freight station as he hurried through an eastern Ohio town. He had an aunt in Winesburg, a black-toothed old woman who raised chickens, and with her he lived until she died. He had been ill for a year after the experience in Pennsylvania and after his recovery worked as a day laborer in the fields, going timidly about and striving to conceal his hands. Although he did not understand what had happened, he felt that the hands must be to blame. Again and again the fathers of the boys had talked of his hands. "Keep your hands to yourself," the saloon keeper had roared, dancing with fury in the schoolyard.

Upon the veranda of his house by the ravine, Wing Biddlebaum continued to walk up and down until the sun had disappeared and the road beyond the field was lost in the gray shadows. Going into his house he cut slices of bread and spread honey upon them. When the rumble of the evening train that took away the express cars loaded with the day's harvest of berries had passed and restored the silence of the summer night, he went again to walk upon the veranda. In the darkness he could not see the hands and they became quiet. Although he still hungered for the presence of the boy who was the medium through which he expressed his love of man, the hunger became again a part of his loneliness and his waiting. Lighting a lamp, he washed the few dishes soiled by the simple meal and, setting up a folding cot by the screen door that led to the porch, prepared to undress for the night. A few stray white bread crumbs lay on the cleanly washed floor by the table, and setting the lamp on a low stool, he began to pick up the crumbs, carrying them to his mouth one by one with unbelievable rapidity. In the dense blotch of light beneath the table the kneeling figure looked like a priest engaged in some service in his church. The nervous, expressive fingers, flashing in and out of the light, might well have been mistaken for the fingers of the devotee going swiftly through decade after decade of his rosary. —March 1916

ADRIANA SPADONI
Real Work

[*Miss Spadoni was another writer who appeared regularly in* The Masses *without achieving any wider fame.*]

He lived across the lightwell from me, in three small rooms, smaller and darker even than mine. On the days when I was quite convinced that all the stories in the world had already been written in every possible way and that I was the only fool left alive in the world, I used to rest and draw peace just sitting behind my curtain at the window and watching.

I believe he was the cleanest old man I have ever seen. He was very tall and straight, with a face of chiseled beauty under his thin white hair. His hands were long and slim and cool looking as if he always washed them in very cold water with some hygienic soap and rubbed them on a crash towel.

From a little after eight till four in the afternoon he sat at a small desk by the window. He never once glanced out into the lightwell or paid any attention to any noise that might rise from the kingdom of the janitress below. The rest of us were always hanging out the window watching one or the other of the janitress's children fall down the area steps. But nothing disturbed him. All day he sat there and wrote, or cut clippings from mountains of newspapers, or read. Sometimes he would stop reading and look up, beckoning with his long thin forefinger, and a little, thin, bowed old woman would come trotting to the desk. In all the months that I watched, before I came to know them, never once did I see him call her in any way but this, so that I pictured her always sitting there, beyond the light from the window, watching and waiting for her summons.

Then he would flick the mass of paper from his desk with one of the fine motions of his long hands, and spreading some particular sheet upon the desk, he would read to her, pointing here and there in emphasis or explanation. She listened attentively, nodding her head and glancing at him from time to time. When he laughed she laughed also, always a little behind, like an echo that never catches up.

At four o'clock he left the window. At five the blinds in the second window came down, the window was opened a little from the top. A few moments later the little old woman came and sat down at the desk. She always sat for a little while doing nothing at all. Never have I seen anyone who could sit so restfully, so utterly at peace. Then after an interval she would fold back the curtain and quietly open the window.

It always seemed to me that she did this cautiously, listening with her little gray head cocked like a frightened bird's. And once it was noiselessly opened she leaned upon the sill in perfect contentment, looking up and down the brick walls.

She never spoke. After a while she came to smile and nod to me, but once when I called to her, she drew in hastily, her finger on her lips.

Yet there was not the smallest change at any of the windows that she did not note. In her short half hour there she was like a spectator at a play.

When the light faded in the well she closed the window. Then for perhaps an hour she would sit and read, but never at the desk. A little before eight she began picking up the papers and magazines the old man had left scattered about, piled them in neat piles upon the bench beside the desk —the desk itself she never touched—turned out the light and went to bed. Very early in the morning I would hear her sweeping and putting the "library" to rights.

Twice I met her on the stairs bringing home her marketing in a little basket. She smiled and nodded but fluttered away before I could hold her in talk. It was late in the winter, however, before I came to know her.

It was a stormy night and all the flapping shutters of the rickety old house were possessed of haunting devils. They creaked and cried and begged to be set free, and the wind whistled through the window cracks, and I was very, very sure that all the ideas in the world had been used up ages before, when I became conscious that a light tapping sound had been going on for some time. I hurried to the window and there was my neighbor, leaning from hers and tapping with a feather duster fastened to the broom.

"Have you a bit of mustard?" she called softly. "He's quite bad."

But before I could reassure her, she drew in and closed the window, making the motion for silence, her finger on her lip.

In a few moments she let me quietly in, took the mustard, and drew my head down to hers.

"Thank you, dearie. I don't know how I came to let the mustard all run out. I ALWAYS keep a bit on hand. "Shussh," she added, "I wouldn't want him to hear, my dear. He would never forgive it letting anyone know. Mr. B——— is terrible proud." With that she pushed me gently into a chair and vanished. In a moment I heard her in the room beyond, crooning over the old man. His panting breaths grew easier. In a little while she came out, drawing the door partly to behind her.

"I don't know what I should have done without you. Fancy my letting the mustard run out like that. But it's a long time since he had a spell." And then, just as if I had known her always, she began to talk, in a kind of soft, gentle flow, like the motion of a shallow river through a flat meadow.

"He's so proud. It would kill him if anybody knew about his spells. Now if it was me, my dear, I'm afraid I wouldn't have the courage to keep it all to myself like that. I would want a bit of sympathy. I always was a powerful one for sympathy. Mr. B——— says it's weakness to need other people, but I always did like 'people.' I guess it's because he's so educated he don't need them. He's very finely educated, my dear. He was ready for the bar, they've all been barristers in his family, when, when——— He's had a lot of trouble, indeed he has. If it weren't for his WORK I don't know what he would have done. It has been a wonderful thing. Without it he would have been very lonely, I'm afraid."

I took one of the worn hands in mine. "He has you. He doesn't need anybody else."

"No, dearie, it isn't that." She blushed faintly under her withered skin. "I'm really not a worthy companion for Mr. B———. He should have married an educated woman like himself. She could have helped him in his work."

"Is—is he writing a book?" I ventured.

"Oh, no, dear," she whispered back. "With his clippings, I mean. He has been clipping for ten years now. See." She trotted to a curtained corner and drew aside the curtain. Almost to the ceiling they reached, bundles and bundles of paper clippings. Each was carefully tied with string and a card hung loosely. She dropped the curtain and came back. "He has millions," she whispered, "millions, all tied and labeled. He can put his hand on any subject in a moment. That," she pointed to an old chest of drawers behind the desk, "is full of pictures. He can get a picture to illustrate any article in a twinkling."

"Does he expect—is he going—to USE them in any way?" I gasped, weak with the thought of all those millions of words that had not been allowed to die.

"Oh, no, dearie; it's his WORK. He's been doing it now for ten years. It's quite wonderful, only I can't explain very well, but if he will consent to see you, I'm sure you would be interested. But we see so few people, my dear, practically none at all. Mr. B——— says so few people have a 'sense of values these days.' It's just 'hurry and babble.' That's the reason we don't live in a front apartment. He says all the bustle and silly hurry about nothing distracts him from his work. I did

miss the cars back here terrible at first, but then I have no WORK. If I had Mr. B———'s education perhaps I'd feel the same. Would you like to come over sometime and talk to Mr. B———?"

"I don't know," I answered helplessly while Mr. B———'s "education" loomed fearfully before me. "Do—you think—he———"

There was a sound from the next room. She rose quickly. "I think I can manage it. You just keep a lookout, dearie, and I'll beckon you some day. About three. He grows a little weary then and really needs some relaxation." Then she trotted softly into the next room and I let myself out quietly.

It was four days before I saw her smiling and beckoning from the bedroom window and I went over. The old man at the window turned his swivel chair and his clear, gray eyes smiled a welcome.

"I would rise," he said courteously, "but my limb incapacitates me," and I saw that his foot was sadly twisted and that he walked with a cane. "I must thank you," he continued. "Mrs. B——— has told of your great kindness the other night." His long, slim hand disclaimed my protest that it was nothing. "You are mistaken. Real kindness is very rare in these days of 'babble and hurry.'"

"But among fellow workers, Mr. B——— ..."

"Ah," he said softly, "that is rarer still. There are few real workers. It's all bustle and hurry. There's no method, no routine." He rolled the words like tidbits between his clean, chiseled lips. "And there's nothing possible without routine. Routine and method." The little old woman nodded and crossed her hands in her lap as one settling to hear and enjoy. "Where would my work be if I had no system? I can't imagine any work that would so soon become confused without routine as clippings. Each subject has its allotted moments just as the finished bundle has its allotted place. In the morning I read science and travel and art and politics and mark the passages worthy of saving. Then in the afternoon from one till three I clip. From three to four I devote myself to illustrative pictures. By that time I am a little tired and the mental strain is not so great. Then each day I practise calligraphy, quite a lost art now, and attend to my mail." . . .

When I went away, an hour later, just outside the door the little old woman took both my hands in hers.

"You've done him lots of good, dear. And you will come again, won't you? You see," she added wistfully, "I'm not brilliant like you and Mr. B——— and I can't talk to him the way you do, but I'll enjoy listening. It'll be quite a treat."

—July 1915

JOHN REED
Mac—American

[*Reed became an almost legendary figure through his exploits as foreign correspondent, chronicler of the Bolshevik Revolution (in his* Ten Days That Shook the World*), and founder of the American Communist party. He was also an editor of* The Masses, *a poet, and an accomplished short-story writer, as this piece indicates.*]

I met Mac down in Mexico—Chihuahua City—last New Year's Eve. He was a breath from home—an American in the raw. I remember that as we sallied out of the Hotel for a Tom-and-Jerry at Chee Lee's, the cracked bells in the ancient cathedral were ringing wildly for midnight mass. Above us were the hot desert stars. All over the city, from the *cuartels* where Villa's army was quartered, from distant outposts on the naked hills, from the sentries in the streets, came the sound of exultant shots. A drunken officer passed us, and, mistaking the *fiesta*, yelled "Christ is born!" At the next corner down a group of soldiers, wrapped to their eyes in *serapes*, sat around a fire chanting the interminable ballad of the "Morning Song to Francisco Villa." Each singer had to make up a new verse about the exploits of the Great Captain. . . .

At the great doors of the church, through the shady paths of the Plaza, visible and vanishing again at the mouths of dark streets, the silent, sinister figures of black-robed women gathered to wash away their sins. And from the cathedral itself, a pale red light streamed out—and strange Indian voices singing a chant that I had heard only in Spain.

"Let's go in and see the service," I said. "It must be interesting."

"Hell, no," said Mac, in a slightly strained voice. "I don't want to butt in on a man's religion."

"Are you a Catholic?"

"No," he replied. "I don't guess I'm anything. I haven't been to a church for years."

"Bully for you," I cried. "So you're not superstitious either!"

Mac looked at me with some distaste. "I'm not

a religious man," and here he spat. "But I don't go around knocking God. There's too much risk in it."

"Risk of what?"

"Why when you die—you know. . . ." Now he was disgusted, and angry.

In Chee Lee's we met up with two more Americans. They were the kind that preface all remarks by "I've been in this country seven years, and I know the people down to the ground!"

"Mexican women," said one, "are the rottenest on earth. Why they never wash more than twice a year. And as for Virtue—it simply doesn't exist! They don't get married even. They just take anybody they happen to like. Mexican women are all ——, that's all there is to it!"

"I got a nice little Indian girl down in Torreon," began the other man. "Say, it's a crime. Why she don't even care if I marry her or not! I—"

"That's the way with 'em," broke in the other. "Loose! That's what they are. I've been in this country seven years."

"And do you know," the other man shook his finger severely at me, "you can tell all that to a Mexican Greaser and he'll just laugh at you! That's the kind of dirty skunks they are!"

"They've got no Pride," said Mac, gloomily.

"Imagine," began the first compatriot. "Imagine what would happen if you spoke like that about a woman to an AMERICAN!"

Mac banged his fist on the table. "The American Woman, God bless her!" he said. "If any man dared to dirty the fair name of the American Woman to me, I think I'd kill him." He glared around the table, and, as none of us besmirched the reputation of the Femininity of the Great Republic, he proceeded. "She is a Pure Ideal, and we've got to keep her so. I'd like to hear anybody talk rotten about a woman in my hearing!"

We drank our Tom-and-Jerries in the solemn righteousness of a Convention of Galahads.

"Say Mac," the second man said abruptly. "Do you remember them two little girls you and I had in Kansas City that winter?"

"*Do* I?" glowed Mac. "And remember the awful fix you thought you were in?"

"Will I ever forget it!"

The first man spoke. "Well," said he. "You can crack up your pretty senoritas all you want to. But for *me*, give me a clean little American girl." . . .

Mac was over six feet tall—a brute of a man, in the magnificent insolence of youth. He was only

THE MASSES

JANUARY 1916   10 CENTS

FRANK WALTS

APRIL, 1917   15 cents

the MASSES

twenty-five, but he had been many places and done many things. Railroad Foreman, Plantation Overseer in Georgia, Boss Mechanic in a Mexican Mine, Cow-Puncher, and Texas Deputy-Sheriff. He came originally from Vermont. Along about the second Tom-and-Jerry, he lifted the veil of his past.

"When I came down to Burlington to work in the Lumber Mill, I was only a kid about sixteen. My brother had been working there already a year, and he took me up to board at the same house as him. He was four years older than me—a big guy, too; but a little soft. . . . Always kept bulling around about how wrong it was to fight, and that kind of stuff. Never would hit me—even when he got hot at me; because he said I was smaller.

"Well, there was a girl in the house, that my brother had been carrying on with for a long time. Now I've got the cussedest damn disposition," laughed Mac. "Always did have. Nothing would do me but I should get that girl away from my brother. Pretty soon I did it, too; and when he had to go to town, we certainly just glued ourselves together. . . . Well, gentlemen, do you know what that devil of a girl did? One time when my brother was kissing her, she suddenly says 'Why you kiss just like Mac does!'"

"He came to find me. All his ideas about not fighting were gone, of course—not worth a damn anyway with a real man. He was so white around the gills that I hardly knew him—eyes shooting fire like a volcano. He says, "—— —— you, what have you been doing with my girl?" He was a great big fellow, and for a minute I was a little scared. But then I remembered how soft he was, and I was game. 'If you can't hold her,' I says, 'leave her go!'

"It was a bad fight. He was out to kill me. I tried to kill him, too. A big red cloud came over me, and I went raging, tearing mad. See this ear?" Mac indicated the stump of the member alluded to. "He did that. I got him in one eye, though, so he never saw again. We soon quit using fists; we scratched, and choked, and bit, and kicked. They say my brother let out a roar like a bull every few minutes, but I just opened my mouth and screamed all the time. . . . Pretty soon I landed a kick in — a place where it hurt, and he fell like he was dead."
. . . Mac finished his Tom-and-Jerry.

Somebody ordered another. Mac went on.

"A little while after that I came away South, and my brother joined the Northwest Mounted Police. You remember that Indian who murdered the fellow out in Victoria in '06? Well, my brother was sent out after him, and got shot in the lung. I happened to be up home visiting the folks—only time I ever went back—when my brother came home to die. . . . But he got well. I remember the day I went away he was just out of his bed. He walked down to the station with me, begging me to speak just one word to him. He held out his hand for me to shake, but I just turned on him and says "You son of a ——!" A little later he started back to his job, but he died on the way. . . ."

"Gar!" said the first man. "Northwestern Mounted Police! That must be a job. A good rifle and a good horse and no closed season on Indians! That's what I call Sport!"

"Speaking of Sport," said Mac. "The greatest sport in the world is hunting niggers. After I left Burlington, you remember, I drifted down South. I was out to see the world from top to bottom, and I had just found out I could scrap. God! The fights I used to get into. . . . Well anyway, I landed up on a cotton plantation down in Georgia, near a place called Dixville; and they happened to be shy of an overseer, so I stuck.

"I remember the night perfectly, because I was sitting in my cabin writing home to my sister. She and I always hit it off, but we couldn't seem to get along with the rest of the family. Last year she got into a scrape with a drummer—and if I ever catch that— Well, as I say, I was sitting there writing by the light of a little oil lamp. It was a sticky, hot night, the window screen was just a squirming mass of bugs. It made me itch all over just to see 'em crawling around. All of a sudden, I pricked up my ears, and the hair began to stand right up on my head. It was dogs—bloodhounds— coming lickety-split in the dark. I don't know whether you fellows ever heard a hound bay when he's after a human. . . . Any hound baying at night is about the lonesomest, *doomingest* sound in the world. But this was worse than that. It made you feel like you were standing in the dark, waiting for somebody to strangle you to death—and *you couldn't get away!*

"For about a minute all I heard was the dogs, and then somebody, or some Thing, fell over my fence, and heavy feet running went right past my window, and a sound of breathing. You know how a stubborn horse breathes when they're choking him around the neck with a rope? That way.

"I was out on my porch in one jump, just in time to see the dogs scramble over my fence. Then somebody I couldn't see yelled out, so hoarse he couldn't hardly speak, 'Where'd he go?'

" 'Past the house and out back!' says I, and started to run. There was about twelve of us. I never *did* find out what that nigger did, and I guess most of the others didn't either. We didn't care. We ran like crazy men, through the cotton field, and the woods swampy from floods, swam the river, dove over fences, in a way that would tire out a man in a hundred yards. And we never felt it. The spit kept dripping out of my mouth, that was the only thing that bothered me. It was full moon, and every once in a while when we came out into an open place somebody would yell 'There he goes!' and we'd think the dogs had made a mistake, and take after a shadow. Always the dogs ahead, baying like bells. Say, did you ever hear a bloodhound when he's after a human? It's like a bugle! I broke my shins on twenty fences, and I banged my head on all the trees in Georgia, but I never felt it. . . .''

Mac smacked his lips and drank.

"Of course," he said, "when we got up to him, the dogs had just about torn that coon to pieces."

He shook his head in shining reminiscence.

"Did you finish your letter to your sister?" I asked.

"Sure," said Mac, shortly. . . .

. . . .

"I wouldn't like to live down here in Mexico," Mac volunteered. "The people haven't got any Heart. I like people to be friendly, like Americans."
—April 1914

Verse

[*The Masses* published a great many poems, some of which were reprinted in Genevieve Taggard's beautiful collection of verse from The Masses and the Liberator entitled May Days. *Most of The Masses editorial staff were also poets, and the arguments over whether or not to publish particular poems were often heated. The magazine's poetry was especially important in shaping its image, for the editors most clearly and persistently expressed their views on love and revolution in verse. Although the poems were consistently good, they ran the gamut from mere doggerel to poetry of an exceptionally high quality indeed. The variety of styles, degrees of excellence, and range of subjects show* The Masses *at its most catholic, exciting, and influential best.*]

HARRY KEMP
Resurrection

I hope there is a resurrection day,
For bodies, as the ancient prophets say,
When Helen's naked limbs again will gleam
Regathered from the dust of death's long dream,—
When those who thrilled the ages, being fair,
Will take the singing angels unaware
And make God's perfect meadows doubly sweet
With rosy vagrancy of little feet.
—March 1916

JOSEPHINE BELL
A Tribute

[*This poetic salute to Alexander Berkman and Emma Goldman led to Miss Bell's indictment under the Espionage Act. She did not, however, stand trial with the other Masses editors, for the judge dismissed her indictment after reading "A Tribute."*]

Emma Goldman and Alexander Berkman
Are in prison,
Although the night is tremblingly beautiful
And the sound of water climbs down the rocks
And the breath of the night air moves through
    multitudes and multitudes of leaves
That love to waste themselves for the sake of
    the summer.

Emma Goldman and Alexander Berkman
Are in prison tonight,
But they have made themselves elemental forces,
Like the water that climbs down the rocks:
Like the wind in the leaves:
Like the gentle night that holds us:
They are working on our destinies:
They are forging the love of the nations:

. . . . . .

Tonight they lie in prison.
—August 1917

HALL ALEXANDER
Three Poems

LOOKING TOWARD O'CONNELL BRIDGE

It cost two hundred lives!
What of it?
I got shot through the wind-pipe
And made a hideous noise
When I breathed.
But I laughed like hell
When I saw the green rebel flag
Waving in Sackville street.

THOROUGHLY PAGAN

A bourgeois lady told me
That hers was a pagan mind. . . .
That she loved to dream of dryads
Dancing through autumnal forests,
Of weak sexless men,
Of powerful brutes in satin,
And of serious-faced monkeys, on gilded
    chairs, in boudoirs decorated in Chi-
    nese red,
Listening to the music of flutes.

I CURSED A WOMAN

It was the only time I cursed a woman . . .
She was prying into the private affairs
Of a wash-woman
Who had applied for charity . . .
That social investigator . . .
I called her a bitch.
I was angry at the time.
It was the only time I swore at a woman.
                              —May 1917

MAX EASTMAN
At the Aquarium

Serene the silver fishes glide,
Stern-lipped, and pale, and wonder-eyed!
As through the aged deeps of ocean,
They glide with wan and wavy motion.
They have no pathway where they go;
They flow like water to and fro.
They watch with never-winking eyes,
They watch with staring, cold surprise
The level people in the air,
The people, peering, peering there,
Who wander also to and fro,
And know not why or where they go,
Yet have a wonder in their eyes,
Sometimes a pale and cold surprise.
                              —December 1912

SEYMOUR BARNARD
On Reading the New Republic

Ah, pause, Appreciation, here
    Sophistication doubly nice is;
See polished paragraph appear
    Anent some cataclysmic crisis.

Note raw-boned, rude, impulsive thought
    Arrested here and subtly twitted;
Note youth comporting as he ought,
    And naked truth correctly fitted.

Not passion's stress, but aftermath!
    Opinion's peaceful realignment!
Here ordered logic takes its path
    Along the line of most refinement.

To tune the nation's raucous voice
    Be these the accents sorely needed;
A calm discriminating choice
    By pleasant dalliance preceded.

And here beyond the stir of strife,
    Where distant drones the blatant babble,
Ah, tread the promenade of life
    A pace behind the vulgar rabble.
                    —November-December 1917

LAURA BENET
Gardens of Babylon

Huddled chimneys grey, forlorn,
In the deadened light of a city morn.
Roof tops ranging, red and high,
Tenement windows glaring, dry.
And—Flower pots!
Gaily caparisoned flower pots!
Nodding against the sky!

Fire escapes alive with the green
Of scarlet runner and Indian bean,
Caught in a handful of black dirt
Carried home in a baby's skirt.
Flower pots!
Verdantly growing flower pots!
Lifting their blooms on high!

Jack and the Beanstalk's magic might—
Vines spring up in a single night.
Old faces soften, children stare
At the slender gardens in the air.
Flower pots!
Meagre little clay flower pots!
Bring the glow of the country there!
                              —March 1914

WILL HEFORD
Welfare Song

Sing a song of "Welfare,"
   A pocket full of tricks
To soothe the weary worker
   When he groans or kicks.
If he asks for shorter hours
   Or for better pay,
Little stunts of "Welfare"
   Turn his thoughts away.

Sing a song of "Welfare,"
   Sound the horn and drum,
Anything to keep the mind
   Fixed on Kingdom Come.
"Welfare" loots your pocket
   While you dream and sing,
"Welfare" to your pay check
   Doesn't do a thing.

Sing a song of "Welfare,"
   Forty 'leven kinds,
Elevate your morals,
   Cultivate your minds.
Kindergartens, nurses,
   Bathtubs, books, and flowers,
Anything but better pay
   Or shorter working hours.

—September 1913

DOROTHY DAY
Mulberry Street

[*Contemporary readers, who know Miss Day as the leader of the Catholic Worker movement in the United States, may be surprised to know that she was at one time a poetess. During this period of her life she served as an editorial assistant to Floyd Dell, and her experiences on* The Masses *became the basis for her only novel,* The Eleventh Virgin.]

A small Italian child
Sits on the curbing,
Her little round, brown belly showing
Through a gap in her torn pink dress.
Her brother squatting beside her
Engrossed in an all-day sucker,
Turns sympathetically
Wipes her nose with the end of his ragged shirt
And gives her a lick.

—July 1917

WILLIAM ROSE BENET
The Laughing Woman

Once I heard a woman laughing—
Not like laughter of the women you have heard;
Syllables whose beauty blinds you, and reminds
    you
Of a brook in sunlight, or a sweet, leaf-hidden
    bird.
   Though shot through with notes of pain—
And then there is that laughter of an old, old,
    evil woman,
   Raising red and burning mists within the brain.

In the mad, gin-reeking dance-hall,
Through the brainless oaths and shrieks, above
    the smoke
Of stale tobacco, burning to man's yearning
For the swinish, acrid incense—high and shrill
    her babbling broke.
There is laughter that is human
   Though its poignance starts our tears—
And then there is a laughter like the laughter of
    that woman,
   Freezing hearts, and ringing raucous in our ears.

There were mingled in her laughter
Girlish love-words, wittold curses, jests obscene.
And the dancers swarmed around her, sunk pro-
    founder
In their beastly, battening stupor—love grown
    loathly and unclean.
There is laughter—bitter-human
   Though it sears us hot and deep—
And then there is a laughter like the laughter of
    that woman,
   Worse than all the ghastly nightmares known
    to sleep.

Old gray hair, that had been honored
In a life less foul than this, less mad with lust—
Gray hair, defiled, polluted, the refuted,
Boast of Man, the world's white banner dragged
    and trampled in the dust!
There is laughter that is human,
   Though the painfullest, the harshest—Yes—
    and then—
And then there is the laughter of that old, old,
    evil woman.
   And life still crawls with maggots—that were
    men!

—October 1913

P. C.
The Bath

We bathed together.
We splashed, and slipped, and lost the soap, and
    laughed.
Our shoulders shone wet and gleaming.
Sometimes we kissed.
The steamy heavy-sweet air stole on our senses.
The sudsy water enveloped us like a blanket,
Only more closely, more intimately,
Its insidious warmth creeping into our bodies
Like a narcotic.
We almost dozed, with limbs entwined,
But we were swept by gusts of golden kisses.

—May 1917

MARY CAROLYN DAVIES
College

First I became
A copy of a book.

Then I became
A copy of a man
Who was also
A copy of a book.

Now
I would not know
What I am

Except that I have
On my wall
A framed paper
Which explains it fully.

—July 1916

ELIZABETH WADDELL
The Tenant Farmer

His lean cattle are luxuriating on his neighbor's
    green wheat, and presently his neighbor will
    have them impounded.
His fences are rotten and broken; he is not so
    shiftless as merely discouraged.
Last year he gave one-third of his crop to the
    landlord and this year he will give two-fifths.
His corn was late-planted because of the rain, and
    then it was overtaken by the drought.
If the prices of grain and potatoes rise, the prices
    of shoes and sugar are up betimes before them.

His thirteen hours of work are done, and his wife
    is on the last of her fifteen.
She has put the children to bed, and is mending
    overalls by the light of the oil lamp.
Her heavy eyes go shut. She blinks wildly to keep
    them open, and starts up after each lapse,
    fiercely attacking her work.
It is coming on to rain and his roof will leak, and
    in the lowering dark a mile away his cattle are
    grazing, rip, rip, rip, reaping great swaths in the
    green wheat, for every mouthful of which he
    will have to pay—
But he knows it not. He is oblivious to all.
He has read for an hour, and now the paper has
    dropped from his loosened fingers.
Already he with a valiant handful, himself the
    leader, has somehow, he doesn't clearly remem-
    ber how, taken a hundred yards of enemy
    trenches.
He is lying in bed, an arm missing. He is exalted
    in soul but body-shattered, unable to move a
    muscle—
And someone has just pinned a decoration upon his
    breast, and he is peeved considerable because he
    cannot tell and no one will tell him
Whether it is the Victoria Cross, the Iron Cross or
    the Cross of the Legion of Honor.

—August 1916

CLEMENT WOOD
A Breath of Life

Yes, he'll enlist—he'll leap at the chance!

If you think eleven servile hours a day, six days a
    week,
A slatternly wife, a tableful of children all mouths,
A sodden Sunday, and then the long round again,
Can bind him to sanity and peace,
You do not know your brother—
You do not know yourself!

Better the close-locked marching feet,
The music like great laughter, the rough comrade-
    ships—

War is a picnic, a vast game of chance;
You may win,—or earn a quick and bursting death,
Cancelling all these unpaid duty-debts at home.
Then—on to the picnic!
Out of the foul-aired routine!
A breath of life, tho death be the price!

—November 1914

Adam and Eve—The True Story

The Foray

Drawn by John Sloan, February 1913

The Sixth Day

The Night Alarm

MAX EASTMAN
The Lonely Bather

Loose-veined and languid as the yellow mist
That swoons along the river in the sun,
Your flesh of passion pale and amber-kissed
With years of heat that through your veins have
    run,

You lie with aching memories of love
Alone and naked by the weeping tree,
And indolent with inward longing move
Your slim and sallow limbs despondently.

If love came warm and burning to your dream,
And filled you all your avid veins require,
You would lie sadly still beside the stream,
Sobbing in torture of that vivid fire;

The same low sky would weave its fading blue,
The river still exhale its misty rain,
The willow trail its weeping over you,
Your longing only quickened into pain.

Bed your desire among the pressing grasses;
Lonely lie, and let your thirsting breasts
Lie on you, lonely, till the fever passes,
Till the undulation of your longing rests.

—August 1917

MAX ENDICOFF
The Public Library—The Fixture

She is always there,
This long, rangy figure
Of sapped-out middle age virginity.
Her moldy-colored, angular face
Is stitched with a thousand seams,
And her thin, bloodless lips
Twitch incessantly
Until her countenance
Assumes the quality of a flexible mask.

She patters on tip-toe along the marble floor
And guides her queer squint
Along the row of "new" books.
With an open smile of triumph
Her colorless hand with its long talons
Darts out
And seizes upon a volume
Bearing the title:
"A Modern Mother."

—February 1917

[82]

ARTHUR DAVISON FICKE
Tables

Once the altar was sacred;
But now, 1 think, it is the table.
For across tables
Go the words, the looks, the blinding flashes of
    thought
That are truly the race's history.
Fellow-lovers and fellow-poets
Lean their arms on these white surfaces,
And bending forward oblivious above the scat-
    tered silver,
Enkindle each other's souls.
I have never got from a pulpit
What I have got from tables.
I have never been so stirred in the greenwood
As at these curious urban trysting-places.
Nor do I think that heaven itself
Will wholly answer to my need
Unless in obscure streets and squares and avenues
And purlieus outlying the Pillared Place
There are little cafés
Where across tables
Blessed angels whisper wonderful and incredible
    secrets to one another.

—December 1916

HELEN HOYT
Menaia

Silently,
By unseen hands,
The gates are opened,
The bands are loosed.

Unbidden,
Never failing,
In soft inexorable recurrence
Always returning,
Comes mystery
And possesses me
And uses me
As the moon uses the waters.

Ebbing and flowing
Obedient
The tides of my body move;
Swayed by chronology
As strict as the waters;
Unfailing
As the seasons of the moon and the waters.

—October 1915

LOUIS UNTERMEYER
God's Youth

I often wish that I had been alive
Ere God grew old; before His eyes were tired
Of the eternal circlings of the sun,
Of the perpetual Springs, the weary years
Forever marching on an unknown quest,
The yawning seasons pacing to and fro
Like stolid sentinels to guard the earth.
I wish that I had been alive when He
Was still delighted with each casual thing
His mind could fashion, when His soul first thrilled
With childlike pleasure at the blooming sun;
When the first dawn met His enraptured eyes
And the first prayers of men stirred in His heart.
With what a glow of pride He heard the stars
Rush by Him, singing, as they bravely leaped
Into the unexplored and endless skies,
Bearing His beauty like a battle-cry;
Or watched the light, obedient to His will,
Spring out of nothingness to answer Him,
Hurling strange suns and planets in its joy
Of fiery freedom from the lifeless dark.
But more than all the splendid worlds He made,
The elements new-tamed, the harnessed winds;
In spite of these it must have pleased Him most
To feel Himself branch out, let go, dare all,
Give utterance to His vaguely-formed desires;
Let loose a flood of fancies, wild and frank.
Oh, those were noble times; those gay attempts,
Those vast and droll experiments that were made
When God was young and blithe and whimsical.
When from the infinite humor of His heart,
He made the elk with such extravagant horns,
The grotesque monkey-folk, the angel-fish,
That make the ocean's depth a visual heaven;
The animals like plants, the plants like beasts;
The loud, inane hyena; and the great
Impossible giraffe, whose silly head
Threatens the stars, his feet embracing earth.
The paradox of the peacock, whose bright form
Is like a brilliant trumpet, and his voice
A strident squawk, a cackle and a joke.
The ostrich, like a snake tied to a bird,
All out of sense and drawing, wilder far
Than all the mad, fantastic thoughts of men.
The hump-backed camel, like a lump of clay,
Thumbed at for hours, and then thrown aside.
The elephant, with splendid useless tooth,
And nose and arm and fingers all in one.
The hippopotamus, absurd and bland—

Oh, how God must have laughed when first He
    saw
These great jests breathe and live and walk about!
And how the heavens must have echoed him. . . .
For, greater than His beauty or His wrath
Was God's vast mirth before His back was bent
With Time and all the troubling universe;
Ere He grew dull and weary with creating. . . .
Oh, to have been alive and heard that laugh
Thrilling the stars and shattering the earth,
While meteors flashed from out His sparkling
    eyes,
And even the eternal placid Night
Forgot to lift reproving fingers, smiled
And joined, indulgent in the merriment.
And how they sang, and how the hours flew,
When God was young and blithe and whimsical.
—August 1913

FLOYD DELL
Summer

I.
The world—a green valley
Full of morning sunlight and deep cool shadow,
Lovely by-paths half hidden,
And the glimmer of white knees
Dancing toward me.

II.
Cool clasping hands
And fragrant, unperturbed mouth,
Lovely and unconscious bosom
Still
Glad, free, indifferent . . .
Only your eyes
Question me . . .

III.
Who knows?
Pain, as of old,
Anger and self-mockery
And the shame of things spoiled forever . . .
Or joy laughing forgetfully
In Eden.
Who dares?

IV.
Fool that I am, who desire
Neither.
Only perpetually your cool hands
And lovely laughing mouth,
White knees that have brushed the cold dew
    from the grasses,
And the unstirred peace of your bosom.
—February 1917

AMY LOWELL
The Grocery

"Hullo, Alice!"
"Hullo, Leon!"
"Say, Alice, gi' me a couple
O' them two for five cigars,
Will you?"
"Where's your nickle?"
"My! Ain't you close!
Can't trust a fellow, can you."
"Trust you! Why
What you owe this store
Would set you up in business.
I can't think why Father 'lows it."
"Yer Father's a sight more neighborly
Than you be. That's a fact.
Besides, he knows I got a vote."
"A vote! Oh, yes, you got a vote!
A lot o' good the Senate'll be to Father
When all his bank account
Has run away in credits.
There's your cigars,
If you can relish smokin'
With all you owe us standin'."
"I dunno as that makes 'em taste any diff'rent.
Yer ain't fair to me, Alice, 'deed yer ain't.
I work when anythin's doin'.
I'll get a carpenterin' job next Summer sure.
Cleve was tellin' me to-day he'd take me on come
     Spring."
"Come Spring, and this December!
I've no patience with you, Leon,
Shilly-shallyin' the way you do.
Here, lift over them crates o' oranges
I wanter fix 'em in the window."
"It riles yer, don't it, me not havin' work.
Yer pepper up about it somethin' good.
Yer pick an' pick, and that don't help a mite.
Say, Alice, do come in out o' that winder.
Th' oranges can wait,
And I don't like talkin' to yer back."
"Don't you! Well, you'd better make the best o'
     what you can git.
Maybe you won't have my back to talk to soon.
They look good in pyramids with the 'lectric light
     on 'em,
Don't they?
Now hand me them bananas
And I'll string 'em right acrost."
"What do yer mean
'Bout me not havin' you to talk to?
Are yer springin' somethin' on me?"

"I don't know 'bout springin'
When I'm tellin' yer right out.
I'm goin' away, that's all."
"Where? Why?
What yer mean—goin' away?"
"I've took a place
Down to Boston, in a candy store
For the holidays."
"Good Land, Alice,
What in the Heavens fer!"
"To earn some money,
And to git away from here, I guess."
"Ain't yer Father got enough?
Don't he give yer proper pocket-money?"
"He'd have a plenty, if you folks paid him."
"He's rich, I tell yer.
I never figured he'd be close with you."
"Oh, he ain't. Not close.
That ain't why.
But I must git away from here.
I must! I must!"
"Yer got a lot o' reason in yer
To-night.
How long d' you callate
Yer'll be gone?"
"Maybe for always."
"What ails yer, Alice?
Talkin' wild like that.
Ain't you an' me goin' to be married
Some day?"
"Some day! Some day!
I guess the sun'll never rise on someday."
"So that's the trouble.
Same old story.
'Cause I ain't got the cash to settle right now.
Yer know I love yer,
An' I'll marry yer as soon
As I can raise the money."
"You've said that any time these five year,
But you don't do nothin'."
"Wot could I do?
There ain't no work here Winters.
Not fer a carpenter, there ain't."
"I guess yer warn't born a carpenter.
There's ice-cuttin' a-plenty."
"I got a dret'ful tender throat;
Dr. Smiles he told me
I mustn't resk ice-cuttin'."
"Why haven't you gone to Boston,
And hunted up a job?"
"Hev yer forgot the time I went expressin'
In the American office, down ther?"
"And come back two weeks later!

No I ain't."
"You didn't want I should git hurted,
Did yer?
I'm a sight too light fer all that liftin' work.
My back was commencin' to strain, as 'twas.
Ef I was like yer brother now,
I'd ha' be'n down to the city long ago.
But I'm too clumsy fer a dancer.
I ain't got Arthur's luck."
"Do you call it luck to be a disgrace to your folks,
And git locked up in jail!"
"Oh, come now, Alice,
'Disgrace' is a mite strong.
Why, the jail was a joke.
Art's all right."
"All right!
All right to dance, and smirk, and lie
And then in the end
Fer a livin',
Lead a silly girl to give you
What warn't hers to give
By pretendin' you'd marry her,—
And she a pupil."
"He'd ha' married her right enough,
Her folks was millionaires."
"Yes, he'd ha' married her!
Thank God, they saved her that."
"Art's a fine fellah.
I wish I had his luck.
Swellin' round in Hart, Schaffner & Marx fancy
    suits,
And eatin' in rest'rants.
But somebody's got to stick to the old place,
Else Foxfield'd have to shut up shop,
Hey, Alice?"
"You admire him!
You admire Arthur!
You'd be like him only you can't dance.
Oh, Shame! Shame!
And I've been like that silly girl.
Fooled with yer promises,
And I gave you all I had.
I knew it, oh, I knew it.
But I wanted to git away 'fore I proved it,
You've shamed me through and through.
Why couldn't you hold yer tongue,
And spared me seein' you
As you really are."
"What the Devil's the row?
I only said Art was lucky.
What you spitfirin' at me fer?
Fergit it, Alice.
We've had good times, ain't we?

I'll see Cleve 'bout that job agin' to-morrer,
And we'll be married 'fore hayin' time."
"It's like you to remind me o' hayin' time.
I've good cause to love it, ain't I?
Many's the night I've hid my face in the dark
To shet out thinkin'!"
"Why, that ain't nothin'
You ain't be'n half so kind to me
As lots o' fellers' girls.
Gi' me a kiss, Dear,
And let's make up."
"Make up!
You poor Fool.
Do you suppose I care a ten cent piece
For you now.
You've killed yourself for me.
Done it out o' your own mouth.
You've took away my home,
I hate the sight o' the place.
You're all over it,
Every stick 'an stone means you;
An' I hate 'em all."
"Alice, I say,
Don't go on like that.
I can't marry yer
Boardin' in one room,
But I'll see Cleve to-morrer,
I'll make him ———"
"Oh, you fool!
"You terrible fool!"
"Alice, don't go yet,
Wait a minute,
I'll see Cleve ———"
"You terrible fool!"
"Alice, don't go.
Alice ———" (Door slams.)

—June 1916

LOUISE BRYANT
Lost Music

[*A gifted writer in her own right, Louise Bryant
was married to John Reed, who may have inspired this poem.*]

I remember you now, my love.
It was eons ago
That I ran through the tangled woods
After butterflies. . . .

I came to a sparkling pool
And broke its smooth surface
With my white feet.

Suddenly I paused in the mad chase
And beheld you
For the first time.

You smiled
And held out your hand.
I went closer
Like a curious deer.

You were so beautiful
And so strong,
I had to keep gazing
Beastlike.

I looked so droll
Standing there . . .
That you laughed.

I can never forget
The silver music
Of your laughter.

That is how I remembered you
Today . . .
You laughed again.
But there is no joy
In your laughter now.

Oh, my love,
Let us go back
Through all the ages behind us . . .
Until we find the music
That was in your laughter.

—January 1917

REGINALD WRIGHT KAUFFMAN
Prometheus

Across the clean canopy of night the mighty plan-
    ets revolving,
Each on its destined track through trackless space
    and through incalculable aeons,
Measuring miles by the million million, measur-
    ing time by the unit of eternity—
Silent, serene:

In a filthy ten-foot alley the man that cannot
    grow taller than seventy-two inches, whose
    brain is compressed in a cell of bone;
Entombed, and tearing the fleshy walls of his
    tomb with yearnings for an endless life, whose
    life is three score years and ten;
Wearied if he walk a dozen miles, surrendering
    to sleep if he remain awake above sixteen
    hours:

[86]

Which is the happier, stronger, greater?
The stars that see not the man, that perform
    prodigies because they are ordained to perform
    them?
Or the man that sees the stars obey and yet re-
    fuses to obey?
The stars serve and live,
The man defies and is slain:
But the man defies!

—February 1915

HARRY KEMP
Leaves of Burdock

[*Kemp was a writer of various talents whose
small reputation as The Tramp Poet died before
he himself did. A famous Villager in the 1910's
and twenties, he never outgrew his origins and
remained to the end an unreconstructed bohemian.
Unlike that of many bohemians, his own poetry
was highly orthodox in style, and he was most
intolerant of other verse forms, as this little par-
ody of Walt Whitman suggests.*]

Three cheers for God and six more for Infin-
    ity. . . .
By God I shall sing the entire universe, and no
    one shall stop me!
Rocks, stones, stars, wash-tubs, axe-handles, red-
    wood trees, the Mississippi—everything!
Hurrah for me! Superbos, optimos, . . . I, see-
    ing eidolons, proclaim myself, and, through
    myself, all men!
By God, I say I *shall* sing!
I tell you that everything is good . . . Life, death,
    burial, beer, birth, marriage, wedding certifi-
    cates, polygamy, polyandry . . . and he who
    denies himself is also right in his way. . . .
Who said that evil is evil? I say that evil is
    good!
Ultime Thule, Ne Plus Ultra, E Pluribus Unum!
Good is both good and evil . . . evil is both evil
    and good!
Everything is nothing, and nothing is everything . . .
I salute you, camarados, eleves, Americanos, Pis-
    tachios, Cascaretos Mios—I salute you!
I come singing, strong, contemptuous, virile, and
    having hair on my chest as abundant as a hay-
    stack . . .
I, imperturbe, aplomb, sangfroid . . . Hurrah,
    hurrah!

—May 1914

JEAN STARR UNTERMEYER
Deliverance

Just think of me—
Come from the shadows of the womb
To the shadows of this world;
Seeing the sun only through a veil.
On both sides of me walk ghostly shapes;
One on either hand.

Often on a Spring afternoon,
Being misled by the bright glow beyond the hills,
I would run with all the strength and fleetness of
    my youth
Up the long slope!
Hearing only my heart-beats and the rushing of
    the wind.
I stood on the summit and hallooed at freedom.
I was glad, thinking I had outrun my gray com-
    panions;
Glad for one moment—
But as the glow died in my cheeks and in my
    heart
I heard again the evil footfalls, measured and
    slow.
And I knew they were still abreast of me. . . .

Then, on a glad May morning I thought I met
    the Sun.
I had always wished to look him in the face; to
    see him without his veil.
And, in that dazzling moment, I thought: "At
    last, the Sun!"
Such a light and gladness was in that face,
Such a rush of living love.
It was not the Sun.
It was my lover.
I mated with him.
He made me such a bright palace of words that
    I thought I could live in it.
I told him of the shadows and of the veil before
    the face of the Sun;
But he said he had a Magic that would slay my
    grim companions.
And that it was not the Sun that was veiled, but
    my eyes;
And that he could tear those veils away . . .
So in the days that followed I lay in a bright
    dream.
At times I waked for an instant, but then I felt
    the dread presences always with me.

So back into the dream. . . .
And from that dream, half ecstasy, half pain,

Came our child.
And I was glad.
"Now," I said, as I watched him grow like a
    flame,
"Here is a fire to burn away mist—
And here is a golden sword to slay an army of
    shadows!"
And I waited for the miracle.

But the flame danced like a wind-blown butterfly;
And the sword made only a happy clatter;
A game in a nursery. . . .
And the black mist rose and wrapped itself over
    all brightness—
It blotted out the sun,
And lay over the gay colors of flowers,
It hung on the lips of laughter like a sneer. . . .
And the dark guests stayed on—
They put an evil sound into the gentle fall of
    snow;
They crept into the wind and made it a menace.
They pressed dully against me—even in the hour
    of love. . . .

Whence will come the cleansing flame—
Must it be the fire of my own heart?
And the sword of deliverance—
Must it be made with my own hands?
                        —November 1915

E. W. P.
Red Cross

The women sit at long white tables,
Clad in straight white aprons
Like shrouds;
Snipping and folding and stitching all day
That each small unit of their work
May be quite perfect.

What are they thinking of, these women
Bent so intently on their work?
Perhaps the mothers are thinking of their sons
Who may need a woman's care,
And the young girls are thinking, maybe,
Of their proud young sweethearts
Full of unthinking eagerness for war.
Or perhaps they are only thinking
How they must make their work quite perfect
So that the women of the Baptist Church
May see and envy
The patriotic zeal of the Presbyterians.
                        —September 1917

WILL HEFORD
That God Made

This is the Earth that God made.
These are the Timber and Coal and Oil
And Water Powers and fertile Soil
That belong to us all in spite of the gall
Of the Grabbers and Grafters who forestall
The natural rights and needs of all
Who live on the Earth that God made.

These are the Corporate Snakes that coil
Around the Timber and Coal and Oil
And Water Powers and fertile Soil
Which belong to us all in spite of the gall
Of the Grabbers and Grafters who forestall
The natural rights and needs of all
Who live on the Earth that God made.

These are the Lords of Mill and Mine
Who act as if they were divine,
Who can't read the writing on the wall
But admire the skill and excuse the gall
Of the Grabbers and Grafters who forestall
The natural rights and needs of all
Who live on the Earth that God made.

These are the Parsons shaven and shorn
Who tell the workers all forlorn
To pray for contentment night and morn
And to bear and to suffer want and scorn
And be lowly and meek and humbly seek
For their just reward on the Heavenly shore,
But not on the Earth that God made.
—February 1916

EUNICE TIETJENS
The Drug Clerk

The Drug clerk stands behind the counter,
Young and dapper, debonair. . . .

Before him burn the great unwinking lights,
The hectic stars of city nights,
Red as hell's pit, green as a mermaid's hair.
A queer half-acrid smell is in the air.
Behind him on the shelves in ordered rows
With strange abbreviated names
Dwell half the facts of life. That young man
   knows
Bottled and boxed and powdered here
Dumb tragedies, deceptions, secret shames,
And comedy and fear.

[88]

Sleep slumbers here, like a great quiet sea
Shrunk to this bottle's compass, sleep that brings
Sweet respite from the teeth of pain
To those poor tossing things
That the white nurses watch so thoughtfully.
And here again
Dwell the shy souls of Maytime flowers
That shall make sweeter still those poignant hours
When wide eyed youth looks on the face of love.
And, for those others who have found too late
The bitter fruit thereof,
Here are cosmetics, powders, paints—the arts
That hunted women use to hunt again
With scented flesh for bait.
And here is comfort for the hearts
Of sucking babes in their first teething pain.
Here dwells the substance of huge fervid dreams,
Fantastic, many-colored, shot with gleams
Of ecstacy and madness, that shall come
To some pale twitching sleeper in a bunk.
And here is courage, cheaply bought,
To cure a sick blue funk.
And dearly paid for in the final sum.
Here in this powdered fly is caught
Desire more ravishing than Tarquin's, rape
And bloody-handed murder. And at last
When the one weary hope is past
Here is the sole escape,
The little postern in the house of breath
Where pallid fugitives keep tryst with death.

All this the drug clerk knows, and there he stands
Young and dapper, debonair. . . .
He rests a pair of slender hands,
Much manicured, upon the counter there
And speaks: "No, we don't carry no pomade.
We only cater to the high class trade."
—September 1914

JOHN REED
Love at Sea

Wind smothers the snarling of the great ships,
   And the serene gulls are stronger than turbines;
   Mile upon mile the hiss of a stumbling wave
      breaks unbroken—
Yet stronger is the power of your lips for my lips.

This cool green liquid death shall toss us living
   Higher than high heaven and deeper than
      sighs—
   But O the abrupt, stiff, sloping, resistless foam
Shall not forbid our taking and our giving!

Life wrenched from its roots—what wretchedness!
  What waving of lost tentacles like blind sea-
    things!
  Even the still ooze beneath is quick and pro-
    found—
I am less and more than I was, you are more and
  less.

I cried upon God last night, and God was not
  where I cried;
  He was slipping and balancing on the thought-
    less shifting planes of sea.
  Careless and cruel, he will unchain the appalling
    sea-gray engines—
But the speech of your body to my body will not
  be denied!

—May 1916

ROSE PASTOR STOKES
Paterson

*[Mrs. Stokes was a working girl who came out of
the New York slums to marry J. C. Phelps Stokes,
one of the "socialist millionaires," and gain fame
as the most militant of revolutionaries.]*

Our folded hands again are at the loom.
      The air
      Is ominous with peace.
But what we weave you see not through the
  gloom.
'Tis terrible with doom.
      Beware!

You dream that we are weaving what you will?
      Take care!
Our fingers do not cease:
We've starved—and lost; but we are weavers
  still;
And Hunger's in the mill! . . .

And Hunger moves the Shuttle forth and back.
      Take care!
The product grows and grows . . .
A shroud it is; a shroud of ghastly black.
We've never let you lack!
      Beware!

The Warp and Woof of Misery and Defeat . . .
      Take care!—
See how the Shuttle goes!
Our bruiséd hearts with bitter hopes now beat:
The Shuttle's *sure*—and *fleet!* . . .

—November 1913

LYDIA GIBSON
Lost Treasure

You know deep in your heart, it could not last—
  And, when a wind, newborn on some hillside—
      (Some fair tall hill the other side of Crete)
Came laden with the dear and odorous past—
  (Laden with scents of gardens that have died,
    Buried in dust, not any longer sweet).

Then, realized, all the unlovely years
  Lay on your heart, like those old gardens' dust;
    You had forgotten how your life was fair,
For all the memories were dulled with tears
  Since shed, and unsuspected moth and rust
    Ate deep, and naught remembered was but
      care.

So is your treasure lost, vanished away—
  Nothing but wind and half-shut eyes and grass—
    Nothing of now but strivings after then.
And naught heard in the clear air of to-day
  But dusty wings that crumble as they pass—
    You have not strength to make them live
      again.

—May 1914

JOEL ELIAS SPINGARN
Heloise Sans Abelard—A Modern Scholar on a Mediaeval Nun

*[As a professor and critic, Spingarn was in a posi-
tion to speak with authority on this question.]*

In the cool, calm palace of prayer
  She sought her haven of dreams:
She gave up her dower of air,
  Of stars, and cities, and streams.

On the cold, sweet steps of prayer
  She sought what young girls seek:
She laid her bosom bare,
  And asked for the stones to speak.

Who wonders she could not hear
  What silence and stones belie?
Who wonders where love may steer?
  Not I, not I, not I!

O passionate Heloise,
  I, too, have lived under the ban,
With seven hundred professors,
  And not a single man.

—February 1914

SEYMOUR BARNARD
Education: A Community Masque

[*Scott Nearing, the subject of this verse play, was a remarkably prolific Marxist whose dismissal from the faculty of the University of Pennsylvania had made him something of a hero to the younger intellectuals. The topical drama—sometimes in dialogue, sometimes in verse—was a favorite literary idiom in the Village, since as author, actor, or audience, everyone could participate.*]

A STADIUM. (Automobile horns, trolley gongs, heard in the distance. Night.)

The spoken word being essential, according to the authors of masques recently produced, lines are herewith provided. But it is understood that nobody in the audience can hear what is said. Only the few having the price to buy a libretto beforehand, and with time to read it, know what is going on. During the performance late-comers pass between the audience and the scene, and by the time every one is seated, those who have had enough begin to file out. This furnishes the action of the masque.

(Darkness, during which have assembled in the foreground college presidents, professors, instructors and teachers. They sing, while the scene grows brighter and brighter, as though a flood of light were being let in.)

PROLOGUE
ALL

There is a process known to man
Which human-kind is bent to;
It makes of every one it can
What Nature never meant to:

The one who might excel a bit
It levels to the many,
And that poor chap without a wit
Becomes as good as any:

A little turn, a little twist
Of natural adaptation,—
Who should have been a humorist
Turns out to rule the nation:

The affluent without a bent,
The poor, who'd never do more,
Take their D.D.'s with wonderment,
And never see the humor:

(With great fervor.)

From out the past we have amassed
Of each decaying nation,
The learning vast (which proved its last),
And called it Education!

[90]

(Darkness, pierced by a spotlight which throws red and blue rays. A stage appears in the center of the scenic design at the further end of the stadium. Scott Nearing is revealed, suit case in hand, his face toward the audience, and his back toward the University of Pennsylvania. He walks off slowly.)

SCOTT NEARING

Amid the glades of William Penn
I taught of pleasant things, and then
It seemed to me that eager youth
Should be conducted nearer truth:

That truth was of a vulgar stuff,—
That near enough was near enough,—
That things should false and pleasant be,—
Thus, thus they thought at U. of P.

(An invisible orchestra strikes up a march.)

(The trustees of the University of Pennsylvania troop across the open space in the foreground of the stadium. A dim religious light plays upon them. Following a short conference they sing.)

TRUSTEES OF THE UNIVERSITY OF PENNSYLVANIA

A highly paid professor
Should impart a moral tone,
And his views are what we tell him,
Independent of his own;
And for the docile here's a
Prodigality of pelf;
Should he wish to teach what *he* thinks,
Then he ought to pay himself.

(Troop off, repeating the refrain.)

INNER SCENE

(A stage appears just above that upon which Scott Nearing stood. A lavender light, with a hint of yellow, revealing Nicholas Murray Butler on the steps of the library of Columbia University.)

NICHOLAS MURRAY BUTLER

An easy liberality
Is here allowed to function,
Without that prodigality
Extremists view with unction:

"A lissome latitude allowed,"
Our tentative decision;
A recognition of the crowd,—
When it obstructs our vision.

(Simultaneously with the above, four radicals of the faculty of Columbia University dance in the foreground.)

FOUR RADICALS

Ink and anarchy!
Ph. D.!
Rank rebellion

JUNE, 1911   No. 6   PRICE, 5 CENTS

THE·MASSES

A·MONTHLY·MAGAZINE
DEVOTED·TO·THE·INTERESTS
OF·THE·WORKING·PEOPLE

THE BEST NUMBER

OF THE

BEST SOCIALIST MAGAZINE

With an Uncommonsensible Essay

BY

'GENE WOOD

AND

Five Other Splendid Features

THE·MASSES·PUBLISHING·COMPANY·112·E:19TH·ST·NEW YORK

MAY, 1916

10 CENTS

The MASSES

Harbinger of Spring

And history!
We're the bane
Of the faculty,—
Irksome irritation:

Our atypical
Attitude,
Our complaint at
A platitude,
Lends the likeness of
Latitude,
To the Corporation!

(To soft music.)

Dance we now, and let us charm you,
What we say need not alarm you,
We're too few by far to harm you,
Any one will testify.

ACT II

(Darkness, pierced by a crimson shaft. Scott Nearing is shown knocking at the gates of Harvard University.)

SCOTT NEARING

Place Athenian; time, Socratic,
Just a little more than static,
I've a message here for youth,
Ever burning, brightest truth!

A VOICE FROM WITHIN

(To slow, very slow music.)

This is but a seat of learning,
And no place for message burning;
Flame and ardor, inspiration,
Here give way to Education.

INNER SCENE

(The preceding scene darkens. Charles W. Eliot appears on the stage above. The setting represents a five-foot book shelf.)

CHARLES W. ELIOT

In gentle, aphoristic vein
I comment on each timely topic,
Reiterating yet again
Opinions mild and philanthropic:

It little matters what I say
As subject for my peroration,
The unimportant things to-day
Attract the man of Education:

Then let our mental exercise
Ignore the substance for the tissues,
Leave us the lesser things we prize,
The mob, the vulgar vital issues.

INTERLUDE

(Groups of trustees arrive, swathed in a white light. A number of freshmen follow. A green light plays over them.)

TRUSTEES

(To freshmen.)

If after all your schooling
There should happen to survive,
A little of the human
And a little of the live,
If there still persists a notion
That it's well to be of use,
That the human race is worthy
But decidedly obtuse,—

PROFESSORS

(From somewhere in the dark, to freshmen.)

Be, ye unregenerate,
Satisfied to speculate,
Action's for the vulgar
And the ones we fail to educate.

FRESHMEN

If furnished with a good excuse
We've no desire to be of use;
What better reason for stagnation
Than that of Higher Education?

(The freshmen are followed by a pageant of college women, bearing a banner inscribed, "WE DEMAND ALL LABOR FOR OUR PROVINCE.")

COLLEGE WOMEN

Our colleges and seminaries
Supply the world with secretaries,
Though handicapped by certain shirkers
Behold the source of social workers;
We've teachers here, and decorators,
Modistes and some investigators;
O, how the men fear our ingressions
Into the field of the professions!

(A host of children from Gary, Ind., throng the scene. They dance and sing.)

GARY CHILDREN

We children of Gary,
Methodically gay,
Efficiently vary
Our work with our play;

Not only we're taught, but
We're doctored and fed;
O, home it is naught
But a place for a bed.

[93]

(School boys, armed to the teeth, march across.)

SCHOOL BOYS

Ye lads like us, though far away,
(One—two—three—four)
In some such place as Paraguay,
War—war—war—war)

In England, Greece or Timbuctoo,
(Five—six—seven—eight)
Look out, for we're prepared for you:
(Hate—hate—hate—hate)

That you were born without the gates
Of these aroused United States,
Remains the strongest reason yet
For bullet, bomb, and bayonet.

ACT III

(A blue light. Scott Nearing knocks at the doors of Yale.)

SCOTT NEARING

Grimmest, greatest of the lot,
Make a place for homeless Scott;
Here is truth, assertive, searing;
Have you place for it and Nearing?

A VOICE FROM WITHIN

Here is all-enduring knowledge,
Suitable for any college;
That prepost'rous thing you're preaching
Wouldn't mix with what we're teaching.

(Scott Nearing sinks to the ground, where he is seen gradually to fall asleep. Sprites from Ohio wing their way on the scene. They are clad only in leaves and flowers.)

SPRITES

We're from a land without a flaw,
Where Truth is dressed in candor,
As nearly naked as the law
Will guarantee to stand for:

(They lift Scott Nearing.)

Our modest mortal looks away
When naked Truth we show him,
Or turns and runs in sheer dismay
Lest he should seem to know him.

(They fly slowly away, bearing Nearing.)

EPILOGUE

(While the Sprites fly away, the professors, instructors, and teachers have assembled *en masse* in the foreground. They sing.)

[94]

ALL

With perfect equanimity,
With confidence unshaken,
The past in close proximity,
Its echoes unmistaken,—

Unaltered our position is,
Our rule, applied tradition:
To educate, our mission is;
Our object,—inanition.

(Long before this the audience has taken its departure. The masque may therefore be brought to a close.)

—September 1916

UPTON SINCLAIR
Reflections of a Strong Man

[These reflections were reflected between twelve and one o'clock on election night. Later returns, while they illustrate the proverb of Solomon to the effect that all is vanity, do not seem to us to affect the authenticity of these reflections.]

I am elected
A million people dance like dervishes,
They blow tin whistles
And shriek my name.

I am a strong man.
My strong teeth shine,
My children shout with glee,
My wife falls upon my strong bosom
And weeps,
But my strong soul is unmoved.

Alone, I bend my knees,
And thank Thee, Lord,
And my Saviour, Jesus Christ,
That I am a strong man.
That I studied the law and obeyed it.
That I worked hard over my cases and mastered
   them.
That I went every Sunday to the Baptist church.
That I was not too intimate with the
   Rockefellers,
And yet intimate enough.
That I did not get drunk.
That I did not fornicate.
That I did not sympathize.
That I did not have ideas.
That I am a strong man.

I thank Thee, Lord,
And my Saviour, Jesus Christ.
And pretty soon I will get busy,
And show the Mexicans and the railwaymen
How strong I am.

—January 1917

LOUIS GINSBERG
I Am Afraid to Face the Spring

I am afraid to face the Spring;
I haven't any heart to pass
The wayside lilacs blossoming,
The sunlight drowsing in the grass. . . .
It isn't clear to me at all;
My hungry eyes can only see
The shrivelled leaves of days that fall
And drift about me wearily. . . .

I hear that Spring is back again,
That flame-buds kindle all about;
But in my heart the buds of pain
Are swiftly breaking, breaking out!
And yet it's when I see the skies
And pass the lilacs blossoming
(Sweet lilacs laughing windily,
That once she used to give me!)
A sudden mist is in my eyes:
I cannot understand this thing;
I have no heart to face the Spring!
                    —November-December 1917

JAMES OPPENHEIM
Civilization

CIVILIZATION!
Everybody kind and gentle, and men giving up
    their seats in the car for the women . . .
What an ideal!
How bracing!

Is this what we want?
Have so many generations lived and died for this?
There have been Crusades, persecutions, wars, and
    majestic arts,
There have been murders and passions and hor-
    rors since man was in the jungle . . .
What was this blood-toll for?
Just so that everybody could have a full belly and
    be well-mannered?

But let us not fool ourselves:
This civilization is mostly varnish very thinly laid
    on . . .
Take any newspaper any morning: scan through
    it . . .
Rape, murder, villany, and picking and stealing:
The mob that tore a negro to pieces, the men that
    ravished a young girl:

The safe-blowing gang and the fat cowardly pro-
    moter who stole people's savings . . .
Just scan it through: this news of civilization . . .

Away then, with soft ideals:
Brace yourself with bitterness:
A drink of that biting liquor, the Truth . . .

Let us not be afraid of ourselves, but face our-
    selves and confess what we are:
Let us go backward a while that we may go for-
    ward:
This is an excellent age for insurrection, revolt,
    and the reddest of revolutions . . .
                    —August 1914

EDMOND McKENNA
A Question

Ho! you schoolmen, you gang of philosophers
    whose souls are tuned to the crackling of parch-
    ment.
You scholars with your pale brows immersed in
    antique customs, interpreting ancient rites.
You capon priests, who, when you want to appear
    impressive condemning women dress yourselves
    in women's clothes (true feminists I think);
You gray haired jurists (some of you bald) who
    also try to look majestic in women's clothes
    while you get rich selling justice;
You too, you beardy, lusty fellows (although at
    that some of you are consumptive), you who
    howl the long prayers of Democracy to the shuf-
    fling, sweaty brothers around the holy soap box
    at night on a street corner;
Poets too and fellows who try to copy the sunlight
    on stretched cloth;
Gentlemen all, in a way of speaking;

Attention now! I put you a question.
Why is it that I can walk all day through the fields
    and woods breathing the fine air and maybe
    plucking a wild rose to pieces and never think
    evil or of a cruel or an ugly thing,

And yet when I reach the edge of the city again
    when the evening is coming down,
When I stop to contemplate a rotten fence with
    filth oozing through into a stinking alley where a
    ragged child is making mud pies and eating
    fever,
I can think of nothing but your laws and systems,
    your philosophies and religion?
                    —June 1914

[95]

Views and Reviews

FLOYD DELL
Behind the Constitution

"By calm meditation and friendly councils, they had prepared a Constitution which, in the union of freedom with strength and order, excelled every one known before. . . . In the happy morning of their existence as one of the powers of the world, they had chosen justice for their guide; and while they proceeded on their way with a well founded confidence and joy, all the friends of mankind invoked success on their endeavor as the only hope for renovating the life of the civilized world."

So wrote the pious historian Bancroft. It is the most popular view of the origin of our Constitution. In school histories, in editorials, in sermons, in political speeches, and in disquisitions from the bench, it is the only one to be found. We are expected to believe that our political institutions were conceived in a happy mood of exalted unselfishness by men who sought only to earn the applause of a grateful and astonished universe. Nevertheless there have been some cynical doubts in many minds.

These doubts have been confined almost exclusively to Socialists. Radicals of other creeds have generally been content to accept the idealistic view of the origin of the Constitution, and have mourned over our latter-day perversion of the fathers' fine intentions. Surely the patriot statesmen of 1787 had no thought that the Senate would ever be the bulwark of the moneyed interests, and the courts their last refuge against the anger of the people! But the Socialist's cynicism remained unqualified. He thought, if you asked him, that the patriot fathers knew just what they were doing. It didn't strain his imagination, exercised as it was by some impressive vistas sketched by Karl Marx, to see in the attitude of the framers of the Constitution a friendliness to the moneyed interests and a real fear of the people.

And now this Socialist cynicism has been justified by a book—"An Economic Interpretation of the Constitution of the United States," by Charles A. Beard, professor of politics in Columbia University. It is such a book as appears only once in a decade—a book at once delightful and impressive. It is written by a man who is both a profound historical scholar and (as not every historical scholar is) a skilful writer. Some happy turn of phrase, some quiet and effective bit of satire, lights up every page. We have not had in America a book of such combined scientific and literary worth since Veblen's "The Theory of the Leisure Class."

Professor Beard's standards of historical workmanship are nothing if not exigent. He puts forth this volume as something frankly fragmentary, based though it is on much severe research. He points out that if it were possible to have a financial biography of all those persons connected with the framing and adoption of the Constitution— "perhaps about 160,000 men altogether"—he would have the materials he wants for his scientific study of the economic forces which created the Constitution. But the records at the Treasury Department are incomplete, the tax lists of various States have been lost, and he has not had the time to examine fully even the few tons of those that are available. Most of his readers, however, will be well satisfied with what he has brought us.

His volume is, in fact, an extraordinary broad survey of the personalities and the conditions of the period which produced the Constitution. He has a record of the vote, the opinions and the financial interests of practically every man who was prominent in the struggle out of which the Constitution came. And from this record he has been able to make the most illuminating generalizations about the economic forces which determined the issue of that struggle.

It is more than interesting to read the records of Baldwin, Bassett, Bedford, Blair, Blount and the others down tó Washington and Wythe. Some of them were men of wealth and standing from New England, some of them men of wealth and standing from the South, but all were men of wealth and standing. Most of them were large owners of public securities, and many of them extensive speculators in western lands. They had been chosen by Legislatures, most of which were elected by a restricted suffrage, to attend this convention, whose secret object they were known to favor. Practically all of them were undemocratic in their sympathies—or perhaps it would be more accurate to say, aristocratic in their fears. And they all were clearly aware of the economic advantages which would accrue to themselves by the change. As Williamson, a member of the Convention from North Carolina, put it in a letter to Madison: "I conceive that my opinions are not biassed by private Interests, but having claims to a considerable Quantity of Land in the Western Country, I am fully persuaded that the Value of those lands must be increased by an efficient federal Government."

As these eminent land speculators knew, an efficient federal government would make war on the Indians and give them a chance to sell their lands to bona-fide settlers. They also knew that an efficient federal government would have to redeem at its face value the paper certificates issued by the Confederacy, which they had bought at five cents on the dollar from the original holders. And they knew, moreover, that an efficient federal government, with a sufficiently undemocratic constitution, would put a stop to the attacks on private property in the State Legislatures.

For there were communists in those days. There is a distinct communist idea at the bottom of the demand of Shay and his "desperate debtors" for relief. "We all fought," they said, "for the land in America in the war. And now that we have won, it belongs to all of us." All they wanted in reality was to keep the land they already had, instead of turning it over to their wealthy creditors and then going to jail. They were put down, as usual, by the militia. But populistic schemes for the issuance of paper money had gained so much favor among the small farming class that the financiers were frightened. Something must be done.

They did it. The Convention called to revise the Articles of Confederation promptly threw the Articles of Confederation overboard and illegally drew up a new plan of government, which was submitted to Congress with a demand for a popular vote. The popular vote itself, carefully engineered, carried the Constitution over an almost overwhelming popular disapproval to a bare success. It was an act which, as one historian has said, if committed by Julius Cæsar or Napoleon Bonaparte, would have been pronounced a *coup d'état*. It was a *coup d'état*. It put property in the saddle. And it was meant to put property in the saddle.

So much is admitted in that remarkable document, the Federalist. On account óf the restrictions upon suffrage, it was not then necessary, as it is now, for politicians to put a democratic mask on their intentions. Madison and Hamilton and Jay could explain to their fellow capitalists just what the Constitution was for. Madison even foresaw the rise of a landless proletariat, and explained how the Constitution would secure "private rights against the danger of such a faction and at the same time preserve the spirit and form of a popular government." The judiciary was expressly designed, it is explained, as the crowning counterweight to "an interested and overbearing majority." And, perhaps most important of all, it would lend the power of a nation to the enforcement of contracts and the collection of debts.

The Federalist stands, indeed, as a predecessor to Professor Beard's book. It is itself, as Professor Beard points out, an economic interpretation of the Constitution. It reveals the Constitution as a conscious entrenchment in power of the exploiting class. And again the Socialist scepticism is justified.   —January 1914

FLOYD DELL
Mr. Dreiser and the Dodo

Theodore Dreiser is an interesting example of an intellectual species that is fast becoming extinct. His attitude toward the world has become so rare among thinking people that one comes upon it with a sense of awe, as one would meet a megatherium in a park. Mr. Dreiser is impressive in all his books, and not least of all in his new one. It is an account of a trip through Europe,* and it shows, even more clearly than his novels, the philosophy of—what shall I call it?

*"A Traveler at Forty," by Theodore Dreiser. $2 net. The Century Company.

There is a philosophy which disposes of revolutionists more completely than any other. It disposes of them, not by hating them, or by ignoring them, but by accepting them as Interesting. According to this philosophy, the revolutionist is a part of life just as much as the artist, the fine lady and the prostitute. They are all interesting. This man's zeal for revolution is an expression of temperament—and nothing more. As such it is admirable. He plans his utopias, the artist paints, the fine lady dresses for the ball, the prostitute smiles invitation to a new man . . . and life goes on. It has always been so, it always will be so. A mad world, my masters, but an interesting one!

This is my philosophy of Theodore Dreiser. It is a philosophy which has been apparent in all his writings. In his novels he has given a broad and impartial account of life as he has seen it lived. Nothing has been too common or mean to escape his observation, nothing too ugly or evil to arouse his scorn. He has described the just and the unjust with a calm and even balance. He has looked on our enthusiasms and our disappointments, our dreams and our lusts, as might some cynical and compassionate god: and we have been properly awed.

It was Theophile Gautier, about the middle of the nineteenth century, who started the idea that the gods were cynical about human affairs. The idea was characteristic of the period. Cynical? Not so the gods of the Greeks—they descended *ex machina* in their godlike anxiety to see that things went right on earth, and the noise of men's quarrels reechoing through Olympus testified to the importance of human affairs. Not so the god of Job, who answered him categorically out of a whirlwind. And not so the god of Bernard Shaw, who waits on his servant to find truth and establish it. Anyone who believes in his own power will have a powerful god—or a philosophy of revolution: it is the same thing. But the mid-nineteenth century—

It was a period dominated by what was called Darwinism—the idea that change came into the world with a tragic tardiness, and that the only way to help the process was to let it alone. People sometimes talk as though Darwin put the idea of evolution in people's heads. He did establish a mechanical and deadly conception of evolution. He made people think of change as something outside human effort. With the chill of his doctrine he froze the blood of revolution for a generation. Darwinism descended like a blight upon the world and upon men's minds.

Conceive yourself in the Darwinian frame of mind. Forget all you have ever learned in histories about the past, and all you have learned in dreams about the future. Then look about you—see how the fly is devoured by the sparrow, and the sparrow by the shrike (whatever that is), and the shrike probably by the cat. That is "natural selection," and it results in the "survival of the fittest." Then observe the same process going on in the industrial world: No, no, don't interfere because it would spoil the natural condition of "free competition"; and, besides, it wouldn't be any use to try, on account of the "iron law of wages"! . . .

Nothing is more certain than that we don't live in that kind of world now. We know better. We have revised our notions of biology to take revolution into account. And we have dislodged enough sticks from the woodpile of economics to know there is a nigger in there somewhere. Besides, we just can't look on while the process is processing. We have to do something about it ourselves, even if it is only to pull judiciously at other people's coat-tails.

Mr. Dreiser calls this, when he runs across it in his travels, the efflorescence of a temperament. It is more than that: it is the solemn knowledge that according to whether you lift your hand or stay it, the world will be different. We have seen changes in machinery, and changes in institutions, and changes in men's minds—and we know that nothing is impossible. We can have any kind of bloody world we bloody want.

We are in the twentieth century. Mr. Dreiser is still in the nineteenth. For purposes of fiction that is all right. It is absurd to quarrel with an artist about the means by which he achieves his effects. "Sister Carrie" justifies mid-nineteenth century pessimism; a book as good would justify Swedenborgianism, or the theory that we live on the inside of the earth. But when Mr. Dreiser comes to write about modern Europe he needs a modern mind. Sympathy isn't enough; it takes understanding. And Mr. Dreiser simply doesn't understand the most outstanding features of contemporary European life. Firm in the impression that things are to-day essentially what they were yesterday, he dwells upon those aspects of social life which might well have attracted an observer of forty years ago. He draws it, while yet it is there to draw, with vivacity and charm: but he does not see ten minutes into the future. And he conceives the past so naively in terms of the mid-nineteenth century, that he talks of the Renaissance as though Lorenzo the Magnificent were a kind of Charles T. Yerkes.

All passes. Lorenzo the Magnificent is gone, and gone that magnificent curiosity about life which created the Renaissance. Gone too is the mid-nineteenth century, and gone the stark grandeur of its philosophic pessimism. One representative of that period remains, one only, the last survivor of a great and pitiful race. And through his eyes we can take one last look at mid-nineteenth century Europe—a Europe of street-corners and drawing-rooms, cafés and cathedrals, repartee and women, and over all a sense of lovely futility as of flowers and toys.   —February 1914

FLOYD DELL
Sweetness and Light

[The Masses *was seriously interested only in the radical press and considered most other periodicals beneath contempt. The* New Republic *was an exception to this rule, however, and if the editors were less impressed by Walter Lippmann & Company than they might have been, they at least favored the* New Republic *with their attention.*]

The New Republic Book: Selections from the First Hundred Issues. (Republic Publishing Co., Inc.)

It is difficult to realize that the *New Republic* is only a hundred weeks old. So thoroughly has it established itself among our best American institutions, and in the regard of our best people, that it seems as though it must have been conceived at the same time as the Constitution, if not actually brought over in the Mayflower. Not that there is anything antiquated about the *New Republic;* for as everyone knows, and as itself does not deny, it represents the most deliberately liberal and carefully enlightened thought in THESE STATES. But so deliberated is this liberalism, so utterly final this enlightenment, that it comes like an utterance from the Ancient of Days. Or, since we do not wish to imply that the *New Republic* is ever gravid, let us say that it comes like an expression of opinion from the Ancient of Days in one of the more urbane and graceful but none the less authoritative moments of his discourse.

An institution at once political and literary, it combines as it were the dignity of W. D. Howells with that of the Supreme Court. And if we were told that these worthies had set up shop only two years ago, and in that space of time filled the more immediate universe with a sense of their importance, we should not be more incredulous than we

are inclined to be about the *New Republic's* hundred weeks of life. A mere hundred weeks? Impossible! Say rather a hundred years. . . .

Yes, decidedly, for the first few years of its life would probably have been spent in the passionate celebration of some new vision of life or the reckless espousal of unpopular causes (cf. the editorial follies of the Transcendentalists or of J. G. Whittier); but eventually these faults of youth would have been overcome. In twenty-five years a weekly journal might have learned to address itself acceptably to those who desire enlightenment without shock; in fifty years it might have acquired the art of extracting the shock from any idea whatever; in seventy-five years it might have established such utter confidence in its decorum that any idea which appeared in its pages became, by virtue of its presence there, correct. In a hundred years it might have become the *New Republic.*

Yet, in spite of probabilities, we can by an effort go back in memory to the time, two years ago, when the *New Republic* was not. It seems strange. A United States of America without the *New Republic* in it. There was only a void, inconspicuous but acute, on library table-tops, and in after-dinner conversation. And then, sprung serene and immortally middle-aged from the editorial brain of Mr. Walter Lippmann and his associates, appeared the *New Republic.*

There was in that first issue—or should have been, we really cannot trouble to look it up—an article on the Freudian interpretation of dreams, and one on the music of Leo Ornstein; there were editorials saying that it was to be hoped that the pants manufacturers would see the reasonableness of the strikers' demands, and that President Wilson should confiscate the German ships interned in American ports; a causerie telling what a nice old gentleman saw out of the train window as he sat with a volume of Henry James on his lap, and a review of a volume of poems, in which (the review, not the poems) there was an estimate of the political future of Colonel Roosevelt and quotations from Veblen and Havelock Ellis; an essay by Rebecca West in which Ibsen was denounced most convincingly as a mid-Victorian chatterer and Santa Teresa exalted as the first (and with one exception the only) feminist; and an article, with map, showing the far-reaching effects of General Bing's victory on the upper branch of the Euphrates. All (except the Rebecca West article) was written with sobriety and restraint, and all (except the editorial advising the confiscation of the German ships) was marked, not to say indelibly branded, by unmistakable literary style. The editorial on confiscating the German ships, which was to reappear from time to time whenever a crisis arose which involved the destiny of the nation, seemed hastily and rather crudely written, as if under the compulsion of a deep conviction which could not stop to palter with literary form.

One hundred times in as many perilous weeks since then it has presented us the best liberal thought; and always in the most agreeable manner. One hundred times it has run the risk of losing its progressive poise. It is perhaps as a proof of its unscathed escape that it issues this volume, befittingly bound in blue-gray board covers with a black and white label, and giving, as the preface modestly says, "A sample of liberal opinion in the United States" (1914-16).

You don't put in your thumb and pull out a plum, however; urbanity takes both time and space. Thus, in an article on Brandeis it is stated at the beginning that "one public benefit has already accrued from the nomination of Mr. Brandeis. It has started a discussion of what the Supreme Court means in American life. . . . Multitudes of Americans believe seriously that the nine Justices embody pure reason, that they are set apart from the concerns of the community, regardless of time, place and circumstances, to become the interpreter of sacred words with meaning fixed forever and ascertainable by a process of ineluctable reasoning. Yet the notion not only runs counter to all we know of human nature; it betrays either ignorance or false knowledge of the actual work of the Supreme Court as disclosed by two hundred and thirty-nine volumes of United States reports."

We pause, by the bye—not to doubt that the *New Republic* is fully conversant with the contents of those 239 volumes but to wonder by precisely what means it became so. Did Mr. Lippmann read them all himself, or were they divided among the editorial staff; and which volumes did "Q. K." read? But, however it was, the erudition of the *New Republic* produces, as always, its effect. No one would venture to disagree with a journal which, before setting forth what it thought of the attack on Brandeis, prepared for the task by reading 239 volumes of law reports. Brandeis had been attacked because he was "too radical," and because he was a Jew. Some liberals might have shown anger at such malevolent prejudices. But not the *New Republic*. No, it was an opportunity to undermine, quietly and tactfully, the popular notion of the Supreme Court. Bellicose propagandists might object that these subterranean operations go so far down that when the mine explodes it does no damage. There are mischievous notions about the function of the Supreme Court which are held by the Supreme Court; and there are mischievous notions about it held, one ventures to say, by most of the readers of the *New Republic;* but no one who reads the polite satire of the *New Republic* is likely to wince.

That is the beauty of reading the *New Republic*. One always agrees with it; and conversely, it always appears to agree with its readers. The appearance may be deceptive. Frequently it is, for Mr. Lippmann and his associates are not at all satisfied with existing politics, industry, education or international relations, and they have fairly definite ideas as to how the things ought to be changed. But with such infinite sweetness does the *New Republic* diffuse its light that no one would think of taking it for a beacon.

Of course, if the *New Republic* went at its readers hammer-and-tongs it wouldn't be—the *New Republic*. It subsists upon the conviction which it irradiates, that the truth is something that can be assimilated in an agreeable manner. It is a monument to the pleasant belief that thought is something that doesn't hurt.

There have been rifts in this serenity of course. But the *New Republic* so obviously wants to avoid the raw earnestness of youth, the passion of propaganda, the angry and eloquent speech of naked idealism, that we take from a recent *New Republic,* where it looked unhappy and made the *New Republic* look unhappier still, this quotation from Bertrand Russell—and put it here where it belongs:

"Men fear thought as they fear nothing else on earth—more than ruin, more even than death. Thought is subversive and revolutionary, destructive and terrible; thought is merciless to privilege, established institutions, and comfortable habits; thought is anarchic and lawless, indifferent to authority, careless of the well tried wisdom of the ages. Thought looks into the pit of hell and is not afraid. It sees man, a feeble speck, surrounded by unfathomable depths of silence; yet it bears itself proudly, as unmoved as if it were lord of the universe. Thought is great and swift and free, the light of the world, and the chief glory of man."
—April 1917

CHARLES W. WOOD
Is Seeing Believing, and Other Questions

George Bernard Shaw is one of my most promising pupils. We are both misunderstood in much the same way, as anyone is bound to be who has such a simple faith in life. We both have an undeserved reputation for being clever. Several million people say Shaw is clever. One man says the same thing about me. That, in fact, is the main difference between us: it is only a trifling difference, as the average intelligence of both groups of appraisers is about the same.

We are not clever. We are not as clever as many of our critics. The things we say sound clever only because they are so simple—because of our childlike acceptance of life.

Everybody indulges in sin, for instance, but nobody but myself actually favors it. I like sin fully as well as I like salvation. I've tried both and I know. As far as I can see, everybody else likes it too, although nobody else says so. Now, it isn't the least bit clever of me to say so. When I sin, I'm glad, but when clever people sin, they're sorry. That's the stamp of cleverness—getting one's psychology all tied up with complicated contradictions.

It wouldn't do, of course, for everybody to be like me. If people weren't sorry for their sins, we wouldn't have any religion. And if they didn't like to sin, there wouldn't be any people. For now, as formerly, we are conceived in sin: and until some other equally pleasant method is discovered, we shall doubtless stick to that.

And so, perforce, most everybody is compelled to become a philosopher. A philosopher is a person who ignores the evidence of his eyes and ears and solves the problems of life through the time-honored system of kidding himself. G. B. S. and I are not philosophers. We are different from most people, but the difference is the other way around. Most people won't believe their eyes and ears, even when they have good ones. They either kid themselves on their own hook, or swallow whole the dope that somebody else kidded himself with some sacred centuries ago.

But here's the point. And it is one that must be grasped in order to understand such people as Shaw and me. That is, that people's eyes and ears don't always lie down on the job just because their philosophies and religions tell them to. And ever and anon, we who have escaped from said philoso-

Drawn by Pablo Picasso, September 1916

A Portrait

phies and religions say something startling. It is startling because your eyes and ears believe it but your philosophy and religion don't.

"That's all wrong," says your philosophy. "It's contrary to Scripture." Or, "It doesn't agree with Article II, section 6."

But your eyes and ears understand it and applaud. They tell you it's just what they've been waiting for. They say it agrees exactly with what they've been listening to and looking at since they were knee-high to a philosophy-hopper.

This is incipient rebellion and the reigning belief is perturbed. And so from the throne of your sacred belief, you answer, cleverly, that we are clever; that we don't mean what we say; that we have a cunning knack of twisting things out of their right relation, and that we are not to be taken seriously but to be enjoyed. Shaw and I are two delectable sins, according to you, to be enjoyed and atoned for.

This is really clever—of you—letting your senses accept us while your beliefs go serenely on.

It is your way of granting limited autonomy to your eyes and ears in order to ward off a revolution in your thinking department. It happens every time a Shaw play comes to town.

Look at "Getting Married," playing at the Booth Theater. Critics have been calling it clever simply because it isn't. It is a sensation simply because it presents the case for matrimony just as it actually stands, instead of presenting it in the usual kid-yourself fashion. One critic wrote half a column of guesses as to whether Shaw actually believes in marriage.

Of course we believe in marriage. We have seen it with our own eyes. If we were as clever as some of the Christian Scientists, say, we might not believe in it even then. We might think it was an error, a psycho-optical illusion, a metaphysical mirage, or whatever the proper name is for something that exists and doesn't.

Would people get married if they knew what they were in for? That's the big question in the play. Shaw doesn't answer it. He makes the audience answer it, and the New York audience loudly answers "No." That's what makes the audience mad. Shaw's appeal to their common nonsense. For the audience has seen matrimony too, even while they are kidding themselves into thinking that they haven't.

It should be explained that men would marry even if they did know what was ahead. So would women, even if they saw the thing clearly. But if the man and the woman both knew—that's a different matter.

A man is often willing to descend from the glory of the lover to the dull business of being a husband, because those are the terms which society imposes. If he knew that the act would wreck and ruin his sweetheart's life as well, he might also see it through. She usually prefers ruin to loss of reputation: that's her lookout and a fellow can't spend his whole life in being kind to somebody else. But if she knew also what the terms of marriage really are—physically, socially, economically and psychologically—if she knew it meant good-bye to romance, if she knew it meant that her lover could court her no longer, what then? She might still want children, but "Getting Married" deals with that as well. Lesbia, who wanted children but didn't want a husband around the house, is by no means an overdrawn character. There are thousands of Lesbias, only those in actual life kid themselves into thinking they want the husband too. Then when they get him, they beat him up—either with broomsticks and pokers or with reproaches or dumb agony.

Incidentally, Shaw knows how to give the devil his due. When the average religious playwright depicts a clergyman, he makes him as big a ninny as himself. Shaw created a bishop who is a real man. William Faversham catches the idea and, philosophy aside, "Getting Married" is one of the keenest pieces of good drama that I ever saw.

Did you ever wonder what sort of drama the extreme left wing of the radicals would thrill to most, if they had their own untrammelled theater? Fortunately, you don't have to wonder any longer. The secret is out. Right in the greenwich villagest part of Greenwich Village, at the extreme left of the Liberal Club, they now have such a theater. They call it the Playwrights' Theater, and it's owned body and soul by the Provincetown Players. The players are all radical, the playwrights are radical, the audience is radical. Everything about the place, from the opening hour to the atmospheric pressure, is radical. And one number on the radical bill sent the whole audience into several minutes of thunderous applause. What do you suppose it was.

It was a sketch by no less a radical than Eugene G. O'Neill. It was called "Bound East for Cardiff," and depicted in a masterly way a tragic scene on shipboard where a dying sailor was saying his last goodbye to his pal. It was a realistic sketch with lines that rang true throughout, and it was acted by George Cram Cook, William Stuart and others in a way that would do credit to the best-trained professional cast. The hard life of the sea was the theme, the longing for a simple home in the country and for the realization of a pure woman's love its human appeal. Any man or woman who was human could scarcely escape being affected, and I did not wonder at the dozen or so curtain calls.

But what interested me most was this. "Bound East for Cardiff" was a sketch which I am sure would make a hit at the Palace, or any one of the ultra bourgeois vaudeville houses. There was not a line in it which any ordinary theater-goer would not wish his daughter to hear. There was not a suggestion anywhere of any antagonism to the sacred ideals of conventional society. It was just human, that's all, and mighty well acted. Just the sort of thing which radicals (and almost all other people) will thrill to most.

Oh, yes, they did have their fling of radicalism too. "King Arthur's Socks," by Floyd Dell, was somewhat devilish and somewhat more Dellish. Max Eastman as "Lancelot Jones"—no, I won't say it. Someone in the audience said something very much more to the point. He said that Lancelot Jones played "Max Eastman" remarkably well. Can a man love one woman and want to kiss another? Also, does a girl become bad if she wants to be bad and can't? These are problems which only the devil and Dell can answer, and they sometimes leave us guessing. But they come nearer being answered at the Playwrights' Theater than any other place I know.

War is just too cute for anything. The invasion of Belgium by those jolly German generals was awfully romantic. They never really had anybody shot. The just jollied the pretty American girls who happened along, had them married by sudden military orders to men they didn't intend to marry, and then gossiped with occasional chauffeurs concerning subsequent silhouettes on the curtains of the bridal chambers. If you don't believe this is a correct picture of war, see "Arms and the Girl" at the Fulton Theater.

No, it isn't a farce. It's drama. It's realistic like a pair of rose goggles. Natural and free like a canary bird. People go to the theater, you know, to be amused. Blessed are the playwrights who know how to turn the trick. Grant Stewart and Robert Baker know how. They know how to keep all the disturbing things out of a play, like ideas and human life. And they know how to dress up what remains, so that it looks and sounds just lovely.

Most assuredly, "Arms and the Girl" will be a success. Why, I liked it myself, even while I was sore at myself for being lulled by this very evident euthanasia of stagecraft. Writers on *The Masses* ought in all conscience to hate such unreal drama; and they ought to hate it all the more for its plausible semblance of reality. But between you and me, they don't. They'll damn such plays roundly, and praise such productions as "Under Sentence"; but ten to one they'll sit through plays of the first sort with considerable more docility.

I wish Irvin S. Cobb and Roi Cooper Magrue would rewrite Hamlet. I wish they would fix up the last act, at least, so that it would come out strong for psychoanalysis as a cure for melancholy. Then they might do for Shakespeare what they did for themselves when they manufactured the last act of "Under Sentence."

"Under Sentence" is a play of tremendous realism and no stagecraft. The plot is rankly unreal and melodramatic, but there ar a few scenes of the tensest and most gripping sort. It is an extraordinary prison play; and if the authors had been content to let it go at that, it might have accomplished wonders for prison reform. But they were not content. They tried to make it a prison reform play; and trying to underwrite prison reform is too much like trying to dramatize the immediate demands of the Socialist Party platform. Due largely to the acting of Felix Krembs as a broken prisoner, the play is, with all its faults, one of the really big achievements of the season. In the interest of the propaganda, I wish they had cut the propaganda out.

Did you ever swap wives with your next-door neighbor? It's lots of fun. No, not for you or the wives, but for the audience. When a couple of gentlemen do it these nights at the Shubert Theater, everybody laughs. I'd like to know why. Possibly it is because Charlotte Greenwood is so funny, but it seemed to me that the crowd saw a big joke in the idea itself.

"So Long, Letty" is a musical farce. Wifeswapping isn't done in really truly drama. It isn't done anywhere except in farce and in Brooklyn and a few other places. And when it is done in Brooklyn, nobody thinks it's funny. Everybody pretends to think it is disgusting. If it is funny at the Shubert Theater, why isn't it funny in Brooklyn? And if it is disgusting in Brooklyn, why isn't it disgusting at the Shubert Theater? I don't pretend to know. I'm just asking.

I knew a fellow once who married a woman and couldn't get along with her worth a cent. Still they stuck together. If they have farces after society becomes civilized, that ought to make a great theme.
—January 1917

FLOYD DELL
We Wonder

Some of our friends tell us it isn't good taste to criticise our esteemed contemporary, the *New Republic,* in the way we do. The charge of bad taste pains us deeply, but it seems to us that it is hardly relevant. The *New Republic* is not so much a magazine as a political institution, comparable in its way to the Progressive Party. We all know with what forward-looking deals the Progressive Party was formed, and how it fell into the hands of

Roosevelt and other plausible reactionaries. The significance of its betrayal and *débacle* is now known to everyone, thanks to the journalistic custom which makes it perfectly good taste to criticise a political party. If anyone falls under its influence now it is a symptom of his own weaknesses, and not anybody else's fault. The folly and failure in which Progressivist idealism becomes mired and stuck are plain for all to see. Not so plain, perhaps, are the ironic follies and failures into which the New Republican idealism is being led. We sincerely hope that our innate courtesy will not prevent us from making some of them rather clearer before we get through.

The *New Republic* came into existence at a time when there was a peculiar and tremendous need of analytic and constructive thinking in regard to social and political institutions. Clearly, it intended to do its best to fulfill this need for America—not, to be sure, in such a way as to alarm anybody. In the politest and subtlest manner possible it was going ahead to revalue all our national and international values. And for a time it seemed as though this compromise, this soft disguise of the raw terrors of free thought, was all that would be required of it. But the war, which by opening a new era to the speculative inquiry and expert manipulation of this group of bold though graceful intellects, had given them an unexampled opportunity, presently brought them face to face with the necessity of making a practical decision which would in itself curtail that opportunity. It was nothing less than a decision about war itself.

The *New Republic* was by the nature of its intellectual ostentions pledged—among its other obligations to the era just dawning upon the world—to assist in the discovery and installation of efficient political and social means of preventing war between nations. A crude kind of consistency might have seemed to require that it should not give its support to the popular theory that the way to promote peace was to continue the present war indefinitely. Yet, as it happened, the only way to gain a hearing for the new doctrine of Peace was to acquiesce in some measure in the old doctrine of War. The *New Republic* did not actually intend at first to accept War as a substitute for Peace. It began with what seemed a merely realistic determination to accept this war as an existing fact, not to be unduly cavilled about. It continued by hoping, less and less skeptically, for it to bring forth good fruits—though it was considerably surprised and not a little alarmed when it brought

forth the Russian Revolution. But long before this latter incident, the conversion of the *New Republic* to War had been for practical purposes complete. It had taken War to its bosom, and its own doubtful past as an ambiguously pacifist journal was forgotten. Vanished were the days when it had seemed to our substantial citizens a kind of Yellow Book of Ideas, or, as a famous ex-President is said to have called it, "a pornographic version of the *Nation*." It was now more like a scholarly version of Mr. Hudson Maxim's photo-play, "The Battle Cry of Peace."

That this compromise was so complete, being more nearly, perhaps, a surrender, was due entirely to the logic of events. If the *New Republic* had appeared to be too coolly aloof from the popular pro-Ally enthusiasm, it would have lost its opportunity to utter the counsels of moderation—or at least its chance of being heard. Its belief that the Germans are, in spite of everything, a civilized people who must eventually be readmitted into the amity of nations, would have been generally dismissed as stuff bought with the Kaiser's gold—an accusation which an ambitious political periodical could hardly be expected to bring upon itself. By joining the procession, it could make itself a power for good. It was, moreover, not in human nature to continue to be skeptical of the benefits of a war upon which its approval had been, however reluctantly, bestowed. Amiable associations improve bad manners, and a war patronized by the *New Republic* could not but turn out to be a better war than anybody had hoped. Thus the entente cordiale between War and the *New Republic* was established, and their relations improved to such an extent that when the assistance of the *New Republic* was asked in a little matter like pushing the United States into the shambles, it was given freely and heartily.

But, nevertheless, the *New Republic*—characteristically enough—finds itself unwilling to surrender the field of intellectual enterprise which it had originally staked out for itself. It remembers uneasily that it had intended to help bring a lasting peace to a war-weary world. It does not yet realize how thoroughly it has committed itself to the program of militarism. Having assisted in inflicting conscription on an unwilling nation, it proceeds to suggest with the most virtuous air in the world that it is really not right to conscript men who consciously object to war; and doubtless it congratulates itself upon being able to speak up for the poor conscientious objector with a voice that

Drawn by George Bellows, July 1916

At Pettipas

[This lithograph showing Robert Henri, John Yeats (the painter, and father of William Butler Yeats), and others in a popular New York restaurant is one of the best known of Bellows' works.]

is heard in the Union League Club and the White House.

We have some doubts of the effectiveness of such mild and courteous protestations in behalf of liberty. Perhaps those who are engaged in destroying our liberties are not after all the best ones to defend them. But to this dual personality of the *New Republic* we do owe a certain debt. Unconscious as it still is of the nature of its relations to militarism, the *New Republic* occasionally behaves as no ordinary militarist publication would dare to do. It occasionally gives away the whole show.

It did this notably in the days before the war when it innocently pointed out, and succeeded in making very clear, the fact that our alleged neutrality was no neutrality at all—that we were deliberately doing everything we could to defeat Germany! Everybody knew it, but it wasn't being admitted by the pro-Ally partisans just then.

A second admission, to the effect that this war was not wanted by the people of the United States, but was put over on them by a small group of intellectuals, was commented on in our last issue. For the second time the *New Republic* had said things that good militarists shouldn't say.

And now the *New Republic* has "spilled the beans" again. In its issue of May 12th, it admits that under the same circumstances as now exist, not only would Germany, however thoroughly punished for it in this war, use the submarine again as she is using it now, but—

"so would any nation, including the United States, which was being blockaded by a superior fleet and was in danger of being crushed as a result of the blockade." (Italics ours.)

The upshot of the article is a plea for an inter-

[105]

national arrangement which would establish the "freedom of the seas," and incidentally draw the sting from British navalism; an arrangement, indeed, which would protect the world from the menace of Germany and of their submarines by simply giving Germany and others no excuse for using them—which is an odd enough ending for an editorial based on the premise that American participation in the war is a contribution to the cause of democracy. Dr. Jekyll and Mr. Hyde are getting rather mixed up. They actually tread on one another's toes. This melange, we understand, is called in some quarters "constructive idealism."

We quote from a book written by one of the editors of the *New Republic*: "The mind of Europe collapsed. The appeal to arms was the result of that criminal recklessness which decides to hack its way through when no other solution presents itself to the mind." Having written that, the author helped dragoon the United States into the process so eloquently described. Some minds are like that.

Being pacifist and militarist both at once involves difficulties, however. We wonder, for instance, whether the editors of the *New Republic* are, as militarists, going to enlist for the trenches, or, as pacifists, going to stay at home and try to work out the problem of peace. Or will they take the ground that in helping to spread the snare of conscription for the feet of others they have already done their bit and should be allowed to walk free? We wonder. —July 1917

FLOYD DELL
The Science of the Soul

[*Although psychoanalysis was not well known to the general public at this time, the Village already considered Freud, if not quite old hat, slightly passé. The* avante-garde *intellectuals were ready for stronger, or at any rate more exotic, meat, as this pioneer review of Jung's* Psychology of the Unconscious *shows.*]

For twenty-odd centuries the philosophers have attempted to discover the nature and the workings of the human soul. One of the earliest subjects of speculation, it has been the last to yield its secrets. When in the seventeenth century Newton reduced the falling of a stone and the wheeling of the stars in their courses to a simple formula, men were still about as far from the heart of the mystery as Plato had been. It is not strange, for the nearer

we come to ourselves the more infinitely complex do facts appear to become. A man's hand *is* a mystery that rivals the ribb'd universe—or whatever it was that Walt Whitman asserted. And when the soul turns its gaze inward upon itself it encounters a cloudy chaos, in comparison to which the revolutions of planets and electrons are simple and orderly matters. When, in the nineteenth century, Darwin formulated the great theory of biological progress which linked the highest achievements of mankind with the lowliest beginnings of life on the globe, the soul of man was still an unanswered riddle.

Nevertheless, quite outside the sublime theorizings of the philosophers, in the humble study of mental disease, facts about the mind were being discovered which were the beginnings of a new science of the soul. Bit by bit in the last two hundred years the data of psychic phenomena have been accumulated. It waited, however, the advent of some bold investigator whose mind could pierce through these phenomena and discover their underlying laws. It is clear that when this should be done we would have a generalization as momentous to the world as Newton's; a discovery as startling and revolutionizing in its effects as Darwin's. Such was, in fact, the nature of the discovery and the generalization made by Sigmund Freud.

The world has not yet had a chance to realize the significance of the Freudian theory of the nature and processes of the soul. When it does, a new light will have been shed on education and morality, to mention only the most obvious territories in which its influence is bound to operate. A new direction will in fact have been given to our thinking, and the shape and color of our lives will be changed as surely as the discovery of the uses of steam changed the landscape of the earth.

There are two chief reasons why the significance of the new discoveries about the soul are slow to affect society at large—aside from the fact that so revolutionary a discovery must necessarily lie under deep suspicion and win its way against the resistance of a natural conservatism. One of these reasons, to put it bluntly, is the apparent inability of these discoverers to write—in the orderly and logical fashion commonly demanded of scientists. There is, it is true, something in the study of fundamental psychic processes which destroys respect for logic by revealing its factitiousness. Nevertheless, the result is unhappy. If Darwin had been no more careful a writer than

Freud, or Huxley than Jung, and if either of them had had the romantic notions about what constitutes a clinching argument that Freud and Jung display, we might all still be believing that species were created one Friday and Saturday in the year 4004 B. C.

The other reason is that this discovery is still complicated and involved with a theory of the treatment of neuroses, out of which it sprang. Freud had tried hypnotism on his patients, and wanted something better to get at the hidden part of their minds, and so elaborated the technique of dream analysis; a fact which has a little, but not much more importance than the apple which is supposed to have fallen on Sir Isaac Newton's head and set him thinking about gravitation. Darwin's generalization was illustrated and proved by a host of observations, from which, however, the generalization itself has been set free. We do not think of the theory of "mutation" in terms of the Dutch primroses—was it primroses?—by which it was originally worked out. Our conception of the germ theory of disease is not cluttered up with the particular slides which were used in originally demonstrating it. But it is the misfortune of the new discovery that practically all its literature deals with the technique of psychoanalysis rather than the more significant revelations achieved through the use of that instrument.

It is from that situation that Jung has apparently sought to deliver the new science, by means of his book, "Psychology of the Unconscious."[1] More exactly, the book is a loose exemplification of the contribution which he himself has already made to this growing science, in setting it free from some of the entanglements incident to its origin.

By means of the technique of dream analysis, Freud has discovered that the "unconscious," the hidden part of the mind, is full of "complexes," knotted groups of emotions and thoughts, which have been "repressed," thrust back out of consciousness as shameful. He found, moreover, that these repressed complexes were sexual in character. Repression, that is to say, was shown to be one way in which the mind deals with emotional force—"libido"—which cannot find free play in civilized life. It is, however, a poor way, for the repression may give rise to a symptom called neurosis. What other way is there of dealing with this emotional force? It is clear that in many people the "libido," meeting the barrier which civilization puts up against its absolutely free play, transcends those barriers in the "sublimated" form of artistic or other expression. Such, roughly, is the core of the Freudian hypothesis. It had, however, some sub-theories which seemed scarcely less important. One of these dealt with the original causes of repression. It was at first Freud's belief, based upon his patients' childhood memories long forgotten and recovered by dream analysis, that some early shock which had produced a painful impression and been repressed into the unconsciousness, was responsible for later-appearing neuroses: a theory which he later found untenable, but not before it had set afoot some very valuable investigations into the psychology of childhood and infancy. Another theory was based upon the universal emergence, among neurotic persons, of a morbid emotional attachment to a parent; the so-called "father-" or "mother-complex." Into the exposition of these theories, which was, to begin with, almost entirely from the practitioner's viewpoint, was imparted an intolerable garrulousness on the subject of sex and dreams; this was, perhaps, inevitable, for the shock with which conservative minds received the news that sexual emotions could not be repressed without morbid consequences, and the skepticism of other minds with regard to the significance of dreams seemed to require endless explanations, in the reverberations of which the real significance[2] of the Freudian discoveries was almost lost.

Jung's chief contributions to this young science were: first, he freed the term "libido" from exclusively sexual connotations, so that it became equivalent to the Life Force, the whole sum of human energy. Second, he finished the destruction of Freud's early notion that neuroses were due to incidents occurring in childhood; he showed that the emergence of infantile memories is due to the fact that the life energy, having turned away from the real or present world, goes into the past, where it revives infantile memories and fantasies. The effect of this revision is to take attention away from the past and place it in the present; for it is Jung's conviction that the cause of neurosis is a refusal or

[1] "Psychology of the Unconscious," a Study of the Transformations and Symbolisms of the Libido: A Contribution to the History of the Evolution of Thought, by Dr. C. G. Jung. Authorized translation, with introduction, by Beatrice M. Hinkle, M. D. Moffat, Yard & Co., $4 net. For sale by Masses Book Shop.

[2] I.e., the loss of a vast portion of the psychic energy of the race in neuroses (insanity) as the result of a blocking of its path into the outer world of reality—a blocking for which civilization may be, and certainly to a large extent is, to blame.

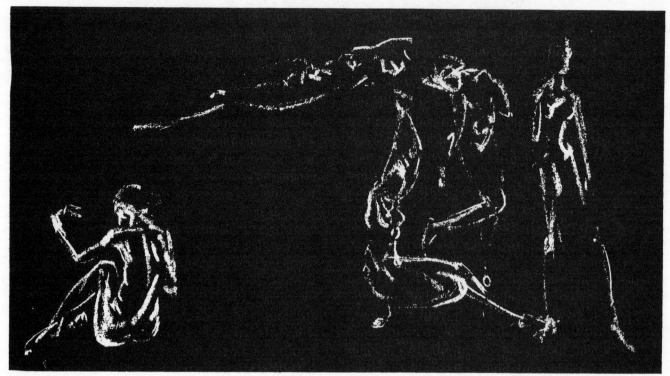

Melodies

[Davies was in many ways an unlikely addition to the Masses' *group. A quiet, bespectacled man, he owed his position in the art world to a group of lady patrons whom he handled with considerable skill. Although he had little interest in politics, he was devoted to* The Masses *and gave it a large amount of his work. Because a steady market existed for his drawings, this was a financially more substantial contribution than the donations of many other less fortunately situated artists. Davies proved to be a deeper and more*

failure to meet the difficulties and dangers of life in the actual world.[3] If this is true, then the specific contents of the patient's dream is a matter of no great consequence, except as it may serve to show him with what subjects his unconscious mind is occupied—a healthful revelation of his basically animal nature. With the revisions of Jung we have in sharper outlines, cleared of the labyrinthine detail of dream interpretation and the monotonous insistence on sexual matters, a revolutionizing science of man's psychical life: a science which explains the obscure causes and effects of his acceptance or refusal of the difficult realities of life.

We come now to Jung's very remarkable book, "Psychology of the Unconscious." At first glance it does not seem at all to fit in with the description of his attitude as stated above. It is a long analy-

sis of a book in which an American girl records certain fantasies; but this is merely the starting point: the explanation proceeds to involve all the myth, legend, and folk-lore of five continents, with liberal excerpts from Byron, Shakespeare and Goethe; it becomes a history of various important events in the life of mankind, from the discovery of fire to the rise of Christianity, with a whole volume of scholarship tucked away in notes at the back. And, above everything, it is an account of the "mother-complex" in all its forms, transformations and ramifications. It is, in short, not exactly what one would expect.

The explanation appears to be this. Jung found this new science deeply involved in detailed study of dreams, and confused by an erroneous estimate of the sexual character of the unconscious activities of the mind. From his point of view it was a pity to waste so much energy in interpreting dreams, since all dreams were, in the end, one dream—the dream of escape from the realities and difficulties and dangers of life. It was a pity to put so much

---

[3] It will be noticed that Jung's revision puts on the individual the responsibility for failure to adjust his psychic energies to reality: but this failure may still be, not so much a failure to *adapt his desires* to reality, as a failure to *remould reality* nearer to the heart's desire! Even if civilization is at fault, man must face it, and if he cannot endure it, must re-shape it.

complex man than his colleagues realized. When, as president of the American Association of Painters and Sculptors, he became responsible for the Armory Show, he revealed an unexpected strength and purposefulness. Thus, while his influence as a painter was negligible, his triumphant management of this greatest event in the history of American art gained him an assured place in our cultural history. He further astonished his colleagues when, upon his death, it was discovered that he had secretly maintained two separate households for many years. The determination and persistent attention to detail which both these feats entailed were hardly suggested by his light, agreeable paintings.]

emphasis on sex, since the sexuality of the unconscious is an infantile sexuality whose desire is to return to the rest and comfort of the mother's breast, or the more perfect peace of the mother's womb.

Now it was impossible for Jung to analyze all the dream-fantasies in the world and show that they all meant the same thing. But he could analyze all the myth-fantasies in the world and show it, and he pretty nearly did. If his exposition fails of persuasiveness in detail, it is extremely impressive in its total effect. And his treatment of the sexuality of the unconscious very effectively reduces it to the motif of this universal myth-fantasy —the desire to escape from reality. By an exhaustive analysis of fantasy he has shown us once for all its superficial character; and he has shown the superficial character of unconscious sexuality by the same gigantic process: and he has put in place of these the thing which actually underlies both—the refusal of the individual to meet the terms of life.

Life is in its preliminary aspect an acceptance of the necessity of adapting oneself to changing realities. The first such necessity comes to the infant when it is compelled to take its food in some other way than from the mother's breast; and all subsequent dealings with changing realities have something of the painful and childish quality of "weaning" in them. They are succeeded by the necessity not merely to accept new realities but to impose one's own will upon them. That is even more painful, and it is from that necessity that the too-sensitive soul recoils into a dream which is an imaginative restoration of the conditions of infantile irresponsibility and peace. Thus all ascending life, all struggle, adventure, effort, is an "escape from the mother"; and all relapsing life, all cowardice, hypocrisy, evasion, surrender, and substitution of the easy dream for the difficult reality, whether it take the form of a belief in paradise to come, or a mere putting off till an imaginary tomorrow of the thing that should be done today, or some more dangerous neurotic compensation, is a "return to the

mother." The facts are not quite so simple as this: for rest, the return, the retiring into oneself for the obscure nourishment of dreams, is a preliminary to all great effort. But in that return lies the danger. If one's Life Force comes out again to the real world it is with renewed power; but it may become beguiled by the dream and not come out. *The dream thus possesses the double quality of savior and destroyer,* and the greatest problem of any man's life is to determine, if such a thing is possible, which it shall be. Such is the contribution of Jung.

And thus the way is left clear for the next great step of psychic science: to investigate more fully the quality of that dangerous moment when the dream either destroys or saves. Here, as in other of Jung's writings, there are hints of tremendous suggestiveness, and the book is well worth reading by the seeker after knowledge for those hints alone. It is far from being a popular account of either the achievements or the possibilities of psychoanalysis; but it is a profound and valuable work, and the best that has yet appeared on the subject. It is indispensable to the student who wishes to keep in touch with science as it is being made—who wishes to stand in the forge and see the sparks fly as the sword of a new and splendid and terrible knowledge is being hammered out.

—July 1916

RANDOLPH BOURNE
The Vampire

[*Bourne was near the end of his short, brilliant life when this review appeared in* The Masses. *Most of his work had been done for journals like* The Seven Arts, *but his militant opposition to American entry into the war had made him almost unpublishable, and he was being sustained at the end by small commissions which his remaining friends were able to find for him.*]

Regiment of Women, by Clemence Dane. New York: The Macmillan Company. $1.50.

Feminism has its cruel and dark products, and there is nothing darker than the type of woman which is portrayed with a great deal of power in this first novel by Clemence Dane. The writer has struck straight in at one of the sorest places of the modern feminist world, and good feminists will have to do much explaining to counteract the rather deadly effect of this very revealing study. She has sensed a situation which extreme feminist doctrines tend directly to cultivate, and she has created a type of woman which must inevitably become rather common in the manless world which women are trying to make for themselves. The detached point of view of the author, and the coolness with which she makes man triumphant, causes one to wonder a little that the book could have been written by a woman. Yet the way she delivers

the situation into the man's hand is proof enough that it could only have been written by a woman. No man would make his hero fatuous in the desirable role of deliverer.

The story is set in the unwholesome atmosphere of an English school for girls, with its faded, neurotic teachers and the tense, hectic life of the adolescent girls. The drama has to do with the mutual loves of Clare, an older teacher who is not faded; of Alwynne, a fresh and adorable young teacher; and Louise, a sensitive school-girl of thirteen. Clare is hard, brilliant, mature, one of those women in whom affection takes almost exclusively the form of a lust for power. She masters both girls, plays them off against each other, flatters and scorns them at her pleasure. The sensitive child breaks under the strain, and, in a frenzy of innocent despair at Clare's calculated harshness, kills herself. Clare, with her instinctive talent for self-righteousness, manages to convey all the remorse and guilt to Alwynne's naive young soul. Alwynne, wan and harried, spends her vacation with friendly relatives in the country, but is pursued by nightmares of Louise. Roger, a kind young cousin, takes her in hand, and the battle is on between him, backed by Alwynne's gentle old aunt, and the masterful Clare. He wins in a precipitous marriage with Alwynne, and Clare is left forlorn by her fireside.

It is an exciting, and not greatly overwrought story. The murky psychology is traced with uncanny insight. The unhealthy but boundless adoration that Clare is able to excite in these girls is not exaggerated. A woman like Clare is able to play on their wistfulness, their vagueness, their good-hearted trustfulness, as upon an instrument. She is fastidious, beautiful, sure, brilliant, experienced. She is kind to them, and they feel in her all the qualities they lack. She becomes all this for them, robs them of their self-confidence, draws to her all their emotion, so that their happiness hangs on her favor. And she soon learns every nook and cranny of their naive young souls. She knows when to disdain and when to be sweet, when to threaten and when to cajole. She feeds on their adoration, and strips them of all emotional perspective. There can be no emotional slavery so devastating as the love which such a vampire-woman exacts from younger girls. They wallow in their own bondage. They can never love anyone as they love their friend. Only this is noble, divine love. Man's loves are worthless. "She's like a cathedral, Roger, a sort of mystery. She's the sort of wonderful person you just worship." "You see, she thinks—we both think, that if you've got a—a really real woman friend, it's just as good as falling in love and getting married and all that—and far less commonplace. Besides the trouble—smok-

ing you know—and children. Clare hates children. Me? I love them. That's the worst of it. When I grow old, I'd mean to adopt some—only Clare wouldn't let me, I'm sure. Of course, as long as Clare wanted me, I shouldn't mind. To live with Clare all my life—oh, you know how I'd love it."

The dramatic struggle of Roger to break this unholy infatuation and turn Alwynne's love towards himself is very skillfully worked out. This kind of bondage, however, is so tenacious and is so incredible to most men that he could hardly have succeeded without the help of wise old Elsbeth, who understands the terrific jealousy and will to power which the vampire-woman has. "You don't know Clare," she tells him. "If once she knows, she'll never let the child go."

"But if Alwynne were engaged to me?"

"She'll never allow it. She'll play on Alwynne's affection for her."——

"My dearest cousin! The age of sorcery is over. You talk as if Alwynne were under a spell."

"Practically she is. Of course Clare would put it on the highest grounds—unsuitability—a waste of talents. She pretends to despise domesticity. Alwynne would be hypnotized into repeating her arguments as her own opinion."

"Hypnotism?"

"Oh, not literally. But she really does influence some women, and young girls especially, in the most uncanny way. I've watched it so often."

"She's not married?"

"She hardly ever speaks to a man. I've seen her at gaieties when she was younger. She was always rather stranded. Men left her alone. Something in her seemed to repel them. I think she fully realized it. And she's a proud woman. There's tragedy in it.——Clare, with that impish nature of hers, may hurt Alwynne."

"I should think she has already, often enough."

"Yes, but Alwynne has never realized that it was deliberate. She is always so sure that it was her own fault somehow. If once she found that Clare was hurting her for—for the fun of it, you know—for the pleasure of watching her suffer—as I'm sure she does—it might end everything. Alwynne hates cruelty. A little more, and she will be disillusioned."

But Roger does not like the role of feminine intrigue which he is to play if he will win. Probably Alwynne would never have been saved if Clare, as such women usually do, had not overreached her power and destroyed herself. Alwynne is incredibly loyal up to the last. To Roger she flares out:

"Do you think I'm going to desert Clare for you, even if, even if—" She stopped suddenly.

He beamed.

"You do. Don't you, darling?" he said.

"I don't. I don't. I don't want to. I mustn't. I don't know why I'm even talking to you like this. It's ridiculous. Of course, there can never be anyone but Clare— What would Clare think of me—when I've let her be sure she can have me always—when I've promised her—"

"At nineteen! Miss Hartill's generous to allow you to sacrifice yourself—"

"It's no sacrifice! Can't you understand that I care for her—awfully. Why—I owe her everything. I was a silly, ignorant school-girl, and she took me, and taught me—pictures, books, everything. She made me understand. You don't know how good she's been to me. I owe her—all my mind—"

"And your peace?" he asked significantly.

"You know I'm grateful. But she's such a dreadfully lonely person. She's queer. She can't help it. She doesn't make friends, though everyone adores her. How could I go when she wants me— How could I care for her so, if she were what you and Elsbeth think?"

Roger's strategy of acquiescence startles her, but it is only her last diabolical interview with Clare that really snaps the bond. Alwynne brings to Clare a birthday gift which she has lovingly worked with her own hands. Clare knows just where to insert the rapier. She has become by this time an anatomist of the soul. She has jeered in the past at Alwynne's impatience and clumsy fingers. Now her satanic power takes this form.

"But you've shown it to me and I've told you that you've learned to work well, so that it has fulfilled its purpose, hasn't it? And now you'd better take it back with you," leading up to a final "Perhaps then, I dislike the hint that you consider my wardrobe inadequate."

The spell is broken. Clare's wanton cruelty has destroyed her own self. Alwynne flies to Roger. The sorcery of that evil love is transformed into healthiness.

The extreme feminist must wince a little when she reads this powerful story. Clare's philosophy of inverted sex-antagonism is a little too much like the doctrines which certain elements of an impressionable younger generation seem to be having inculcated in them as the gospel of true feminism. The Clares in the feminist movement do their cause a very bad turn. Any taint of the vampire in the modern women runs the risk of poisoning the movement. Feminism mustn't stand apologist for the "monstrous empire of a cruel woman."

—June 1917

FLOYD DELL
And So They Were Married

[*As a conspicuous feminist and the Village's leading authority on marriage, Dell was interested in this popular divorce play not so much for its dramatic value, which was negligible, but for the opportunity it afforded him to discuss his favorite subject. His most complete statement on the problem of love and marriage, themes which engrossed much of his attention, was* Love in the Machine Age.]

AN INTRUSION BY F. D.

By an unhappy twist of fortune, I am now engaged in telling you about Jesse Lynch Williams' play,* while over at another typewriter my friend Charley Wood is pounding out his impressions of "The Yellow Jacket." It should have been the other way about. Charley Wood likes ideas, and loves to discuss marriage. In "And So They Were Married" he would have found almost all the ideas ever promulgated on the subject, and he would have added several perfectly new ones himself, and we would all have been happy. Instead of which he is telling you how "The Yellow Jacket" bored him. Actually, the profusion, color, surprise, charm, humor, pathos and sheer magical loveliness of "The Yellow Jacket" bored him. Of course, there are no ideas in that play; there is only beauty of the first order. But when I reproach him on his callousness, he looks up and with a forefinger poised severely over one of the keys, replies irrelevantly that he never pretended to be a dramatic critic. As if that had anything to do with it? The trouble is not that he isn't a dramatic critic (which he is), but that he isn't a child. He is grown up—excessively. At that, I think he really enjoyed "The Yellow Jacket" as much as I did; only he is ashamed to admit the fact. Five years ago, when "The Yellow Jacket" was first put on, I sat behind a stockbroker who laughed and almost cried by turns at the play, and then complained between the acts that he couldn't understand it. He understood it as well as I did— but he didn't know that what he understood was all there was to understand. Charley Wood is like that, only different. He wanted some Chinese sociology. Instead he got butterflies. He doesn't like to chase butterflies. Most everybody else does.

---

*Performed for the first time at the Belasco Theater, Jan. 12, by the pupils of the American Academy of Dramatic Arts and the Empire Theater Dramatic School.

But I do wish that when he finds himself unable to sympathize with our childlike amusements he wouldn't pretend that he is too "low-brow" to do so. . . . I have just looked over his shoulder, and I feel compelled to state that Mr. Wood, as a matter of fact, never reads the *Saturday Evening Post* at all. He carries about with him Professor Santayana's "Life of Reason," in two large volumes.

Well, if I must, in spite of my incapacity for dealing with the subject, write about this marriage drama, I will begin by saying that it is better than Shaw's "Getting Married"—in spite of its labored propaganda, in spite of its selection of "types" for characters, in spite of everything. It is better than Shaw because it deals sympathetically with a situation the crux of which is that a man and a woman want each other—a desire with which Mr. Shaw prefers not to deal. These lovers happen, quite delightfully, to be idealists, and, quite naturally, they don't like to spoil their relationship by getting married. The man is, perhaps, not quite in earnest; he appreciates the comfort which accrues from behaving like everybody else, he believes himself strong enough to overcome the perils of matrimony, and he feels that almost inevitable masculine condescension toward the female which makes it seem his duty to "protect" her. But the girl is so much in earnest that a pack of scandalized relatives ramp up and down the stage for several acts trying to circumvent her horrific plans. Knowing as one does from the title that the marriage is going to happen, one is occupied for some forty minutes wondering how it *can* happen without a most abject crawl on the part of the playwright. The arguments against marriage have been so complete, the girl's determination is so final, that there seems no way out. But the author finds one which does not lose him our respect. I won't tell what it is; for sometime, it is to be hoped, the play will be seen on the regular stage, and it would be a pity to reveal the surprise. But if perchance you have a daughter whose rash idealism you wish to circumvent, the book is published by Scribner's.

But, after all, I think too much fuss was made over that ceremony. What's a little ceremony or two, between lovers? They would have been married just as surely if they had dispensed with it. For they were good-hearted, honest people who expected and intended the relationship to last forever. They were going to share the same house and have the same interests and the same friends and the same thoughts. Two different individuals, blown together from the ends of the world by the winds of a passion older than humanity itself, they expected to make of their momentary and illusory unity a social fact, to build their relationship solidly and securely into the world of work and friendship—and they expected the magic which made them yearn to each other across the gulfs of division, to endure within that elaborate structure. I hope it did. But I wish Mr. Williams would write another play, timed several years later. That would be a play about marriage. This one isn't.

—March 1917

CHARLES W. WOOD
The Prevention and Cure of Childhood

Children under seventeen, I understand, were not allowed to see " 'Ception Shoals" at the Princess Theater.

Because " 'Ception Shoals" deals particularly with the problems that concern children under seventeen.

" 'Ception Shoals" is a serious play which aims to expose the crime of keeping young girls ignorant. Advanced New York therefore welcomed the play, lauded it, patronized it—and kept its young girls away.

The place for young girls, says New York, is at the leg-shows; at the burlesques; at the Midnight Frolics or the Cocoanut Grove; at the melodramas where the fellow with the bushy, black eyebrows finally gets all mussed up by the handsome arrow-collar boy; or at the white-slave films, where vice and virtue are as easy to distinguish as day and night, and not at all complicated as they are in actual experience. There are enough places to send our daughters, says brilliant, clever, intellectual New York, without letting them into places where they might learn something.

"Father, what is conception?" asks Nazimova, playing the part of a girl who has never been allowed to see another living person. "Tell me, how do women conceive?" That's all. That's the sole reason why young women weren't allowed to see this drama.

At all hazards, our young women must be protected. Pack them off to the farces and follies, where life is symbolized by a row of feet pointed at the ceiling and mating isn't mentioned except in jest. When they are safely out of the way, we old men can face intrepidly the problems of adolescent womanhood. For we are an advanced lot, we New Yorkers. If we decided to have a course in dieting, we would confine it to people who can't eat.

By the way, " 'Ception Shoals" is worth seeing, especially if you are young and threatened with adolescence. There are several things I didn't like about it: the last act was cluttered up, for instance, with a lot of perfectly superfluous tragedy—but the lambasting given to many of the sacred rules of society is fully worth the price of admission. I think I'd go anyway, if I were you, children; and if they didn't let me in, I'd keep New York busy answering why.

Dearly beloved: We are now going to talk about ourself. We never read anything and we can prove it. We never heard of Prof. Santayana; and when Floyd Dell alleged last month that said professor was our sole literary indulgence, we supposed that he was talking about a versatile soap-boxer we have occasionally heard in New York, who guarantees to answer any question on any subject in any language: his name is something like that.

So much for our superior intellect. Our specialty is chasing butterflies. But when we do chase butterflies, we chase them like a child, not at all like the artists and literati of our acquaintance. Our idea of chasing a butterfly is to chase a butterfly. Theirs is to throw a brick or a ham-sandwich across the room and yell: "There's a butterfly—chase it." When they spring that on us, we chase ourself.

For instance, one of our artistic friends once dragged us into Bruno's garret to see an exhibition of Clara Tice's "nudes." "Marvellous color and motion," he told us. No doubt. But they didn't look like nudes to us. They looked like neckties. For this, they say we are lacking in imagination.

We have imagination, but imagery to us must be built out of things we see. Children can't conceive of God, but they can imagine a heavenly Father. And their heavenly Father has to have whiskers and pants and all the other things that childhood inevitably associates with fatherhood. So does ours. And when a sad atheist once pointed out to us that God couldn't have shown Moses his back parts (Exodus xxxiii : 23), simply because an infinite being can't have any rear, we did just what all real children will do in the face of such intellectual sophistry: we let infinity go to the devil and hung on to our heavenly Father, coat-tails and all.

Confirmed adults cannot do this: and neither can those in their second childhood—imagists, futurists, cubists, and the whole legion of lost souls

floundering around in the hades they call "Modern Art." They have forgotten the combination. When their imaginations get to soaring like kites, they let go the string. Children would know better. They know that in order to make the darn thing keep going up they've got to keep pulling it down. They never had to have Prof. Santayana explain the principle either; and if these modernists were as simple as they think they are, they'd get wise.

I've been altogether too humble before these highbrows. When they raved over "The Yellow Jacket," and I couldn't, I apologized. I apologize no longer. My advice to the whole bunch is to go and see Maude Adams at the Empire Theater and learn again how glorious the world of imagery can be.

J. M. Barrie's kite soars higher than most because Barrie never lets go the string. In "A Kiss

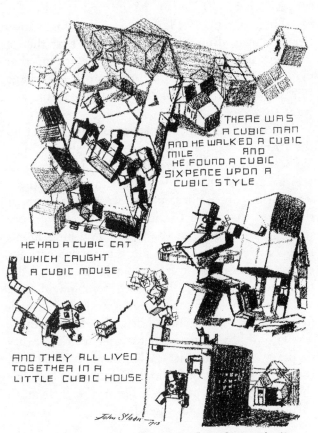

Drawn by John Sloan, April 1913

A Slight Attack of Third Dimentia Brought on by Excessive Study of the Much Talked of Cubist Pictures in the International Exhibition at New York

[*Sloan's art was representational but, as this good-natured comment on cubism indicates, he was amused rather than shocked by the non-representational art displayed in the famous Armory Show.*]

for Cinderella," he has pulled down a little harder, and gone up a little further, than in "Peter Pan." That's saying a lot: but "Peter Pan" depended rather too much upon the ability of the electrician to produce satisfactory fire-flies, while "A Kiss for Cinderella" depends almost altogether on the well-known childhood of the human race and upon Maude Adams.

Concededly, Maude Adams is not an actress. But she is Maude Adams; and there isn't an actress on earth who can be that. She is more than an actress: she's an inspiration, a religion, a ministering angel to a world that still longs to dream but has almost forgotten how. In "A Kiss for Cinderella" she and Barrie give a wonderful demonstration. She isn't a revolutionist, so far as I know, but she makes one revolutionist feel that the revolution is worth fighting for. Some revolutionists may be so discouraged that they would rather see Andrieff's "Life of Man," played by the Washington Square Players in their subscription performance. But that made me feel that the jig was up; and if I ever get into the spirit of that play, I'll throw the human race into the garbage can. Maude Adams made me dream again and want to go on fighting.

And in that dream, let me repeat, nobody let go the string. Cinderella was a London slavey. The big scene was in a corner of Cinderella's head. It was a ball—slipper and prince and all; but there was nothing in the dream that wasn't made up of the things the actual Cinderella knew. The prince was the policeman on the beat. The king in his gorgeous robes had a still more gorgeous cockney dialect. The rivals were animated pictures from the studio where she had been scrubbing floors, and the bishop who married her to the policeman-prince was a solemn stuffed penguin. Beauty there was in limitless measure; but it was not the beauty made by tired imagists who have emancipated themselves from the feelings of humanity. It was the beauty that grew like a lily in the little dark corner of Miss Thing's head.

G. K. Chesterton is always logical. He doesn't know it but he is. He is the first person who ever proved to me conclusively, by logical syllogism, that the whale swallowed Jonah, that Joshua told the sun where to get off and that Jesus was born of the Virgin Mary. It was in his book "Orthodoxy," which a good Methodist let me take after the usual line of argument had seemed to fail.

Chesterton, you will remember, proves all these things by first proving that Santa Claus does come down the chimney, that the cow did jump over the moon and that the Spanish Inquisition was a humanitarian reform movement.

It is quite possible to prove anything if you only begin by proving everything: and the stunt, when done by Chesterton, is decidedly entertaining. Some critics have intimated that "Magic" is dull; but they were of the morose and hopeless type who couldn't see any fun in a Billy Sunday revival.

"Magic" is a play with a purpose. In order to appreciate it thoroughly, you must understand that. Even Billy Sunday wouldn't be funny if he meant to be. An unbeliever challenging God is a sorry spectacle; but Billy bossing the Almighty is a scream. Chesterton defending Fairyland is every bit as good: and if "Magic" can only break through the lines and reach the New York public who are not in the habit of attending theaters, it should become the season's success.

As in all of Chesterton's works, it sets out to prove the unprovable; to prove, in fact, that nothing is really provable except that which cannot be proved. And if New York goes to see the play, I haven't the slightest doubt that New York will be convinced.

The particular Q. E. D. in this instance is the existence of fairies, elves and little devils. I had my doubts, myself, about these things until I saw the play. But there was a conjurer in it who did all the ordinary conjuring tricks and one more. It was admitted that pulling rabbits from a hat, or a bowl of gold-fish from a silk handkerchief, is a mere trick. But when a red light back stage was made to turn blue, it was apparent to all that something more than mere trickery was involved. The one skeptic in the cast, too stubborn to admit the truth, went insane. Of course. What else was there for him to do? The audience is well satisfied in the end, however, when it is revealed that the transformation was made by a battalion of devils who are finally sent back to hell.

Far be it from me to suggest that the audience had had experience with electric light companies. I don't believe they thought of any such thing. I believe it was all accepted in the Chestertonian meaning, that the preachers are right when they speak of the renaissance of faith now spreading throughout the world, that New York is ripe for the revival and that Billy Sunday will score his greatest triumph here.

Billy's big show, by the way, will be reviewed faithfully in this department, if we have to pay our own way in.

Even if you don't like "Magic"—and I can't understand why you should not—you will still find it worth while to attend the show. Galsworthy's "A Little Man" is put on as a curtain raiser.

It was written before the war. It shows a whimsically humorous meeting of a number of national types, and one little man, without nationality, who proves himself to be altogether man. It is sentimental, yes, but you can't help applauding; for Man looms up so infinitely superior to nationality that everybody sees the point.

And then—here's a joke. The curtain dropped and the orchestra began "The Star Spangled Banner." Everybody stood up except one timid reviewer and his wife. He almost stood too: he hates to make a scene except on paper.

"We might as well stand," he whispered, "there isn't any way to make an effective protest."

"Protest!" she answered. "I'm not protesting. If any one wants to stand up, I have no objections."

Annette Kellermann is now at the Hippodrome in place of Anna Pavlowa. When I first heard the news, I wanted to see the Big Show again: it seemed to me the one thing needed to make it just about the biggest possible. Not Annette on the screen, but Annette herself, diving and swimming and disporting like a water-nymph in a great crystal tank, illumined wondrously so that every motion of her beautiful free body could be watched by the audience.

I went to the show and they wouldn't let me look: at least, not at all as I wanted to look at it. It was all there, just as described, and I had to admit that it was magnificent. But out in front of the crystal tank, the producers had put on another show—bears and frogs, and "Toto" as a "funnyfish," and a fearfully expensive layout of alligators and clowns, all efficiently calculated to disturb and distract. It was all well done, too: that was the worst of it. It seemed to me like producing a perfectly fine bass-drum solo simultaneously with a Strauss waltz—just to let the listeners take their choice. —April 1917

ANNA STRUNSKY WALLING
Memoirs of Jack London

[Although William English Walling was one of the most fervent pro-war socialists and broke with The Masses *over America's entry into the war, his wife did not share his convictions, and this charming personal recollection was therefore a tacit gesture of support for the hard-pressed magazine.]*

"Take me this way: a stray guest, a bird of passage, splashing with salt-rimed wings through a brief moment of your life—a rude and blundering bird, used to large airs and great spaces, unaccustomed to the amenities of confined existence."

So he wrote in a letter to me dated Oakland, December 21, 1899, in the twenty-fourth year of his life. A bird of passage, splashing with salt-rimed wings not only through my life but through life itself, and not for a brief moment but for eternity. For who shall say when that of wonder and beauty which was Jack London will pass from the earth? Who that ever knew him can forget him, and how will life ever forget one who was so indissolubly a part of her? He was youth, adventure, romance. He was a poet and a social revolutionist. He had a genius for friendship. He loved greatly and was greatly beloved. But how fix in words that quality of personality that made him different from everyone else in the world? How convey an idea of his magnetism and of the poetic quality of his nature? He is the outgrowth of the struggle and the suffering of the Old Order, and he is the strength and the virtue of all its terrible and criminal vices. He came out of the Abyss in which millions of his generation and the generation preceding him throughout time have been hopelessly lost. He rose out of the Abyss, and he escaped from the Abyss to become as large as the race and to be identified with the forces that shape the future of mankind.

His standard of life was high. He for one would have the happiness of power, of genius, of love, and the vast comforts and ease of wealth. Napoleon and Nietzsche had a part in him, but his Nietszchean philosophy became transmuted into Socialism—the movement of his time—and it was by the force of his Napoleonic temperament that he conceived the idea of an incredible success, and had the will to achieve it. Sensitive and emotional as his nature was, he forbade himself any deviation from the course that would lead him to his goal. He systematized his life. Such colossal energy, and yet he could not trust himself! He lived by rule. Law, Order and Restraint was the creed of this vital, passionate youth. His stint was a thousand words a day revised and typed. He allowed himself only four and one-half hours of sleep and began his work regularly at dawn for years. The nights were devoted to extensive reading of science, history and sociology. He called it getting his scientific basis. One day a week he devoted to the work of a struggling friend. For recreation he boxed and fenced and swam—he was a great swimmer—and he sailed—he was a sailor before the mast—and he spent much time flying kites, of which he had a large collection. Like Zola's, his first efforts were in poetry. This no doubt was the secret of the Miltonic simplicity of his prose which has made him the accepted model for pure English and for style in the universities of this country and at the Sorbonne. He had always wanted to write poetry, but poets proverbially starved—unles they or theirs had independent incomes—so poetry was postponed until that time when his fame and fortune were to have been made. Fame and fortune were made and enjoyed for over a decade, but yet the writing of poetry was postponed, and death came before he had remembered his promise to himself. Death came before he had remembered many other things. He was so hard at work—so pitifully, tragically hard at work, and it was a fixed habit by now. He forgot what he wrote in a letter to me when we were little more than boy and girl:

January 18, 1892.
"As for my not having read Stevenson's letters—my dear child! When the day comes that I have achieved a fairly fit scientific foundation and a bank account of a thousand dollars, then come to be with me when I lie on my back all day long and read, and read, and read, and read.

"The temptation of the books—if you could know! And I hammer away at Spencer and Haeckel and try to forget the joys of the things unread."

The time came when he had that bank account of $1,000 and an assured income of over $60,000 a year in addition, but he did not return to the simple and beautiful existence of the poet and the student of which he had dreamt. He paid the ultimate price for what he received. His success was the tragedy of his life. He mortgaged his brain in order to meet the market demands, and fatigue and over-stimulation led him to John Barleycorn and to the consequent torture of what he called the White Logic. He had written forty-four books. Sometimes a vertigo seized him. What had a strong, normal man to do with labor that involved

so puny a tool as the pen? He longed for a man's work. He conceived the idea of cultivating his Valley of the Moon. He would put the money he earned by his pen into a vast agricultural experiment; he would make arid land fertile. He would grow eucalyptus trees and raise horses. That was creative work in a sense that the stories he was writing so prolifically (four books a year) were not creative; he had not time to remember that the same pen that wrote these pot-boilers had written short stories of immortal beauty like "The Odyssey of the North" and "The White Silence," and books of such greatness as "Martin Eden" and "The Call of the Wild," and essays of unparalleled brilliance like those in "The Kempton-Wace Letters," the book we wrote together.

His was not a vulgar quest for riches. In his book "The Game" he explains the psychology of the prize fighter to whom the ring is symbolic of the play and the purpose of life itself. To become inordinately rich through the efforts of his pen was his way of "playing the game." It appealed to his sense of humor and his sense of the dramatic to house members of the I. W. W., Comrades of the Road, or Mexican Revolutionists in a palace. The best was none too good for them or for any man. Not only had the Abyss not been able to swallow him up; the Abyss had risen with him.

Here is a letter written from Oakland, Cal., January 21, 1900:

Do you know, I have the fatal faculty of making friends, and lack the blessed trait of being able to quarrel with them. And they are constantly turning up. My home is the Mecca of every returned Klondiker, sailor or soldier of fortune I ever met. Some day I shall build an establishment, invite them all, and turn them loose upon each other. Such a mingling of castes and creeds and characters could not be duplicated. The destruction would be great.

"However, I am so overjoyed at being free that I cannot be anything but foolish. I shall, with pitfall and with gin, beset the road my visitors do wander in; and among other things, erect a maxim rapid-fire gun just within my front door. The sanctity of my fireside shall be inviolate. Or, should my heart fail me, I'll run away to the other side of the world."

This is exactly what he did in Glen Ellen, in beautiful Sonoma Valley, California. He built a mansion, surrounded by fifteen hundred acres, where he kept open house, and when his heart failed him he did run away to the other side of the world. He went to the South Sea Islands and to Hawaii. He made the memorable and extraordinary cruise of the Snark, purporting to be away from the world for seven years.

Only a youth as intense as his could feel as

deeply as he did the flight of time, and could so eagerly hoard the hours. Life was very short. One should have no time to dally. It was his working creed. It had been given to him to see so much of life. Child of the people that he was, he had never had a childhood. He had early seen struggle and been forced to struggle. He thought himself "harsh, stern, uncompromising." Of course he was not. It is only that he had few illusions, and that the sensitive nature of childhood and youth had suffered at what he had beheld in the Abyss and beyond. This suffering and this reaction against what is called organized society, but is in reality a chaotic jungle, became the basis of his world philosophy.

The following is from a letter written December 21, 1899:

"Life is very short. The melancholy of materialism can never be better expressed than by Fitzgerald's 'O Make Haste!' One should have no time to dally. And further, should you know me, understand this: I, too, was a dreamer, on a farm, nay, a California ranch. But early, at only nine, the hard hand of the world was laid upon me. It has never relaxed. It has left me sentiment, but destroyed sentimentalism. It has made me practical, so that I am known as harsh, stern, uncompromising. It has taught me that reason is mightier than imagination; that the scientific man is superior to the emotional man. It has also given me a truer and a deeper romance of things, an idealism which is an inner sanctuary and which must be resolutely throttled in dealings with my kind, but which yet remains within the holy of holies, like an oracle, to be cherished always but to be made manifest or to be consulted not on every occasion I go to market. To do this latter would bring upon me the ridicule of my fellows and make me a failure. To sum up, simply the eternal fitness of things."

Sincerity was the greatest trait of his character. He never made pretensions and he built neither his work nor his life on sophisms and evasions. If literature is marketable and had a price and he put the products of his brain for sale, then he could not stoop to pretend that he was following art for art's sake and was not writing for money. But it would not be seemly and according to "the eternal fitness of things" to offer wares for which society would not pay him lavishly. If you make yourself marketable at all, you must also be indispensable. With the cold-bloodedness of the "economic man" which he claimed to be, he set to work to achieve this. In those days Marie Corelli was perhaps the most financially successful novelist. He threatened to study her art in order to discover just those qualities which made her success inevitable and to make them a part of himself. In all this he was frank, and by his avowal of his program and his

object he invited from his friends haranguing and attack. Many set themselves up to be better than he, who were in reality only envious of his strength of purpose.

The following letter bears this out:

962 East 16th St.,
Oakland, California,
February 3, 1900.

DEAR ANNA:—

"Saturday night, and I feel good. Saturday night, and a good week's work done—hack work, of course. Why shouldn't I? Like any other honest artisan by the sweat of my brow. I have a friend who scorns such work. He writes for posterity, for a small circle of admirers, oblivious to the world's oblivion, doesn't want money, scoffs at the idea of it, calls it filthy, damns all who write for it, etc., etc.,—that is, he does all this, if one were to take his words for criteria. But I received a letter from him recently. *Munsey's* had offered to buy a certain story of him, if he would change the ending. He had built the tale carefully, every thought tending toward the final consummation, notably, the death by violence of the chief character. And they asked him to keep the tale and to permit that character, logically dead, to live. He scorns money. Yes; and he permitted that character to live. 'I fell,' is the only explanation he has vouchsafed for his conduct."

From overwork and from turning art into a toilsome trade, the natural reaction set in, and he, the most generous of natures, was often obsessed by a kind of cynicism. His soul was sick with all the adulation which his success brought him. Why had these people, now eager to flatter him, not seen what was in him before he was "discovered"? A story for which he had received five dollars from the *Overland Monthly* and which had not brought him a word of praise from anybody, suddenly became great when it was found between the stiff covers of a book. So he held lightly the praise and the kindness of people, and he suffered from a melancholy which made him question not only the worth of the world but of life itself. He had achieved so much, only to find it was not worth having. There was no intrinsic value in anything. He suffered from melancholia. He was obsessed by suicidal ideas. As with Tolstoy, there was a time when he kept a loaded revolver in his desk ready to use it against himself at any time.

January 5, 1902.

"I look back and remember, at one in the morning, the faces I saw go wan and wistful—do you remember? Or did you notice?—and I wonder what all the ferment is about.

"I dined yesterday on canvasback and terrapin, with champagne sparkling and all manner of wonderful drinks I had never before tasted warming my heart and brain, and I remembered the sordid orgies and carouses of my youth. We were ill-clad, ill-mannered beasts, and the drink was cheap and poor and nauseating. And then I dreamed dreams, and pulled myself up out of the slime to canvasback and terrapin and champagne, and learned that it was solely a difference of degree which art introduced into the fermenting."

It was in his twenty-sixth year that he began to sign all his letters "Yours for the Revolution" and thousands in this country and in the countries across the sea took up the phrase. He had served the revolutionary cause from his earliest youth. He had talked Socialism on street corners and had addressed the regular Sunday night meetings at the "Locals." He had let his name stand on the Socialist political ticket for school director and for mayor, and when he became famous he came East and lectured, choosing Socialist subjects. In a letter dated February 22, 1908, he says: "Back again after four months of lecturing. I rattled the dry bones some. Spoke at Yale, Harvard, Columbia, University of Chicago, and a lot of speeches for the Socialist Party." He was a Revolutionist. "The imposing edifice of society above my head holds no delight for me. It is the foundation of the edifice that interests me. There I am content to labor, crowbar in hand, shoulder to shoulder with intellectuals, idealists, and class-conscious workingmen, getting a solid pry now and again and setting the whole edifice rocking. Some day, when we get a few more hands and crowbars to work, we'll topple it over, along with all its rotten life and unburied dead, its monstrous selfishness and sodden materialism. Then we'll cleanse the cellar and build a new habitation for mankind, in which all the rooms will be bright and airy, and where the air that is breathed will be clean, noble and alive."

They have toppled it over in Russia, and how sad it is that Jack London should have passed into the silence, out of the sight of the red banners waving over a free people and out of the reach of the voices of millions singing the International!

He wrote "The People of the Abyss," a story of the London slums. It was on the occasion of his first visit to Europe. He did not even go to see his publishers. He dropped out of sight and lost himself in the abyss of human misery, and the result was the strongest indictment against modern society written in our time, a "Les Miserables" in sociological form. To do this he compelled himself to live as a slum dweller. He cut himself off from his money and walked the streets seeking employment, starving and homeless.

London, August 25, 1902.

"Saturday night I was out all night with the homeless ones, walking the streets in the bitter rain, and, drenched to the skin, wondering when dawn would come. Sunday I spent with the homeless ones, in the fierce struggle for something to eat. I returned to my rooms Sunday evening, after thirty-six hours continuous work and short one night's sleep. To-day I have composed, typed and revised 4,000 words and over. I have just finished. It is one in the morning. I am worn out and exhausted and my nerves are blunted with what I have seen and the suffering it has cost me."

And again: "I am made sick by this human hell-hole called London Town."

He had social wisdom. He understood the class struggle and he believed in the international organization of the people. He understood that international humanity in our present evolution had only one enemy, which was international capitalism, and that economic and social forces in society were clarifying the minds of the people and strengthening their hearts and investing them with weapons with which to give successful combat to their enemy. Society was a battlefield upon which were ranged in conflict the forces of the people against the oppressors and exploiters of the people. His place was in the ranks of the people. His success and his genius did not exempt him from bearing revolutionary arms. They were only proof of the basic truth of social democracy, of the force of environment, of the fiction of blood and aristocracy. He had faith and vision and the courage not to be overawed by the mighty of this world.

R. M. S. "Majestic,"
July 31, '02.

"I sailed yesterday from New York at noon. A week from to-day I shall be in London. I shall then have two days in which to make my arrangements and sink down out of sight in order to view the Coronation from the standpoint of the London beasts. That's all they are—beasts—if they are anything like the slum people of New York—beasts, shot through with stray flashes of divinity.

"I meet the men of the world in Pullman coaches, New York clubs, and Atlantic liner smoking rooms, and, truth to say, I am made more hopeful for the Cause by their total ignorance and non-understanding of the forces at work. They are blissfully ignorant of the coming upheaval, while they have grown bitterer and bitterer towards the workers. You see, the growing power of the workers is hurting them and making them bitter while it does not open their eyes."

He wrote an essay called "What Life Means to Me" which takes its place with Kropotkin's "Appeal to the Young" and Oscar Wilde's "The Soul of Man Under Socialism," and its closing sentence rings with his faith in the rise of the common man.

"The stairway of time is ever echoing with the wooden shoe going up, the polished boot descending."

I am attempting a difficult and marvelous thing when I attempt to write of the youth of one so young as Jack London! One has to speak of him in terms of feeling rather than thought and no one understands better than he how difficult that is. I quote from a letter dated—

962 East 10th St.,
Oakland, California,
December 27, 1899.

"Thinkers do not suffer from lack of expression; their thought is their expression. Feelers do. It is the hardest thing in the world to put feeling, and deep feeling, into words. From the standpoint of expression, it is easier to write a 'Das Capital' in four volumes than a simple lyric of as many stanzas."

He flaunted his physical bases. He was an idealist without any illusions. He was avid for truth, for justice, and he found little of it at hand. He was an individualist who was consecrated to the cause of mankind. As long as he lived he would strip the veils from truth and be a living protest against all the evils and injustices of society.

962 East 16th St.,
January 21, 1900.

"The highest and the best had been stamped out of me. You know my life, typified mayhap by the hastily drawn picture of the forecastle. I was troubled. Groping after shadows, mocking, disbelieving, giving my own heart the lie oftentimes, doubting that which every doubt made me believe. And for all, I was a-thirst. Stiff-necked, I flaunted my physical basis, hoping that the clear water might gush forth. But not then, for there I played the barbarian."

What was this "physical basis" which he flaunted in those days? He justified war. He said that as long as we accepted the aid of a policeman and the light of a street lamp from a society that legalized capital punishment, we had no right to attack capital punishment. He believed in the inferiority of certain races and talked of the Anglo-Saxon people as the salt of the earth. He inclined to believe in the biological inferiority of woman to man, for had he not watched women and men at the Piedmont Baths and had the women not shivered on the brink of the swimming pool, "not standing up straight under God!" He believed that right made might. He fled from civilization and systematically avoided it. He had a barbarian's attitude toward death, holding himself ready to go at any time, with total indifference to his fate. He held that love is only a trap set by na-

ture for the individual. One must not marry for love but for certain qualities discerned by the mind. This he argued in "The Kempton-Wace Letters" brilliantly and passionately; so passionately as to again make one suspect that he was not as certain of his position as he claimed to be. Later, Jack became the most mellow of thinkers, as passionately promulgating his new ideas as he had then assailed them. He now believed in romantic love, he had helped in the agitation for woman suffrage and was jubilant over its success in California. He was now an absolute internationalist and anti-militarist. He now laughed at himself when he recalled how in the Russian-Japanese War he had been on the Russian side although all Socialists wanted Russia beaten for the sake of the revolutionary movement. The Russians were white men and the Japanese were not. He had looked on a wounded Russian foot and had felt the thrill of "consciousness of kind." It was a white foot, a foot like his own. He made his loathing of capital punishment the theme of his most ambitious book, "The Star Rover." And his former belief in sensation for the sake of sensation, leading him to experiment with drugs and drink, he repudiated in his classic, "John Barleycorn." He had come far —he had come out on the other side of everything he had before adhered to, as all who knew him were convinced that he would.

I see him in pictures, steering his bicycle with one hand and with the other clasping a great bunch of yellow roses which he had just gathered out of his own garden, a cap moved back on his thick brown hair, the large blue eyes with their long lashes looking out star-like upon the world— an indescribably virile and beautiful boy, the kindness and wisdom of his expression somehow belying his youth.

I see him lying face down among the poppies and following with his eyes his kites soaring against the high blue of the California skies, past the tops of the giant sequoias and eucalyptus which he so dearly loved.

I see him becalmed, on "The Spray," the moon rising behind us, and hear him rehearse his generalizations made from his studies in the watches of the night before of Spencer and Darwin. His personality invested his every movement and every detail of his life with an alluring charm. One took his genius for granted, even in those early years when he was struggling with all his unequalled energies to impress himself upon the world.

I see him seated at his work when the night is

hardly over, and it seems to me that the dawn greets and embraces him, and that he is part of the elements as other less generic natures are not. I see him on a May morning leaning from the balustrade of a veranda sweet with honeysuckle, to watch two humming birds circling around each other in their love ecstasy. He was a captive of beauty—the beauty of bird and flower, of sea and sky and the icy vastness of the Arctic world. No one could echo more truthfully the "Behold, I have lived" of Richard Hovey, with which he

closed the essay which sums up his world philosophy, "Human Drift."

"Behold, I have lived!"

He lived not only in the wide spaces of the earth, under her tropic suns and in her white frozen silences, with her children of happiness and with her miserable ones, but he lived in the thought always of life and death, and in the timeless and boundaryless struggle of international socialism.

—July 1917

Drawn by Hugo Gellert

III
The Class Struggle

THE late Progressive Era was a time when the problems created by industrialization were both simpler and more pressing than they are today. For that very reason men were confident that solutions could be found to the vexing questions posed by the new order. Especially for radicals the battle lines were clearly drawn. On one side stood the embattled and virtuous proletarian, worn down by the merciless exactions of the profit system, but destined to seize power and bring about a new reign of justice and plenty—that is, if he was not misled by false prophets and labor fakers. On the other side loomed the giant figure of the capitalist oppressor who daily ground the faces of the poor and accumulated vast fortunes to be lavished on follies and amusements.

There was enough truth in this stereotyped appraisal of the state of the nation to generate the appropriate emotions in those who fought the industrial wars. There *was* a class struggle going on, and the army of wage earners needed all the direct, vivid symbolism and inflated imagery they could get. The day of "people's capitalism," "industrial relations," and "labor-management partnerships" had not yet dawned, although glimpses of it could be seen on the horizon, and scientific management was beginning to make itself felt. Art Young's top-hatted, pot-bellied plutocrats had their counterparts in real life and everyone knew who they were.

As radicals, *The Masses'* editors were obliged to think little of the political arena, because it was not elections which decided what kind of social order was to obtain in America. Although this section includes some prescient political reporting, *The Masses* knew that it was the National Association of Manufacturers and not the Republican party that determined the conditions of American life and labor. Yet the magazine failed in not following through and attempting to isolate and evaluate the dynamic elements within the ranks of organized capital. If national policy was really being made behind closed doors and not on the floor of Congress, then it behooved a fearless radical publication which proposed to get at the root of things to try to find out what was really going on. Of course there were obvious problems involved, since revolutionaries do not normally have easy access to the corridors of power. But capitalism was not all of a piece; there were crucial differences between the grasping, acquisitive mining companies and industries like the railroads which were becoming organized and acquiring a measure of sobriety and decorum. Some business leaders were simple Darwinists who would bring down the temple rather than treat with a union head, while others were looking forward to the day when the entire economy would be rationalized and the more disagreeable aspects of competition eliminated. These and other vital distinctions were not apparent to *The Masses'* editors, whose ideological blinders prevented them from usefully analyzing the ruling classes. But it was a blindness they shared with most radicals—which is not to excuse them, but only to say that if American radicalism had had another, finer perception of reality the Left would have developed very differently.

In dealing with that aspect of reality with which they were most concerned—the industrial wars—*The Masses'* editors require no apologies, for they brilliantly executed the task they were superbly equipped to do. When it came to reporting the great strikes of their day, they were without peer. If you send a poet to report a strike you are likely to get something rather special—hence, Max Eastman's "The Nice People of Trinidad," a masterpiece of sensitive interpretation. The newspapers and better periodicals published reams of material on these great strikes, but none uncovered the human realities that lay beneath the flow of events. For this you needed the imaginative sympathy which *The Masses* possessed in abundance, and most other journals had not at all.

These stories graphically illustrate the relatively simple issues over which industrial disputes were waged a half-century ago. Often so primitive a demand as union recognition was considered utopian; life and death battles were fought to win another five or ten cents an hour. The very innocence of these demands inspires a certain nostalgia today when negotiations involve issues of such complexity that even the bargainers hardly understand them, or when strikes are called over grievances so unintelligible and subconscious that they can be articulated only in terms of longer coffee breaks.

Another noteworthy feature of *The Masses'* era was the absence of poverty as an independent social problem. Today we see the poor as anomalies who have no important relations with other elements of the economy or with the rest of society. We speak of "pockets of poverty" against which war can be waged without affecting the great majority of Americans. *The Masses* entertained no such comfortable illusion. If you lived, as most of the group did, in Greenwich Village, the poor were all around you, and if you went to the zones of industrial combat you knew that there was an ocean of poverty surrounding the islands of middle-class plenty.

If their ideology handicapped the editors in dealing with the capitalist class, it enabled them to see that most social problems were parts of the greater problem of industrial capitalism. The general welfare required neither more charity nor more elevated sentiments; it demanded a fundamental reconstruction of the social order. One looks in vain through *The Masses* for isolated reflections on poverty; what can be found is a wry awareness of the condition of the poor. No other subject except war elicited such bitter humor or such irony from the staff. *The Masses* could be sentimental, as Alice Beach Winter's mawkish pictures of ragged waifs attest, but more characteristic was Art Young's cartoon in which the slum child observes that the stars are thick as bedbugs.

The Masses knew that the poor, who lived up tight against it, were abraded by the machinery of justice every day of their lives. Social workers and philanthropists judged the unruly poor and found them wanting in the necessary civilities, but *The Masses'* artists took them as they were and neither patronized nor derided them. The magazine was full of drunks, tawdry working girls, brutalized laborers, all living on the edge of subsistence and taking what crude pleasures their short, hard, violent lives afforded them. Here was no idealized proletariat bursting with heroic virtues, but a people struggling to make it from one day to the next—people who were sometimes comic, sometimes picaresque, and always worth noticing.

Of course there were other kinds of poverty in which *The Masses* was not much interested—particularly that of the hard-working, dues-paying, God-fearing men and women who sent their children to school and managed under appalling conditions to preserve their dignity and self-respect. These were the people who made up the settlement houses' constituency, and we know about them for that reason. But it was the drama of the streets which attracted the artist's eye. Thanks to *The Masses* we have not a photographic reproduction but a vivid impression of the rich, turbulent, and endlessly varied life of the urban poor in the early years of the century.

Drawn by K. R. Chamberlain

The Capitalist Order

[*The Masses' most telling commentaries on the essential nature of capitalism were pictorial.*]

Drawn by Art Young, December 1912

A Compulsory Religion

[*One of Art Young's gifts as a political cartoonist was his ability to take stock images and labels and give them a horrifying reality. In cartoons like this he breathed life and power into the tiredest clichés of socialist folkore.*]

"The trouble with the world is the insane worship of money."

How often we hear this thundered from the pulpit, emphasized in the press and in ordinary conversation. Yes, that's the trouble. But what drives people to this insanity?

In the first place, life is a fight for food, shelter, and clothing. No matter how high the price of food soars, we must struggle to pay the cost. No matter how high the cost of apparel goes, we must keep a degree of comfort and a decent appearance. No matter how far the landlord advances his rent, we must struggle to pay for shelter.

We must fight to get these things or die, and the average man does die fighting for them between 45 and 50 years of age.

You might truthfully write over the tombstones of four-fifths of the human race: "Died fighting for food, shelter, and clothing—in a world of plenty."

The fear that they will not get the necessities of life, and that their children will suffer for them, drives the restless spirits on.

It is this kind of a civilization that breeds an insane worship of money. That some men want more, after they have been assured a life of comfort, merely emphasizes the tragic baseness of this mad movement.

In a world that is running amuck, individuals cannot stop, even if they would, for back of it all is the original cause: FEAR.

A stampede of cattle carries all with it, even if one of the herd is ready to stop.

So, bend your back to the lash, cringe, crawl, prostitute yourselves mentally and physically, bribe, graft, do anything to get money. "Get it," says father to son; "Marry for money," says mother to daughter.

Under the circumstances, how can the average individual worship any God—but Mammon?

Drawn by Art Young, February 1913

"I Like a Little Competition"—J. P. Morgan

November 1913

One Day of Civilization
Shall We Allow Socialism to Destroy This Splendid Fabric?

Drawn by John Sloan, October 1913

NATIONAL ASSOCIATION OF MANUFACTURERS: "If that keeps on itching back there, I'll have to scratch."

[The timelessness of some problems is illustrated by this cartoon, which could have been drawn as easily yesterday as half a century ago.]

Complete History of Capitalism in Five Chapters

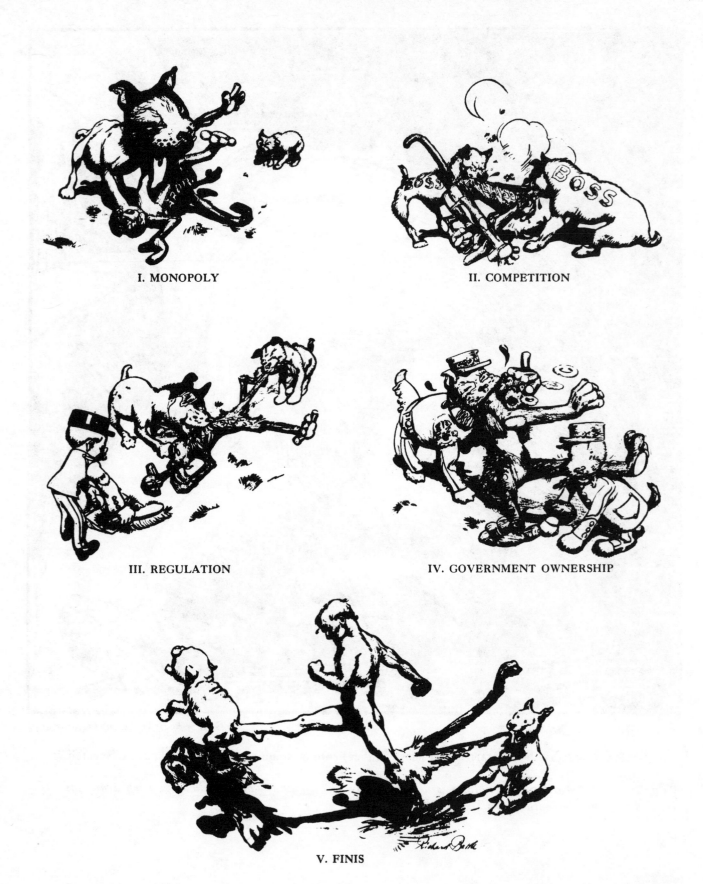

I. MONOPOLY

II. COMPETITION

III. REGULATION

IV. GOVERNMENT OWNERSHIP

V. FINIS

Drawn by Richard Battle, January 1914

The Political Order

[*Before America's entry into the war, one of the most urgent questions facing the socialist movement was its relationship to political Progressivism. The left socialists were, of course, for revolution and against reform. But this theoretical commitment was increasingly less useful as a guide to political action, and* The Masses *agonized endlessly over the tactical problems created by the Progressive surge. Woodrow Wilson aggravated the problem, for Wilson, the intellectual in politics, appealed to the radical intelligentsia (despite his capitalist affiliations) much as Leon Trotsky, who was both a radical intellectual and a man of power, was to do a few years later. It was more than a coincidence that Eastman, who had especially ambivalent feelings toward Wilson, became almost the first American supporter of Trotsky. Some of the following articles demonstrate the various and contradictory responses of* The Masses *group to Wilson, as do Eastman's article, "*The Masses *at the White House," and his editorial endorsing Wilson's plan for a League of Nations which appear later in this volume.*]

MAX EASTMAN
Knowledge and Revolution

"Political Action *versus* Direct Action" is a foolish expression born of the dogmatic mode of thinking. Direct action means strikes and all that they involve. As a method of social revolution, it means large strikes, including the possibility of a class strike in a nationwide crisis. "Political Action" means campaigning and voting. As a method of social revolution, it means class-conscious voting, including the possibility of a complete expropriation of capitalists by an unpropertied majority. "*Versus*" means opposed to. So far from being *opposed to* each other, political action and direct action always have, and always will accompany each other.

"Which is the correct method?" This question cannot be answered, because both of them are correct methods. Adopting a strong, positive attitude toward one does not involve adopting a negative attitude toward the other. Throwing your heart and strength into one does not involve a repudiation of those whose heart and strength are in the

other. The incorrect method is that of the man who adopts one, and then spends his time and energy denouncing the other.

Which is the more important method?—This too is a dogmatist's question. It cannot be answered in general, because now one and now the other is more important. All these questions of method are to be answered differently at different times, at different places, in different circumstances. They are forever new questions, arising in new conditions, and depending for a correct answer upon our exercise of a free and intelligent judgment. Therefore, the one thing continually important is that we keep our judgment free. Tie up to no dogma whatever.

These observations are suggested by John Sloan's picture. It is a picture, drawn with the artist's license, of events at polling-places in the twelfth congressional district of New York. That was where Meyer London, the Socialist, got within a few hundred votes of United States Congress. It is a matter of public rumor that he was deprived of legitimate ballots by methods of the kind indicated. But John Sloan was, or tried to be, a watcher at these polls, and his verdict is a good deal better than a rumor. It is both an actual and a symbolic portrayal of one thing that may happen when political action alone is resorted to for an attack upon private capital.

Jack Ketchel could fight out of his class because he swung both arms at once. He never spent any time arguing with himself about which one to swing first. He just walked through. We recommend his example to the revolutionary movement.

Wisconsin is the fountain source of Progressivism. It is the scene of the chief political success of Socialism. It is noted for the most advanced type of public education.

Michigan is the fountain source of nothing but the Roosevelt boom. It is behind New Jersey in Socialist politics. It is noted chiefly for scab-made furniture and Ty Cobb.

Nevertheless Michigan voted even on Woman Suffrage, and Wisconsin went against it more than two to one.

I do not bring this forward in proof of the fact that sex equality is a question by itself, because to me the fact needed no proof. I merely point to it as an illustration. "Advanced education" does not include it. Progressivism does not include it. Socialism does not include it. Let us honestly admit this. The question of sex equality, the economic, social, political independence of woman stands by itself, parallel and equal in importance to any other question of the day. The awakening and liberation of woman is a revolution in the very process of life. It was not an event in any class or an issue between classes. It is an issue for all humanity. It is not an event in history. It is an event in biology. The race that shall fight the struggles of life in the future depends for its heredity upon the accomplishment of this change. It will be a heroic race only if it has the twofold inheritance of independent virtue and true knowledge that this change portends.

Saint-Simon, Fourier, Karl Marx and Frederick Engels were men who grasped the real origin and damning effect of the subjection of women and stood for the revolution that is now on. Almost from the first use of the word "Socialism" the freedom of woman has been united with it; and because of the size of those men's minds the liberation of woman has been demanded by the platform of the International party. Socialists may well congratulate themselves upon that. But they need not pretend that for this reason woman's freedom is subordinate to, or logically included in, their political success. Let the Wisconsin vote teach them that it is not. Members of the Socialist party in America, on the whole, have been like every other group of sexually selfish men. None of them got up and actively went into the suffrage propaganda until after they saw that suffrage was coming, and they would soon have to be asking for women's votes. Then they became ardent over this plank in their platform, which was not due to them at all, but only to the men that are gone, and they decided they could even afford to join the suffragists of all classes in their fight for political liberty. Up to that time they stood solid behind the declaration of the Stuttgart Congress that "the Socialist women should not carry on this struggle for complete equality of right of vote in alliance with the middle class women suffragists, but in common with the Socialist parties, which insist upon woman suffrage as one of the fundamental and most important *reforms*," etc.—a declaration in flat contradiction of the established policy of the International upon all other matters, which is *to join with the bourgeoisie in their fight for a uni-*

versal franchise wherever the political revolution is not completely accomplished.

In other words, they stood for sex equality, not fightingly as they stood for masculine democracy, because they felt the great possibility and the great principle, but passively and tamely, because it had been written into their platform by greater men than they. Every Socialist must know in his heart that this is the true history of the matter, and therefore we merely point to the Wisconsin vote as an illustration. Sex equality is a question by itself. Answer it.

We said last month that there was no real issue among the big parties, that upper class politics in America is pure sport. We said this in the heat of the campaign, and we do not hold anyone responsible for it. Only we wish to point out that such statements are not accurately true. There was a real issue between Taft and Wilson on the one side and Roosevelt on the other. It was more of an issue than has been to the front in American politics for a long time. It was a conflict of two economic theories. The question was: What shall the capitalists do about monopoly? Shall they through their government try to destroy monopolies and restore free competition? Or shall they accept monopolies as inevitable, regulate them, supervise them, and ultimately adopt them into the government and run them for the good of the capitalist class as a whole, with incidental benefits to the working people?

That, as near as I can tell, was the issue between the big parties. And speaking theoretically, the nation declared for free competition by electing Woodrow Wilson. As we know that free competition is dead, however, that declaration on the part of the nation was not very significant. It was only a matter of saying a good word for the departed. We do not want anybody to take it too seriously, but we do want to point out to those Socialists who were carried away as we were by the heat of the campaign, that whatever may have been the attitude of the politicians, hundreds of thousands of citizens in this country voted honestly and earnestly upon the question: What are capitalists going to do about monopoly?

As a matter of fact, I do not believe a majority of the nation ever declared for free competition. I divide the vote that elected Wilson into three large classes. In the largest class I put the Democrats who voted straight just because they voted straight. They voted for Woodrow Wilson because Thomas Jefferson was a great and talented gentleman. In the next largest class I put the small businessmen who are fools enough to think that free competition can be restored, and a Democrat government is going to restore it. In the third class I put the big businessmen, who are smart enough to know that competition can not be restored, and a Democrat government will only pretend to restore it.

Many of those small businessmen will discover the folly of a legal pretense at competition, and come gradually over into the party that advocates regulation. Some of the big businessmen, too, will weary of the bother that attends a policy of public pretense, and decide that inasmuch as they pretty well regulate the government they may as well let the government regulate them. That is to say, with increasing numbers all kinds of businessmen will come round to the programme of progressive capitalism.

There is success in the future for the Progressive Party. Government ownership of the trusts is going to be advocated by the trusts that own the government pretty soon. And nothing could be more dangerously foolish than the statement of many Socialist campaigners that the Progressive Party is a mere flash in the pan, and will go up in smoke after this election. The Progressive platform—government control, with labor reform on the side—is the next step in the evolution of Capitalism. And the party that advocates this platform is to become the chief enemy of those who demand a genuine industrial democracy such as can be inaugurated by a united struggle of the unprivileged and by that means alone.

We do not mean that the Progressive Party is an enemy in that its measures if adopted will retard the progress of the social revolution. Quite the contrary. The more government ownership they introduce the better we like it; the more labor legislation the better we like it—only provided there is enough clear thought and independent volition in the Socialist movement to keep clear the issue between us. The Progressive Party is the chief enemy because it will appear to be fighting with us. Some of its future members are in our own ranks. We must fight them back on their own side, fight the Progressive Party so hard that nobody will ever be in the slightest degree confused about the difference between us.

We intend a social revolution, to be accomplished by a class-conscious struggle against capital and privilege. They intend a social amelioration to be accomplished by the enlightened self-interest of the privileged, combined with a little altruism and a great deal of altruistic oratory. Essentially they represent the *enlightened* self-interest of capitalists. We represent the *enlightened* self-interest of the workers, and the fight goes on.

Now, when Socialists say, "Oh, the Progressive Party is a mere flash in the pan—it will go up in smoke," they show that they are afraid of the Progressive Party. They are afraid that it will somehow crowd out, or eat up, the Socialist movement. And when they stand up with their fists in their eyes and complain that "Teddy stole all the planks out of our platform!" they show again that they are afraid of the Progressive Party. They are afraid that the Bull Moose will swallow them up. And I really think he will. I think the Bull Moose will swallow up every member of the Socialist Party who cannot see the difference between a working-class revolution and the evolution of state ownership and industrial efficiency within the capitalist class.

The advent of this state-capitalist-welfare-workers' party in the political arena will be the best thing that ever happened to Socialism in America. It will purge the Socialist party of sympathizers. And if those of us who are left will only stand up to our faith with courage and with clear heads, we will have a line drawn in this country between the party of the people and the parties of the people's money, sixty-five times as quick as we would have if the Bull Moose had never come out of the woods.

Right in the midst of our excitement over the campaign arrived a cablegram from London stating, on the authority of Edmund Gosse, that the English language was worn out. Coming at such a time, this news would have been about as severe a shock as the country could stand, but for one redeeming circumstance. Edmund Gosse is a literary man, and he only meant to speak from an aesthetic point of view. For practical purposes he seemed to think the language might do for a while yet, and he certainly finds strong corroboration in the fact that it has survived another electoral campaign on this side of the Atlantic.

Here is what he says: The poetry of the future "will be largely written in languages which have been subjected to less wear and tear—languages which have not so extensive and complicated a literature and in which simple things can still be said without affectation and without repetition."

And here is what we think of it: We think it is not the language, but Edmund Gosse and all the other library poets that are worn out. We think it is entirely true that great poetry will never be written by anyone who has spent his life burrowing in an extensive and complicated literature. It will never be written by anyone who has specialized in letters. It will be written by persons who are innocent of the smell of old books. Let Edmund Gosse burn up his library, and all the shelvings in his mind, and go down to the street, and out into the fields and quarries and among the ships and chimneys, the smoke and glory of living reality in his own time; let him learn to love that, and language only as it enriches that—then when he speaks of the poets of the future we will listen. For he will be a poet, and not merely a taster of the connotations and the music of ancient phrases. The poetry of England is wonderful, a treasure house, but those who live in that house will never add to its riches. Poets are lovers of the adventure of life. And the adventure of life is ever new, and words are as young as the minds that use them. In a continually unfolding world their flavors are continually altered and refreshed. Only in the musty chambers of a house of books does the language cease from change, or could it by any effort of a decadent imagination be conceived to be used up or worn by those who spoke it in the past.

It is a well-known fact that Andrew Carnegie has a great deal of trouble getting rid of his money. It sticks to him like burrs to a cow's tail. It makes him uncomfortable all over. I wish we might do something to help him. The trouble seems to be that he lacks imagination. That is the trouble with most rich men. Either they were born rich, in which case they never grew up, or else they got rich, and in the process of getting, they dried up their imaginations.

Andrew has got so in the habit of taking money that when it comes to the reverse process he is just as awkward as if he never saw any. Did you ever notice those dime machines they have on the Fifth Avenue bus, how they reach right out and grab your money before it even touches the slot? Well, you can imagine how hard it would be to get a dime to go through one of these things in the opposite direction. And that's about the way it is with a millionaire. A millionaire with a genuine reverse action has yet to be discovered.

I believe it is over fifty years now that Andrew Carnegie has been grabbing money out of the purses of the wretched. It is a matter of public record that he has cleaned the change out of more pockets and the independence out of more hearts than almost any other antagonist of organized labor in this country. He's an automatic collector. Now, how can you expect a man like that to know how to give away money? You take an ordinary man—take yourself, for instance—when you've picked a nickel off the palm of a blind beggar in the church door, and gone home and got to feeling bad about it, you know perfectly well what to do. You take your hat and hurry over and put the nickel back where you got it, with a half a dime added for the sake of salvation. It is not a difficult problem. But Andrew Carnegie has got so in the habit of picking up these nickels, that when he gets to feeling uncomfortable he doesn't know how to break himself of it. He hunts all 'round the house, and looks out of the window, and searches under the bed, trying to find a "worthy person." Of course it is really difficult to find a person worthy of having the tears of widows, and the blood and bones of dead children, bestowed upon him in the shape of legal tender, and if you refuse to look among the kinsmen of the departed, it is practically impossible. And so in a kind of desperation Andrew picks out the ex-President. We mustn't laugh at him, and we mustn't allow the republic to feel insulted. We must understand that after all he didn't want to pension the ex-President; he didn't want to pension anybody; it was only the last resort of a man driven to distraction by his own bad habits. *He can't stop taking money*—that's the trouble with him. And how is he going to get rid of it? Something's got to be thought of, and an ex-President, take him all around, is not a bad receptacle for a little of the small change. He may not really be what you would call "worthy," but at least he has done all the harm he is ever going to do, and he isn't likely to take any action towards getting the money back to its original sources. I think it might be a good plan to pension the defeated candidates. They've had their day, too, and nothing to show for it but a bunch of newspaper clippings. Anyway, we mustn't judge millionaires the way we judge people who have an imagination. We must remember that we are not millionaires ourselves, and we don't know what it is to get so uncomfortable and have to go tearing 'round the premises looking for a "worthy person."

The Socialist war congress spoke softly, but it carried a big stick. The stick that it carried was

Drawn by Art Young, July 1913

Forward–Backward?

PRESIDENT WILSON: "I summon all forward-looking men to my side."
VICE-PRESIDENT MARSHALL: "Hold on, fellers, you'll bump into socialism!"

not altruism, it was not ethics, it was not supernormal idealism. The stick that it carried was the possibility of educating the self-interest of the working people, who do the shooting and the getting shot.

It is a nice thing when ladies and gentlemen of a peaceable disposition meet together and abjure the horrors of war. They do not do any harm. And when they invent tribunals and other devices to replace war after it is gone, they do a very real service. They make everything ready for the Power to arise that shall abolish it. The Power has arisen. The warlike have met together and abjured the horrors of war. The revolutionary proletariat has declared war against war, and their soft declaration is worth fifty million echoing resolutions of humanitarian societies, and all the peace bequests of all the tyrants that ever wore the

mantle of philanthropy.

"The time has passed when the working classes of the world should shoot down one another for the profit of capitalists, the pride of dynasties or the exigencies of secret treaties. If the governments suppress the possibility of evolution and force the proletariat to desperate measures, the responsibility for what happens will rest on the shoulders of the governments."

Remember these words, for they mark an epoch in the martial history of the world. During the last week of November, the International State, the congress of the working-classes of all countries, met in extraordinary session at Basel, Switzerland, in the face of a general military crisis, delivered this manifesto to their exploiters, the patriots of Europe. Behind this manifesto lies the power that is greater than nations, the power that created war and will destroy it—the will of the people to live.   —January 1913

[135]

ALLEN L. BENSON
Our New President

Some men are so fearful lest others shall sometimes fool them that they fool themselves all the while. I know no class of men of whom this is more true than it is of Socialists. Therefore we now hear much about the "adroitness" of Woodrow Wilson, or of "old Doc Wilson," as some of these gentlemen are pleased to call him. They believe Wilson is trying to fool them. They never pause to consider how absurd is such a belief. They never contemplate the solemn fact that if the President were twice as adroit as he is, he could not possibly hope to fool gentlemen who have reserved the exclusive privilege of fooling themselves.

I am not so afraid of being fooled by others as I am of being fooled by myself. I would rather be fooled by others once in a while than to fool myself all of the while. Also do I know something of the danger of too hastily tying a blue ribbon to a new broom. Yet, notwithstanding this consideration, I am frank to affirm that on the twenty-sixth day of March (the day I write this) I have a very warm feeling toward Mr. Wilson.

Not because I believe in his economic philosophy. I don't believe in it. Not because I believe in the measures he advocates. I don't believe in them. Not even because I believe he will lighten by a feather's weight the load upon the back of the working class. I don't believe he will lighten this load. I like Wilson because he seems to have a fairly tight grip on the fact that things cannot much longer go on in this country as they have been going. And I like him because he seems to be approaching the great problems of the Presidency with the realization that the best way to serve the people is not to serve the plutocracy first. To me Wilson in the White House is like a breath of fresh air in my lungs.

I frankly admit that this is because I have lived forty years in a tannery—nationally and politically speaking. The fumes from the White House, so long as I have known it, have been fierce. They were fierce long before I knew it. Grant felt at home there—but he had been a tanner. The stench of his administrations nauseated everybody but himself and the grafters who passed gold bricks to him while he smoked. Hayes, though not so stolid and stupid, was no more inspiring. Garfield, politically speaking, was so crooked that he could hide behind a corkscrew. Arthur knew all about corkscrews but nothing about the Presiden-

tial duty of serving the people. Cleveland might have been a great man if heredity and environment had not decreed otherwise. Harrison lived and died a corporation lawyer. McKinley will be remembered in history only as the man who made Mark Hanna famous. And Roosevelt? Yes, Roosevelt—the "Terrible Teddy," the "Eat-em-alive" gentleman, the man who fought, bled, and fried in the White House for more than seven years without even so much as cutting the price of a pretzel—the man who put the *organ* in Morgan and then set it to playing "He Certainly Was Good to Me!" Terrible Teddy—when shall we see his like again? Not this side of hell, I hope. "Come over and meet me some dark night" he wrote to Harriman when he wanted campaign contributions. "Harriman, you are a malefactor of great wealth and an undesirable citizen," he said some months later when Harriman, fried of his fat, was no longer of any use to him.

These men constitute the background in front of which Woodrow Wilson now stands. Is it any wonder that Wilson looms large? Would not a spindling schoolboy look like a Jack Johnson beside a bunch of hunchbacks?

But in keenness of perception and sincerity of purpose, I believe Mr. Wilson will be found no spindling. I have watched him as carefully as I could for more than a year. He has been changing, and is still changing so rapidly that it is difficult to keep cases upon him. But gentlemen who are not so afraid of being fooled that they fear to open their eyes, will observe that Wilson's changes all tend to make him keener in his determination to put a crimp in some of the grafters. A few years ago he was a fine example of the smug aristocrat. All he wanted was to "knock Bryan into a cocked hat," and prevent the initiative, the referendum and the recall from getting anywhere. The grafters nominated him for Governor of New Jersey, believing that he would wear a plug hat gracefully and turn his back whenever they wanted to pull off anything. Wilson kicked the stuffing out of the bunch, from old Jim Smith down, and went about it to put a little justice into Jersey.

I first heard Wilson speak at the banquet of the American Periodical Publishers' Association in Philadelphia a year ago last winter. As I sat there I was captivated. He had imagination. I could see that. He had vision. I could see that. And he had the most wonderful faculty of choosing what seemed to be the precise word that he needed to convey a given idea.

The next day I began to think over what Wilson had said. After beholding a beautiful landscape, did you ever fall out of a balloon? If you never have, you don't need to try it to get the sensation. Find Wilson's Philadelphia speech. Read it. Sleep over it. Then try to figure out what it means. To me it had melted almost to nothing. It so little resembled an administrative chart that, beside it, the celebrated portrait of "A Nude Descending a Staircase" almost made one feverish.

During the campaign there was much more of the same, sprinkled here and there with something more nearly definite. The first effect of actual election to the Presidency seemed to overwhelm him with a sense of what was to be his responsibility. I remember how I despaired of him the next morning. Some Princeton students had called to congratulate him. He met them upon the lawn. He hopped up on a chair. And the best news he could give them was to caution them against expecting him to do anything. The substance of what he said was that our wrongs were so deeply seated that no one administration could be expected to bring about much improvement.

Perhaps I was so afraid of being fooled that I fooled myself. I still believe, however, that when Woodrow spoke then he was suffering from an aggravated case of cold feet. But I have observed no such symptoms since. With the exception of McAdoo, his Cabinet seems to me to be creditable. McAdoo is too close to Wall Street and Charlie Murphy to look good. But during the campaign he was also close to Wilson, and the effect of association counts for much. Moreover, he knows something about finance, about which Wilson probably knows little, and it is a fair assumption that Wilson wanted to put the Treasury Department in charge of some one who understood the game.

Certainly Morgan did not get much nourishment when he sent two of his partners to Wilson to perpetuate the scheme for robbing China by means of a loan. I do not now recall the exact words of the President's statement, but the substance was: "Get the hell out of here, or I will have you pinched."

I like that kind of talk. I do not overestimate its importance. I realize that, of itself, it can never emancipate the working class. The emancipation of the working class is the only thing about which I much care. But a man who talks that way can do much to emancipate the workers. He himself may not know it, but he can. He can split the Democratic party up the back. The Democratic party must be split up the back before the Socialist party

can do much business. And, if Wilson proceeds as he has started, the Democratic party in four years will be as great a wreck as the Republican party.

If Wilson plays the game as he has begun, how can a split be avoided? He has taken what he believes to be the side of the people. At any rate, he has not taken the side of Wall Street. He tells the people that if the men whom they elected last fall shall prove unfaithful he hopes they will "be gibbeted throughout all history."

Does Wilson want to be gibbeted? If he does, I have absolutely failed to understand him. I believe Wilson has a pretty thorough understanding of the critical nature of this country's condition. I believe he honestly wants to prevent a smash. I must also assume that he realizes that, whether he will or no, history will insist upon passing judgment upon him. I do not believe Wilson wants to go down in history with George III. and James Buchanan.

He will be compelled to, however, if he refrains from fighting the men who control the Democratic party. History will surely hang those fellows up by the heels. They would all be hanged by the neck now if theft were properly defined by law and capital punishment were still the penalty for theft. Wilson must go the route or land in the ditch. If he were a jackass or a crook, I should expect him to land in the ditch. Believing that he is neither, I am prepared to see him do business.

I thoroughly expect to see Wilson stiffen up the backbone of this country by imbuing it with a greater conception both of its rights and its wrongs. Except by way of clearing the ground for those who are to come after him, I have no hope that he will accomplish anything else. Toward the trusts, which embody nearly every wrong from which we suffer, he is reactionary. As an exponent of capitalistic individualism he is as blind as a bat, or nearly so. But he wrote the finest inaugural address since Lincoln's second one, and I believe he believes what it contains. As a Socialist I fundamentally differ from him, but up to and including this twenty-sixth day of March, I respect him. That does him no good, but it does me good.

—May 1913

W. L. STODDARD
Pitiless Publicity

Washington, Any Monday Noon.—Just came from one of Wilson's "conferences" with the newspapermen. The meeting took place in the President's circular office, quiet, green and white, and remote. We stood around the back wall while Wilson stood around behind his desk, and about three officials, including Joe Tumulty, stood around in the northeast part of the picture.

We were all polite about the questions we asked. We are allowed to ask anything we want to, but we find that we don't want to ask many questions on some subjects: Such as wages and poverty, and whether the Democratic party represents the working people. These questions get chilled on our lips. If by any chance we ask one of them we are rebuked, not in words, but by the dignity of the President and by the holy quiet of the circular room, the bare desk, and the three officials, like open-faced spies, watching.

The only things we found out to-day were that the President is still interested in the same legislative program that he was interested in last week; that he hasn't yet made up his mind about those appointments; that there isn't any truth in the despatch this morning from El Paso; that the troops have not yet been ordered withdrawn from Colorado; that there is no warrant for the Government's taking over the mines.

We herd ourselves out of the round room, the more elaborate of us bowing to the Presence, and walk back to report this news to the world. A man who might have talked through our hands and over the wires to the people, had nothing to say. That he said it eloquently was the greater pity. He had no vision to set before the country this morning.   —January 1915

JOHN REED
Roosevelt Sold Them Out

The Editor of the *New York Evening Mail* was advising the German-Americans to vote for Roosevelt. Someone asked him why. He replied, "I know he is anti-German, but the Germans should support Roosevelt because he is the only exponent of German Kultur in the United States."

When Theodore Roosevelt was President, a delegation from the State of Michigan went to Washington to plead with him the cause of the Boer Republic, then fighting for its life against the British Government. One of the delegates told me that Roosevelt answered them, cold as ice: "No, the weaker nations must yield to the stronger, even if they perish off the face of the earth."

When Germany invaded Belgium, Colonel Roosevelt, in *The Outlook,* told us that was none of our business and that our policy of isolation must be maintained even at the expense of the Belgian people.

These instances showed the peculiar Prussian trend of the Colonel's mind, and we were at a loss when he subsequently took up cudgels for that same Belgium which he had so profoundly damned, and came forward as the champion of the "weak nations." Could it be chivalry? Could it be a sympathy with the cause of democracy? We held off and waited, skeptical as we were, and soon the Snake was discerned gliding through the Colonel's grass. All this talk about Belgium insensibly changed into an impassioned pleading for enormous armies and navies in order that we might live up to our international obligations, and into a violent attack upon the Wilson administration for not doing what the Colonel had told it to in the first place. And the particular point he kept emphasizing was the administration's cowardly refusal to crush the Mexican people!

After General Leonard Wood and the ambitious military caste in this country had whispered in the Colonel's ear, and after the munitions makers and the imperialist financiers had given the Colonel a dinner, and after the predatory plutocrats he fought so nobly in the past had told him they would support him for President of the United States, "Our Teddy" came out for the protection of weak nations abroad and the suppression of weak nations at home; for the crushing of Prussian militarism and the encouragement of American militarism; for all the liberalism, including Russia's, financed by the Anglo-French loan, and all the conservatism of the gentlemen who financed it.

We were not fooled by the Colonel's brand of patriotism. Neither were the munitions makers and the money trust; the Colonel was working for their benefit, so they backed him. But large numbers of sincere people in this country who remembered Armageddon and "Social Justice" imagined that Roosevelt was still on the side of the people. Most of these persons had flocked to his standard in 1912 flushed with a vision of regenerated humanity, and had given up a good deal of their time, money and position to follow Democracy's new Messiah. Four years of dictatorship by George W. Perkins and the Steel Trust, four years in which the Colonel had patiently allowed his crusaders to perish politically in droves, four years of contradiction and change until he was screaming at the top of his lungs for blood-thirstiness, obedience and efficiency, had not dimmed their faith.

These people were not militarists; they were for peace, not war; they were not for universal service of any kind, nor obedience to corporations. They were for Roosevelt; they thought that, after all, he stood for Social Justice. So they blindly swallowed what he advocated and shouted, "We want Teddy!"

In 1912 Theodore Roosevelt issued his Covenant with the American People, assuring them that he would never desert them, and affirming the unalterable principle of Social Justice for which he stood. This Covenant was the Progressive Party's reason for being. Indeed, if they had not believed the Covenant with the American people would be resuscitated, I doubt if the Progressives, after those four long years of silence and neglect, would have risen to blindly follow Colonel Roosevelt again. They had had their knocks. They had made their sacrifices. They knew that as Progressives they could not come to power in 1916. But when that call came, all over the country in a million hearts the spark of almost extinct enthusiasm burst into flame, and the feeling of a holy crusade of democracy, which had stirred men and women four years ago, again swept the country.

Not the intelligent radicals—no matter how much they wanted Teddy, they knew he would betray them when it suited him—but the common, ordinary, unenlightened people, the backwoods idealists, as it were.—they trusted Teddy. Hadn't he said he would never desert them? It was to be another Armageddon, and they would sacrifice to the cause as they had sacrificed before.

Little did they know that Theodore Roosevelt, in New York, was referring to them as "rabble," and planning how he could shake himself free from enthusiasts, from idealists, from the dirty and stupid lower classes. Little did they know that he was saying impatiently about them "You can't build a political party out of cranks. I have got to get rid of the 'lunatic fringe.'" And by "lunatic fringe" he meant those people who believed in Social Justice and wanted to put it into effect.

The call to the Progressive Convention spoke of trying to reach a basis of understanding with the Republican Party. To this the Progressives assented; some because they wanted to get back into the Republican fold, and others because they wanted to force Roosevelt and Social Justice upon the Republicans and upon the country. And if the Republicans would not take Teddy and Progressivism why then hadn't Teddy made a covenant with them? They would go it alone again as they had in 1912—the Party of Protest, the noble forlorn hope. And so they came to Chicago, inarticulate, full of faith, stirred by a vague aspiration which they would put into words later. Teddy was not Teddy to them; he was Democracy—he was justice and fairness and the cause of the poor. Also he was Preparedness; but if Teddy said Preparedness meant Justice and Liberty, then Teddy must be right. The platform of the party shows how completely these crusaders of 1913 had replaced principles with Roosevelt—there is no social justice in it.

I looked down from the platform of the Auditorium in Chicago upon that turbulent sea of almost holy emotion; upon men and women from great cities and little towns, from villages and farms, from the deserts and the mountains and the cattle ranches, wherever the wind had carried to the ears of the poor and the oppressed that a leader and a mighty warrior had risen up to champion the Square Deal. The love of Teddy filled those people. Blind and exalted, they sang "Onward Christian Soldiers!" and "We Will Follow, Follow Teddy!" There was virility, enthusiasm, youth in that assembly; there were great fighters there, men who all their lives had given battle alone against frightful odds to right the wrongs of the sixty per cent of the people of this country who own five per cent of its wealth. These were not Revolutionists; for the most part they were people of little vision and no plan—merely ordinary men who were raw from the horrible injustice and oppression they saw on every side. Without a leader to express them, they were no good. We, Socialists and Revolutionists, laughed and sneered at the Progressives; we ridiculed their worship of a Personality; we derided their hysterical singing of Revival Hymns; but when I saw the Progressive Convention, I realized that among those delegates lay the hope of this country's peaceful evolution, and the material for heroes of the people.

On the platform was another crowd—the Progressive leaders. Now at the Republican Convention I had seen Barnes and Reed, Smoot and Penrose, and W. Murray Crane and those other sinister figures who fight to the death against the people. Well, the crowd on the platform of the Progressive Convention looked much the same to me; George Perkins of Wall Street, James Garfield, Charles Bonaparte, et al. Among this furtive, cold group of men there was no spark of enthusiasm, no sympathy for Democracy. Indeed, I passed close to them once and I heard them talking

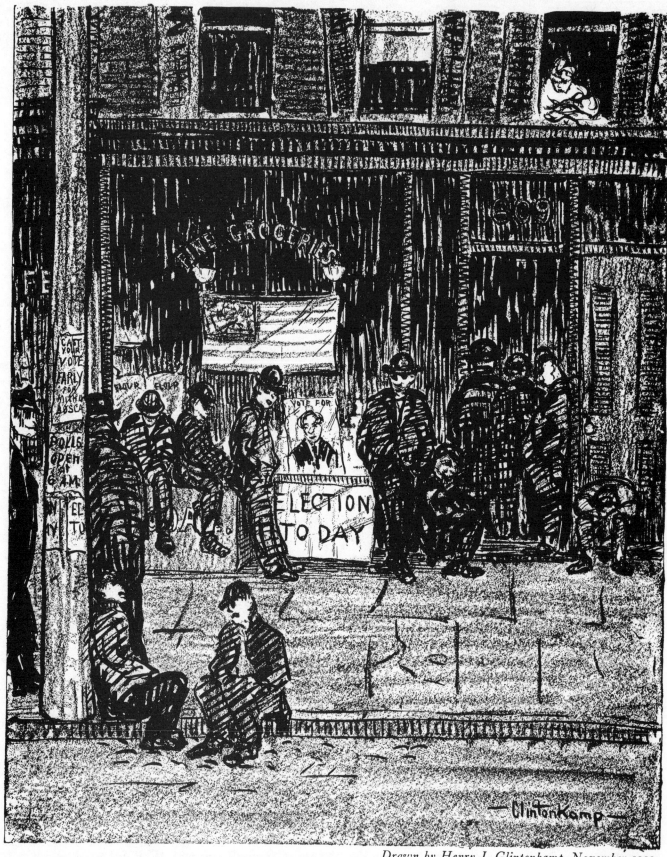

Drawn by Henry J. Glintenkamp, November 1913

Voting Machines

about the delegates on the floor. They called them "the cheap skates!" And yet this inner circle, whose task it was to use the Progressives as a threat to the Republicans, but not to permit them to embarrass the Colonel, were, as I knew, Theodore Roosevelt's confidants, his lieutenants in the Convention.

The Republican Convention was sitting only a few blocks away, thoroughly controlled by Penrose, Smoot, Crane, Barnes, et al. This the Progressive delegates learned; and they learned that Theodore Roosevelt could not under any circumstances be nominated there. They clamored for Teddy. Roaring waves of sound swept the house, "We want Teddy! Let's nominate Teddy now!" Only with the greatest difficulty did the Gang persuade them to wait. "The call for a Convention," they said, "had emphasized the necessity of getting together with the Republicans in order to save the country. We ought to appoint a Committee to confer with the Republican Convention as to a possible candidate that both parties might support."

"We want Teddy. We want Teddy!"

"Wait," counseled Perkins, Penrose, Garfield and the rest of the Gang, "it will do no harm to talk with them."

Governor Hiram Johnson of California thundered to the delegates: "Remember Barnes, Penrose and Crane in 1912! We left the Republican Convention because the bosses were in control. They are still in control. The only word we should send to the Republican Convention is the nomination of Theodore Roosevelt!"

"It won't do any harm to talk it over with them," counseled the gang. "We have here a telegram from Theodore Roosevelt recommending that we discuss matters with the Republicans." And they read it aloud.

Flaming Victor Murdock leaped to the stage. "You want Teddy!" he cried. "Well, the only way you will get him is to nominate him now!"

"I will tell you the message we ought to send to the Republican Convention," shouted William J. McDonald. "Tell them to go to Hell!"

Well did they know—Murdock, McDonald and Johnson—that the Colonel was liable to sell them out. Well did they know that the only way to put it up squarely to Roosevelt was to nominate him immediately, before the Republicans had taken action.

"Wait!" counseled the Gang, cold, logical, polished and afraid. "It will do no harm to appoint a Committee to consult with the Republicans. If we go it alone, Theodore Roosevelt and Social Justice cannot be elected."

And so the Committee on Conference was appointed, because the delegates trusted Perkins, Garfield, Bonaparte—and Roosevelt. What the Republicans thought about it was indicated in the composition of *their* Conference Committee: *Reed Smoot, W. Murray Crane, Nicholas Murray Butler,* Borah and Johnson.

"God help us!" cried Governor Hiram Johnson. "Tonight we sit at the feet of Reed Smoot and Murray Crane!"

And literally he did; for he was appointed as one of the Progressive Committee upon which sat *George W. Perkins* and *Charles J. Bonaparte.*

Upon the platform of the Progressive Convention the next morning word was spread quietly around that the Colonel, over the telephone, had requested that his name not be put in nomination until the Republicans had nominated their man. The Committee made its report, inconclusive from every point of view, and little by little the feeling that Roosevelt must be nominated grew as the time went on. Only the Gang held the Convention in check by insisting that the Committee must have another session with the Republicans. And then, like a thunderbolt, came Roosevelt's second message from Oyster Bay, recommending as a compromise candidate the name of Senator Henry Cabot Lodge of Massachusetts! Henry Cabot Lodge, the heartless reactionary, who is as far from the people as any man could be! It threw a chill over the assembly. They could not understand. And now the nominations had begun in the Republican Convention, and the Gang in control of the Progressives could control no longer. Bainbridge Colby of New York was recognized and nominated Theodore Roosevelt; Hiram Johnson seconded the nomination; and in three minutes the rules had been suspended and Roosevelt was adopted by acclamation. "Now," said Chairman Raymond Robins, "the responsibility rests with Colonel Roosevelt, and I have never known him to shirk any responsibility, no matter how insignificant or tremendous it might be. I believe that Colonel Roosevelt will accept." And the convention adjourned until three o'clock.

How the Republicans nominated Hughes by an overwhelming majority is now ancient history; and how the Progressives, full of hope and enthusiasm and girding themselves for the great fight, returned to receive Roosevelt's acceptance, I saw. The bands played, and exultingly, like children, the standards moved up and down the aisles. Prof. Albert Bushnell Hart of Harvard raved about the hall waving a huge American flag.

"No one man or two men or three men can own the Progressive Party," shouted Chairman Robins, referring directly to George W. Perkins. "This is to be a people's party, financed by the people. I call for subscriptions to the campaign fund from the floor." In twenty minutes, with a burst of tremendous enthusiasm, $100,000 had been pledged by the delegates in the gallery. It was a magnificent tribute to the spirit of the "cheap skates."

And then it began to be whispered about the platform that Theodore Roosevelt's answer had arrived; it said that if the Convention insisted upon an answer at once, he must decline—that before accepting the Progressive nomination Colonel Roosevelt must hear Justice Hughes' statement; that he would give the Progressive National Committee his answer on June 26th; that if the Committee thought Justice Hughes' position on Preparedness and Americanism was adequate he would decline the Progressive nomination; however, if the Committee thought Justice Hughes' position inadequate, he would consult with them upon what was best to be done. This we, the newspapermen, and George Perkins and the Gang knew for an hour before the Convention adjourned, yet not one word was allowed to reach the delegates on the floor. Skilfully, Chairman Robins announced that in accordance with the will of the delegates, he was going to see that the Convention adjourned at five o'clock sharp—though no one had asked for this. The collection of money went merrily on, and those who gave did so because they thought Theodore Roosevelt was going to lead them in another fight. Only Governor Hiram Johnson and Victor Murdock sounded the note of bitterness and the certainty of betrayal.

"God forgive us," cried Governor Johnson, "for not acting the first day as we ought to have acted!"

Victor Murdock was even more disillusioned. "The steam roller has run over us," he cried. "We must never again delay making our decisions."

And then, at four minutes to five o'clock, Chairman Robins announced perfunctorily another communication from Theodore Roosevelt, and read it; and before the Convention had time to grasp its meaning, it had been adjourned and was pouring, stunned and puzzled, out through the many doors into the street. It took several hours for the truth to get into those people's heads that their Messiah had sold them for thirty pieces of political silver. But they did understand finally, I think.

That night I was in the Progressive Headquarters. Big bronzed men were openly weeping. Others wandered around as if they were dazed. It was an atmosphere full of shock and disaster. Yes, the intelligent radicals had known it would come, but they did not think it would come this way, so contemptuously, so utterly. They thought that the Colonel would have left them some loophole as he left himself one. They did not realize that the Colonel was not that kind of a man, that his object was to break irrevocably with the "cranks" and the "rabble"—to slap them in the face by the suggestion of Henry Cabot Lodge as a Progressive candidate. But now they were left, as one of them expressed it, "out on a limb and the limb sawed off."

As for Colonel Roosevelt, he is back with the people among whom alone he is comfortable, "the predatory plutocrats." At least he is no longer tied to Democracy. For that he undoubtedly breathes a sigh of relief. And as for Democracy, we can only hope that some day it will cease to put its trust in men.   —August 1916

Drawn by Mell Daniell

The Industrial Wars

[One of the distinguishing marks of The Masses was the ability of its contributors, who were nearly all highly skilled professionals. Hence, the reportage which The Masses printed, while it was anything but unbiased, was of a very high order. Although The Masses did not cover as many stories as the labor historian might wish, it did report most of the great strikes of its day.]

JOHN REED
War in Paterson

[The Masses was intimately concerned with the I.W.W.'s Paterson strike just outside New York. Many of the staff were able to visit the strikers and conceived a great admiration for them, and for the Wobbly leaders as well. After the experience described here, John Reed went on to organize the great pageant in Madison Square Garden which united the efforts of proletarians and leftist intellectuals and was an enormous aesthetic success—though a financial failure. Max Eastman made this strike the central event of his novel, Venture.]

There's war in Paterson. But it's a curious kind of war. All the violence is the work of one side—the Mill Owners. Their servants, the Police, club unresisting men and women and ride down law-abiding crowds on horseback. Their paid mercenaries, the armed Detectives, shoot and kill innocent people. Their newspapers, the Paterson *Press* and the Paterson *Call*, publish incendiary and crime-inciting appeals to mob-violence against the strike leaders. Their tool, Recorder Carroll, deals out heavy sentences to peaceful pickets that the police-net gathers up. They control absolutely the Police, the Press, the Courts.

Opposing them are about twenty-five thousand striking silk-workers, of whom perhaps ten thousand are active, and their weapon is the picket-line. Let me tell you what I saw in Paterson and then you will say which side of this struggle is "anarchistic" and "contrary to American ideals."

At six o'clock in the morning a light rain was falling. Slate-grey and cold, the streets of Paterson were deserted. But soon came the Cops—twenty of them—strolling along with their nightsticks under their arms. We went ahead of them toward the mill district. Now we began to see workmen going in the same direction, coat collars turned up, hands in their pockets. We came into a long street, one side of which was lined with silk mills, the other side with the wooden tenement houses. In every doorway, at every window of the houses clustered foreign-faced men and women, laughing and chatting as if after breakfast on a holiday. There seemed no sense of expectancy, no strain or feeling of fear. The sidewalks were almost empty, only over in front of the mills a few couples—there couldn't have been more than fifty—marched slowly up and down, dripping with the rain. Some were men, with here and there a man and woman together, or two young boys. As the warmer light of full day came the people drifted out of their houses and began to pace back and forth, gathering in little knots on the corners. They were quick with gesticulating hands, and low-voiced conversation. They looked often toward the corners of side streets.

Suddenly appeared a policeman, swinging his club. "Ah-h-h!" said the crowd softly.

Six men had taken shelter from the rain under the canopy of a saloon. "Come on! Get out of that!" yelled the policeman, advancing. The men quietly obeyed. "Get off this street! Go home, now! Don't be standing here!" They gave way before him in silence, drifting back again when he turned away. Other policemen materialized, hustling, cursing, brutal, ineffectual. No one answered back. Nervous, bleary-eyed, unshaven, these officers were worn out with nine weeks' incessant strike duty.

On the mill side of the street the picket-line had grown to about four hundred. Several policemen shouldered roughly among them, looking for trouble. A workman appeared, with a tin pail, escorted by two detectives. "Boo! Boo!" shouted a few scattered voices. Two Italian boys leaned against the mill fence and shouted a merry Irish threat, "Scab! Come outa here I knocka you' head off!" A policeman grabbed the boys roughly by the shoulder. "Get to hell out of here!" he cried, jerking and pushing them violently to the corner, where he kicked them. Not a voice, not a movement from the crowd.

A little further along the street we saw a young

woman with an umbrella, who had been picketing, suddenly confronted by a big policeman.

"What the hell are *you* doing here?" he roared. "God damn you, you go home!" and he jammed his club against her mouth. "I *no* go home!" she shrilled passionately, with blazing eyes. "You bigga stiff!"

Silently, steadfastly, solidly the picket-line grew. In groups or in couples the strikers patrolled the sidewalk. There was no more laughing. They looked on with eyes full of hate. These were fiery-blooded Italians, and the police were the same brutal thugs that had beaten them and insulted them for nine weeks. I wondered how long they could stand it.

It began to rain heavily. I asked a man's permission to stand on the porch of his house. There was a policeman standing in front of it. His name, I afterwards discovered, was McCormack. I had to walk around him to mount the steps.

Suddenly he turned round, and shot at the owner: "Do all them fellows live in that house?" The man indicated the three other strikers and himself, and shook his head at me.

"Then you get to hell off of there!" said the cop, pointing his club at me.

"I have the permission of this gentleman to stand here," I said. "He owns this house."

"Never mind! Do what I tell you! Come off of there, and come off damn quick!"

"I'll do nothing of the sort."

With that he leaped up the steps, seized my arm, and violently jerked me to the sidewalk. Another cop took my arm and they gave me a shove.

"Now you get to hell off this street!" said Officer McCormack.

"I won't get off this street or any other street. If I'm breaking any law, you arrest me!"

Officer McCormack, who is doubtless a good, stupid Irishman in time of peace, is almost helpless in a situation that requires thinking. He was dreadfully troubled by my request. He didn't want to arrest me, and said so with a great deal of profanity.

"I've *got* your number," said I sweetly. "Now will you tell me your name?"

"Yes," he bellowed, "an' I got *your* number! I'll arrest you." He took me by the arm and marched me up the street.

He was sorry he *had* arrested me. There was no charge he could lodge against me. I hadn't been doing anything. He felt he must make me say something that could be construed as a violation

of the Law. To which end he God damned me harshly, loading me with abuse and obscenity, and threatened me with his night-stick, saying, "You big —— —— lug, I'd like to beat the hell out of you with this club."

I returned airy persiflage to his threats.

Other officers came to the rescue, two of them, and supplied fresh epithets. I soon found them repeating themselves, however, and told them so. "I had to come all the way to Paterson to put one over on a cop!" I said. Eureka! They had at last found a crime! When I was arraigned in the Recorder's Court that remark of mine was the charge against me!

Ushered into the patrol-wagon, I was driven with much clanging of gongs along the picket-line. Our passage was greeted with "Boos" and ironical cheers, and enthusiastic waving. At Headquarters I was interrogated and lodged in the lockup. My cell was about four feet wide by seven feet long, at least a foot higher than a standing man's head, and it contained an iron bunk hung from the side-wall with chains, and an open toilet of disgusting dirtiness in the corner. A crowd of pickets had been jammed into the same lockup only three days before, *eight or nine in a cell,* and kept there without food or water for *twenty-two hours!* Among them a young girl of seventeen, who had led a procession right up to the Police Sergeant's nose and defied him to arrest them. In spite of the horrible discomfort, fatigue and thirst, these prisoners had *never let up cheering and singing* for a day and a night!

In about an hour the outside door clanged open, and in came about forty pickets in charge of the police, joking and laughing among themselves. They were hustled into the cells, two in each. Then pandemonium broke loose! With one accord the heavy iron beds were lifted and slammed thunderingly against the metal walls. It was like a cannon battery in action.

"Hooray for I. W. W.!" screamed a voice. And unanimously answered all the voices as one, "Hooray!"

"Hooray for Chief Bums!" (Chief of Police Bimson).

"Boo-o-o-o!" roared forty pairs of lungs—a great boom of echoing sound that had more of hate in it than anything I ever heard.

"To hell wit' Mayor McBride!"

"Boo-o-o-o!" It was an awful voice in that reverberant iron room, full of menace.

"Hooray for Haywood! One bigga da Union!

Hooray for da Strike! To hell wit' da police! Boo-o-o-o! Boo-o-o-o! Hooray! Killa da A. F. of L.! A. F. of *Hell,* you mean! Boo-o-o-o!"

"Musica! Musica!" cried the Italians, like children. Whereupon one voice went "Plunk-plunk! Plunk-plunk!" like a guitar, and another, a rich tenor, burst into the first verse of the Italian-English song, written and composed by one of the strikers to be sung at the strike meetings. He came to the chorus:

"Do you lika Miss Flynn?"
(Chorus) "Yes! Yes! Yes! Yes!"
"Do you lika Carlo Tresca?"
(Chorus) "Yes! Yes! Yes! Yes!"
"Do you lika Mayor McBride?"
(Chorus) "No! *No!* NO! *NO!!!*"
"Hooray for I. W. W.!"
"Hooray! Hooray!! Hooray!!!"

"Bis! Bis!" shouted everybody, clapping hands, banging the beds up and down. An officer came in and attempted to quell the noise. He was met with "Boos" and jeers. Some one called for water. The policeman filled a tin cup and brought it to the cell door. A hand reached out swiftly and slapped it out of his fingers on the floor. "Scab! Thug!" they yelled. The policeman retreated. The noise continued.

The time approached for the opening of the Recorder's Court, but word had evidently been brought that there was no more room in the County Jail, for suddenly the police appeared and began to open the cell doors. And so the strikers passed out, cheering wildly. I could hear them outside, marching back to the picket-line with the mob who had waited for them at the jail gates.

And then I was taken before the Court of Recorder Carroll. Mr. Carroll has the intelligent, cruel, merciless face of the ordinary police court magistrate. But he is worse than most police court magistrates. He sentences beggars to *six months' imprisonment* in the County Jail without a chance to answer back. He also sends little children there, where they mingle with dope-fiends, and tramps, and men with running sores upon their bodies—to the County Jail, where the air is foul and insufficient to breathe, and the food is full of dead vermin, and grown men become insane.

Mr. Carroll read the charge against me. I was permitted to tell my story. Officer McCormack recited a clever *mélange* of lies that I am sure he himself could never have concocted. "John Reed," said the Recorder. "Twenty days." That was all.

And so it was that I went up to the County Jail.

In the outer office I was questioned again, searched for concealed weapons, and my money and valuables taken away. Then the great barred door swung open and I went down some steps into a vast room lined with three tiers of cells. About eighty prisoners strolled around, talked, smoked, and ate the food sent in to them by those outside. Of this eighty almost half were strikers. They were in their street clothes, held in prison under $500 bail to await the action of the Grand Jury. Surrounded by a dense crowd of short, dark-faced men, Big Bill Haywood towered in the center of the room. His big hand made simple gestures as he explained something to them. His massive, rugged face, seamed and scarred like a mountain, and as calm, radiated strength. These slight, foreign-faced strikers, one of many desperate little armies in the vanguard of the battle-line of Labor, quickened and strengthened by Bill Haywood's face and voice, looked up at him lovingly, eloquently. Faces deadened and dulled with grinding routine in the sunless mills glowed with hope and understanding. Faces scarred and bruised from policemen's clubs grinned eagerly at the thought of going back on the picket-line. And there were other faces, too— lined and sunken with the slow starvation of a nine weeks' poverty—shadowed with the sight of so much suffering, or the hopeless brutality of the police—and there were those who had seen Modestino Valentino shot to death by a private detective. But not one showed discouragement; not one a sign of faltering or of fear. As one little Italian said to me, with blazing eyes: "We all one bigga da Union. I. W. W.—dat word is pierced de heart of de people!"

"Yes! Yes! Dass righ'! I. W. W.! One bigga da Union"—they murmured with soft, eager voices, crowding around.

I shook hands with Haywood, who introduced me to Pat Quinlan, the thin-faced, fiery Irishman now under indictment for speeches inciting to riot.

"Boys," said Haywood, indicating me, "this man wants to *know* things. You tell him everything"—

They crowded around me, shaking my hand, smiling, welcoming me. "Too bad you get in jail," they said, sympathetically. "We tell you ever't'ing. You ask. We tell you. Yes. Yes. You good feller."

And they did. Most of them were still weak and exhausted from their terrible night before in the lockup. Some had been lined up against a wall, as they marched to and fro in front of the mills, and herded to jail on the charge of "unlawful assemblage"! Others had been clubbed into the patrol-wagon on the charge of "rioting," as they stood at the track, on their way home from picketing, waiting for a train to pass! They were being held for the Grand Jury that indicted Haywood and Gurley Flynn. *Four of these jurymen were silk manufacturers, another the head of the local Edison company—which Haywood tried to organize for a strike—and not one a workingman!*

"We not take bail," said another, shaking his head. "We stay here. Fill up de damn jail. Pretty soon no more room. Pretty soon can't arrest no more picket!"

It was visitors' day. I went to the door to speak with a friend. Outside the reception room was full of women and children, carrying packages, and pasteboard boxes, and pails full of dainties and little comforts lovingly prepared, which meant hungry and ragged wives and babies, so that the men might be comfortable in jail. The place was full of the sound of moaning; tears ran down their work-roughened faces; the children looked up at their fathers' unshaven faces through the bars and tried to reach them with their hands.

"What nationalities are all the people?" I asked. There were Dutchmen, Italians, Belgians, Jews, Slovaks, Germans, Poles—

"What nationalities stick together on the picket-line?"

A young Jew, pallid and sick-looking from insufficient food, spoke up proudly. "T'ree great nations stick togedder like dis." He made a fist. "T'ree great nations—*I*talians, Hebrews an' Germans"—

"But how about the Americans?"

They all shrugged their shoulders and grinned with humorous scorn. "English peoples not go on picket-line," said one, softly. " 'Mericans no lika fight!" An Italian boy thought my feelings might be hurt, and broke in quickly: "Not all lika dat. Beeg Beell, *he* 'Merican. *You* 'Merican. Quinl', Miss Flynn, 'Merican. *Good! Good!* 'Merican workman, he lika talk too much."

This sad fact appears to be true. It was the English-speaking group that held back during the Lawrence strike. It is the English-speaking contingent that remains passive at Paterson, while the "wops," the "kikes," the "hunkies"—the "degraded and ignorant races from Southern Europe" —go out and get clubbed on the picket-line and gaily take their medicine in Paterson jail.

But just as they were telling me these things the keeper ordered me to the "convicted room," where

I was pushed into a bath and compelled to put on regulation prison clothes. I shan't attempt to describe the horrors I saw in that room. Suffice it to say that forty-odd men lounged about a long corridor lined on one side with cells; that the only ventilation and light came from one small skylight up a funnel-shaped airshaft; that one man had syphilitic sores on his legs and was treated by the prison doctor with sugar-pills for "nervousness;" that a seventeen-year-old boy *who had never been sentenced* had remained in that corridor without ever seeing the sun for over *nine months;* that a cocaine-fiend was getting his "dope" regularly from the inside, and that the background of this and much more was the monotonous and terrible shouting of a man who had lost his mind in that hell-hole and who walked among us.

There were about fourteen strikers in the "convicted" room—Italians, Lithuanians, Poles, Jews, one Frenchman and one "free-born" Englishman! That Englishman was a peach. He was the only Anglo-Saxon striker in prison except the leaders— and perhaps the only one who *had been* there for picketing. He had been sentenced for insulting a mill-owner who came out of his mill and ordered him off the sidewalk. "Wait till I get out!" he said to me. "If them damned English-speaking workers don't go on picket *I'll* put the curse o' Cromwell on 'em!"

Then there was a Pole—an aristocratic, sensitive chap, a member of the local Strike Committee, a born fighter. He was reading Bob Ingersoll's lectures, translating them to the others. Patting the book, he said with a slow smile: "Now I don' care if I stay in here one year." One thing I noticed was the utter and reasonable irreligion of the strikers—the Italians, the Frenchman—the strong Catholic races, in short—and the Jews, too.

"Priests, it is a profesh'. De priest, he gotta work same as any workin' man. If we ain't gotta no damn Church we been strikin' t'ree hund'd years ago. Priest, he iss all a time keeping working-man down!"

And then, with laughter, they told me how the combined clergy of the city of Paterson had attempted from their pulpits to persuade them back to work—back to wage-slavery and the tender mercies of the mill-owners on grounds of religion! They told me of that disgraceful and ridiculous conference between the Clergy and the Strike Committee, with the Clergy in the part of Judas. It was hard to believe that until I saw in the paper the sermon delivered the previous day at the Presbyterian Church by the Reverend William A. Littell. He had the impudence to flay the strike leaders and advise workmen to be respectful and obedient to their employers—to tell them that the saloons were the cause of their unhappiness—to proclaim the horrible depravity of Sabbath-breaking workmen, and more rot of the same sort. And this while living men were fighting for their very existence and singing gloriously of the Brotherhood of Man!

The lone Frenchman was a lineal descendant of the Republican doctrinaires of the French Revolution. He had been a Democrat for thirteen years, then suddenly had become converted to Socialism. Blazing with excitement, he went around bubbling with arguments. He had the same blind faith in Institutions that characterized his ancestors, the same intense fanaticism, the same willingness to die for an idea. Most of the strikers were Socialists already—but the Frenchman was bound to convert every man in that prison. All day long his voice could be heard, words rushing forth in a torrent, tones rising to a shout, until the Keeper would shut him up with a curse. When the fat Deputy-Sheriff from the outer office came into the room the Frenchman made a dive for him, too.

"You're not producing anything," he'd say, eyes snapping, finger waving violently up and down, long nose and dark, excited face within an inch of the Deputy's. "You're an unproductive worker—under Socialism we'll get what we're working for—we'll get all we make. Capital's not necessary. Of course it ain't! Look at the Post Office—is there any private capital in that? Look at the Panama Canal. That's Socialism. The American Revolution was a smugglers' war. Do you know what is the Economic Determinism?" This getting swifter and swifter, louder and louder, more and more fragmentary, while a close little circle of strikers massed round the Deputy, watching his face like hounds on a trail, waiting till he opened his mouth to riddle his bewildered arguments with a dozen swift retorts. Trained debaters, all these, in their Locals. For a few minutes the Deputy would try to answer them, and then, driven into a corner, he'd suddenly sweep his arm furiously around, and bellow:

"Shut up, you damned dagos, or I'll clap you in the dungeon!" And the discussion would be closed.

Then there was the strike-breaker. He was a fat man, with sunken, flabby cheeks, jailed by some mistake of the Recorder. So completely did the strikers ostracize him—rising and moving away when he sat by them, refusing to speak to him, absolutely ignoring his presence—that he was in a pitiable condition of loneliness.

"I've learned my lesson," he moaned. "I ain't never goin' to scab on working-men no more!"

One young Italian came up to me with a newspaper and pointed to three items in turn. One was "American Federation of Labor hopes to break the Strike next week;" another, "Victor Berger says 'I am a member of the A. F. of L., and I have no love for the I. W. W. in Paterson,'" and the third, "Newark Socialists refuse to help the Paterson Strikers."

"I no un'erstand," he told me, looking up at me appealingly. "You tell me. I Socialis'—I belong Union—I strike wit' I. W. W. Socialis', he say, 'Worke'men of de worl', Unite!' A. F. of L., he say, 'All workmen join togedder.' Bot' dese organ-i-zashe, he say, 'I am for de Working Class.' Awri', I say, I am de Working Class. I unite, I strike. Den he say, 'No! You *cannot* strike!' Why dat? I no un'erstan'. You explain me."

But I could not explain. All I could say was that a good share of the Socialist Party and the American Federation of Labor have forgotten all about the Class Struggle, and seem to be playing a little game with Capitalistic rules, called "Button, button, who's got the Vote!"

When it came time for me to go out I said goodbye to all those gentle, alert, brave men, ennobled by something greater than themselves. *They* were the strike—not Bill Haywood, not Gurley Flynn, not any other individual. And if they should lose all their leaders other leaders would arise from the ranks, even as *they* rose, and the strike would go on! Think of it! Twelve years they have been losing strikes—twelve solid years of disappointments and incalculable suffering. They must not lose again! They cannot lose!

And as I passed out through the front room they crowded around me again, patting my sleeve and my hand, friendly, warm-hearted, trusting, eloquent. Haywood and Quinlan had gone out on bail.

"You go out," they said softly. "Thass nice. Glad you go out. Pretty soon we go out. Then we go back on picket-line"—   —June 1913

Drawn by Maurice Becker, April 1913

Sunday

LOUIS UNTERMEYER
Sunday

It was Sunday—
Eleven in the morning; people were at church;
Prayers were in the making; God was near at
hand—
Down the cramped and narrow streets of quiet
Lawrence
Came the tramp of workers marching in their
hundreds;
Marching in the morning, marching to the grave-
yard,
Where, no longer fiery, underneath the grasses,
Callous and uncaring, lay their friend and sister.
In their hands they carried wreaths and drooping
flowers,
Overhead their banners dipped and soared like
eagles—
Aye, but eagles bleeding—stained with their own
heart's blood—
Red, but not for glory—red, with wounds and
travail,
Red, the buoyant symbol of the blood of all the
world. . . .
So they bore the banners, singing towards the
grave-yard,
So they marched and chanted, mingling tears and
tributes,
So, with flowers, the dying went to deck the dead.

Within the churches people heard
    The sound, and much concern was theirs—
God might not hear the Sacred Word—
    God might not hear their prayers!

Should such things be allowed these slaves—
    To vex the Sabbath peace with Song,
To come with chants, like marching waves,
    That proudly swept along. . . .

Suppose God turned to these—and heard!
    Suppose He listened unawares—
God might forget the Sacred Word,
    God might not hear their prayers!

And so (oh, tragic irony)
    The blue-clad Guardians of the Peace
Were sent to sweep them back—to see
    The ribald song should cease;

To scatter those who came and vexed
    God with their troubled cries and cares.
Quiet—so God might hear the text,
    The sleek and unctuous prayers!

Down the rapt and singing streets of little Law-
rence
Came the stolid columns; and, behind the blue-
coats,
Grinning and invisible, bearing unseen torches,
Rode red hordes of anger, sweeping all before
them.
Lust and Evil joined them—Terror rode among
them,
Fury fired its pistols, Madness stabbed and
yelled. . . .
Down the wild and bleeding streets of shuddering
Lawrence
Raged the heedless panic, hour-long and bitter;
Passion tore and trampled men once mild and
peaceful,
Fought with savage hatred in the name of Law
and Order.
And, below the outcry, like the sea beneath the
breakers,
Mingling with the anguish rolled the solemn or-
gan. . . .
Eleven in the morning—people were at church—
Prayers were in the making—God was near at
hand—
It was Sunday!
                                —April 1913

MAX EASTMAN
Class War in Colorado

"For eight days it was a reign of terror. Armed miners swarmed into the city like soldiers of a revolution. They tramped the streets with rifles, and the red handkerchiefs around their necks, singing their war-songs. The Mayor and the sheriff fled, and we simply cowered in our houses waiting. No one was injured here—they policed the streets day and night. But destruction swept like a flame over the mines." These are the words of a Catholic priest of Trinidad.

"But, father," I said, "where is it all going to end?" He sat forward with a radiant smile.

"War!" he answered. "Civil war between labor and capital!" His gesture was beatific.

"And the church—will the church do nothing to save us from this?"

"The church can do nothing—absolutely nothing!"

"Yes, this is Colorado," he said. "Colorado is 'disgraced in the eyes of the nation'—but *soon it will be the Nation!*"

I have thought often of that opinion. And I have felt that soon it will, indeed, unless men of

[149]

strength and understanding, seeing this fight is to be fought, determine it shall be fought by the principals with economic and political arms, and not by professional gunmen and detectives.

Many reproaches will fall on the heads of the Rockefeller interests for acts of tyranny, exploitation, and contempt of the labor laws of Colorado—acts which are only human at human's worst. They have gone out to drive back their cattle with a lash. For them that is natural. But I think the cool collecting for this purpose of hundreds of degenerate adventurers in blood from all the slums and vice camps of the earth, arming them with high power rifles, explosive and soft-nosed bullets, and putting them beyond the law in uniforms of the national army, is not natural. It is not human. It is lower, because colder, than the blood-lust of the gunmen themselves.

I put the ravages of that black orgy of April 20th, when a frail fluttering tent city in the meadow, the dwelling place of 120 women and 273 children, was riddled to shreds without a second's warning, and then fired by coal-oil torches with the bullets still raining and the victims screaming in their shallow holes of refuge, or crawling away on their bellies through the fields—I put that crime, not upon its perpetrators, who are savage, but upon the gentlemen of noble leisure who hired them to this service. Flags of truce were shot out of hands; women running in the sunlight to rescue their children were whipped back with the hail of a machine gun; little girls who plunged into a shed for shelter were followed there with forty-eight calibre bullets; a gentle Greek, never armed, was captured running to the rescue of those women and children dying in a hole, was captured without resistance, and after five minutes lay dead under a broken rifle, his skull crushed and three bullet holes in his back, and the women and children still dying in the hole.

It is no pleasure to tell—but if the public does not learn the lesson of this massacre, there will be massacres of bloodier number in the towns.

For you need not deceive your hearts merely with the distance of it. This is no local brawl in the foothills of the Rockies. The commanding generals are not here, the armies are not here—only the outposts. A temporary skirmish here of that conflict which is drawing up on two sides the greatest forces of the republic—those same "money interests" that have crushed and abolished organized labor in the steel industry on one side, and upon the other the United Mine Workers of America, the men who stand at the source of power. This strike in Colorado does not pay—in Colorado. It is a deliberately extravagant campaign to kill down the Mine Workers' Union, kill it here and drain and damage it all over the country. And you will neither know nor imagine what happened at Trinidad, until you can see hanging above it the shadows of these national powers contending.

It is not local, and moreover it is not "western." You cannot dismiss the bleeding here with that old bogus about the wild and woolly west. Fifty-seven languages and dialects are spoken in these two mining counties. The typical wage-laborers of America—most of them brought here as strike-breakers themselves ten years ago—are the body of the strike. Trinidad with its fifteen thousand has more of the modern shine, more ease and metropolitan sophistication than your eastern city of fifty thousand. It is just a little America. And what happened here is the most significant, as it is the most devastating human thing that has happened in America since Sherman marched to the sea.

Between one hundred and fifty and two hundred men, women, and children have been shot, burned, or clubbed to death in these two counties in six months. Over three hundred thousand dollars' worth of property has been destroyed. And the cause of this high record of devastation, in a strike so much smaller than many, appears bodily in the very first killing that occurred. On the 6th day of last August, Gerald Lippiat, a union organizer, was shot dead on the main street of Trinidad by Belcher and Belk, two Baldwin-Feltz detectives, one of whom was at that time out on bail under a murder charge in his home state of West Virginia. That was three months before the strike, and for three months before that these two detectives and others had been in this district engaged in the business of *spotting union members for discharge from the mines*—a fact which illumines Rockefeller's statement that only ten per cent of his employees were union men.

"Just let them find out you were a union *sympathizer*," I was told by a railroad man, "and that was enough to run you down the cañon with a gun in the middle of your back. It was an open shop for scabs—that's the kind of an open shop it was."

And this fact, verified on all sides, is not only sufficient ground for a strike, but it is ground for a criminal indictment under the laws of Colorado. So indeed are most of the complaints of the miners, for Colorado has a set of excellent mining laws stored away at the capitol. Five out of the seven demands of the strikers* were demands that their employers should obey the laws of the State —an incident which shows more plainly than usual what the State is in essence, an excellent instrument for those who have the economic power to use it.

I quote these formal demands in a footnote, but I think for human purposes the informal remarks of Mrs. Suttles, who tried to keep a clean boarding-house at the Strong mine, and "doesn't care a damn if she never gets another job, so long as she can tell the truth and put her name to it," are more valuable.

"What was the complaint? Well, it was everything. It was dirt, water, scrip, robbery. They kept everybody in debt all the time. Lupi was fired and compelled to pick up his own house and move it off the property, because he wouldn't trade at the company store. Why, I says, if the Board o' Health even, would come up here and take a look at the water out o' this boarding-house—show me any human being that'll drink refuse from a coal mine! It was hay, alfalfa, manure—everything come right through the pipes fer the men to drink —and if that ain't enough to make a camp strike, I'd like to know what *ain't!* It was black an' dirty an' green an' any color you want to call it—and when I'd enter a complaint they'd say, 'Who's kickin'?' An' I'd tell 'em the man's name, an' they'd say, 'Give him his time! Let him get to hell out o' here, if he don't like it!'

"I give 'em a bit o' their own medicine, too. They had a couple o' these millionaire clerks down here from Denver oncet, an' they didn't have enough of the La Veta water brought down for their own table. I heard these fellers ask for a drink, an' I took in a little of this warm stuff right out o' the mine. Do you suppose they touched it? 'What's good enough for a miner,' I says, 'is good enough for you.' I wanted to tell that before the Congress committee so bad I was just bustin', an' you can say it's the truth from me, an' I don't care what happens to me so long as I'm tellin' the truth." She doesn't care what happens to her, Mrs. Suttles doesn't, but she cares what happens to other people, and I'm happy to be her mouthpiece.

You will know from her that there is nothing we are accustomed to call "revolutionary" in the local aspect of this strike. One sees here only an uprising of gentle and sweet-mannered people in favor of the laws they live under. In the mines they had learned to endure, and in the tents they surely did endure, smilingly as I have it from those who know, without impetuous retaliations, more hardship and continuous provocation than you could imagine of yourself—if indeed you can imagine yourself tenting four months in the winter snow for any cause. Patient and persistent and naturally genial—yet the militia, and the mine operators, and all the little priests of respectability of Trinidad are full of the tale of those "blood-thirsty foreigners," "ignorant," "lawless," "unacquainted with the principles of American Liberty."

As a pure matter of fact, so long as those foreigners remained "ignorant" and "lawless," their employers were highly well pleased with them. But when they began to learn English, and acquire an interest in the laws, and also in the "principles of American liberty," straightway they became a sore and a trouble to their employers—because their employers were daily violating these laws and these principles at the expense of *their* lives and *their* happiness, and they knew it. That was the trouble. And their employers, from Rockefeller down to the mine boss, are perfectly well aware of this, having brought them here in the first place for the express purpose of supplanting English-speaking Americans who knew their rights and had rebelled.

When you hear a man talking about "blood-thirsty foreigners," you can be perfectly sure there is one thing in his heart he would like to do, and that is drink the blood of those foreigners—especially if he happens to be one of these hatchet-faced Yankees.

The strike was declared on September 23, and the companies, having imported guards for about two weeks before that, were ready for it. They were ready to evict the miners from their houses, dumping their families and furniture into the snow, and in many of the mines they did this. Those

<hr>

*These are the formal demands of the miners:

1. Recognition of the union.

2. Ten per cent advance in wages on the tonnage rates and wage scale (in accordance with the Wyoming day wage scale).

3. Eight hour day for all classes of labor in and around the mines and coke-ovens.

4. Pay for all narrow work and dead work (including brushing, timbering, removing falls, handling impurities).

5. Check weighmen elected by others without interference.

6. The right to trade in any store, and choose boarding-place and doctor.

7. Abolition of the guard system.

But let it be understood that the strike is not directed against any specific evil or evils, but against an entire system of peonage incredible to behold in this century — a system, against which unionism is absolutely the only defense. Recognition of the union or feudal serfdom in these mines — that is the issue.

miners who owned the houses from which they were evicted, having paid for them although they were built upon the company's land, must have received at this point a peculiarly fine taste of "American Liberty." That is almost as fine as having a tax deducted from your wages, to pay for a public school privately owned and situated upon private property, or being compelled to pay fifty cents toward the salary of a Protestant town minister when you are a Roman Catholic. Miners in one case were not allowed to pass through the gate of the mining camp, in order to get their mail from a United States Post Office located within the gate called "Private Property"—another sweet taste of "American Liberty." Was it such fortunes as this, I wonder, that led one of the strikers to run back among the blazing tents in order to rescue an American flag, "because he just couldn't see that burn up"?

Early in October, say the strikers, an automobile containing Baldwin-Feltz gunmen stopped under the hills and fired into the Ludlow tent colony in the plain.

Early in October, says the superintendent of the Hastings mine, an automobile containing men coming to work in the mines was fired on from the vicinity of the tent colony. The reader may solve this problem for himself. I can only picture the location of the mines and the colony, and let it stand that guerrilla warfare between the strikers and those men imported for their shooting ability, was frequent and was inevitable.

The mining camps are in little cañons, running up into a range of hills that extends due north and south, and the Ludlow tent colony was out on the wide plain to the east of these hills by the railroad track. It stood just north of the junction of the main line of the Colorado & Southern with branch lines running up to the mines. In short, it held the strategic point *for warning strike-breakers on incoming trains.* And to those who cannot believe the story of its destruction for the sheer wantonness of it, that little fact will be of interest. The tent colony at Holly Grove, West Virginia, shot up in the same wantonness by the same gunmen last year, was similarly situated. These tent colonies are white flags on the gatepost, flashing the signal "Quarantine" to the initiated, and it is very important for the unsanitary business within that they be removed.

So the gunmen would issue down the cañons, or shoot from the hills, and the strikers would sally out to each side of the colony, and shoot into the

cañon or the hills. And this occurred often in the days of October, leading up to the pitched battle on the 28th, when the people in that vicinity seemed to be breathing bullets, and Governor Ammons ordered John Chase into the field with the militia.

The militia came avowedly to disarm both sides, and prevent the illegal importation of strike-breakers, and they were received with cheers by the "lawless" strikers, who surrendered to them a great many if not all of their arms. For a week or two, in fact, the militia did impartially keep the peace. And the reason for this is that it had been asserted by the mine-owners, and believed by the Governor, that that famous "ten per cent of union men" were forcibly detaining the rest of the strikers in the colonies, and that as soon as the ninety per cent had the protection of the militia they would return to work.

In the course of the two weeks it became evident, however, that this happy thought was founded upon a wish, and that something else would have to be done to get the men back into the mines. Therefore the guns surrendered by the strikers were turned over to the new gunmen, and the protection of illegally imported strike-breakers began again. Began also the enrolling of Baldwin-Feltz gunmen in the Colorado militia; the secret meetings of a military court; the arresting and jailing by the hundred of "military prisoners"; the search and looting of tent colonies under color of military authority; and the forcible deportation of citizens. By such means and many others John Chase, riding about in the automobiles of the companies, made his alliance with invested capital perfectly clear to the most "ignorant" foreigner in the course of less than a month.

Thence forward we have to lay aside and forget the distinction between the private gunmen of the mine owners, and the state militia of Colorado—a fact which reveals more plainly than usual what the army is in essence, a splendid weapon for those who have the economic power to use it.

On November 25th, the strikers for the second time asked the operators to confer, and the operators refused.

On November 26th, Baldwin-Feltz Belcher was shot on the streets of Trinidad, not two blocks from where he had shot Lippiat in August. The militia cleared the streets, and indiscriminate arrests followed, strikers even being taken to jail, I am assured, in the automobiles of their employers. *Habeas corpus* proceedings were laughed at.

Personal liberty, the rights of a householder, of free speech, of assemblage, of trial by jury—all these old fashioned things dropped quietly out of sight, not only in the case of Mother Jones, which is notorious, but also in the case of the striking miners one and all. The State and organized capital were married together before the eyes of men so amiably and naturally that, except in retrospect, one hardly was able to be surprised.

Sunday, April 19th, was Easter Sunday for the Greeks, and they celebrated that day in the happy and melodious manner of their country, dancing out of doors in the sunlight all morning with the songs of the larks. In the afternoon they played baseball in a meadow, two hundred yards from the tents, the women playing against the married men, and making them hustle, too. It was a gay day for the tent colony, because all the strikers loved the Greeks and were borne along by their happy spirits. Especially they loved Louis Tikas for his fineness and his gentle and strong way of commanding them. To all of them he seemed to give the courage that was necessary in order to celebrate a holiday with merriment under the pointed shadows of two machine guns.

But in the very midst of that celebration eight armed soldiers came down from these shadows into the field. Standing about, they managed to place themselves exactly on the line between the home-plate and first base, and during a remonstrance from the players, one of them said to another, "It wouldn't take me and four men to wipe that bunch off the earth." After some discussion among themselves, the players finally altered the position of their bases, and the soldiers decided not to interfere again. One of them said, "All right, Girlie, you have your big time today, and we'll have ours tomorrow!"

On Monday morning, at about 8:30, Major Hamrock called the tent colony on the telephone, and asked Louis Tikas to surrender a mine-worker who, he asserted, was being held in the colony against his will. The person in question was not in the colony, and Tikas said so. But the major insisted, so Tikas arranged to meet him on the railroad track, half way between the two encampments, and discuss their disagreement. Tikas went to the meeting place, and the major was not there. He returned, called him on the telephone, and again agreed to meet him alone at the railroad station.

They met and continued their discussion, but while they were talking a troop of reinforcements appeared over the hill at one of the military camps. The machine-gun at the other camp was already trained upon the colony, and a train-man tells me that at that time he saw militia-men running down the track, ready to shoot.

"My God, Major, what does this mean?" said Tikas.

"You stop your men, and I'll stop mine," is the major's answer as reported. But before Tikas got back to the colony, the strikers had left in a body, armed. Three bombs were fired off in the major's camp—a prearranged signal to the mines to send down all the guards, officers, and strike-breakers they were able to arm. And immediately after the sounding of this signal, at the order of Lieutenant Linderfelt, the first shot was fired by the militia.

It is incredible, but it is true that they trained their machine guns, not on the miners who had left their families and made for a railroad cut to the southeast, but on their families in the tent colony itself. Women and children fled from the tents under fire, seeking shelter in a creek-bed, climbing down a well, racing across the plain to a ranch-house. "Mamma tried to protect us from the bullets with her apron," said Anna Carich to me—a little girl of twelve years.

She herself plunged down the ladder-stair into the well—but no sooner arrived there than she had to go back and call her dog. "I says to him, 'Come on, Princie. Come on in!' but he was afraid or something, and when I stuck my head out, the bullets came as though you took a mule-whip and hit it on the floor. Papa pulled me back in, and Princie was killed. Maybe he wanted to go back after his puppy." I guess that was it, for it was way off at the rear of the colony that I saw him lying in the grass.

There were women and children too that did not leave their homes in this volley, but simply lay flat or crawled into the earth-holes under the tents. And to these Tikas returned, and he spent the day there, caring for them, or cheering them, or lying flat with a telephone begging reinforcements for the little army of forty that was trying to fight back two or three hundred—rifles against machine guns. But reinforcements came only to the militia, for they controlled the railroad, and in the evening, after a day's shooting, they took courage under their uniforms, and crept into the tent-colony with cans of coal-oil, and set torches to the tents. I quote here the verdict of the Coroner's jury: "We find that [here follow twelve names of women and children] came to their death by asphyxiation, or fire, or both, caused by the burning of the tents of the Ludlow Tent Colony, and that the fire on the tents was started by militia-men, under Major Hamrock and Lieutenant Linderfelt, or mine guards, or both."

When that blaze appeared, Louis Tikas, who had left the tent colony for a moment, started back to the rescue of those women and children who would be suffocated in the hole. He knew they were there. He was captured by the soldiers then. It is likely he did not tell his captors where he was going and what for? The women and children were left dying, and Louis Tikas was taken to the track and murdered by K. E. Linderfelt or his subordinates.

Linderfelt is a man who had his taste of blood in the Philippines, in the Boer War, and with Madero in Mexico. He was second in command of this gang—a lieutenant. "Shoot every son-of-a bitchin' thing you see moving!" is what a train-inspector heard him shout at the station. And in that command from that man, brought here by the Rockefeller interests as an expert in human slaughter, you have the whole story of this carnage and its cause.

Is it a thing to regret or rejoice in that Civil War followed, that unions all over the state voted rifles and ammunition, that militia-men mutinied, that train-men refused to move reinforcements, that armed miners flocked into Trinidad, supplanted the government there, and with that town as a base, issued into the hills destroying? For once in this country, middle ground was abolished. Philanthropy burned up in rage. Charity could wipe up the blood. Mediation, Legislation, Social-Consciousness expired like memories of a foolish age. And once again, since the days in Paris of '71, an army of the working class fought the military to a shivering standstill, and let them beg for truce. It would have been a sad world had that not happened.

I think the palest lover of "peace," after viewing the flattened ruins of that little colony of homes, the open death-hole, the shattered bedsteads, the stoves, the household trinkets broken and black—and the larks still singing over them in the sun—the most bloodless would find joy in going up the valleys to feed his eyesight upon tangles of gigantic machinery and ashes that had been the operating capital of the mines. It is no retribution, it is no remedy, but it proves that the power and the courage of action is here.   —June 1914

MAX EASTMAN
The Nice People of Trinidad

Pearl Jolly says that after she escaped from the blazing tents at Ludlow, she spent the night with a crowd of children, out of bullet-shot, in the cellar of Baye's ranch, a mile away. The next morning she crept up to the telephone to listen for news. And this is what she heard:

Mrs. Curry, the wife of the company's physician at the Hastings mine, was talking with Mrs. Cameron, the wife of the mine superintendent.

"Well, what do you think of yesterday's work?" she said.

"Wasn't that fine!"

"They got Fyler and Tikas."

"Wasn't that fine!"

"The dirty old tent-colony is burnt down, and we know of twenty-eight of the dirty brutes we've roasted alive down there."

Later she heard two men discussing the same subject.

"We have all the important ones we wanted now," they agreed, "except John Lawson and the Weinburg boys."

Pearl Jolly is a cool, clever and happy-hearted American girl, the wife of a miner. She stood in her tent making egg sandwiches for the people in the holes, while bullets clattered the glassware to the floor on all sides of her.

"Tikas asked me if I was afraid to stay," she said. "I was, but I stayed."

When Pearl Jolly tells you exactly what she heard over the telephone, correcting you if you misplace a monosyllable, it is difficult to retain the incredulity proper to an impartial investigator. But still it is possible, for the thing she heard is a shade too barbarous to believe. The quality of cruelty is a little strained. And so I shook hands with Pearl Jolly and hastened away from her honest face, in order to do my duty of disbelieving.

Subsequently I heard with my own ears, not from professional gunmen or plug-uglies, but from the nicest ladies of Trinidad, sentiments quite equal in Christian delicacy to those she plucked out of the telephone. And I quote these sentiments verbatim here because they prove, as no legal narrative ever can prove, where lay the cause of the massacre of Ludlow, in whose hearts the deliberate plan of that Indian orgy was hatched.

A visit to the general manager of the Victor American Company, an introduction from him to his superintendents, Snodgrass at Delagua and

Cameron at Hastings, a charming and judicial lecture from these gentlemen, had netted us nothing more than a smile at the smoothness with which a murder business can be conducted. Not an armed man was in sight as we drove into the camp, not a question asked at the gate, everything wide open and free as the prairie. Did we wish to see the superintendent? Oh, yes—his name was Snodgrass. We had mislaid our letter of introduction? Well, it would hardly matter at all, because in fact the general manager happened to be telephoning this morning and he mentioned our coming.

So began a most genial conversation as to the humane efforts of the companies to conduct the strike fairly and without aggression upon *their* side, whatever indiscretions might be committed by the miners. I had just come up from the black acre at Ludlow, where I had counted twenty-one bullet holes in one wash-tub, and yet when that Snodgrass assured me that there had been no firing on the tent-colony at all I was within a breath of believing him. There are such men in the world, mixing cruelty and lies with a magnetic smile, and most of them out of politics are superintendents of labor camps.

So we learned nothing to corroborate Mrs. Jolly from the company's men—except, perhaps, an accidental remark of Mr. Cameron's "town marshal," A. W. Brown, that the strikers got so obstreperous last fall that he "really had to plant a few of 'em" —a remark we may set down to the vanity of one grown old as a gunman in the company's service. Excepting that, the men behaved as men of the world have learned to behave under the eyes of the press.

And for this reason we turned to the women.

We secured from the librarian at Trinidad a sort of social register of the town's elite. We selected—and "we" at this point means Elsa Euland, who was representing the *Independent*—selected and invited to a cup of afternoon coffee at the Hotel Corinado a dozen of the most representative ladies of the elegance of the town. And as the town's elegance rests exclusively upon a foundation of mining stock, these ladies were also representative of the sentiment of the mine-owners in general.

There was Mrs. McLoughlin, who is Governor Ammon's sister and the wife of an independent mine-owner—an active worker also in the uplift or moral betterment of the miners' wives.

There was Mrs. Howell, whose husband is manager of the Colorado Supply Company, operating the "Company Stores," of which we have heard so much.

Mrs. Stratton, whose husband heads a commercial college in Trinidad.

Mrs. Rose, whose husband is superintendent of the coal railroad that runs up from Ludlow field into the Hastings mine.

Mrs. Chandler, the Presbyterian minister's wife.

Mrs. Northcutt, the wife of the chief attorney for the coal companies, the owner also of the bitterest anti-labor newspaper of those counties, the *Chronicle-News*.

One or two others were there, but these furnished the evidence. And they furnished it with such happy volubility to our sympathetic ears, and note-books, that I feel no hestitation in reproducing their words exactly as I copied them there.

"You have been having a regular civil war here, haven't you?" we asked.

"It was no war at all," said Mrs. McLoughlin. "It was as if I had my home and my children, and somebody came in from the outside and said, 'Here, you have no right to your children—we intend to get them out of your control'—And I tell you I'd take a gun, if I could get one, and I'd fight to defend my children!"

A mild statement, by what was to follow, but to my thinking a significant one. For what exists in those mining camps—incorporated towns of Colorado, with a United States postoffice and a public highway, all located within a gate called "Private Property"—what exists there, is a state of feudal serfdom. The miners *belong* to the mine-owners in the first place, and what follows follows from that.

"Then you attribute the fighting," I said, "solely to these agitators who come in here where they don't belong and start trouble?"

"Just these men who came in here and raised a row. There was nothing the matter. We had a pretty good brotherly feeling in the mines before they came."

"Yes," said Mrs. Northcutt, "I've had a hired girl from the mining camps tell me how much money the miners get—but *they never save a cent.* 'I tell you we live high,' she would say, 'we buy the very best canned goods we can get.'"

"Yes—the men who are *willing* to work make five and six dollars a day. Of course the lazy ones don't. But the majority of them in the Delagua camp just simply *cried* when the strike was called! They didn't want to go out."

"Isn't that strange," I said. "How do you account for 80 or 90 per cent of them going out when they didn't want to?"

"Well, the union compelled them—that's all. You know all the good miners have left here now. That is always the way in a strike. The better class go on to other fields."

"Then you feel that the low character of the strikers themselves is what made it possible for these trouble-makers to succeed here?"

"That's it exactly—they are ignorant and lawless foreigners, every one of them that caused the trouble. I've thought if only we could have a tag, and tag all the foreigners so you could recognize them at a glance—I believe if Roosevelt were here he'd deport them."

This subject of the native iniquity of every person not born on American soil was then tossed from chair to chair for the space of about an hour. It is the common opinion in Trinidad society. We even heard it voiced by a Swedish lady of wealth, who had herself been less than ten years in America.

"Americans, you know, won't work in the mines at all."

"I wonder why that is."

"Well, I don't know. They don't want to go under ground, I suppose," was one answer. Another was:

"These people are ignorant, you see, and that's why they will do the menial work."

"I see," I said.

"And you must understand that our town was absolutely turned over to these people for a week. They were armed with guns and singing their war songs in the streets. The policemen knew they could do nothing and stayed home. I kept my children in the basement."

"Was the larger part of the town sympathetic to the strikers?"

"Well, those of us who weren't sympathetic thought best either to keep still or pretend we were!"

"I understand. And what did they do?"

"Had control of the town, that's all! And don't hesitate to say that we didn't have any mayor."

"What became of your mayor?"

"The mayor received some letters and he was called suddenly away, that's what became of him! And the sheriff—they say he went to Albuquerque for his wife's health—but his wife stayed at home."

"You know our church is right next door to the union headquarters, and on Sunday morning there was such a crowd of these people around there that we couldn't get to church. I wasn't going to

pick my way through these people to get to church" —this is the minister's wife speaking—"so I called up the chief of police and asked him to clear the street. He said he had no authority, it was a county matter. So I called up the sheriff's office, and they said they couldn't do it. Finally we had to call up the labor union secretary himself!"

"Has the church done anything to try to help these people, or bring about peace?" we asked.

"I think it's the most useless thing in the world to attempt it," she answered. And there followed the story, which I had also from a priest himself, of how a Catholic father was reported as a scab and compelled to stop preaching because he taught that "Idleness is the root of evil," and tried to advise the men to return to work.

"Christianity could prevail, of course," was her conclusion, "but we haven't enough of it."

"You haven't a spiritual leader in the community, have you?" said the least tactful of us.

"We haven't a spiritual *community!*" said the minister's wife.

"And how do you feel about the disaster at Ludlow?" we asked. It was Mrs. Northcutt who answered.

"I think there has been a lot of maudlin sentiment in the newspapers about those women and children. There were only two women, and they make such a fuss about those two! It was their own fault, anyway."

"You mean that the papers are to blame for all the trouble they have caused?"

"The sensational papers," she added. "They're looking for something to sell their papers, that's all."

"I guess that's true," I said, and thanked God they were.

"The worst that has come out of this strike," Mrs. Northcutt continued, "is the way those poor militia boys have been treated. They've just had abuse heaped upon them. Yes, my heart has felt very sore for those boys who came down here full of patriotic feelings!"

"And General Chase certainly was a fine man," said another, "one of the Lord's own! Do you know that at the time they broke up the Mother Jones parade a woman stuck her hatpin in the general's horse, and the horse threw him off?"

"That was just it—the low things they would do!" came the refrain. "And he hasn't a bit of cowardice in him. He rode around all day just the same! I tell you the soldiers behaved themselves nobly down here."

"And yet people object," said Mrs. Stratton, "because they occasionally got drunk—didn't General Grant get drunk? Did they expect a lot of angels to come down here and fight a lot of *cattle?*"

Mrs. Stratton had touched the key-word—*cattle*—and from that word ensued a conversational debauch of murder-wishing class-hatred of which I can only give a suggestion.

"That's it," said Mrs. Rose, "they're nothing but cattle, and the only way is to kill them off."

I think one of us winced a little at this, and the speaker rested a sympathetic hand on her shoulder. "Nothing but cattle, honey!" she said.

"They ought to have shot Tikas to *start with*," added the minister's wife, a woman of more definite mind than the others. "That's the whole trouble. It's a pity they didn't get him first instead of last."

"You know, there's a general belief around here," she continued, "that those women and children were put in that hole and sealed up on purpose because they were a drain on the union."

"Yes, those low people, they'll stoop to anything," agreed Mrs. Northcutt.

"They're brutal, you know," continued the minister's wife. "They simply don't regard human life. And they're ignorant. They can't read or write. They don't know anything. They don't even know the Christmas story!"

"Is that possible!" I gasped.

"Yes, sir; there was a little girl, one of the daughters of a miner, and she was asked on Christmas day what day it was, and she said, 'Well, it's somebody's birthday, but I've forgotten whose!'"

"All you ladies, I suppose, are members of the church?" we asked in conclusion.

"Oh, yes; all of us."

"Well—we are glad to have met you all and found out the true cause of the trouble," we said.

And here I turned to Mrs. Rose—whose word comes, remember, straight from the mine above Ludlow. "What do you seriously think," I said, "is the final solution of this problem?"

"Kill 'em off—that's all," she answered with equal seriousness.

So that is how I returned to my original faith in Pearl Jolly's story of what she heard over the telephone. And when she tells me that while she was assisting in lifting twelve corpses out of that black pit, the soldiers of the National Guard stood by insulting her in a manner that she will not repeat, and one of them said, "Sorry we didn't have more in there for you to take out," I believe that, too.

When a train despatcher at Ludlow and his assistant both assure me that at 9:20 A. M. on Monday, the 23d of April, from their office, square in front of the two military camps, they saw and heard the militia fire the first shot, and that the machine guns were trained directly on the tent-colony from the start, although never a shot was fired from the colony all day, I believe that.

This "Battle of Ludlow" has been portrayed in the best of the press as a "shooting-up" of the tent-colony by soldiers from a distance, while armed miners "shot-up" the soldiers to some extent, also, from another distance.

The final burning and murder of women and children has been described as a semi-accidental consequence, due perhaps to irresponsible individuals.

I want to record my opinion, and that of my companions in the investigation, that this battle was from the first a deliberate effort of the soldiers to assault the tent-colony, with purpose to burn, pillage and kill, and that the fire of the miners with their forty rifles from a railroad cut and an arroyo on two sides of the colony was the one and only thing that held off that assault and massacre until after dark. It was those forty rifles that enabled as many of the women and children to escape as did escape.

Every person in and in the vicinity of the colony reports the training of machine guns on women and children as targets in the open field. Mrs. Low, whose husband kept a pump-house for the railroad near the tent-colony, tells me that she had gone to Trinidad the day of the massacre. She came back at 12:45, alighted at a station a mile away, and started running across the prairie to save her little girl whom she had left alone in a tiny white house exactly in the line of fire. They trained a machine gun on her as she ran there.

"I had bought six new handkerchiefs in Trinidad," she said, "and I held them up and waved them for truce flags, but the bullets kep' coming. They come so thick my mind wasn't even on the bullets, but I remember they struck the dust and sent it up in my face. Finally some of the strikers saw I was going right on into the bullets—I was bound to save my little girl—and they risked their lives to run out from the arroyo and drag me down after them. I didn't know where my baby was, or whether she was alive, till four-thirty that afternoon."

Her baby, as I learned, had run to her father in the pump-house at the first fire, and had been followed in there by a rain of .48-calibre bullets, one of which knocked a pipe out of her father's hand while she was trying to persuade him to be alarmed. He carried her down into the well and they stayed there until nightfall, when a freight train stopped in the line of fire and gave them a chance to run up the arroyo where the mother was hiding.

This has all grown very easy for me to believe since that bloody conversation over the coffee cups. And when citizens of Trinidad testify that they saw troops of armed soldiers marching through on their way to Ludlow at midnight of the night before the massacre, that too, and all that it implies, is easy to believe. It prepares one's mind for the testimony of Mrs. Toner, a French woman with five children, who lay all day in a pit under her tent, until the tent was "just like lace from the bullets." At dark she heard a noise "something like paper was blowing around."

"I looked out then, and the whole back of my tent was blazing, with me under it, and my children. I run to a Mexican tent next door, screaming like a woman that had gone insane. I was fainting, and Tikas caught me and threw water in my face. I was so thrubled up, I says, 'My God, I forgot one, I forgot one!' and I was going back And Mrs. Jolly told me, 'It's all right. They're all here.' And I heard the children crying in that other hole, the ones that died, and Mrs. Costa crying, 'Santa Maria, have mercy!' and I heard the soldier say, 'We've got orders to kill you and we're going to do it!'"

" 'We've got plenty of ammunition, just turn her loose, boys' they said.

"Oh, I tell you, that was one of the saddest things was ever went through! When I was lying in my tent there, Mr. Snyder come running in to me with his two hands out just like this. 'Oh, my God, Mis' Toner,' he said, 'my boy's head's blown off. My God, if your children won't lay down, just knock 'em down rather 'n see 'em die.' He was just like wild.

"I didn't like to say it before the children—but I was going to have this baby in a day or two, and when I got to that tent I was having awful pains and everything. And there I had to run a mile across the prairie with my five children in that condition. You talk about the Virgin Mary, she had a time to save her baby from all the trouble, and I thought to myself I was havin' a time, too.

"He was born in a stable, I says, but mine come pretty near bein' born in a prairie. Look at him—I had everything nice for him, and here he's come, and he didn't have hardly a shirt to his name."

Mrs. Toner sat up languidly from a dark and aching bed in a tiny rented room in Trinidad.

"I lost everything," she said. "All my jewelry. A $35 watch and $8 chain my father gave me when he died. A $3 charm I'd bought for my husband. My fountain pen, spectacles, two hats that cost $10 and $7, my furs, a brown suit, a black one, a blue shirt-waist, a white one—well, just everything we had left. I don't believe the Turks would have been half so mean to us."

"Whom do you blame for it?"

"Do you know who I blame? Linderfelt, Chase and Governor Ammons—I think one of 'em as bad as the other. If Linderfelt had got any of my children I bet I'd have got him by and by. But then it's the coal companies, too, for that matter—if they wouldn't hire such people.

"They searched my tent eight different times, tore up the floor, went through all my trunks, and drawers. One of the dirty men asked me for a kiss. I picked up my iron handle, and I says, 'If you ask me that again I'll hit you between the teeth.'

"If they hadn't brought those bloodhounds in here there'd have been no trouble. They started it on us every time. They'd often threatened to burn it up, you know, but we said, 'Oh, that's just talk.'

"Look at him! I tell you it's a wonder he was born at all!

"Just the same I'd go through the same performance again before I'd scab. I'd see the rope first. I was the first woman in that colony and I was the last one out—alive. They took my husband up to the mine, and offered him $300 a month to run a machine. He'd been getting $2.95 a day before, and they offered to pay up his back debts at the store, too.

" 'You'll need a wash-tub to come after your pay,' they said.

" 'Yes,' he said, 'why didn't you offer me that before the strike?'

"Oh, we ain't bluffed out at all—only I'll never go back and live in a tent. I brought my children out alive and I'm going to keep 'em alive.

"You know the children run cryin' when they see a yellow suit—even the Federals. All yellow suits look alike to them!"

I have trusted Mrs. Toner's own words to convey, better than I could, the spirit of the women on strike. But I wish I could add to that a portrait of the young Italian mother, Mrs. Petrucci, who survived her babies in that death-hole at Ludlow—sweet, strong, slender-fingered, exquisite Italian Mother-of-God! If there is more fineness or more tenderness in the world than dwells in those now pitifully vague and wandering eyes, I have lived without finding it.

It would be both futile and foolish, I suppose, to pretend that there is hatred, ignorant hatred of dwarfed and silly minds, only upon the "capital" side of this struggle. Yet I must record my true conviction, that the purpose to shoot, slaughter, and burn at Ludlow was absolutely deliberate and avowed in the mines and the camps of the militia; that it was an inevitable outcome of the temper of contemptuous race and class-hatred, the righteous indignation of the slave-driver, with which these mine-owners met the struggle of their men for freedom; and that upon the strikers' side is to be found both more of the gentleness and more of the understanding that are supposed to be fruits of civilization, than upon the mine-owners'. It will be granted, perhaps, even by those who love it, that our system of business competition tends to select for success characters with a fair admixture of cruel complaisance, and that those excessively weighted with human love or humility gravitate toward the bottom? At least, if this *is* granted to begin with, it will be heartily confirmed by the facts for anyone who visits the people of Las Animas County.

"Revenge?" said Mrs. Fyler to me—and Mrs. Fyler's husband was caught that night in the tent-colony unarmed, led to the track and murdered in cold blood by the soldiers—"Revenge? We might go out there and stay five years to get revenge, but it would never get us back what we lost. It would only be that much on our own heads."—July 1914

INEZ HAYNES GILLMORE
At the Industrial Hearings

The old City Hall, where the hearings of the Federal Commission on Industrial Relations were held, was a curious frame for the picture within it.

The beautiful Board of Estimate room with its airy colonial lines and chaste coloring, the crystal chandeliers, the stiff pewlike seats, the canopied dais on which the Commission sat . . . and outside a tablet telling that near this spot George Washington, First President of the United States, read the Declaration of Independence.

And within this white, cool, exquisitely proportioned spaciousness, an audience constantly at the boiling-point of emotion—single-taxers, socialists, anarchists, members of the A. F. of L. and of the I. W. W., poets, novelists, dramatists, investigators of all kinds, reformers and revolutionists of every description. . . . To look into those rows of eyes, eager, intense, shadowed, many of them, by the melancholy of Israel or glowing with the rebellion of Russia, was like looking into the barrels of rows of guns.

That room seemed a lingering and beautiful expression of a long-established and indifferent past within the husk of which a passionate and disorderly present was struggling for the expression of its needs.

The juxtaposition which the world at large found most poignant was that of Mother Jones, the venerable labor-agitator, and John D. Rockefeller, Jr. The newspapers pictured and paragraphed that strange meeting; but no one can describe the thrill—half of hope and half of horror—which ran through the audience. It was as though it were not a simple meeting of two persons, but a portent of good or evil.

The days of the hearing were full of such impressive juxtapositions—of personalities, of ideas, of facts. Such were the testimonials of Miss Tarbell and Mrs. Petrucci. Miss Tarbell had found the employing class leaning toward the Golden Rule because, in effect, it pays:

"There is a silent revolution in American industry, towards the end of doing as you would be done by. Throughout American business on the side of management, there is a growing feeling that the common man is worth a great deal more than the employers dreamed. The most important thing in the world is this common man; to give him full opportunity and full justice is the greatest work that can be done.

"Everywhere you will find this idea at work, that it is not well to ignore him, to deny his rights. Employers are struggling to express in the best possible way that feeling in their business. *Sometimes the forms of expression are tentative, sometimes very full expressions are found.*"

One remembered this easy optimism of Miss Tarbell's when hearing, a few days later, the testimony of Mrs. Petrucci. Chairman Walsh drew from her an account of her experiences in the massacre at Ludlow, and, in detail, the story of the death of her three children, smothered in a cellar in the tent-colony. Chairman Walsh asked her

about her children. "How old was the youngest?"
—"Three. He would have been four yesterday."
Then he asked her about her mental condition the
first of those nine days of stupor that followed that
hideous night.

"What were you thinking?"

"I wasn't thinking of anything."

How different it would have been if Mrs. Petrucci had known what Miss Tarbell knows—that
employers are struggling to express in the best possible way their feeling that it is not well to deny
the common man his rights! She could have con-
soled herself with that.

Then there was the testimony of Antoni Wiater,
pick and shovel operator for the Liebig plant of
the American Agricultural Chemical Company of
Roosevelt, N. J., and that of A. Barton Hepburn,
director in that company.

Wiater's story, shorn of its interruptions, hesita-
tions and inarticulatenesses, was this. There had
been a period when, although there were seven in
the family, he was fairly prosperous. He was earning three dollars a day. By working every day in
the week, Sundays and holidays and at night, he
managed to break even, and sometimes to save as
much as five dollars a month. Then came work at
the Liebig plant at two dollars a day—and hard
times. Toil as hard as he could, cutting down
every possible superfluous expense, and even with
his wife taking in washing, he ran behind steadily.
He did not drink or chew, although he smoked a
pipe. He never went to the theater, or to the
movies; nor did the children. His shoes cost two
dollars and fifty cents, but they only lasted a
month, because he worked in acid. He had had
but one suit in nine years. On top of this came the
cut from two dollars a day to one-sixty—and he
struck.

Soon afterward Mr. Hepburn was questioned.
He professed the usual ignorance in regard to
labor conditions in the industry which he helped to
control. But, unlike other capitalists who had testified, Hepburn had one burning instant of emotion.

Q.—Did you hear about the shooting in Roosevelt?

A.—*Yes, and I was very much surprised!*

It was interesting to learn what these leaders of
the world of capital thought about labor. The
New York hearings of the Commission were notable in that they brought so many of these leaders
into the open and compelled them to register their
opinions. As to these opinions, the capitalists
seemed to divide into four classes:

First—Those who pretend to neither knowledge
nor interest in the conditions of labor or in industrial unrest—like Morgan.

Second—Those who know all about these conditions, but will not admit that they know; who
with their backs against the wall, are fighting labor
—like Berwind, Belmont, and the Rockefellers.

Third—Those who understand the conditions
and are willing to give way to labor—to give way
a little, though not seriously enough to cut profits
—like Perkins and Guggenheim.

Fourth—Those who think a paternalistic system
in industry will settle the question—like Ford.

From this point of view, Morgan made a very
interesting witness. He is handsome, debonair,
charming. He has the manner of what we call "the
gentleman" and the accent of what we call "culture." One feels that he would make a delightful
dinner-guest, an ideal week-end visitor. He knew
nothing about labor conditions, had no opinions in
regard to them, and frankly admitted it. He was
often a little amused by the questions of the Commission and sometimes a little bored. . . . Once or
twice it obviously got to him that the situation
might be important. And then a shade fell across
his face. When that shadow fell, it was as though
the predatory condor-like visage of his dead father
peered terrifically for an instant through his amiable eyes. . . . When Commissioner Weinstock
questioned him in regard to collective bargaining,
he asked what collective bargaining was. And when
Chairman Walsh asked him if he thought a long-
shoreman could live on ten dollars a week, he made
the answer that has already, as the *Call* says, become a classic: "If that's all he can get and he
takes it, I should say it's enough." It has been suggested that this ignorance was an affectation, that
his whole attitude was a bit of acting. That is
impossible. Not Irving, nor Salvini, could have
turned out such a finished piece of acting.

In comparison with Morgan, Perkins was alert
and astute. He had plenty of mental spryness and
dapperness. There can be no doubt that Mr. Perkins knows that there is industrial unrest. There
was an air about him of regretful candor in regard
to it, one might almost say of sympathetic alarm.

Ford aroused a great deal of friendliness in the
audience; for one reason because he unquestionably
believes in what he is doing, and for another, because of his announcement that he is willing to employ ex-convicts. He displayed rather a shame-
faced attitude in regard to his benefactions. You
felt that he really did not enjoy talking about

Drawn by George Bellows, July 1913

Splinter Beach

them. Ford does not understand yet that his system is only another phase of the charity he deprecates.

The two days and a half in which John D. Rockefeller, Jr., and the one hour in which John D. Rockefeller, Sr., were on the stand were of course the events of the Commission. Superficially young Rockefeller's attitude seemed ideal. He was courteous, apparently frank, seemingly ready and willing to answer questions. It was an hour perhaps before it developed that he was a master of the art of evasion. He had a system and he kept to it—to profess in his attitude toward labor the maximum of abstract nobility and the minimum of concrete information. In other words, whenever he could answer a specific question with a general statement, he did. When facts in regard to labor were demanded of him, he professed ignorance.

When an actual case was presented for his comment he answered almost without variation, "I could not form an opinion unless I knew all the circumstances." Chairman Walsh put one question to him certainly four—and I think five—times. Only when he concluded, "Mr. Rockefeller, I must ask you to answer this question by either a *yes* or a *no,* or put yourself on rcord as not being willing to answer it," did he depart from his general statement. Indeed one of the most interesting phases in this battle of two days and a half was the contrast between the two men: Walsh suave, bland, absolutely undeflectable but informed always with the warmth of his Celtic quality; Rockefeller gentle, Christianish, but cold as steel and unmalleable as stone. Gradually, however, Walsh's masterly questioning drew a web about the witness, and Rockefeller made the most important admission of the three weeks' hearing; that he could conscientiously, acting as director in the Rockefeller Foundation in the morning, advise one course of action, and, acting as director in the Colorado Fuel and Iron Company in the afternoon of the same day advise an exactly opposite course of action.

The extraordinary temperamental coldness of young Rockefeller I have never seen equalled except in the case of his father. It was not a superficial coldness. It went deep and was all-permeating. Young Rockefeller's face moved only with the mechanism of speech, never at the urge of emotion. I studied him one morning when he talked with Mother Jones, on the watch for one gleam of appreciation of a character so remarkable, one sparkle of enjoyment of a personality so forthright. Not a gleam, not a sparkle came into that icy mask.

When in response to the call "Mr. Rockefeller," John D. Rockefeller, Senior, appeared at the door of the ante-room, a hushed murmur ran through the audience. Had he been one of the crowned heads of Europe, there could scarcely have been a greater sense of dramatic tension. Rockefeller is a remarkable looking man. Given the clothes of the period, he would have emerged with absolute authenticity from the portrait of some aged medi-aeval monarch. Age has mummified him a little, but it has not made him physically meagre. The skin of his head is parchment drawn so tightly over the skull that the bones seem exposed. The straight gray hair of his wig looked glued to that parchment. A line drawn from the top of his forehead to the tip of his nose would make a perfect right-angle with a line drawn from the tip of his nose to the point of his chin. His ears are small, beautifully modeled, flat to his head. His eyes are blue, austere, remote. When he looked off into the audience, his glacial gaze seemed to come from a great distance and to go a great distance. It did not seem possible that he saw us as human beings.

He had been preceded on the stand by Carnegie. Now Carnegie—it developed through his testimony—has no more real social vision than Rockefeller. But Carnegie, though mentally a little broken, radiated warmth, sympathy, enjoyment. He was like a little Santa Claus, jumping up and down on the stand, joking the newspaper-men and the Commissioners, bubbling with infectious laughter and good-humor. When he turned his wide, happy grin on the auditors, he gathered them all in to the last I. W. W. in the hall. In contrast the

Rockefeller coldness seemed more than normally frigid. Rockefeller also showed the effects of eighty-odd years on his mentality, but not so much as Carnegie. Carnegie could not "get" all the questions nor could he answer them all that he got. But Rockefeller got them all and answered them all. It was as though the machinery of his mind moved automatically, answering with adequate accuracy though without interpretive comments. He seemed a shell of a man from which the personality —no, you could not feel that that shell had ever housed anything so vibrant as personality—the cold spirit had departed. With Carnegie, you felt that the thinking apparatus was broken, leaving the warm personality untouched.

Like his son, Rockefeller professed always the maximum of abstract nobility in his relation to labor. The young Rockefeller has, I believe, expressed a desire to know the truth about Colorado, even to go there with Mother Jones on a tour of investigation. We all welcome the idea of that pilgrimage! Personally, however, until something is done about those hundreds of indictments in Colorado, I feel———— Well, I'll quote in full a remarkably apposite poem from "The Shropshire Lad":

> When I came last to Ludlow
>   Amidst the moonlight pale,
> Two friends kept step beside me,
>   Two honest lads and hale.
>
> Now Dick lies long in the churchyard,
>   And Ned lies long in jail,
> And I come home to Ludlow
>   Amidst the moonlight pale.

Let me confess that I brought to these hearings a kind of apprehension. I had seen a few of the big figures in the world of labor. I had seen none of the big figures in the world of capital, but I had attributed to them a great and sinister ability, simply because they were mysterious and inaccessible. It has always seemed to me that the most cruel thing about life is not its artificial inequalities but its real inequalities. I mean that some people seem to be born beautiful, charming, able, enterprising, efficient, resourceful, while others are born the reverse. "Now," I said to myself, "I am going to see some of these great 'Captains of Industry,' these 'Napoleons of Finance.' It may be that I shall discover that they have been unfairly dowered by Nature with a commanding genius. It may be that I shall be forced to the conclusion that it is futile for labor even to attempt to fight capital!"

But I did not get that impression of superhuman

ability on the part of the leaders of capital. It seemed to me that they contrasted to their great disadvantage with the leaders of labor. I felt this particularly when I compared their craft, their cunning, their fox-like evasions and downright mendacity, with the frankness, sincerity, candor, straightforwardness, the passionate conviction and the forthright expression of a man like Lawson. And when I put them beside the big labor men of the Pacific Coast, Andrew Gallagher, Anton Johansen, Austin Lewis, Paul Scharrenborg, and Olaf Tveitmoe, they seem to belong not only to another generation, but to another century, to another world. Indeed, the investigation of the Commission convinced me that they are of an order that is passing. How long that passing will take and at what expense—of spiritual courage, mental anguish, bodily suffering, death—nobody knows. It would be foolish to prophesy, futile to conjecture. But at last we have let the light in on them. It is not so much that we see them as they are, as that they have shown us what they are. The writing did not appear on the wall. They wrote it there themselves. —March 1915

FRANK BOHN
Fire in the Steel Trust

[*Bohn had a Ph.D. in economic history and was the leading theoretician of American syndicalism. He was a regular contributor to* The Masses.]

It was a real battle—not a ridiculous piece of medievalism such as is now going on in Europe. It was a Twentieth Century conflict such as is becoming a familiar story in the newspapers. The unarmed militia of the working class, like the forces of Jackson at New Orleans a hundred years ago, won a qualified victory from the organized and disciplined army of capitalism.

"No, I tell you, I never see anything like it. I was there in Pittsburgh in '77 among the railroad men. Somebody filled an engine and five cars full of oil, set it afire, and run it forty miles an hour into the round house where the Pinkertons was livin'. But this East Youngstown business! In my forty years a' strikes an' strikers I never see the like. It was a patch a' hell sizzlin' in its own juice."

I had just come to town and a few old friends were entertaining me in the "Puddlers Saloon."

Another one of the old ones agreed heartily with the view already expressed. "It looked at first," he said very quietly, "as though the golden dreams of my youth had come true. I had read in the labor papers about such things as twenty thousand unskilled, unorganized men coming out on strike and standing together like a rock, but I had never imagined what it was to see it with my own eyes. I too have waited a long time. I was slated to make a speech from the wagon in Chicago in 1887 when the 'stool' pitched the bomb. When I heard it blow of course I skedaddled. I run home and says to the wife—I says 'We K. of L. officials has got to cut the town.' I went on a train with over a hundred others and we dropped off any old place on the prairie. At three the next morning the Pinkertons and the Police came to my house to arrest me. Well, those times is gone and the real fight is on at last."

THE MIGHT OF THE MASS

The Youngstown Sheet and Tube Company employs 15,000 men. Two-thirds of these were unskilled and they received 19½ cents an hour before the strike. This concern spent $7,000,000 in improvements last year. Its common stock since the war started has risen from 85 to 340. Not a single group of workers received a cent increase. On December 27th 10,000 "Hunkies" struck. Two weeks later they carried the 5,000 skilled and semi-skilled on and up for a ten per cent increase. The Republic Iron & Steel Company employs 9,000 men and the Carnegie Steel Company, which is part of the Steel Trust, has 10,000. All these received a flat ten per cent increase.

Thirty cents a day more might not seem very much to a New York bricklayer, but the steelworker in Youngstown has literally starved on his 19½ cents an hour. Three dimes more a day has given him a taste of victory—which is more to be desired even than a taste of fresh meat.

Before the strike the craft unions did not have a single organized group of workmen in the steel industry. Since the strike a half dozen organizers, machinists, pipe-fitters, etc., have been here on the job, successfully organizing their crafts in every steel mill in Youngstown.

YOUNGSTOWN

To get a view of Youngstown fixed in your imagination, conceive on the horizon fifteen miles distant a dark and ugly cloud. If it is night, this cloud is illuminated by flashes of fire. You come closer and at last into the clouds—you are among the suburbs of this workshop of 110,000 inhabitants. On one side the mills of The Youngstown Sheet & Tube Company occupy exactly four miles of the Valley of the Mahoning River. Above it is the Republic Iron & Steel Company. On the other side are hundreds of acres of dingy shacks. You conclude at once that they are the cheapest and meanest habitations occupied by human beings in the whole world.

The central part of the town is like other American industrial cities of its size. A few thin sky-scrapers shoot up at intervals. There is a beautiful new postoffice paid for by the Federal Government, of course. There is one good hotel. Citizens tell you that the new court house cost just two millions of dollars. The rear wall and top story made of cement blocks are already cracking to pieces. Everywhere smoke—dirt—dust—mud—grime. Prosperous looking business men with dirty faces and dirty hands and dirty linen. Everybody breathing dirt, eating dirt—they call it "pay dirt," for Youngstown clean would be Youngstown out of work and out of business and starving to death. So dirt is the one essential part in the life of the community. Everybody loves it.

THE STRIKE

On December 27th fifty pipe fitters in the Republic Iron & Steel Company struck for an increase of 25 cents a day and won in about five minutes. The news was too good! Two hundred laborers went out in a body for 25 cents a day increase and began to picket the gates. They "made it stick." Skilled and semi-skilled couldn't work without the Hunkies. Then, too, the skilled were not averse to an increase themselves. On the third and fourth day the furnaces were stopped—which is the essential thing in an iron and steel strike.

On January 5th the Electric Shock of the real thing ran along the lines of the strikers' army. Its sure sign was the battle cry, "General Strike." Nobody knows who started it. There has been a small Slavic Local of the I. W. W. at Youngstown. A dozen or more A. F. of L. organizers, Craft Unionists and general headquarters men had come to town. Probably no organization and no individual was responsible. It was instinctive. Crowds of strikers moved upon the Youngstown Sheet & Tube Company plant. Voluntary committees organized themselves and went to New Castle, to Sharon and to Niles. Their demands had focalized—25 cents an hour minimum for a ten-hour day, time and a half for overtime and double time on Sundays and holidays.

The officials of the Steel Trust, who manage the Carnegie Steel Company at Youngstown, were wise. They saw what was coming and at once

posted bulletins informing their workers that 22 cents an hour for unskilled labor would be the rate after February 1st and that everybody would get a 10 per cent increase.

JIM CAMPBELL WANTS THE MILITIA

The dominant mind among the employers was Mr. James Campbell, president of The Youngstown Sheet & Tube Company. "Jim" Campbell is a perfect representative of his class—the "self-made" American Capitalist. From a clerk in a flour and feed store he has become the employer of 15,000 men in a town of 110,000 men, women and children. "Jim" Campbell usually has his way about most everything in Youngstown. Now the mind of "Jim" Campbell worked quite as correctly as that of the strikers. The strikers kept saying to one another—"Keep together, stay in bunches; if 20 of you speak 17 different languages, make motions and laugh and shout. Everybody come out night and morning when shifts are changed. Speak sweetly to the men who are going to the mill and plead with them with tears in your eyes to join your forces. If that doesn't help, try some other method, but keep it up." As a matter of fact nearly everybody *had* come out of the shops, except stationary engineers and firemen and the clerks, who kept up a bluff of work among the furnaces.

"Jim" Campbell said to his colleagues that crowds would have to be dispersed—that the assembling of crowds meant success for the strikers, that what they wanted was a full brigade of militia, 2,000 strong, who would keep East Youngstown swept clean of "disorder" and "lawlessness." They appealed to the Governor through the local authorities.

On Friday morning Adjutant General Weybrecht came from Columbus and looked over this situation. He went into conference with Mayor Cunningham, the Sheriff, "Jim" Campbell and other capitalists. In that conference he declared that the militia was not needed and that he was going back to Columbus.

"The militia not needed," shrieked Campbell and his distinguished fellow citizens—25,000 men asking for a twenty per cent increase in wages and *the militia not needed*. What are we supporting the militia for, anyway?

THE MASSACRE

In the afternoon there was another conference without the Adjutant General. That conference closed at 4:30. At five o'clock about 200 strikers were in the vicinity of the bridge-head on the raised street, from which the employees cross the bridge over a dozen railroad tracks to get into the plant. Six company guards, armed with repeating rifles, came out and took up their station on the bridge. There was not a single striker on the bridge, which is company property. They were in the public street. It was the Orthodox Greek and Russian Christmas. The strikers had been celebrating by parading in quaint costumes and feasting in their homes. There were thousands in the streets who were not specially interested in picketing on such a holiday.

The six company guards first raised their rifles and fired one shot over the heads of the pickets, who refused to retreat. The guards then emptied their repeating rifles into the crowd. They were at a point blank range—not over forty feet away. Forty dead and dying men fell to the ground.

THE FIRE OF REVENGE

Probably every striker in East Youngstown was on the scene within ten minutes. What they accomplished was told in headlines throughout the country next day. The guards retreated to the far end of the bridge and took cover. It was impossible for the strikers to get into the mill or lay hold of the guards.

Their action was absolutely instinctive. Society had committed treason and murder against them. In their power was a half million dollars' worth of property, about which was thrown the guarding power of the sanctity of the law. They took such revenge as the situation made possible. Here, unprotected, was the bank and post office, an office building or two and a dozen considerable stores. Scattered among these were a score of smaller buildings. The mob made no distinction. It threw dynamite through the windows and doors and retreated long enough for the fuses to set it off. A shoe repair shop owned by a Slavic Socialist and strike sympathizer went with the rest.

"How *could* they dynamite the bank?" asked an astounded and perplexed small business man. "Didn't they have their savings in it?"

Mr. Jim Campbell got his militia the next morning—two full regiments of them. There was no more picketing, no more crowds on the street. Every informed working man in Youngstown knows that 25 cents an hour would have been secured had it not been for the "riot" and fire.

The "riot" and fire lasted from 5:15 in the evening until one o'clock in the morning. The East Youngstown police ran away. At two o'clock the next morning, when the streets were deserted except by a few drunks, a posse of brave citizens moved like ghosts among the ruins and drove the few remaining intoxicated men away from the beer cases and whiskey casks which had been carried out of the burning saloons and piled in the open. This act of heroic public service has resulted in a rancorous debate as to who is to be first in public esteem and praise. The argument resembles that between the friends of Sampson and those of Schley after the battle of Santiago. City Solicitor E. O. Diser says that he did it. He will be rewarded with nothing less than Republican nomination for Congress. His claim is disputed by the friends of the Honorable Mr. Martin Murphy, Democrat and former constable of East Youngstown.

East Youngstown has 8,000 inhabitants and 400 voters. The kind of government resulting therefrom may be imagined. "Justices of the Peace," when they fine a prisoner $5.00 and costs, are permitted by law to pocket $3.95 of the $5.00. Before the strike a foreign working man was arrested for "trespassing" on the railroad track while going to work: "A dollar and costs," said the Justice. The laborer had just been the recipient of a month's pay and in his innocence he drew out a twenty dollar gold piece. The Judge saw the coin and quickly changed the fine to twenty dollars and costs.

PROFSSOR FAUST REAPS A HARVEST

In Youngstown there is a principal of a school known as Professor Faust. The Professor lacks none of the philosophic qualities of his great namesake. But, of course, modern industrial America has changed the means of expression. The Faust of classical lore never had such an opportunity as came to the Youngstown savant.

For Professor Faust has just recently been elected Justice of the Peace.

After the militia came, the police returned to town and under their protection arrested some three hundred strikers. The cells were packed and Prof. Faust held court in the county jail. He came close to his game for fear some might escape him. There was no jury impaneled. There was no evidence taken. No witnesses were called. Whether the prisoners had been present or not in East Youngstown during the riot and fire did not concern the "Court." Only one distinction was made.

Those who had lawyers to defend them were fined $1.00, $2.00 and $3.00 apiece. Those that came before the Professor undefended were fined from $10 to $50 apiece. During the four days that followed the strike, Prof. Faust's share of the fines amounted to more than a year's salary as Principal of Schools. It amounted to exactly 1,648 units of the coinage of these United States of America—each one of the 1,648 bearing on the one side the insignia "Liberty," and on the other side "In God We Trust."

The advocates of "law and order" in Youngstown thought that the "fair name of their city" would not be clean of the aspersions cast upon it by the newspapers of Akron, Canton and New Castle unless at least a hundred strikers were sent to the penitentiary, but the big employers wouldn't listen to this. Workers are mighty scarce these days, and "Jim" Campbell and his colleagues didn't care a rap about the small business men who lost their little all in the fire. Three days after the strike the Youngstown newspapers began to say that the community was more or less responsible for what had happened, that the "poor working people" had never been brought close enough to the tender bosom of the community. As soon as magnates began to talk about the dangerous scarcity of labor and to express fear that foreign working people from other towns would be kept away by drastic action, the Youngstown *Vindicator* began to editorialize in answer to the question as to what "Christ would do to the striking workers if he came to Youngstown." So, although there are still over a hundred workers in jail, some of them every day are enabled to borrow the amount of their fines from loan sharks. In the end probably not more than fifteen or twenty of them will have to go to the penitentiary.

NOTE.—As I am hurriedly completing this statement, the attorney for several of the men in jail calls and informs me that the prosecuting attorney is selecting the Socialists and I. W. W. members for criminal prosecution—that not the slightest effort had been made to arrest a single company guard, and that nothing would be left undone in the way of furnishing "an example" to future strikers. "The Iron Heel," says their attorney, "is coming down on their necks."

—March 1916

The Progress of Poverty

JOHN REED
A Taste of Justice

[*Perhaps more than anything else in this volume, Reed's short piece on the unequal application of the law demonstrates the qualities that made him a great reporter.*]

As soon as the dark sets in, young girls begin to pass that Corner—squat figured, hard-faced "cheap" girls, like dusty little birds wrapped too tightly in their feathers. They come up Irving Place from Fourteenth Street, turn back toward Union Square on Sixteenth, stroll down Fifteenth (passing the Corner again) to Third Avenue, and so around—always drawn back to the Corner. By some mysterious magnetism, the Corner of Fifteenth Street and Irving Place fascinates them. Perhaps that particular spot means Adventure, or Fortune, or even Love. How did it come to have such significance? The men know that this is so;

at night each shadow in the vicinity contains its derby hat, and a few bold spirits even stand in the full glare of the arc-light. Brushing against them, luring with their swaying hips, whispering from immovable lips the shocking little intimacies that Business has borrowed from Love, the girls pass.

The place has its inevitable Cop. He follows the same general beat as the girls do, but at a slower, more majestic pace. It is his job to pretend that no such thing exists. This he does by keeping the girls perpetually walking—to create the illusion that they're going somewhere. Society allows vice no rest. If women stood still, what would become of us all? When the Cop appears on the Corner, the women who are lingering there scatter like a shoal of fish; and until he moves on, they wait in the dark side streets. Suppose he caught one? "The Island for her! That's the place they cut off girls' hair!" But the policeman is a good sport. He employs no treachery, *simply*

[166]

Drawn by Alice Beach Winter, January 1913

"He ain't got no stockin's, he's poorer nor me."

stands a moment, proudly twirling his club, and then moves down toward Fourteenth Street. It gives him an immense satisfaction to see the girls scatter.

His broad back retreats in the gloom, and the girls return—crossing and recrossing, passing and repassing with tireless feet.

Standing on that Corner, watching the little comedy, my ears were full of low whisperings and the soft scuff of their feet. They cursed at me, or guyed me, according to whether or not they had had any dinner. And then came the Cop.

His ponderous shoulders came rolling out of the gloom of Fifteenth Street, with the satisfied arrogance of an absolute monarch. Soundlessly the girls vanished, and the Corner contained but three living things: the hissing arc-light, the Cop, and myself.

He stood for a moment, juggling his club, and peering sullenly around. He seemed discontented about something; perhaps his conscience was troubling him. Then his eye fell on me, and he frowned.

"Move on!" he ordered, with an imperial jerk of the head.

"Why?" I asked.

"Never mind why. Because I say so. Come on now." He moved slowly in my direction.

"I'm doing nothing," said I. "I know of no law that prevents a citizen from standing on the corner, so long as he doesn't hold up traffic."

"Chop it!" rumbled the Cop, waving his club suggestively at me, "Now git along, or I'll fan ye!"

I perceived a middle-aged man hurrying along with a bundle under his arm.

"Hold on," I said; and then to the stranger, "I beg your pardon, but would you mind witnessing this business?"

"Sure," he remarked cheerfully. "What's the row?"

"I was standing inoffensively on this corner, when this officer ordered me to move on. I don't see why I should move on. He says he'll beat me with his club if I don't. Now, I want you to witness that I am making no resistance. If I've been doing anything wrong, I demand that I be arrested and taken to the Night Court." The Cop removed his helmet and scratched his head dubiously.

"That sounds reasonable." The stranger grinned. "Want my name?"

But the Cop saw the grin. "Come on then," he growled, taking me roughly by the arm. The stranger bade us good-night and departed, still

grinning. The Cop and I went up Fifteenth Street, neither of us saying anything. I could see that he was troubled and considered letting me go. But he gritted his teeth and stubbornly proceeded.

We entered the dingy respectability of the Night Court, passed through a side corridor, and came to the door that gives onto the railed space where criminals stand before the Bench. The door was open, and I could see beyond the bar a thin scattering of people of the benches—sightseers, the morbidly curious, an old Jewess with a brown wig, waiting, waiting, with her eyes fixed upon the door through which prisoners appear. There were the usual few lights high in the lofty ceiling, the ugly, dark panelling of imitation mahogany that is meant to impress, and only succeeds in casting a gloom. It seems that Justice must always shun the light.

There was another prisoner before me, a slight, girlish figure that did not reach the shoulder of the policeman who held her arm. Her skirt was wrinkled and indiscriminate, and hung too closely about her hips; her shoes were cracked and too large; an enormous limp willow plume topped her off. The Judge lifted a black-robed arm—I could not hear what he said.

"Soliciting," said the hoarse voice of the policeman, "Sixth Av'nue near Twenty-third——"

"Ten days on the Island—next case!"

The girl threw back her head and laughed insolently.

"You ——" she shrilled, and laughed again. But the Cop thrust her violently before him, and they passed out at the other door.

And I went forward with her laughter still sounding in my ears.

The Judge was writing somthing on a piece of paper. Without looking up he snapped:

"What's the charge, officer?"

"Resisting an officer," said the Cop surlily. "I told him to move on an' he says he wouldn't——"

"Hum," murmured the Judge abstractedly, still writing. "Wouldn't, eh? Well, what have you got to say for yourself?"

I did not answer.

"Won't talk, eh? Well, I guess you get——"

Then he looked up, nodded, and smiled.

"Hello, Reed!" he said. He venomously regarded the Cop. "Next time you pull a friend of mine——" suggestively, he left the threat unfinished. Then to me, "Want to sit up on the Bench for a while?"

—April 1913

MARY FIELD
Bums—A Story

He came slouching out of McDougal Street. The battered toes of his shoes pointed in no particular direction. His head hung. His eyes roved. Now and then as he shuffled along he stopped to cough and spit in the gutter. On the corner he hesitated, stood still, then as if blown by a gust of wind, he drifted into Washington Square. The park benches were pretty well occupied though it was not yet nine o'clock. He recognized the men who sprawled over the seats as members of his fraternity. They wore no emblem, yet he knew them as fraternity brothers, knew them by their rusty clothes, by the glance that flashed the password "out-of-work."

Chucky thought at first he would sit down by McGillvery, but McGillvery was licking his lips as if he had had a breakfast, so Chucky changed his mind and scuffled along down the path to an unoccupied bench. Back of the bench, tied to a tree, was a wire basket for waste paper. Over it was a sign that said "For a clean city." Chucky pulled out one of the newspapers, a yesterday's copy, and slouched down on the seat. He hunted out the Want columns. It made him think he was looking for work. It was his last effort at respectability.

"Wanted Help—Male." Chucky was glad he had gone three years to Public School and wasn't like the ignorant old Dago across the path. He could read. He straightened his thin shoulders a bit with the sense of superior education, and as he swept one eye down the column of wants, he watched with the other what he thought to be the envious glance of the Dago. "Wanted an artist, an acrobat, an automobile hand," on down through the A's into the B's, he read slowly. Queer it was, how many barbers were wanted, and box-makers, and bunchers for cigars. Why hadn't he been a barber, or an artist? It was just as Sandy said, "If ye're a carpenter, it's ditch-diggers is wanted; if ye're a ditch-digger, it's carpenters they's hollerin' after."

Ah, here was what he was looking for! He pounced upon the tiny letters. "Wanted, a non-union baker."

"Alright! That's me!"

He read on. "Must be single and ready to leave city."

"The job's all square on the non-union part and the bakin', but what's a feller to do with a wife?"

Somewhere, he didn't know just where, he had a wife. He was married. It was an excuse for not taking the job—and no railway fare! That was another reason. This looking for a job was funny business! Seemed like everybody had work who didn't want it, or wanted work who didn't have it!

Listlessly he let the paper drop. He had made his usual morning effort. He had tried to find work. He wasn't wholly a bum,—yet. He leaned forward, feeling a little weak, put his elbows on his knees and sunk his head in his open hands. He didn't think. He didn't muse on the problem of unemployment. He didn't dream of anything higher, or better, or different. He didn't feel sad or happy. He had drifted on the surface of existence out of the struggling current into a kind of stagnant marsh. Hunger, the cough, cold,—these were his only sensations of pain. Food, whiskey, the sun,—these his sensations of joy. And in the great city all six sensations could be more or less easily obtained, especially the first three. So Chucky was not thinking of any white-haired mother who made crullers, and put a candle in the window at night, and sang at the organ, "Where is my wandering boy?" The fact was, he didn't remember whether his mother's hair was white or red, or even whether she had any hair. Her very existence was dubious. Nor was his conscience troubling him about the whereabouts of his wife and children. They had drifted beyond memory.

He watched without interest some silly ants tugging with all their tiny might at a dead fly. After ten minutes of their valuable short lives they gave it up, and in solemn procession disappeared into a crack. For want of anything else to do, Chucky mashed one of them with his dilapidated boot. He followed vaguely the whirl of a dying leaf as it danced a last dance.

Legs passed him—legs with creases in the trousers. These legs always walked briskly, crushing the fallen leaves. They always terminated in a pair of well blacked boots. Other legs passed. They scuffed along slowly, and out of the frayed pants always protruded a pair of battered shoes like his own. Women's skirts swished before him. Without so much as glancing up, he knew the waist and hat that went with each skirt. Little legs scampered by. Many were as thin as the twigs overhead, a few were chubby. Now and then an iron brace, a crutch clicked along on the pavement. (Chucky didn't call this knowledge of life and of clothes, knowledge. His knowledge was the baking

Drawn by John Sloan, May 1913

"Circumstances" Alter Cases

"Positively disgusting! It's an outrage to public decency to allow such exposure on the streets."

trade. He called that only knowledge, which can be bought and sold.)

Now a peculiar pair of legs was approaching— the kind in the creased trousers, but there was something wrong, for they did not walk briskly. They paused, and Chucky felt someone sit down beside him at the other end of the bench. Out of the corner of an eye he saw him take a paper from his pocket and open it, fluttering out its wide pages like wings. Then the man coughed. The cough Chucky instantly recognized. It spoke the language of his fraternity. It made Chucky straighten up slowly, and look stealthily at his bench-mate. Legs

with creased trousers didn't usually cough like that. Chucky took a good look at him. Correct! Hat brushed; face smooth shaven; collar clean; tie, vest, and coat with the shoulders padded; and finally, proof perfect that the stranger belonged to the Society of Creased Trousers—a watch-fob! Then with the same sweeping glance that took in these outer items of respectability, Chucky noted, not without surprise, that the stranger had spread the pages of his paper open to the Want Columns.

"Damn it!" thought Chucky, spitting to relieve his perplexed mind. "What's the bull? Ten o'clock, creased trousers, want columns, watch-fob, cough! He must be one o' dem high-up rummies—or mebbe a gumshoe!"

At the thought of the stranger's being a detective, Chucky slowly shook himself together. He moved like an old, mangy dog who loathes to leave a sunny spot. He edged toward the end of the seat —but—well—he would wait a minute. There was plenty of time. He guessed they weren't lookin' fer *him,* anyway.

"Hello, pard," said the stranger quietly.

"'Lo," growled Chucky, sidling still farther away. He wasn't used to having well fitted trousers address him—excepting blue ones that said "move on."

"There doesn't seem to be much doing for anyone but canvassers and messenger boys!"

"Yup," admitted Chucky. Then he had a new idea. Perhaps the guy was off in the head and— that watch chain! Slick Goldman's was a good fence. With five dollars one could live. He thought of food. He felt a little dizzy. He slid back a bit nearer the stranger.

"Y'ain't lookin' fer a job?" he ventured.

"Sure."

"I see they's jobs repairin' leaky roofs, or sellin' sewin' machines."

"Nothing doing, pard." The stranger folded the paper neatly and put it back in his coat pocket. With the folding of the paper, a terrible fear clutched Chucky's heart. Maybe the guy would be going, and the fob!—Again he felt the dizziness, again the cough. This time the man coughed too, as racking a cough as Chucky's.

"Fierce, old pard, isn't it?" panted the stranger when he got a little breath.

"I'm thinkin' o' goin' Sout' fer my helt dis Fall!" grinned Chucky. "I read a avertisement wot says 'Out o' blizzards into Bliss,' an' you don't need nuttin' but railroad fare an' hotel money!"

The stranger turned sidewise toward Chucky, crossed his knees, put his elbow on the back of the seat, and rested his head on his palm.

"Tell me," he said, "how'd you get here?"

Chucky, suspicious of all the world, looked up into his face. The eyes looking straight into his were blue and serious. Fine lines, like those in a kindly old man's face, radiated from the corners of these eyes. Two deep lines as if cut in the flesh ran from the nostrils to the corners of the mouth. Yet this man was young—not much older than Chucky.

"How'd I get here? Come up McDougal," an-swered Chucky, avoiding the glance and the question. His eyes involuntarily sought the fob. It held him hypnotized. Instinctively he located the park policeman. It meant breakfasts and whiskeys for an eternity.

"How *did* you get here?" insisted the stranger, his eyes compelling an answer. "What's your trade?"

"Baker."

"Always worked at it?"

"Twenty years! Ever since I was a kid."

"Bad luck?"

Chucky was silent. His past was not vivid. It was hard to isolate any facts. Hunger, cold, the cough,—these were the chief memories.

"Married?"

"Yup."

"Children?"

"Yup. Say, y' takin' de census?"

"No," said the stranger. "I'm a bum, like yourself, and I'm taking notes."

"Crazy for sure," Chucky mused. Crazy guys were easy! Whiskey and pot-roast he'd buy with the five dollars——

"Where are they—the children?"

"Dunno. Some died, I guess. Never had steady work. Got the cough young. The bosses wouldn't hire me. Las' place I worked—God, they're all alike! Bakin' bread in a basement. 'Twas wetter'n a pump, and hotter'n hell, and col' when yer come out, and the flour a flyin' in yer face, and I took sick, couldn't do a lick o' work fer a year. Got kind o' used to settin' aroun', and the ol' woman done scrubbin' an' "—he stopped. His breath came laboriously. The stranger's grave eyes were still upon him. They compelled him. They drew him. He was a "fer-sure queer guy."

"And so—," helped the stranger.

"And so, one day, I come home, been trampin' to fin' work, and the ol' woman and the kids is gone. Left word she'd got sick o' s'portin' me. S'pose she had. So I took to settin' aroun'. Ain't so strong anyway, but if I had work—I was lookin' fer a job this mornin'. But they say there's a law now as to employin' lungers in bakeries. But wots a lunger goin' to do, damn it!"

"A baker, you say?"

"Yup."

Chucky leaned back against the seat, spread out his thin, dirty fingers beside him and looked up pensively at the leafless trees.

"Where'd you work?"

"Ev'rywhere." He made a circle with his head

to indicate the whole city. "Soon's I'd get t' coughin', the boss says me fer the fresh air!"

"Ever work at Bradfield's?"

For answer Chucky laughed—a strange, distorted sound, the laugh of a gargoyle.

"Bradfield's? That's were I took the sickness first! That's the hell o' the basement I'm speakin' about particular, and that's where when I come back to the boss, he says its nixie on the lungers. I tol' him to go to hell, and he hollers at me an'—" The rest of the story came gurgling a few words at a time between spasms that shook the ill-fitting clothes.

And now it was the stranger's turn to laugh; not the careless laugh that usually went with creased trousers and watch fobs; not even the coarse laugh that gurgled out of a whiskey bottle,—a grim, horrible laugh that made Chucky shiver and look almost in terror over his shoulder. Once he had believed in the devil.

"So you worked at Bradfield's?"

"Y'bet. Damn 'em!" He was planning how he could end matters; how he could grab that fob and run.

"Funny, ain't it!" grimaced the stranger, unconsciously reflecting Chucky's rhetoric. "You ain't got a job because you're sick and poor, and I ain't got a job because I'm sick and rich. Never did anything in my whole life; just bum around. Didn't need to; father made piles of money. I was wild, you know, like all young chaps without work and with plenty of cash. Got the cough, not from working, like you, but from *not* working, as you might say—I'm sick of loafing. I'd like a job all right. Tired of being bored. But I'm like you, see? I'm a lunger, and they can't use me in my father's office any more than they could down in the cellar with the bakers. I'm a bum." The mockery had faded from his eyes, the laugh died on his lips. "I'm a bum," he whispered softly.

"Damn it!" said Chucky sympathetically. "It's a hell o' a worruld."

"So you worked at Bradfield's?" Then before Chucky could "damn 'em" again' he added, "I'm Bradfield's son."

With a gasp Chucky drew in his breath. He felt as if he were being dropped twenty stories in an elevator. When he recovered, the stranger was standing up in front of him, and Chucky's chance at the watch-fob was gone. The stranger drew something from a side pocket, and extended his arm.

"I'd like to make sure you have something hot for dinner to-day," he said.

As Chucky clutched a half a dollar in his scrawny paw, the other bum walked away toward the avenue.

"I wisht I hadn't been so dam' slow," mumbled Chucky.

—May 1913

HELEN FORBES
The Hunky Woman

The kitchen clock struck five. Down in the cement-floored laundry the tired washerwoman straightened her bent shoulders while she counted the slow strokes, then she went on with her work of sprinkling the freshly dried linen. When the last damp roll was placed in the clothes-basket she covered the whole with a wide Turkish towel, shoved it under the table and went upstairs.

Mrs. Atwood was waiting to give her the day's wages; this perfect housekeeper made it her duty to pay *personally* every worker she employed, using that point of contact as an opening wedge to an intimate knowledge of their conditions and needs.

"You'll be here early tomorrow for the ironing, won't you, Annie?" She spoke in a tone that invited confidence.

"Yes." And the stubby fingers snatched the money from Mrs. Atwood's outstretched hand.

The woman did not lift her eyes high enough to see the smile, her ears did not catch the friendly tone, and she turned away with a movement that seemed sullenly abrupt. She threw her shawl over her shoulders, twitched it close at her throat, and without a word of farewell opened the back door and went out into the foggy night.

Mrs. Atwood stood at the window and watched the squat ugly figure as it stumped down the narrow path to the alley. There was something stolid, something typical of the woman's race in the very way her dingy skirt drabbled over the rain-soaked grass.

This creature baffled all Mrs. Atwood's attempts at establishing a bond of sympathy. Many a Bridget and Maggie had profited by their mistress's advice and by the very tangible assistance that never failed to accompany it. But Annie Szorza, this woman from Central Europe, was beyond anything in Mrs. Atwood's previous experience. It seemed impossible to touch the inner consciousness of this stolid lump, this self-regulating machine that arrived at the kitchen door promptly on Monday and Tuesday mornings, coming from no known place and working all day long without complaint, without any sign of enjoyment.

Peasant-fashion, Annie Szorza walked home from her work. The lighted cars flashed by as she plodded along the wet pavement, yet it did not occur to her that she might stop one of them and ride. Shaking with the chill of the penetrating fog and drizzle, she shuffled through the mud and wet, her eyes fixed on the ground, just as a tired horse hangs his head as he draws the empty wagon back to the barns at the end of the day.

Her home was the upper floor of a two-storied shack that occupied a corner of a great tract of waste land lying on the main thoroughfare between the business section of the city and the fashionable residences. Behind the unpainted shanty the hill rose steeply, as barren as a hillside in Thibet; in front of it, but partly hidden beneath

the bluff, ran the river. And crowning the desolation, the house was propped on either side by gigantic billboards, hideous, with glaring advertisements. Yet the shanty owed its existence to these monstrosities; without their help it would have tumbled into ruins, it was so old and ramshackle.

When Annie reached the house she stopped downstairs at Mrs. Tapolsky's to get her children. The babies were glad to see her, but she did not lean over to kiss them; she was too tired. Carrying the smaller child and pushing little Annie ahead of her she stumbled up the unlighted stairs to her own tenement.

Then the last section of her day began. She put the baby in the center of the great bed that filled half the room and proceeded to get supper. Experience had taught little Annie what to do.

Drawn by Maurice Becker, February 1913

Beware of Pickpockets

She seated herself on a box under the table where she was out of the way of her mother's blundering haste, and found consolation in her thumb.

At last everything was ready.

It was the baby's turn first. From his post on the bed he watched the warm milk being poured into his cup and set up an eager howl. He was hungry.

A sharp rap sounded on the door and the knob rattled. Annie put the milk back on the stove and hurried to see who was outside.

Pressing her back with the opening door, a policeman pushed his way into the room.

"You're here, are you," and the man strode heavily across the room and flung open the cupboard door. "Where's your man?"

At all times English speech came slowly to Annie and now she could not frame an articulate reply. The muttered syllables might have been Ancient Egyptian for all the policeman understood.

"Where's your man? Answer!"

"My man he ain't here. I dunno."

"Well, I got you anyway. Put on your bonnet and come along."

"What you want?" asked Annie. Then she added, "I don't work no more to-night."

The man burst into a roar. "She thinks I've got her a job!"

"What you want?" she repeated anxiously.

"You can guess all right. Your carryings-on with your old man has been found out. His brother-in-law's come over from the old country and caught him, see? Next time you'd better make yourself safe with a real husband."

The woman caught the meaning of the words. "He is my husband!" she cried indignantly. "The priest—"

"That'll do! Come along!" and he seized her by the arm.

Annie tried to pull herself loose. "My babies! I ain't fed my babies yet. By and by I go."

The man's voice changed to a roar. "When I say come I mean it! I can't be waiting here all night. You'll have to leave the kids."

Although the baby had been screaming all this time, little Annie had kept quiet, watching with frightened eyes. She knew that crying would do her no good; she could have nothing to eat until her brother had his milk. But when she saw her mother pushed toward the stairs she realized there was no immediate prospect of supper for either of them and she burst into a yell that drowned the baby's cry.

"Oh, my babies, my babies!" sobbed the mother over and over again. "My babies ain't had nothing to eat!"

As the patrol-wagon jolted over the cobbles she entreated incessantly, "I go back one little minute, please! Just one little minute!"

It was not until she reached the station-house that she accepted the inevitable, but all night long she sat on the edge of her cot swaying back and forth in her misery. "Oh, my babies, my babies!"

Her husband was routed out from some hiding place and after a few days the case came up for trial. The indignant brother-in-law proved that Szorza had left a wife and family in Europe, but since Annie was not responsible in any way she was dismissed with kindly warnings and advice.

But Annie was absorbed in the hope of seeing the children. Once or twice she had tried to tell the matron of her trouble, but she began so stupidly and used such broken English that she failed to make herself understood.

"Of course you left your babies. You'd not be bringing them to jail would you?"

After that Annie could do nothing but wait. Probably Mrs. Tapolsky was taking care of them; she would come up to see why they were crying so long. But Mrs. Tapolsky was an old woman and it tired her to be with the children even a few hours. What had she done with them?

In that city of coal-dust and fog, night often prolongs itself far into the morning hours and at eleven o'clock Annie walked home beneath lighted streetlamps. With the accumulated energy of her days in prison, she pushed forward in a straight line, men and women standing aside as she pushed on, regardless of the rules of the road. Teamsters drew in their horses directly over her head, boys with heavy pushcarts dug their heels between the cobbles and threw their weight backwards until they resembled acrobats, automobiles swerved and she escaped by a hair's breadth.

Panting, she stopped outside Mrs. Tapolsky's door to listen and catch her breath; then she rushed into the room without knocking.

Mrs. Tapolsky rose, pressing her hand to her heart, while her spool and scissors clattered to the floor. "What do you mean, scaring me so? Where have you been, you wicked woman?"

"My babies! Where are they?"

"Eh! What do you care? You do not deserve to know. They are not here."

"Upstairs then." And she was trampling over-

Drawn by Boardman Robinson, May 1915

"Wha's the celebration about, M's Milligan?"
"Sure, me boy's comin' home today. He was sentenced to ten years in the penitentiary, but he got three years off for good conduct."
"Ah! I wish I had a son like that!"

head before Mrs. Tapolsky guessed what she meant.

The upper floor was as empty as the room below. Back she came to Mrs. Tapolsky. "Where are they?" Her round dark eyes looked out of a face green with weariness and fear and anxiety.

"Why did you leave them?" And not until Annie's story was done would the stolid old woman tell a word of what had happened. She began at last, speaking slowly and severely, as though she still held Annie responsible for what had happened.

Mrs. Tapolsky had gone around the corner to buy her supper when the patrol-wagon came and the street had calmed down before she returned, and though she heard the children crying, she was too busy to care to learn what was the matter with them. At supper her husband complained of the noise, but she reminded him of how often their own babies had cried themselves to sleep. By and by the house was still.

In the middle of the night she was awakened by the children's screaming; it seemed strange that she did not hear the thud of their mother's feet. As she sat up in bed, leaning on her elbow to listen and wonder, the boy stopped crying. He broke short off, with a curious sob. And little Annie's cry became fainter and fainter until she too was quiet again.

Early next morning Mrs. Tapolsky went upstairs; she felt sure that Annie was ill and in need of help. Finding the door unlocked, she entered.

Little Annie was lying on the floor, and on the bed, thrown back among the pillows, was the baby, dead.

The neighbors looked down upon Hunkies, so nobody gossiped with the Tapolskys, and they remained in ignorance of what had happened to Mrs. Szorza. As the hours passed by, and then the days, their fears changed to righteous anger; surely nothing but deliberate desertion was keeping her away. On the third day Tapolsky notified the city and they carried off the baby; he said it was his own grandchild, to avoid explanations. Mrs. Tapolsky wrapped the little girl in a corner of her shawl and took her to the Associated Charities.

That was all. Mrs. Tapolsky made no attempt to soften the ugly story, and she stopped speaking without a word of sympathy, waiting to see what the mother would do, and looking at her curiously.

That evening Mrs. Atwood told her perplexity to her husband. "There," she said, "I might as well try to be nice to the ironingboard. I'd get exactly the same response."

"Then what's the use of bothering? You can't understand her because there's nothing to understand. These Hunkies are all alike; as much emotion in a Hunky as there is in a bump on a log."

"But she's such a good laundress."

"No doubt. That's what she's meant for. Hunkies are brought over here to work; they're only half human."

While she listened Annie sat perfectly quiet. It seemed as if she did not understand. But when she saw that Mrs. Tapolsky had no more to tell, she rose and went out. Mrs. Tapolsky took her shawl from the hook and followed, instantly realizing what her neighbor had in mind. The two were alike in that action took the place of speech. Together they climbed the rickety flight of stairs that led over Grimes Hill to Dover Street and the Temporary Home.

When little Annie was given back to her, the mother held her close, as if she could never bear to put her down again, but when they were out of sight of the institution she gave the child to Mrs. Tapolsky.

"Take her," she said, "I go find work by Mrs. Atwood." And half-running, she hurried down the street.

Without really understanding how kind Mrs. Atwood meant to be, Annie did know that of all her employers she was the fairest and most considerate, and now the woman turned to her in this great trouble.

"Have you been sick?" asked Mrs. Atwood.

"Naw. I been to jail."

"To jail!" echoed the horrified woman. "Mercy!"

But Annie interrupted. She had no notion of the best way to tell what had happened; it seemed to her that the result of her imprisonment was the only important thing now. In her mind the tragedy completely outweighed the injustice. "My baby die." Her face was hard and set in her respectful effort not to break down in Mrs. Atwood's presence.

This statement, following on the heels of the previous announcement, suggested but one thing to Mrs. Atwood. "You killed your baby?" Her voice was terrible.

"Yes!" Annie shrank back against the wall and covered her face. And then her courage and anger came back together. "No! That policeman!"

As she listened to the broken explanation, mere scraps and hints of unintelligible horrors, Mrs. Atwood felt annoyed at what was plainly a badly made up lie; such terrible things could not happen. At last she said, "There is no need of telling me any more. You are not speaking the truth."

The heavy lines in Annie's dull face moved strangely; square and stupid, with short nose and wide nostrils, it resembled the face of an ape. The sight of her was repulsive.

Mrs. Atwood continued, turning away her eyes. "How could I ever trust you, after the way you failed me last week? You left the clothes all damp. They might have been ruined."

"I don't do that once more."

"How could I tell that? I'm sorry for you if you need work and can't get it, but I can't think of trying you again." Then Mrs. Atwood's voice grew colder still. "And I will not have anyone in my house who has been in jail."

"That's what my man did, not me!"

It was a cry of despair, but Mrs. Atwood did not recognize it.

"I'm not so certain that it was altogether your husband's fault. Things like that don't happen in this country. Besides, there is nothing more to be said about it; I have engaged someone else."

The back door closed and Annie found herself on the steps outside.

"I told you," said Mr. Atwood that evening, "those Hunkies are just animals."

"I guess you're right," sighed Mrs. Atwood.

—May 1916

IV
Moral
Issues

THE common denominator of the material in this section is that while all these subjects (except the Negro) were matters of vital concern to *The Masses,* they were of no interest whatsoever to orthodox socialists. The official position on prostitution, for example, was that it originated in economic want and would vanish when decent wages for decent work prevailed. *The Masses* paid lip service to this principle but was never able to adopt the matter-of-fact position entirely. The editors apparently had little contact with real, live prostitutes and entertained slightly romantic, faintly exotic notions about them. Selling one's flesh, they seemed secretly to believe, was not quite the same as selling one's labor.

A more middle-class and respectable enthusiasm of *The Masses* was its passionate commitment to feminism. By 1912 the feminist drive for "Votes for Women" and "Equal Pay for Equal Work" had become respectable, even if most Americans were still dubious about their desirability. But *The Masses'* feminism had far less mundane origins. To the editors free love, not votes for women, was the burning question. Unfortunately, the lamentable condition of public opinion made it impossible for *The Masses* really to come to grips with the problem. Its high-minded sensuality found expression in glowing nudes and erotic poetry—a form of expression which protected it from Anthony Comstock and the Post Office while communicating its real feelings to friend and foe alike.

The group's real problem was that its leading spirits were mostly men, and so the male feminist's point of view dominated. Max Eastman was a feminist before he was a socialist; one of his first public acts was to organize the Men's League for Women Suffrage. Floyd Dell's first book was *Women as World Builders* (1913). But Dell's relationship to the Woman Movement was more complicated, and he later developed serious reservations about the whole business. He was never as uncritical of feminism as many of his admirers thought. At the peak of his Village days he wrote a one-act play, *What Eight Million Women Want* (which took off from Rheta Childe Dorr's popular book of that title), that raised some questions about feminist motivations.

In 1926 Dell published *Intellectual Vagabondage,* in which he pointed out the crucial difference between the male and female approach to women's rights. Men admired emancipated women because they were more like men, that is, "more interested in ideas, more honest, and less finicking." Men looked forward to the emergence of woman as the Glorious Playfellow, equally at home in bed and boardroom. Women, on the other hand, were more ambivalent because men were not only the favored sex whom they were struggling to equal, but also the major obstacle to the realization of their ambitions. Feminists could hardly help being anti-masculine to some extent, and this became more apparent after they won the vote. Thus, while the victorious suffrage campaign was the high point of the Woman Movement, it was a demoralizing triumph, because it removed the one point on which feminists could agree and exposed the confusion which the suffragists' popular front had temporarily obscured. A case in point was the Woman's party, whose uncompromising tactics helped win the vote. In the 1920's the Woman's party turned cranky and sour and soon was attacking protective labor legislation for women on the grounds that it was discriminatory. What had been the advance guard of feminism in the Progressive Era ended up in the reactionary camp during the twenties.

If there was irony in one of *The Masses'* more straightforward causes turning out to be so tangled and complex, then its stand on birth control was just as productive of misunderstandings. Planned Parenthood, or Neo-Malthusianism as it was often called, was a touchy, dangerous subject from the very beginning. In our overpopulated world even Roman Catholics have been known to speak well of family planning, but before the wars it was almost safer to peddle dope than contraceptives. Both Margaret Sanger and Emma Goldman became convinced of the need for birth control through their nursing experiences. Both sought to relieve the misery of the poor by eliminating the destructive physical and economic consequences of excessive child-bearing. Both studied contraceptive techniques in Europe and sought to awaken the radical conscience of America to the need for birth control. There the resemblance ends.

[179]

Emma Goldman had too many irons in the fire to concentrate her energies on birth control alone, although she rendered yeoman service to the cause as her speech in this section shows. Margaret Sanger began her crusade with a series of articles on feminine hygiene in the socialist *New York Call.* This failed, largely because she was cutting too close to the bone, and one morning she opened the *Call* to discover a blank space under her title "What Every Young Girl Should Know" except for the words "NOTHING, by Order of the Post Office Department."

Mrs. Sanger's next step was to start her own magazine, *The Woman Rebel,* a highly idiosyncratic periodical whose brief career was equally unrewarding. More frustration ensued when the birth-control clinics she opened in the slums were closed by the police and neither the urban masses nor the Socialist party rallied to her side.

Since the poor had let her down, Mrs. Sanger turned increasingly to the middle- and upper-class women who were most receptive to her appeals. But they had more reason for aiding her than a desire to uplift the demoralized poor. They were attracted by the greater sexual freedom which contraception promised them, and, as Mabel Dodge tells us, Mrs. Sanger was a persuasive advocate of the Gospel of Sex. The sexual bohemianism which was to enter bourgeois life after the war was just beginning to make itself felt. Feminism started it; psychoanalysis was to supply it with a powerful rationale. In time, middle-class women, assisted by the flood of guide books to better living through intercourse—the production of which has today become a minor industry in America—would believe that orgasm was not only a possibility but a right. Margaret Sanger anticipated this surge of interest by some years. While her pioneering status was a source of much discomfort in the beginning, the ultimate success of her movement was assured.

A finer sex life was not something to which *The Masses* could object. What must have distressed the editors, however, was that as Mrs. Sanger became identified with women of means in pursuit of a more private vision, she herself inevitably became less radical and less concerned with the plight of the toiling masses who had been the original source of her inspiration. The crusade for birth control finally became a self-propelled vehicle which needed little help and less sympathy from the Left.

The one aspect of *The Masses* which is most likely to shock modern readers is its hugely irreverent, not to say sacrilegious, treatment of religion. The workings of a half-century have drawn the sting from much of what the magazine had to say about art and life, yet the old force still adheres to its anti-clericalism. This not only lets us feel a touch of the striking power which *The Masses* had for its contemporaries but also tells us something important about ourselves.

Although we often think of the United States as having grown progressively more secular since the fundamentalist struggles of the 1920's, in many ways organized religion commands a greater influence now than it did in *The Masses'* time. In recent years church attendance has grown more rapidly than the population, while immigrant groups who seemed to be moving away from their historic churches have in the third generation come back to them again. We see evidences of the increased social influence of religion on every hand—the insertion of "under God" into the Pledge of Allegiance, the virulent public reaction to the Supreme Court's prayer decision, and the persecution of Mrs. Murray for her strident atheism are only a few examples of religion's new power. The postwar religious revival may not signify a renewal of the ancient faiths, but it certainly does mean that organized religion is more important today than it has been for many years. Despite the liberal, ecumenical flavor of the revival, the persistence of socio-religious groups as an increasingly consequential part of the national life has led some sociologists to believe that we may be moving toward a compartmentalized rather than a pluralistic society. Gerhard Lenski in *The Religious Factor* (1961), for instance, argues that a heightened sense of religious loyalty might well lead to a diminished concern with spiritual and ethical values, and an exaggeration of the political elements from which few churches are entirely free.

This does not suggest that a new age of repression is at hand, but only that *The Masses'* treatment of religion is dated mainly in its particulars. The magazine did not shock the secular audience for which it was designed, but it profoundly disturbed that fraction of the general public which was exposed to it. *The Masses* was irreverent to the point of blasphemy, but it was part of the well-established tradition of nineteenth-century skepticism which in America owed more to Robert Ingersoll than to Karl Marx. Now that a kind of public piety has returned, while the old free-thought movement has largely passed away, the sacrilegious quality of *The Masses* is, perhaps, all the more potent. The major religions have changed a great deal in the half-century since *The Masses* leveled its guns against them. Yet in a very real way there is now less room in America for the straightforward anti-clericalism which the magazine served up. Consequently, to many of us *The Masses* on religion is fresher, bolder, and more exciting than ever it was in its own day.

Time has not been so kind (if that's the word) to *The Masses* in the matter of race relations. Even the moderately perceptive reader who leafs casually through the magazine will be astonished by the profusion of fat mammies, dancing bucks, and fuzzy-headed, watermelon-eating black children. Especially in its early years the Negro was a comic staple which *The Masses* used again and again in what strikes modern sensibilities as a peculiarly tasteless manner. That this well-established tradition might have deeply offended Negroes never occurred to the editors, nor, it must be emphasized, did it to the overwhelming majority of their fellow Americans.

The truth is that, despite the efforts of some historians to rehabilitate the Progressive Era, it was not a good time for Negroes. The Civil Rights movement as we know it did not exist, and the newly formed NAACP's slender resources were wholly committed to fighting the most elemental brutalities and prejudices. Race leaders had neither time nor strength to waste on little magazines like *The Masses,* whose editors were, in any case, sympathetic to the aspirations of colored people.

The reasons for *The Masses'* lack of awareness are easy to locate. Racism was so prevalent during these years that merely avoiding the infection was itself something of an achievement. Men of good will were preoccupied with the plight of the immigrant masses who filled the great cities and were lightning rods for all that was base and ignoble in the Northern character. There were few Negroes in the cities and it was easy to see their difficulties as a separate and largely Southern problem. The urban Negro was never more invisible.

In viewing *The Masses'* humorous material on the Negro, then, it is important to bear in mind that the staff was very far from thinking it damaging to the cause of racial equality. Most of it drew on a rich comic tradition which almost no one regarded as offensive, and to which Negro leaders were not in the habit of objecting. Max Eastman knew Walter White and other prominent Negroes, and to his knowledge none of them found *The Masses* at all disagreeable. When Claude McKay, the West Indian poet who became an editor of the *Liberator,* joined the group he was much impressed with their easy, natural response to him as a man and not just as a man of color. But their color-blindness, which in these racially conscious days is almost enviable, was the obverse of their insensitivity. Not until the wartime labor shortages created black ghettos in the North was the Left as a whole to discover the Negro.

The Prostitute

[*As socialists the* Masses *group dutifully maintained the Marxist view that prostitution resulted from capitalist exploitation which forced the daughters of the poor into the only unskilled labor where work was regular and wages high. However, as romantics, the contributors tended to idealize the prostitute, and as bohemians to see her as the vital antithesis to bourgeois morality. All of these strains are apparent in the following items.*]

JOHN REED

A Daughter of the Revolution

That night there was one of those Paris rains, which never seem to wet one as other rains do. We sat on the *terrasse* of the Rotonde, at the corner table—it was a warm night, though November—Fred, Marcelle and I, sipping a Dubonnet. The cafés all closed at eight sharp because of the war, and we used to stay until then almost every night before we went to dinner.

Next to us was a young French officer with his head done up in a bandage, and his arm comfortably around Jeanne's green-caped shoulder. Beatrice and Alice were farther down along under the glare of the yellow lights. Behind us we could peek through a slit in the window-curtain and survey the smoke-filled room inside, an uproarious band of men sandwiched between girls, beating on the table and singing, the two old Frenchmen at their tranquil chess-game, an absorbed student writing a letter home, his *amie's* head on his shoulder, five utter strangers and the waiter listening breathlessly to the tales of a muddy-legged soldier back from the front. . . .

The yellow lights flooded us, and splashed the shining black pavement with gold; human beings with umbrellas flowed by in a steady stream; a ragged old wreck of a man poked furtively for cigarette-butts under our feet; out in the roadway the shuffling feet of men marching fell unheeded upon our accustomed ears, and dripping slanted bayonets passed athwart a beam of light from across the Boulevard Montparnasse.

This year all the girls at the Rotonde dressed alike. They had little round hats, hair cut short, low-throated waists and long capes down to their feet, the ends tossed over their shoulders Spanish-

fashion. Marcelle was the image of the others. Besides, her lips were painted scarlet, her cheeks dead white, and she talked obscenities when she wasn't on her dignity, and sentimentalities when she was. She had regaled us both with the history of her very rich and highly respectable family, of the manner of her tragic seduction by a Duke, of her innate virtue—and had remarked proudly that she was no common ordinary street-walker. . . .

At this particular instant she was interlarding a running fire of highly-flavored comment upon what passed before her eyes with appeals for money in a harshened little voice; and I thought to myself that we had got to the bottom of Marcelle. Her comments upon things and persons were pungent, vigorous, original—but they palled after while; a strain of recklessness and unashamed love of life held only a little longer. Marcelle was already soiled with too much handling. . . .

We heard a violent altercation, and a tall girl with a bright orange sweater came out from the café, followed by a waiter gesticulating and exclaiming:

"But the eight anisettes which you ordered, *nom de Dieu!*"

"I have told you I would pay," she shrilled over her shoulder. "I am going to the Dome for some money," and she ran across the shiny street. The waiter stood looking after her, moodily jingling the change in his pockets.

"No use waiting," shouted Marcelle, "There is another door to the Dome on the Rue Delambre!" But the waiter paid no attention; he had paid the *caisse* for the drinks. And, as a matter of fact, the girl never reappeared.

"That is an old trick," said Marcelle to us. "It is easy when you have no money to get a drink from the waiters, for they dare not ask for your money until afterward. It is a good thing to know now in time of war, when the men are so few and so poor." . . .

"But the waiter!" objected Fred. "He must make his living!"

Marcelle shrugged. "And we ours," she said.

"There used to be a *belle type* around the Quarter," she continued after a minute, "who called herself Marie. She had beautiful hair—*épatante*, —and she loved travelling. . . . Once she found herself on a Mediterranean boat bound for Egypt without a *sou*,—nothing except the clothes on her back. A monsieur passed her as she leaned against the rail, and said, 'You have marvellous hair, mademoiselle.'

" 'I will sell it to you for a hundred francs,' she flashed back. And she cut off all her beautiful hair and went to Cairo, where she met an English lord. . . ."

The waiter heaved a prodigious sigh, shook his head sadly, and went indoors. We were silent, and thought of dinner. The rain fell.

I don't know how it happened, but Fred began to whistle absent-mindedly the *Carmagnole*. I wouldn't have noticed it except that I heard a voice chime in, and looked around to see the wounded French officer, whose arm had fallen idly from the shoulder of Jeanne, staring blankly across the pavement, and humming the *Carmagnole*. What visions was he seeing, this sensitive-faced youth in the uniform of his country's army, singing the song of revolt! Even as I looked, he caught himself up short, looked self-conscious and startled, glanced swiftly at us, and rose quickly to his feet, dragging Jeanne with him.

At the same instant Marcelle clutched Fred roughly by the arm.

"It's *défendu*—you'll have us all pinched," she cried, with something so much stronger than fear in her eyes that I was interested. "And, besides, don't sing those dirty songs. They are revolutionary—they are sung by *voyous*—poor people—ragged men——"

"Then you are not a revolutionist yourself?" I asked.

"I? *B'en* no, I swear to you!" she shook her head passionately. "The *méchants*, the villains, who want to overturn everything——!" Marcelle shivered.

"Look here, Marcelle! Are you happy in this world the way it is? What does the System do for you, except to turn you out on the street to sell yourself?" Fred was launched now on a boiling flood of propaganda. "When the red day comes, I know which side of the Barricades I shall be on——!"

Marcelle began to laugh. It was a bitter laugh. It was the first time I had ever seen her un-self-conscious.

"*Ta gueule*, my friend," she interrupted rudely. "I know that talk! I have heard it since I was so high. . . . I *know!*" She stopped and laughed to herself, and wrenched out—"My grandfather was shot against a wall at Père Lachaise for carrying a red flag in the Commune in 1870." She started, looked at us shame-facedly, and grinned. "There, you see I come of a worthless family. . . ."

"Your grandfather!" shouted Fred.

"Pass for my grandfather," said Marcelle indifferently. "Let the crazy, dirty-handed old fool rest in his grave. I have never spoken of him before, and I shall burn no candles for his soul. . . ."

Fred seized her hand. He was exalted. "God bless your grandfather!"

With the quick wit of her profession, she divined that, for some mysterious reason, she had pleased. For answer she began to sing in a low voice the last lines of the *Internationale*.

"*C'est la lutte finale*——" She coquetted with Fred.

"Tell us more about your grandfather," I asked.

"There is no more to tell," said Marcelle, half-ashamed, half-pleased, wholly ironical. "He was a wild man from God knows where. He had no father and mother. He was a stone-mason, and people say a fine workman. But he wasted his time in reading books, and he was always on strike. He was a savage, and always roaring 'Down with the Government and the rich!' People called him 'Le Farrou.' I remember my father telling how the soldiers came to take him from his house to be shot. My father was a lad of fourteen, and he hid my grandfather under a mattress of the bed. But the soldiers poked their bayonets in there and one went through his shoulder—so they saw the blood. Then my grandfather made a speech to the soldiers—he was always making speeches—and asked them not to murder the Commune. . . . But they only laughted at him——" And Marcelle laughed, for it was amusing.

"But my father—" she went on; "Heavens! He was even worse. I can remember the big strike at the Creusot works.—wait a minute,—it was the year of the Great Exposition. My father helped to make that strike. My brother was then just a baby,—eight years he had, and he was already working as poor children do. And in the parade of all the strikers, suddenly my father heard a little voice shouting to him across the ranks,—it was my little brother, marching with a red flag, like one of the comrades!

" 'Hello, old boy!' he called to my father. '*Ça ira!*'

"They shot many workmen in that strike." Marcelle shook her head viciously. "Ugh! The scum!"

Fred and I stirred, and found that we had been chilled from resting in one position. We beat on the window and ordered cognac.

"And now you have heard enough of my miserable family," said Marcelle, with an attempt at lightness.

"Go on," said Fred hoarsely, fixing her with gleaming eyes.

"But you're going to take me to dinner, *n'est-ce pas?*" insinuated Marcelle. I nodded. *"Pardié!"* she went on, with a grin. "It was not like this that my father dined—hè! After my grandfather died, my old man could get no work. He was starving, and went from house to house begging food. But they shut the door in his face, the women of my grandfather's comrades, saying 'Give him nothing, the *salaud;* he is the son of Le Farrou, who was shot.' And my father sneaked around the café tables, like a dog, picking up crusts to keep his soul and body together. It has taught me much," said Marcelle, shaking her short hair. "To keep always in good relations with those who feed you. It is why I do not steal from the waiter like that girl did; and I tell everybody that my family was respectable. They might make me suffer for the sins of my father, as he did for his father's."

Light broke upon me, and once more the puzzling baseness of humanity justified itself. Here was the key to Marcelle, her weakness, her vileness. It was not vice, then, that had twisted her, but the intolerable degradation of the human spirit by the masters of the earth, the terrible punishment of those who thirst for liberty.

"I can remember," she said, "how, after the Creusot strike was ended, the bosses got rid of their troublesome workmen. It was winter, and for weeks we had had only wood that my mother gathered in the fields, to keep us warm—and a little bread and coffee that the Union gave us. I wasn't but four years old. My father decided to go to Paris, and we started—walking. He carried me on his shoulder, and with the other a little bundle of clothes. My mother carried another—but she had already tuberculosis, and had to rest every hour. My brother came behind. . . . We went along the white, straight road, with the light snow lying on it, between the high naked poplars. Two days and a night. . . . We huddled down in a deserted roadmender's hut, my mother coughing, coughing. Then out again before the sun rose, tramping along through the snow, my father and my brother shouting revolutionary cries, and singing.

'Dansons la Carmagnole

[184]

'Vive le son—Vive le son—
'Dansons la Carmagnole
'Vive le son du canon!'"

Marcelle had raised her voice unconsciously as she sang the forbidden song; her cheeks flushed, her eyes snapped, she stamped her foot. Suddenly she broke off and looked fearfully around. No one had noticed, however.

"My brother had a high, little voice like a girl, and my father used to break off laughing as he looked down at his son stamping sturdily along beside him, and roaring out songs of hate like an old striker.

"'Allons! Petit cheminot,—you little tramp you! I'll bet the police will know you some day!' And he would slap him on the back. It made my mother turn pale, and sometimes at night she would slip out of bed and go to the corner where my brother slept, and wake him up to tell him, weeping, that he must always grow up to be a good man. Once my father woke up and caught her. . . . But that was later, at Paris. . . .

"And they would sing—

'Debout freres de misere!
(Up! Brothers of misery!)
'Ne voulons plus de frontieres
(We want no more frontiers)
'Pour egorger la bourgeoisie
(To loot the bourgeoisie)
'Et supprimer la tyrranie
(And suppress tyranny)
'Il faut avoir du coeur
(We must have heart)
'Et de l'energie!'
(And energy!)

"And then my father would look ahead with flashing eyes, marching as if he were an army. Every time his eyes flashed like that, my mother would tremble,—for it meant some reckless and terrible fight with the police, or a bloody strike, and she feared for him. . . . And I know how she must have felt, for she was law-abiding, like me —and my father, he was no good." Marcelle shuddered, and gulped her cognac at one swallow.

"I really did not begin myself to know things until we came to Paris," she went on, "because then I began to grow up. My first memory, almost, is when my father led the big strike at Thirion's, the coal-yard down there on the avenue de Maine, and came home with his arm broken where the police had struck him. After that it was work, strike,—work, strike,—with little to eat at our house and my mother growing weaker until she died. My father married again, a religious woman, who finally took to going continually to church and praying for his immortal soul. . . .

"Because she knew how fiercely he hated God. He used to come home at night every week after the meeting of the Union, his eyes shining like stars, roaring blasphemies through the streets. He was a terrible man. He was always the leader. I remember when he went out to assist at a demonstration on Montmartre. It was before the Sacré Coeur, the big white church you see up there on the top of the mountain, looking over all Paris. You know the statue of the Chevalier de la Barre just below it? It is of a young man in ancient times who refused to salute a religious procession; a priest broke his arm with the cross they carried, and he was burned to death by the Inquisition. He stands there in chains, his broken arm hanging by his side, his head lifted so,—proudly. *Eh b'en,* the workingmen were demonstrating against the Church, or something, I don't know what. They had speeches. My father stood upon the steps of the basilica and suddenly the *curé* of the church appeared. My father cried, in a voice of thunder, '*A bas* the priests! That pig burned *him* to death! he pointed to the statue. 'To the Lanterne with him! Hang him! Then they all began to shout and surge toward the steps,—and the police charged the crowd with revolvers. . . . Well, my father came home that night all covered with blood, and hardly able to drag himself along the street.

"My step-mother met him at the door, very angry, and said, 'Well, where have you been, you good-for-nothing?'

" 'At a manifestation, *quoi!*' he growled.

" 'It serves you right,' she said. 'I hope you're cured now.'

" 'Cured?' he shouted, roaring through the bloody toothlessness of his mouth. 'Until the next time. *Ça ira!*'

"And true enough, it was at the guillotining of Leboeuf that the cuirassiers charged the Socialists, and they carried my father home with a sabre cut in his head."

Marcelle leaned over with a cigarette in her mouth to light it from Fred's.

"They called him *Casse-téte* Poisot—the Head-breaker, and he was a hard man. . . . How he hated the Government! . . . Once I came home from school and told him that they had taught us to sing the Marseillaise.

" 'If I ever catch you singing that damned trait-

ors' song around here,' he cried at me, doubling up his fist, 'I'll crack your face open.' "

To my eyes came the picture of this coarse, narrow, sturdy old warrior, scarred with the marks of a hundred vain, ignoble fights with police, reeling home through squalid streets after Union meeting, his eyes blazing with visions of a regenerated humanity.

"And your brother?" asked Fred.

"Oh, he was even worse than my father," said Marcelle, laughing. "You could talk to my father about some things, but there were things that you could not talk to my brother about at all. Even when he was a little boy he did dreadful things. He would say, 'After school come to meet me at such and such a church,—I want to pray.' I would meet him on the steps and we would go in together and kneel down. And when I was praying, he would suddenly jump up and run shouting around the church, kicking over the chairs and smashing the candles burning in the chapels. . . . And whenever he saw a *curé* in the street, he marched along right behind him crying, '*A bas les calottes! A bas les calottes!*' Twenty times he was arrested, and even put in the Reformatory. But he always escaped. When he had but fifteen years he ran away from the house and did not come back for a year. One day he walked into the kitchen where we were all having breakfast.

" 'Good morning,' he said, as if he had never gone away. 'Cold morning, isn't it?'

"My step-mother screamed.

" 'I have been to see the world,'-he went on. 'I came back because I didn't have any money and was hungry.' My father never scolded him, but just let him stay. In the daytime he hung around the cafés on the corner, and did not come home at night until after midnight. Then one morning he disappeared again, without a word to anyone. In three months he was back again, starving. My step-mother told my father that he ought to make the boy work, that it was hard enough with a lazy, fighting man to provide for. But my father only laughed.

" 'Leave him alone,' he said. 'He knows what he's doing. There's good fighting blood in him.'

"My brother went off and came back like that until he was almost eighteen. In the last period, before he settled down in Paris, he would most always work until he had collected enough money to go away. Then he finally got a steady job in a factory here, and married. . . .

"He had a fine voice for singing, and could hold

people dumb with the way he sang revolutionary songs. At night, after his work was finished, he used to tie a big red handkerchief around his neck and go to some music hall or cabaret. He would enter, and while some singer was giving a song from the stage, he would suddenly lift up his voice and burst out into the *Ça ira* or the *Internationale.* The singer on the stage would be forced to stop, and all the audience would turn and watch my brother, up there in the top benches of the theatre.

"When he had finished, he would cry 'How do you like that?' and then they would cheer and applaud him. Then he would shout 'Everybody say with me "Down with the Capitalists! *A bas* the police! To the Lanterne with the *flics!*"' Then there would be some cheers and some whistles. 'Did I hear somebody whistle me?' he'd cry. 'I'll meet anybody at the door outside who dared to whistle me!' And afterward he would fight ten or fifteen men in a furious mob in the street outside, until the police came. . . .

"He, too, was always leading strikes, but had a laughing, gallant way that made all the comrades love him. . .·. . He might perhaps some day have been a deputy, if my father had not taught him lawlessness when he was young——"

"Where is he now?" asked Fred.

"Down there in the trenches somewhere." She waved her arm vaguely Eastward. "He had to go with the others when the war broke out, though he hated the Army so. When he did his military service, it was awful. He would never obey. For almost a year he was in prison. Once he decided to be promoted, and within a month they made him corporal, he was so intelligent. . . . But the very first day he refused to command the soldiers of his squad. . . . 'Why should I give orders to these comrades?' he shouted. 'One orders me to command them to dig a trench. *Voyons,* are they slaves?' So they degraded him to the ranks. Then he organized a revolt, and advised them to shoot their officers. . . . The men themselves were so insulted, they threw him over a wall.—So terribly he hated war! When the Three Year Military Law was up in the Chamber, it was he who led the mob to the Palais Bourbon. . . . And now he must go to kill the *Bôches,* like the others. Perhaps he himself is dead.—I do not know, I have heard nothing." And then irrelevantly, "He has a little son five years old."

Three generations of fierce, free blood, struggling indefatigably for a dim dream of liberty. And now a fourth in the cradle! Did they know why they struggled? No matter. It was a thing deeper than reason, an instinct of the human spirit which neither force nor persuasion could ever uproot.

"And you, Marcelle?" I asked.

"I?" She laughed. "Shall I tell you that I was not seduced by a Duke?" She gave a bitter little chuckle. "Then you will not respect me—for I notice that you friends of passage want your vice seasoned with romance. But it is true. It has not been romantic. In that hideousness and earnestness of our life, I always craved joy and happiness. I always wanted to laugh, be gay, even when I was a baby. I used to imagine drinking champagne, and going to the theatre, and I wanted jewels, fine dresses, automobiles. Very early my father noticed that my tastes led that way; he said, 'I see that you want to throw everything over and sell yourself to the rich. Let me tell you now, that the first fault you commit, I'll put you out the door and call you my daughter no more.'

"It became intolerable at home. My father could not forgive women who had lovers without being married. He kept saying that I was on the way to sin—and when I grew older, I wasn't permitted to leave the house without my step-mother. As soon as I was old enough, he hurried to find me a husband, to save me. One day he came home and said that he had found one—a pale young man who limped, the son of a restaurant-keeper on the same street. I knew him; he was not bad, but I couldn't bear to think of marrying. I wanted so much to be free." We started, Fred and I. "Free!" Wasn't that what the old man had fought for so bitterly?

"So that night," she said, "I got out of bed and put on my Sunday dress, and my everday dress over that, and ran away. All night I walked around the streets, and all the next day. That evening, trembling, I went to the factory where my brother worked and waited for him to come out. I did not know whether or not he would give me up to my father. But soon he came along, shouting and singing with some comrades. He spied me.

" 'Well, old girl, what brings you here?' he cried, taking my arm. 'Trouble?' I told him I had run away. He stood off and looked at me. 'You haven't eaten,' he said. 'Come home with me and meet my wife. You'll like her. We'll all have dinner together!' So I did. His wife was wonderful. She met me with open arms, and they showed me the baby, just a month old. . . . And so fat! All was warm and happy there in that house. I re-

Drawn by Stuart Davis, July 1913

LOUIS UNTERMEYER
Any City

Into the staring street
   She goes on her nightly round,
With weary and tireless feet
   Over the wretched ground.

A thing that man never spurns,
   A thing that all men despise;
Into her soul there burns
   The street with its pitiless eyes.

She needs no charm or wile;
   She carries no beauty or power,
But a tawdry and casual smile
   For a tawdry and casual hour.

The street with its pitiless eyes
   Follows wherever she lurks,
But she is hardened and wise—
   She rattles her bracelets, and smirks.

She goes with her sordid array,
   Luring, without a lure;
She is man's hunger and prey—
   His lust and its hideous cure.

All that she knows are the lies,
   The evil, the squalor, the scars;
The street with its pitiless eyes,
   The night with its pitiless stars.
            —July 1913

member that she cooked the dinner herself, and never have I eaten such a dinner! They did not ask me anything until I had eaten, and then my brother lighted a cigarette and gave me one. I was afraid to smoke, for my step-mother had said it was to bring hell on a woman. . . . But the wife smiled at me and took one herself.

" 'Now,' said my brother. 'What are your plans?'

" 'I have none,' I answered. 'I must be free. I want gaiety, and lovely clothes. I want to go to the theatre. I want to drink champagne.'

"His wife shook her head sadly.

" 'I have never heard of any work for a woman that will give her those things,' she said.

" 'Do you think I want work?' I burst out. 'Do you think I want to slave out my life in a factory for ten francs a week, or strut around in other women's gowns at some *couturière's* on the Rue de la Paix? Do you think I will take orders from anyone? No, I want to be free!'

"My brother looked at me gravely for a long time. Then he said, 'We are of the same blood. It would do no good to argue with you, or to force you. Each human being must work out his own life. You shall go and do whatever you want. But I want you to know that whenever you are hungry, or discouraged, or deserted, that my house is always open to you—that you will always be welcome here, for as long as you want.' . . ."

Marcelle wiped her eyes roughly with the back of her hand.

"I stayed there that night, and the next day I went around the city and talked with girls in the cafés—like I am now. They advised me to work, if I wanted a steady lover; so I went into a big department store for a month. Then I had a lover, an Argentine, who gave me beautiful clothes and took me to the theatre. Never have I been so happy!

"One night when we were going to the theatre —as we passed by my brother's house, I thought I would stop in and let him know how wonderful I found life. I had on a blue charmeuse gown—I remember it now, it was lovely! Slippers with very high heels and brilliants on the buckles, white gloves, a big hat with a black ostrich feather, and a veil. Luckily the veil was down; for as I entered the door of my brother's tenement, my father stood there on the steps! He looked at me, I stopped. My heart stood still. But I could see he did not recognize me.

" '*Va t'en!*' he shouted. 'What is your kind doing here, in a workingman's house? What do you mean by coming here to insult us with your silks and your feathers, sweated out of poor men in mills and their consumptive wives, their dying children? Go away, you whore!'

"I was terrified that he might recognize me!

"It was only once more that I saw him. My lover left me, and I had other lovers. . . . My brother and his wife went out to live near my father, in St. Denis. I used sometimes to go out and spend the night with them, to play with the baby, who grew so fast. Those were really happy times. And I used to leave again at dawn, to avoid meeting my father. One morning I left my brother's house, and as I came onto the street, I saw my father, going to work at dawn with his lunch pail! He had not seen my face. There was nothing to do but walk down the street ahead of him. It was about five o'clock—few people were about. He came along behind me, and soon I noticed that he was walking faster. Then he said in a low voice, 'Mademoiselle, wait for me. We are going the same direction, *hein?*' I hurried. 'You are pretty, mademoiselle. And I am not old. Can't we go together some place?' I was in a panic. I was so full of horror and of fear that he might see my face. I did not dare to turn up a side street, for he would have seen my profile. So I walked straight ahead—straight ahead for hours, for miles. . . . I do not know when he stopped. . . . I do not know if now he might be dead. . . . My brother said he never spoke of me. . . ."

She ceased, and the noises of the street became again apparent to our ears, that had been so long deaf to them, with double their former loudness. Fred was excited.

"Marvelous, by God!" he cried, thumping the table. "The same blood, the same spirit! And see how the revolution becomes sweeter, broader, from generation to generation! See how the brother understood freedom in a way which the old father was blind to!"

Marcelle shot him an astonished look. "What do you mean?" she asked.

"Your father—fighting all his life for liberty— yet turned you out because you wanted *your liberty*."

"Oh, but you don't understand," said Marcelle. "I did wrong. I am bad. If I had a daughter who was like me, I should do the same thing, if she had a frivolous character."

"Can't you *see?*" cried Fred. "Your father wanted liberty for men, but not for women!"

"Naturally," she shrugged. "Men and women

THE
DECEMBER 1915 10 CENTS
MASSES

IN THIS ISSUE
"THE ONLY WAY TO END WAR"
BY MAX EASTMAN

NOVEMBER, 1913   10 CENTS

The MASSES

Innocent Girlish Prattle—Plus Environment

"WHAT! HIM? THE LITTLE ——————! HE'S WORSE'N SHE IS, THE ————!"

are different. My father was right. Women must be *respectable!*"

"The women need another generation," sighed Fred, sadly.

I took Marcelle's hand.

"Do you regret it?" I asked her.

"Regret my life?" she flashed back, tossing her head proudly, "*Dame,* no! I'm *free!* ..."

—February 1915

JAMES HENLE
Nobody's Sister

The clock in the corner marked twelve-thirty. The waiter, having brought our drinks, lounged wearily against the wall. My companion set down his glass, looked at me with a deep, impersonal earnestness, and began to speak in a slow, quiet tone that seemed hardly to keep pace with his thoughts:

"I call her nobody's sister. As a matter of fact, she is the sister of us all, though no one ever thinks of her as anybody's sister. She is everywhere and she sees all things, and she knows more than we guess. She meets us at our weakest and our worst and leaves us angered and degraded. Yet has she faith, and the courage of the meek, and the charity born of suffering.

"She endures much, and she unwittingly and unwillingly avenges on us the misery she cannot escape. We pay for our sins and she pays for them, too, so the Devil is satisfied in double measure. And who pays for her sins? My friend, your connection with her may at times have been close, but it is plain you do not understand the honest, simple-hearted little creature. Sins?—she has none, none save those we force upon her. . . . And perhaps when the galleys are emptied and the last form is locked up and the Final Edition goes to press, we, even we, may be found to be blameless.

"Honest? If I cared to be flippant, I would say that she is as honest as the day is long. And even at night. . . . She is honest if honesty consists in giving what you offer for value received. True, she does not give much, but she has not much to give. She gives her body, and with it neither lies nor sighs. She may murmur nothings, but they are part of the conventions of her profession, and are not accepted nor meant to be accepted as more. Other women are different. Mary in 'The Passionate Friends' would have run with the hare and hunted with the hounds. That is the secret desire of every 'straight' woman—to receive all and to risk nothing. It is only when we force her to be 'crooked' that she realizes the futility of attempting to eat her cake and have it too. . . . She is satisfied with dry bread.

"You may call this sickly sentimentality. You very probably have done so. Let me tell you of a friend of mine, a true friend, for our friendship is secure. It is not founded upon moping and moonshine.

"I had spent several hours in her apartment. You could call them joyous hours or sensuous hours or wicked hours. I shall call them plain 'hours.' She had given herself to me as freely as though she loved me, which certainly she did not, and I—well, I had at any rate been ordinarily sociable.

"I rose to go. I noticed that she was getting ready to go, also. It was three o'clock in the morning. 'Where on earth are you going, Marjorie?' I inquired. (What an improvement such a relation is upon the marital state! A husband under the same circumstances would have asked his wife where in hell she was going.)

" 'I'm going to see a friend,' she replied. 'She's had an operation performed on her. She has to keep in bed, and she can't sleep all the time.'

"*Bats!* They are called that because they flit about after nightfall. But Marjorie, whom I now know that I respect in a deep and true sense—you are the kindest and gentlest of little winged creatures. I see you now, dressing to sally forth in the cold, windy, winter darkness, you to whom all men and all hours are alike! I took you to your friend's house and on the steps held your hand for a moment. If I had told you what I thought you would have laughed . . . or cried. For you like to be respected, much as do people a great deal worse, such as politicians and poetasters and pimps.

"I wonder if the world realizes just how much Marjorie is always willing to do for a companion. Do you know that if Marjorie should die and, for such things happen, leave behind her a little one, the baby would be taken care of tenderly and later given a good schooling and a 'chance in life,' better it may be, than Marjorie herself had? This would especially be true if Marjorie were the sort that lived in a 'house' and at her death left behind her half a dozen intimate associates who would assume charge of her child. And please do not laugh when I say that Marjorie herself is the most devoted and faithful of mothers when she is assigned that rôle. I know that this doesn't agree very well with

[191]

the popular notion of gayety and laughter and abandon, nor with the 'uplift' one of anatomical charts and microscopic slides, but I am not responsible for the wrong impressions of others.

"The second point of view is nearer the truth than the first. There is very little gayety in Marjorie's life. Fundamentally my sister (nobody's sister, if you will) is honest. Do not forget that. It is difficult and it hurts her to pretend that she is what she isn't. She must seem glad to receive your embrace—and she might be, but she has received so many embraces. . . . It is nothing against you personally. . . . And to the end she shrinks from certain liberties you take. . . . Upward and downward there are many steps to the ladder. Marjorie may be upon one of them—and so may you. You may not like your work, but you must earn a living; Marjorie may recoil in every nerve when, wearied and worn, she must receive you. . . . Sometimes she seeks to forget this in whiskey or cocaine, and then is the beginning of the end.

"It is strange how much of the old morality Marjorie has preserved. She is 'loyal.' Shakespeare tells us that she dupes all men and is duped by one. I challenge the first clause. Marjorie is too simple and straightforward and businesslike to dupe anyone very long. But she is usually duped by some one. And in spite of everything that he may do she remains true to him, not geographically true, of course, but deeply and spiritually true. He may be, and usually is, a man of unspeakable vices—because men without these vices demand something that Marjorie with all her virtues cannot give. But, vices or no vices, Marjorie is loyal to him to the end, ready and willing to give him her last cent, to shield him and protect him, and to lavish upon him all the kindly care she gets such little chance to give free play. It is silly to say she loves him. It is something bigger than that. He is at once her domineering lover, her stern father and her naughty, erring son.

"I am afraid that I have idealized slightly upon this relationship. Like marriage, it never works out exactly as it should. Too often its golden—or green-back—simplicity is marred by brutality and suspicion, and lack of Faith and Charity. Too often will he accuse her of Holding Out, too often will she reply with bitter recriminations. Let us turn the leaf upon this unfortunate phase of the subject.

"But do not imagine that Marjorie never follows the fortunes, or the fortune, of a 'good man.' Sometimes she marries such a one, and then in most cases she becomes a model wife. . . . She has had her taste of ashes.

"What does Marjorie think about herself and us and the world? What goes on inside her mock-sophisticated little head? It may surprise you to learn that she is not in the least revolutionary. She does not feel that she is greatly wronged. Though she is somewhat dubious concerning the virtue of other women, she half believes that she is suffering for her sins. As a rule, she blames no one for the path she follows, not even that First. 'I was a fool,' is the way she puts it. She makes few excuses. She condemns her own weakness, where wiser people do not, though the cause lay in the cruelly low wages she was receiving. She is something of a stoic. Enduring so much now, she believes that she should have endured more then.

"She thinks that what she does is wrong. There is no attempt at justification, no blind hatred of society. It would be better if there were, but there is no room for such emotions in her kindly little heart. Sometimes she is timidly religious. I doubt not that she prays more sincerely than most of our professed and obsessed reformers. I do not think that she prays for rain.

"So Marjorie is Nobody's Sister. When you approach her you lock your soul and open your purse. To that other world of womankind she is a painted plague. She is cursed and hounded and mulcted and jailed for earning her livelihood by the only means she knows. I wonder if God loves her the less for all this. Nobody's Sister . . ."
—January 1915

A Strange Meeting

Rev. Paul Smith, head of the vice crusade, stood in his own church before the strangest audience ever assembled in San Francisco—or, perhaps, in the world—an audience of over two hundred women of the night life, clad in bedraggled finery and bearing upon their faces the marks of ill health, showing plainly despite the traces of rouge —and exclaimed in a voice of sorrow:

"You have asked me some questions that have been asked ever since the world began and are still unanswered. I cannot answer them. I do not know what is to be done."

The delegation of prostitutes had come voluntarily to the Rev. Smith's church to present to him their side of the vice crusade which he is leading.

At 11 o'clock a body of fifty women reached the Central Methodist Church, at O'Farrell and

Leavenworth streets. From all directions other women were seen approaching in small groups.

Word had got around the local underworld that this dramatic visit was to be made. A crowd of male onlookers had assembled, in addition to motion-picture and camera men and reporters.

The women passed to the church door along a lane in the crowd which filled the street intersection completely and overflowed down the side streets.

On seeing how many of the women there were, the Rev. Smith opened the doors of his church and asked them to step inside to the main auditorium. All men and bystanders were excluded, excepting the newspaper reporters.

As the women passed through the crowd some hung their heads, some stared calmly, while many covered their faces from sight behind cheap muffs or under the collars of their overcoats.

Within the auditorium, when all were seated, and the doors closed, the Rev. Smith arose and addressed them.

"I do not know what this meeting is about," he said. "This morning I received a telephone call from a woman who did not give her name, but said she was the keeper of a house of ill fame, and asked if I would meet a group of women of the underworld and confer with them. I consented.

"If the woman who called me up will step to the platform I should be pleased to have her occupy this chair."

A woman neatly clad in a suit of shepherd's plaid, of intelligent appearance and evidently controlling her nervousness by a strong effort of will, arose and took the seat which the pastor offered.

The Rev. Smith made a brief speech, in which he said:

"I am very glad to have this opportunity to confer with you and to hear a word from the other side of the problem. No person could be more sympathetic than I am. Any person who desires to lead what I consider the right kind of life I will help to the best of my ability.

"How many of you," asked the Rev. Smith, "have children dependent upon you?"

Drawn by John Sloan, August 1913

The Women's Night Court
Before Her Makers and Her Judge

About half the women who crowded the auditorium raised their hands.

"How many of you went into this life because you could not make enough money to live on?"

This time practically every woman in the place raised her hand.

The woman who had come to the platform then arose and in a voice that vibrated with strong emotion told of the problem from the standpoint of herself and her fellow prostitutes.

"We women find it impossible to exist on the wages of $6 or $7 a week that are paid to women in San Francisco," she declared in her opening sentence.

There was a volley of loud applause from the two hundred women in the auditorium.

"Most of the girls here present came from the poor," she continued.

"Nearly every one of these women is a mother, or has someone depending on her. They are driven into this life by economic conditions. People on the outside seem oblivious to this fact.

"These women do not lead a gay or happy life. Many of them hardly ever see the sunlight. It was an unusual experience for them to step outdoors to come to this church this morning.

"There is not one of these girls that would not quit this unhappy life of illness and pain and artificiality if the opportunity was given. But these women haven't anything. How can they do differently?

"You won't do anything to stop vice by driving us women out of this city to some other city. Has your city and your church a different God, that you drive evil away from your city and your church to other cities and other churches?

"If you want to stop prostitution, stop the new girls from coming in here. They are coming into it every day. They will always be coming into it as long as conditions, wages and education are as they are. You don't do any good by attacking us. Why don't you attack those conditions?

"Why don't you go to the big business houses? Why don't you go to the Legislature and change the conditions? Men here in San Francisco say they want to eliminate vice. If they do, they had better give up some of their dividends and pay the girls wages so they can live."

"What do you consider a fair wage?" asked the Rev. Smith.

"Twenty dollars a week."

"Why, statistics show that the heads of the majority of families throughout the country do not make this much," declared Smith.

"That's why there is prostitution," responded the woman.

At this sharp retort the assembled women cheered and stamped their feet for several minutes. Smith colored in confusion and laughed nervously.

"How many of you would work for $8 a week?" was the next question asked by Smith. His question was met with an outburst of laughter.

"But," he insisted, "many girls live respectably on this wage."

"Yes," cried a woman in the audience, "but their mothers and fathers look after them.

"No woman can live without a wage of at least $15 a week."

"How many of you would do housework?" asked Smith. This question brought another burst of laughter from the audience.

"What woman wants to work in a kitchen?" shrilled a voice.

At the close of the meeting the Rev. Smith extended to Mrs. R. M. Gamble, who had been the spokesman of the women, his compliments on her able presentation of the case.

"If you will accept an invitation to come to my house and dictate your statements to a stenographer," he said, "I will try to have it published for the sake of aiding toward a betterment of social conditions." She accepted the pastor's invitation.

The Rev. Smith spoke with a changed demeanor. It appeared that he had been deeply affected by the things that had been said, and his voice was less clear and his bearing less confident.

"You have asked me some very puzzling questions—questions that I cannot answer," he said.

Just before adjournment, when the Rev. Smith was trying to bring the meeting to a speedy close, he was interrupted by a voice from the rear of the room. It came from a pale, slight figure, who demanded:

"Are you trying to reform us, or trying to reform social conditions? You leave us alone. It is too late to try to do anything with us. You give your attention to the boys and girls in the schools and the social conditions that are responsible for the spread of prostitution."

*　　*　　*　　*　　*　　*

The curious reader has probably by this time come to the conclusion that the above is an improbable chapter from a new novel by Upton Sinclair. The sensational setting, the figure of the earnest and startled clergyman, the eloquent speeches of the prostitutes, and the obvious propaganda-motif of the whole, mark it clearly enough as being from the hand of that ingenious fabricator of sociological melodrama. Such things, of course, happen only in Socialist novels.

Nevertheless, in this case, the thing happened in real life. It happened January 25, in San Francisco, as stated. The earnest and bewildered Rev. Smith is a real person, and so are the women who filled his church that morning, and the passionate eloquence of their speeches is as literal as good reporting can make it. The whole story is taken from the pages of the San Francisco *Bulletin* of the same date. —April 1917

LYDIA GIBSON

Lies

Along the gaslit Boulevard
  Under the shadow-spreading trees
    They walk, the slender silhouettes,
Night-hidden, but for outlines hard,
  Slow-stepping, wanly mad to please,
    While, heart-deep, endless Hunger frets.

Or, choked, that hunger long is dead,
  Or, unborn, died before its bliss.
    The curve of feather and of eyes,
Their hot light calling to the bed—
  The breasts borne temptingly to kiss—
Of what Truth are these things the lies?
            —October 1913

Feminism

[The Masses *was unswervingly, but not humorlessly, dedicated to Feminist ideals.*]

FLOYD DELL

Why Mona Smiled

"I know what I'm talking about," said Sudberg. "I was married once. For a whole year. Then I busted it up."

I had met Sudberg in the restaurant at noon. Sudberg is a big blond Norwegian, and a painter. After luncheon he talked.

"If you're just an ordinary human male," he said, "it's all right for you to spend your time playing with women, working for them, taking care of them and their children. Somebody has got to do it! But the artist has something more important to do.

"The artist is different. Women ought to leave him alone, and pick out some ordinary human male to play with and to exploit. But they can't leave the artist alone. Any sort of distinction attracts women. So they capture the poor devil of an artist, and proceed to kill everything in him that attracted them.

"I used to hate my wife—I called her a vampire. I've got over that now. I realize that she was everything that was sweet and lovely. But she was a woman. . . . I couldn't be a lover and a husband and a permanent companion to a woman—and be an artist too.

"Not that I really blame a woman for being a vampire. I've got no use for the sort of women who try to be 'independent.' A woman simply must demand love and support and permanency, and everything else that it uses up a man's life to give."

So said Sudberg; and that evening, in that same restaurant, at the same table, I sat at dinner with Paul Ferens. Ferens is a middle-aged young dramatic critic, and the author of a successful comedy.

"There's nothing like having a wife to make a man do his best," said Ferens. "You hear people talk about marriage spoiling an artist. All rot! I've seen young men with talent waste themselves in a lonely struggle. There's nothing to it. The only thing is for the artist to have a wife.

"I know what I am talking about"—that magic phrase! "If it hadn't been for my wife I should never have been where I am now. The fact is, an artist's job is too big for one person to tackle. It takes two.

"And a woman loves nothing so much as to help some man do what he wants to do. She will give up her own plans any time, to carry burdens for him. Why, a year ago, when typewriter's bills were a serious matter, my wife learned to use the machine, and copied my manuscripts—that in addition to running the house and making everything comfortable for me.

"The line in my play that got the biggest laugh—she fished that out of the waste-basket, where I had thrown it when I was so tired I didn't know what I was doing—she saved it and copied it out for me, along with a dozen other discarded scraps, on the chance that it *might* be of value.

"That's what women are like—real women. They are happiest in helping a man."

"The squaw theory . . ." I suggested.

"Call it what you like," said Ferens, looking around for the waiter. "I don't care. My wife is a good squaw, and it makes her happy."

Presently it was time for Ferens to go to the theatre. His wife wasn't with him, he conscientiously explained, because it was the maid's evening off, and she had to stay at home and look after the baby. Did I want to come along?

No, I didn't. I had another idea, which I didn't explain to Ferens. It was an idea that pleased me. As soon as Ferens had left, I went to the telephone, and half an hour later I was calling on Mrs. Paul Ferens in her apartment uptown. She was glad to see me.

"This is the first time you've ever been here," she said reproachfully. "Just because you were once in love with me, is that any reason you should avoid me forever after?"

"Mona," I said, "I've just been talking to *both* your husbands to-day."

"What!" she said. "Did you see Olaf? What is he doing?"

"When I saw him, he was talking to me about you."

"Oh! Did he say anything particularly nasty about me?"

"He said you were everything that was sweet and lovely."

"Didn't he say I was a vampire?"

"Yes, he did. But you mustn't mind that, Mona."

"Oh, I don't," said Mona. "I know his theory about women. I ought to! What else did he say?"

"You know what he would say. He warned me against women. But what I want to know is this: Mona, were you a vampire?"

Mona shrugged her shoulders. "He insisted on my making him very unhappy, if that's what you want to know. He wouldn't let me work with him, and so I suppose I took up more of his time than I ought in trying to get him to play with me. I did want to share some of his life. What's the use of being married if you don't?"

"And then there's another thing I want to know. Mona, are you a squaw?"

"A squaw! . . . Did Paul say I was a squaw?" Her eyes flashed.

"No, no! I supplied the word myself. Paul said you loved to help."

"Well, that's one way of having some fun together. I do like to help. But if Paul thinks I like to copy manuscript any more than he does, he's mistaken. But that's all there is. . . . Yes, I suppose I am a squaw. . . ."

"Ah!" I said. "Now there's just one thing more I would like to know. What would you have been if you had married me: a vampire? or a squaw?"

Mona sat silent for a moment. A smile, ambiguous, teasing, curiously reminiscent, deepened upon her lips. At last she spoke slowly:

"It would all have depended. . . . But there's one thing I wouldn't have had a chance to be, no matter whom I married. . . ."

"And what," I asked, "wouldn't you have had a chance to be?"

"Myself," said Mona.   —June 1914

Confessions of a Feminist Man

On the day that I left business college, thirty years ago, the odd little old maid in the office slipped a pamphlet into my hands as she bade me good-bye and good luck. "Read it," she said, glancing around as if afraid that the efficient president of the college might just then bustle into the room.

In the hall I looked at the title. It was "The Rights and Wrongs of Women." I was not surprised, for I had heard that Miss Milliken believed in woman suffrage. I had also heard that she was going to be fired from her position as secretary because she had not caught "the spirit of the institution." I stuck the pamphlet in my pocket and went out to look for a job.

I had caught the spirit of the institution all right; and when before the day was over I had got a job as shipping clerk in a paint factory, I felt that my future was assured. I knew that success must come to a young man who was capable, shrewd, energetic, and who gave his whole mind to his work. That was me.

And sure enough, before the year was out I was an accountant. I proved that I had a head for figures. Life meant to me simply success in my career, and naturally enough I forged ahead. Five years later I was making forty dollars a week in another office, ready to step into the shoes of the general sales manager when his asthma should get a little worse. I was a rising young businessman.

I was so much of a businessman that when I fell in love I felt disturbed about the time and thought that the girl was taking from my business. One of my reasons for an early marriage was the idea that when we had settled down I would be able to concentrate my mind again on affairs at the office. So we were married, and after a month's honeymoon in the Maine woods returned home to settle down.

That is to say, after a month of continual association with a woman, a sharing equally of work and play, I tried to go back to my womanless world of business and give to it my old singleness of devotion. I almost succeeded, but there was one fatal flaw. That was breakfast.

At night I was too tired to go to the theater with my wife, or read with her, or talk with her; for I had to get up at six-thirty o'clock and ride for an hour on the cars to get to my office at eight o'clock. Only the excitement of a game of cards could keep me awake in the evening after ten. But in the morning I lingered over my coffee, finding my wife an interesting and delightful companion. I didn't want to leave the house. And she didn't want me to go—for she, too, liked companionship and felt the need of it. I resented the arrangement of life which took me so inexorably from the side of a pleasant playmate. For the first time I was late to work, and listless at my desk.

Those breakfasts, which were my first concession to a standard of life alien to the womanless world in which all my thoughts had centered— those breakfasts played an important part in my career. For I decided not to wait on the sales manager's asthma to give me more leisure. I took another place, where work began at the civilized hour of nine, and which was only half an hour's ride from my home. I had time for my breakfasts now. And I was more of a human being in the evening. I read with my wife, talked with her, went about with her. And I did not regret that my new position offered no such possibilities of promotion as the old.

I had begun to feel that the one-sexed world in which I had been living was inadequate to human needs—that life ought to be lived and shared by men and women together. The reality of my feeling was soon tried by children and illness. I had the choice of assuming a perfunctory responsibility for the affairs of my home, while giving my real energies to my work, or—honestly sharing them.

Drawn by Maurice Becker, January 1917

"They Ain't Our Equals Yet!"

So I ceased to be simply a businessman. I became a woman's friend and helper. It wasn't until later, when the panic threw me out of a job, that I realized the heavy economic disadvantage of the transformation.

I then realized that in losing my original indifference to everything but my work I had lost my original chance for success. Other men, unmarried or able to leave to women what they called "women's affairs," had passed me by. I was, in a business sense, a dead one.

A man who is out of a job may be forgiven many things. I saw myself, who had started out so promisingly on the road to success, thrown aside in the gutter. And why? Because of the enervating influence of a woman. I became bitter, not against my wife so much as against womankind. I saw femininity as a force that softened the masculine will and misdirected its energies. I grew to hate the sight of the pictures of pretty women on the covers of popular magazines. That—I said— is what is sapping the strength of mankind. And once when a little reform organization that I belonged to was considering timidly the project of admitting women to membership, I made a violent speech against it. I said: "Things are going to hell on account of women. I don't want to have any more truck with them. I want to get back out of this feminized, sentimental wallow of a world into a clean, strong, sane, masculine civilization." . . . But when I found an account of my speech in the morning paper, I wanted to hide it away from my wife.

I had another job by this time. But I was still obsessed by the thought that I had lost my chance for business success. And so I had. I couldn't devote myself heart and soul to my work. The fact was, I didn't want to. I had other things to think about. I was changed. And on account of that change I despised myself and hated woman-kind.

I had at any rate begun to take women into account. I was now selling insurance, which gave me some time to myself. And I spent a good deal of that time thinking about women. I soon got over my bitterness, but I kept on thinking about them. I was trying to see their side of the case.

Then one day, in unpacking a box of books, I came across an old notebook of my wife's. Written on the cover was the title, "New Year's Resolutions." I smiled and opened it.

The page before me was dated two years before our wedding, when she was nineteen years old. It read: "I want my life to count for something in particular. I want to be a definite part of the world. Surely there is some one thing I can do. I have a brain and two hands. I am going to find a use for them."

The vague aspirations of youth! I turned to the next year's page. "I know now," it read, "what I want to do. I really know a little about architecture. I will study, and learn more, and then go to work at it. I mean—earn my living by it. That is my job."

I thought of the plans she was always sketching out for our hypothetical house in the country; of the pictures of cathedrals and towers and temples that she pinned to the walls; of the architectural magazine that found its way every month into our home. It was an interest of hers that I had never taken seriously. Now I realized that it might have been a serious matter to her. These things which I had carelessly noticed might be the shattered fragments of her plans for happiness.

I turned to the next page. It was blank. On the first New Year's day after our wedding she had no plans to make; they were already made for her.

The rest of the book was empty, page after page, until at last I came on this, written on the first day of the year of my own bitterness—just two sentences: "I did not deliberately decide to spend the rest of my life sitting in a house and taking care of children. It just happened to me."

I had never read any feminist literature, but I suppose I formulated in my mind that day the whole theory of feminism. I saw that this girl had as much right to resent the limitations which another sex had placed on her life, as ever I had. She had been pent up in a flat, and condemned to spend twenty-four hours of the day with her children. It is true she loved them—I loved them, too, but I was glad to get away from them some of the time. She had been prevented from doing the kind of work she wanted to do. She was tied down to a job that didn't satisfy her, and that she couldn't change. And she got no wages—only support. She was shut off from the life of the world. She wasn't a citizen in the real sense. Nobody asked her what kind of laws she wanted. Nobody cared whether she liked the laws or not. She took care of an individual's children and looked after an individual's meals. But she herself wasn't an individual. She wasn't a free human being. So it was that I became a feminist.

I am now forty-five years old. I have been a failure in my chosen career. I have long since ceased to regret that, for it was a poor career at best. But I have just realized that I deserved to fail.

The other day my wife brought home from the office of a suffrage paper a little pamphlet, yellow with age and carefully bound. It was a copy of "The Rights and Wrongs of Women." I thought of the odd little old maid in the office of the business college. "Read it!" she had begged. I sat down to read it. Thirty years ago I had dropped it on the sidewalk before I went into the paint factory to get my first job and commence my life career.

The first sentences of the little pamphlet that I had never read came home to me. "A woman," it said, "is the same kind of creature as a man. The fact that a woman bears children in her own body does not mean that she has not the same kind of hands and brain that a man has, the same faculty of using them, and the same desire to achieve through their use her own happiness. So long as any woman is denied the right to her own life and happiness, no man has a right to his; and every man who walks freely in his man's world, walks on an iron floor, whereunder, bound and flung into her dungeon, lies a woman-slave."

Rhetorical, yes—but the truth. And when I read that, I knew that it was only just that my life and my happiness, as I once conceived them, should have been wrecked for me by a woman—a woman with her rights and wrongs, of which I knew nor cared nothing, and which I must suffer a little with her to learn.   —March 1914

FLOYD DELL
Adventures in Anti-Land

"Vote no!" the banner screamed at me. I went in. The elevator starter informed me that some noble women, animated by a keen sense of political duty, and fearful that the men of New York State might vote wrong if left to themselves, had set up shop here to teach them what was what. On the third floor I would find them, he said, equipped with campaign literature, speakers, and an educational phonograph. I went up.

I nearly made a mistake and entered a door marked "Mrs. Arthur M. Dodge—Private." Just in time I saved myself from intruding into the sanctum of the high priestess of woman's duty. Everyone knows what woman's duty is—and I blushed to think of what sacred and tender scene I would thus rudely have burst in upon. Mrs. Arthur M. Dodge would have been engaged in suckling a baby, at the very least.

When I entered the other door, the educational phonograph was being played. I gathered that it was an anti-suffrage speech. A very efficient woman in a shirt-waist and stiff collar stood listening. Two men occupied chairs. I also listened, curiously. In a flat metallic voice the machine was saying: "Chivalry must be preserved." Knowing something of the laws of chivalry, I glanced quickly at the two men, expecting them to leap shamefacedly to their feet and offer their chairs to the standing lady. But they continued to sit.

I listened to the machine again. It was saying: "Woman's place is in the home." I looked at the woman. She was nodding approval.

"That's a good record," she said as it finished. The men agreed with her hastily. I picked up a pamphlet from the table, and read: "No such revolutionary change as that which proposes to take woman from the high place she now holds and where men love to leave her, and put her brawling in the market-place, can ever succeed."

When the woman had finished making arrangements for the sale or rent of a certain number of the records, and the men had gone, she turned to me.

"What can I do for you?" she asked.

"Do for me? What could you do for me, but continue to be what you are—a woman! I beg you, dear madam, to preserve those peerless prerogatives inherent in your sex, those charms and graces which exalt you and make you the ornament and devoted companion of man. You are indeed a queen, and your empire is the domestic kingdom. The greatest triumphs you would achieve in public life fade into insignificance, madam,—fade into insignificance, I say, compared with the serene glory which radiates from the domestic shrine, which you illumine and warm by conjugal and motherly virtues!"

I might have said this, quoting from the statement by James, Cardinal Gibbons, which I held in my hand. But I didn't. I was afraid she would think I was crazy. I merely said: "I want to get some of your literature."

"Certainly," she said, and proceeded to sell me fifty cents' worth. At least she charged me fifty cents for it.

In one of the pamphlets I read, while standing there, of the shyness with which the women who opposed woman suffrage had to contend. "They confessed," said the pamphlet, "to a struggle before they could make up their minds to come forward."

I looked at the woman before me with a new admiration. Had she had to struggle with herself before she could come forward and sell anti-suffrage pamphlets? No doubt, no doubt. But, like a Spartan mother, she concealed her agony. She did up my pamphlets without a trace of suffering and took my fifty cents with apparent cheerfulness. One would have thought she actually *enjoyed* being there in that public place and talking to casual strangers. One might even have imagined that she preferred it to the sacred duty of cooking. She looked as if she relished the idea of earning twenty-five dollars a week. Ah! thought I—the heroism and the hypocrisy of woman!

But I was only beginning to learn—Fifty cents! Those pamphlets are worth thousands of dollars to me if they are worth a cent! I learned about women from them. There is that master psychologist, the Hon. Elihu Root, and Mr. Henry L. Stimson, former secretary of war, who has searched out the deepest secrets of Woman's heart. There is Professor William T. Sedgwick, that noted biologist, Curator of Glass Jars in the Massachusetts

Institute of Technology, and Dr. Charles Loomis Dana, who taught physiology in a woman's medical college in the 80's, and more recently became professor of nervous diseases at a place called Bellevue Hospital Medical School—one of the world's leading neurologists. (You haven't heard of them? Well, such is fame!) There is the anonymous schoolboy whose essay on Feminism is reprinted from the *Unpopular Review,* there is the lavender-scented old lady who writes editorials for the New York *Times,* and finally there are the shy but husky-voiced anti-suffrage ladies themselves.

From all these I learned the true nature of woman. And I want to tell you it is something to learn. I can hardly believe it, myself. I thought I knew what women were like. I had some slight experience of the sex, as a son, a brother, a husband, a lover. I had played with them, studied with them, worked beside them in factories and offices, danced with them, dined with them, walked with them, talked with them—And I had all along considered them persons just like men, only nicer—some of them very much nicer. I had confided in them, and listened to their secrets; asked their advice and taken it; sought out their society on all possible occasions; liked to have them about wherever I was, at work or at play, sharing together the glory, the joy, the comedy and the burden of the world. I thought, you see, that they were persons like myself.

Well, they aren't. I know better now. And I shudder to think how I have been deceived. Dr. Charles L. Dana, he of the 1880 medical college, put me on the right track. *"There are,"* he says, and I italicize the words, *"some fundamental differences between the bony and the nervous structures of women and men. The brain-stem of woman is relatively——"* But I cannot go on with it—it is too painful. Suffice it to say that there are differences between the sexes. "I do not say," concedes Dr. Dana magnanimously, "that they will prevent a woman from voting, but they will prevent her from ever becoming a man. . . ." I had not thought of that!

"No one can deny," he says, "that the mean weight of the O. T. and C. S. in a man is 42 and in woman 38; or that there is a significant difference in the pelvic girdle." Ah, that fatal difference in the mean weight of the O. T. and C. S. To think that I had gone among them for years without noticing it!

Dr. Sedgwick, the noted biologist, goes further.

He gives "facts which are not generally discussed in the newspapers." And therefore, of course, not generally known. There is the dark and terrible fact, for instance, that every twenty-eight—no, I cannot bring myself to tell it. It is too sinister, too disillusionizing.

Of course, I knew about these things—quite intimately, indeed. I knew that women had babies, and that every twenty-eight—in short, I knew. But I did not know the dreadful significance of these things. I did not know that they cut woman off forever from political and intellectual life.

But they do! These great scientific authorities say so, and it must be true. These things, innocent as they always seemed to me, have marked woman as a thing apart from the life of mankind. She does not think as man thinks; her whole psychology is deranged by the fact of her sex; much of the time she is practically insane, and at no time is she to be trusted to take part in man's affairs. She is chronically queer; of an "unstable preciosity." She is not in fact a person at all, capable of thinking and acting for herself; others must think and act for her. If permitted to behave as a free and independent human being, she would do injury to herself and the community.

Through all this there runs a strain of dark implication, which I have met before—in the speculations of savage medicine-men on "the mysterious sex." Sir Almroth Wright echoes the chief scientific authority of the Ekoi, in Southern Nigeria, who "as no one can deny" has though deeply upon the fact that woman is marked recurringly with a sanguine sign, and subject to the dreadful magic of childbirth. She is therefore not on any account to be allowed to touch a weapon that is to be used in hunting—her influence would bring bad luck. "The reverberations of her physiological emergencies," says Sir Almroth—how this phrase would please Aiyu, the great witch-doctor who lives near Okuni!

This witch-doctor view of womankind is stated, multiplied, expanded, argued, urged, until, overborne by the weight of authority, I am compelled to accept it as the right one. I hate to do it. It hurts me to believe such things of the girls I have always got along so well with. I don't like it at all. But I must face the truth.

Well; what then? Then, say the pamphlets, keep her close, don't let her out, above all don't let her meddle with men's affairs. I should think not!

Give her the vote? Give her nothing. Keep her

away from me! She gives me the creeps to think of. Have I been associating unawares with that kind of creature? Playing with it, talking to it, touching it—? Let me retire to a monastery.

But the pamphlets puzzle me. Having established these dark facts about woman, they tell you to cherish her, worship her, make her the queen of the kitchen and the nursery and the bedroom, the consolation and delight of your life. *Why, I should like to know?*

I can't get any consolation or delight out of that kind of creature. I can't bear even to read about her. I don't want to cherish her, I don't want to protect her, I don't want anything to do with her. James, Cardinal Gibbons may say what he likes, but I will be damned if I will enjoy the "conjugal virtues" with a woman who isn't fit to vote. If woman is like that, all I can say is—take her away!

Apparently they have persuaded me of too much, these pamphlets. They show not merely that woman isn't fit to vote, they give good reasons for believing that she isn't fit to live.

And yet—can these people be mistaken? I have known women who were mothers; I have seen something of the discomfort and the delight that children bring; I have helped put crying babies to sleep, and felt the delicious softness of infantile flesh against my cheek. And in all this there seemed to be nothing dehumanizing. I never failed to regard woman, in spite of her babies, as a person, a fellow human being.

What if I were right, after all?

Suppose it were true that women are like men, only, to us, sweeter, lovelier, more desirable companions—and with the same sense, the same interests, the same need of work and play?

I could go on living in that kind of world. And, frankly, I can't live in the other. I'd just as soon commit suicide. The nightmare of anti-suffrage oppresses me. I will go back to my own country, where a woman is a person, with a mind and will of her own, fit for all the rough, sweet uses of this harsh and happy life.

—October-November 1915

HORTENSE FLEXNER
The Fire-Watchers

Woman, who the dim centuries ago,
Guarded the fire,
Fed it with twig and branch,
While the strong male with weapon crude,
Ranged the deep woods,

In search of meat and berries and wild fruit;
Woman, who sheltering, hovering near the flame,
Watched its curved leapings, waiting, lonely, still,
With fear and dark foreboding and fierce love;
O, woman, silent watcher of the day,
Inactive, yearning, listening,
Stretching cold hands above the yellow flame
That must not die;
We send to you across the million years,
The kinship call,
Our greeting of despair!
Do we not know as by the hearth we wait,
Watching the falling ash, the glowing heart
Of coal or log,
What were your thoughts, your agonies, your
    prayers?
Do we not tremble with the fear you felt,
And strain to catch the footstep on the flag,
The opening door,
As you the snapping of the underbrush,
The tearing of the cave mouth's matted vine?
Are not our hands, stretched to the blaze, your
    own?
And do our savage hearts not cry,
Out of the wilderness of stone and steel;
"Why always ours to wait, to feed the fire,
"While he, with leap, with joy of strength and life,
"Follows the prey, spends of his fearless youth
"Beneath the open skies?"
Mother of ages, brooding in the dusk,
Forging the chain of empty hours and years,
O why, for us,
The weary after-keepers of the hearth,
Did you not heed the call of wind and toil,
Tread the red embers cold and take your way,
Alone and free,
That all the misery of the faggot load,
The guarding of the flame by those who wait,
Had never been?

—September 1913

MAX EASTMAN
Confession of a Suffrage Orator

It was never a question of making people believe in the benefits of women's freedom, it was a question of making them *like the idea*. And all the abstract arguments in the world furnished merely a sort of auction ground upon which the kindly beauties of the thing could be exhibited. Aristotle, in his hopeful way, defined man as a "reasonable animal," and the schools have been laboring under that delusion ever since. But man is a voluntary

Drawn by Cornelia Barns, March 1915

"My Dear, I'll be economically independent if I have to borrow every cent!"

animal, and he knows what he likes and what he dislikes, and that is the greater part of his knowledge. Especially is this true of his opinion upon questions involving sex, because in these matters his native taste is so strong. He will have a multitude of theories and abstract reasons surrounding it, but these are merely put on for the sake of gentility, the way clothes are. Most cultivated people think there is something indecent about a naked preference. I believe, however, that propagandists would fare better, if they were boldly

aware that they are always moulding wishes rather than opinions.

There is something almost ludicrous about the attitude of a professional propagandist to his kit of arguments—and in the suffrage movement especially, because the arguments are so many and so old, and so classed and codified, and many of them so false and foolish too. I remember that during the palmiest days of the abstract argument (before California came in and spoiled everything with a big concrete example) I was engaged in teaching, or endeavoring to teach, Logic to a division of Sophomores at Columbia. And there was brought to my attention at that time a book published for use in classes like mine, which contained a codification in logical categories of all the suffrage arguments, both pro and con, and a *priori* and a *posteriori,* and *per accidens* and *per definitionem,* that had ever been advanced since Socrates first advocated the strong-minded woman as a form of moral discipline for her husband. I never found in all my platform wanderings but one suffrage argument that was not in this book, and that I discovered on the lips of an historical native of Troy, New York. It was a woman, she said, who first invented the detachable linen collar, that well-known device for saving a man the trouble of changing his shirt, and though that particular woman is probably dead, her sex remains with its pristine enthusiasm for culture and progress.

But the day of the captious logician, like the day of the roaring orator, is past. What our times respond to is the propagandist who knows how to respect the wishes of other people, and yet show them in a sympathetic way that there is more fun for them, as well as for humanity in general, in the new direction. *Give them an hour's exercise in liking something else*—that is worth all the proofs and refutations in the world.

Take that famous proposition that "woman's sphere is the home." A canvass was made at a women's college a while ago to learn the reasons for opposing woman suffrage, and no new ones were found, but among them all this dear old saying had such an overwhelming majority that it amounted to a discovery. It is the eternal type. And how easy to answer, if you grab it crudely with your intellect, imagining it to be an opinion.

"Woman's sphere is the home!" you cry. "Do you know that according to the census of 1910 more than one woman in every five in this country is engaged in gainful employment?

"Woman's sphere is the home! Do you know where your *soap* comes from?

"Woman's sphere is the home!—do you know that in fifty years all the work that women used to do within the four walls of her house has moved out into the ——

"Woman's sphere is the home! Do you know that, as a simple matter of fact, the sphere of those women who most need the protection of the government and the laws is *not* home but the factory and the market!

"Why, to say that woman's sphere is the home

after the census says it isn't, is like saying the earth is flat after a hundred thousand people have sailed round it!"

Well—such an assault and battery of the intellect will probably silence the gentle idealist for a time, but it will not alter the direction of her will. She never intended to express a statistical opinion, and the next time you see her she will be telling somebody else—for she will not talk to you any more—that "woman's *proper* sphere is the home." In other words, and this is what she said the first time, if you only had the gift of understanding, "I like women whose sphere is the home. My husband likes them, too. And we should both be very unhappy if I had to go to work outside. It doesn't seem charming or beautiful to us."

Now there is a better way to win over a person with such a gift of strong volition and delicate feeling, than to jump down her throat with a satchel full of statistics. I think a propagandist who realized that here was an expression primarily of a human wish, and that these wishes, spontaneous, arbitrary, unreasoned, because reason itself is only their servant, are the divine and unanswerable thing in us all, would respond to her assertion more effectively, as well as more pleasantly.

The truth is that any reform which associates itself with the name of liberty, or democracy, is peculiarly adapted to this more persuasive kind of propaganda. For liberty does not demand that any given person's tastes or likings as to a way of life be reformed. It merely demands that these should not be erected into a dogma, and inflicted as morality or law upon everybody else. It demands that all persons should be made free in the pursuit of their own tastes or likings.

Thus the most ardent suffragist might begin by answering our domestic idealist—"Well, I suppose it is a charming and beautiful thing for you to stay in your home, since you are happy there. I myself have a couple of neighbors who have solved their problem of life that way too, and I never have an argument with them. Why? Because they recognize that all people's problems are not to be solved in the same way. They recognize the varieties of human nature. They recognize that each one of us has a unique problem of life to solve, and he or she must be made free to solve it in her own unique way. That is democracy. That is the liberty of man. That is what universal suffrage means, and would accomplish, so far as political changes can accomplish it.

"Let us agree that woman's *proper* sphere is

the home, whenever it is. But there are many women who, on account of their natural disposition perhaps, or perhaps on account of their social or financial situation, cannot function happily in that sphere; and they are only hindered in the wholesome and fruitful solution of their lives by the dogma which you and your society hold over them, and which is crystallized and entrenched as political inequality by the fundamental law."

Thus our agitation of the woman question would appear to arise, not out of our own personal taste in feminine types, but out of our very recognition of the fact that tastes differ. We would propagandize, not because we are cranks and have a fixed idea about what everybody else ought to become, and what must be done about it at once, but because we are trying to accept variety and the natural inclinations of all sorts of people as, by presumption at least, self-justified and divine. We want them all to be free.

Such is the peculiar advantage that the propaganda of liberty has over all the evangelical enthusiasms. It does not at the first gasp ask a man to mortify his nature. It merely asks him to cease announcing his own spontaneous inclinations as the type and exemplar of angelic virtue, and demanding that everybody else be like him. It tries to remove another old negative dogmatic incubus from the shoulders of life, aspiring toward variety and realization. That is what the suffrage propaganda is doing.

It would be folly to pretend, however, that the principle of equal liberty is the only motive behind the suffrage movement. I have said that it is the primary one. It is at least the broadest, the surest, the one upon which the conversion of a person whose taste opposes yours can be most graciously introduced.

But there is yet another way of changing a person's wish, and that is to show him that he himself has deeper wishes which conflict with it. And there is one deep wish in particular that almost all women, and most men possess, and that is a wish for the welfare and advancement of their children. And just as "Woman's sphere is the home" typifies the voluntary force opposing woman suffrage, so "Women owe it to their children to develop their own powers," typifies the force that favors it.

Universal citizenship has meant in human history universal education. That has been, next to a certain precious rudiment of liberty, its chief value. That will be its chief value to women for a long time to come. And by education I do not mean merely political education. I do not mean that it will awaken in women what we call a "civic consciousness," though it will, I suppose, and that is a good thing. I mean that by giving to women a higher place in our social esteem, it will promote their universal development.

We are not educated very much by anything we study in school or see written on the blackboard. That does not determine what we grow up to be. The thing that determines what we grow up to be is the natural expectations of those around us. If society expects a girl to become a fully developed, active and intelligent individual, she will probably do it. If society expects her to remain a doll-baby all her life, she will make a noble effort to do that. In either case she will not altogether succeed, for there are hereditary limitations, but the responsibility for the main trend of the result is with the social conscience.

> "Sugar and spice and everything nice,
> That is what little girls are made of;
> Snips and snails and puppy-dogs' tails,
> That is what little boys are made of."

There is an example of what has been educating us. That kind of baby-talk has done more harm than all the dynamite that was ever let off in the history of the world. You might as well put poison in the milk.

All that is to be ended. And this is the chief thing we expect of women's citizenship. It will formulate in the public mind the higher ideal that shall develop the young girls of the future. They will no longer grow up to be, outside the years of motherhood, mere drudges or parlor ornaments. They will no longer try to satisfy their ambitions by seeing who can parade the most extreme buffooneries of contemporary fashion on the public highway. They will grow up to be interested and living individuals, and satisfy their ambitions only with the highest prizes of adventure and achievement that life offers.

And the benefit of that will fall upon us all—but chiefly upon the children of these women when they are mothers. For if we are going anywhere that a sane idealism would have us go, we must first stop corrupting the young. Only a developed and fully constituted individual is fit to be the mother of a child. Only one who has herself made the most of the present, is fit to hold in her arms the hope of the future.

We hear a good deal about "child-welfare" in these days, and we hear the business of child-welfare advanced as one of the arguments for woman suffrage. To me it is almost the heart of the arguments, but it works in my mind a little differently from what it does in the minds of the people who write the child-welfare pamphlets. I do not want women to have, for the sake of their children, the control of the milk-supply and the food laws, half so much as I want them to have, for the sake of their children, all the knowledge-by-experience that they can possibly get. That is the vital connection between child-welfare and woman suffrage—that is the deeper ideal. No woman is fit to bring children into this world until she knows to the full the rough actual character of the world into which she is bringing them. And she will never know that until we lift from her—in her own growing years —the repressive prejudice that expresses itself and maintains itself in refusing to make her a citizen.

A man who trains horses up in western New York put this to me very strongly. "If you're going to breed race-horses," he said, "you don't pick out your stallions on a basis of speed and endurance, and your mares according to whether they have sleek hides and look pretty when they hang their heads over the pasture fence. And if you're going to raise intelligent citizens you'll have to give them intelligent citizens for mothers." I do not know whether he was aware that an actual tendency to *select* the more intelligent, rather than

a mere training of the intelligence of all, is the main force in racial evolution. But that is what he said. And, either way, it is a piece of cold scientific fact. The babies of this world suffer a good deal more from silly mothers than they do from sour milk. And any change in political forms, however superificial from the standpoint of economic justice, that will increase the breadth of experience, the sagacity, the humor, the energetic and active life-interest of mothers, can only be regarded as a profound historic revolution.

In these broad effects upon the progress of liberty and life, not in any political result of equal suffrage, are to be found an object of desire which can rival and replace the ideal that opposes it. They are the material for the propaganda of the will. And while we noisy orators are filling the air with syllogisms of justice, and prophecies of the purification of politics, and the end of child labor, and what women will do to wars, and the police-department, and the sweat-shops, and the street-cleaning department, and the milk-wagons, and the dairy farms, and how they will reform the cows when they come into their rights, we ought to remember in our sober hearts that those large warm human values, which have nothing to do with logic or politics or reform, are what will gradually bend the wishes of men toward a new age.

—November 1915

Birth Control

[*Radical support for birth control was largely inspired by feminist sympathies. The need to free women from the dangers of excessive childbirth and their bondage to large, unwanted families were the primary reasons advanced by radicals for family limitation. Not surprisingly, the early birth control movement owed a considerable debt to the Left. Before America's entry into the war, birth control was one of the touchiest causes supported by* The Masses. *Many people were arrested for distributing contraceptive literature, and Margaret Sanger was forced at one point to flee the country. A degree of circumspection on the issue was demanded of* The Masses, *which compensated by striking as militant a pose as possible and by raising funds for the victims of Comstockery.*]

MAX EASTMAN
The Woman Rebel

In Margaret Sanger's new magazine, with its motto the old ideal that Lucretius preserved from Epicurus, "No Gods, No Masters," I look for a strong and poised and affirmative expression of the final goal of feminism. In two respects, and these very vital, I am disappointed in the first member. It is not sufficiently strong and it is not affirmative.

Just as a blow landed with your arm at full length is weak, so is a statement which holds no emotion in reserve. I think the Woman Rebel has fallen into that most unfeminist of errors, the tendency to cry out when a quiet and contained utterance is indispensable. Everything it says, so far as I can remember, might be accepted, or at least soberly debated, by anyone devoted to the life of reason. But in a style of over-conscious extremism and blare of rebellion for its own sake, those who incline to the life of reason will be the last to read it. Like the Anarchist Almanac, the Woman Rebel seems to give a little more strength to the business of shocking the Bourgeoisie than the Bourgeoisie really are worth.

And then further, its mood is not affirmative. The clever and original things in it are not assertions of liberty, nor even attacks upon the varieties of bondage. They are attacks upon other feminists who have not gone so far, or have gone in a somewhat different direction from the editors. And that of course is the old story of wasted strength in negativism.

I think this phenomenon might be described, in Freudian language, as a transference of hate from the original object to another object from which one can get a more satisfactory response! The entrenchments of custom and capital and privilege are so impregnable to our attacks—they ignore us and we have no satisfaction, and so we turn upon our own weaker sisters and brothers who will recoil and fight back, and give us an exhaust for our emotions. It is the sad history of every crusade.

But we must thank Margaret Sanger for speaking out clearly and quietly for popular education in the means of preventing conception. And if she goes to court in this fight, we must go too and stand behind her and make her martyrdom—if martyrdom it must be—the means of that very publicity she is fighting to win. There is no more important stand, and no stand that requires more bravery and purity of heart, than this one she is making. And if the virtue that holds heroes up to these sticking points must needs be united with the fault of a rather unconvincing excitedness and intolerance—all right, we will hail the virtue and call it a bargain at the price.   —May 1914

ELSIE CLEWS PARSONS
Facing Race Suicide

[*Mrs. Parsons was the Left's favorite anthropologist. A regular contributor to* The Masses, *the* Dial, *and other progressive journals, she first achieved fame with her textbook,* The Family *(1906), in which she suggested that legal marriage be preceded by trial marriages. She enjoyed a distinguished scientific career culminating in her election to the presidency of the American Anthropological Association in 1940.*]

Sentimentality is always a costly luxury, but one form of it, the indulgence in emotions over the irrelevant or the non-existent, is peculiarly extravagant—and peculiarly American. Encourage an American to express himself, on the native birth-rate, for example, and he will talk to you about the high cost of living, pampered wives, nationality, or the god of an alien, ancient race, all facts, more or less, but irrelevancies, each capable enough of arousing an emotion for itself, but none holding any relation whatsoever to the emotion of regret over the fallen birth-rate which always warms up the speaker's peroration.

If it seems worth while, perhaps you point out to him by way of preliminary that children are no longer economic assets in the family, nor does he want them to be; that army and navy can be as well recruited from other countries as from factory or public school or university; that the supernatural sanction has become a negligible factor in our life; that if intelligence and character are to be reproduced as race traits, only women who want children should bear them, not women who are mothers despite themselves—and he will probably agree with you on all these points.

The air cleared, you may go on to ask him why the kind of woman you and he both admire, or say you admire, the woman of intelligence and character, why should she or why does she have children? I doubt if he has ever thought about it—in this way, as he will say—and as thinking may make him feel uncomfortable and restless, he is almost certain to change the subject—with some appeal to your sense of humor. Having one of course, you drop the subject, or—him.

Why *does* a woman, the kind of woman let us concede we admire, bear children? Surely not from sentimentality, not from powerlessness, not from ignorance. Why does she bear children? Because motherhood is to her an expression of her-

THE
MAY, 1915   10 CENTS

MASSES

WHAT I SAW IN PRISON - - BY FRANK TANENBAUM

NEWS FROM THE FRONT - - BY ROSIKA SCHWIMMER

ISADORA DUNCAN IN THE "MARCHE MILITAIRE"

self, either a direct, simple expression or a more complex expression through her love for another.

Modern as this conception of childbearing is, it is being forced upon the attention of even those conservative and alarmist moralists, the race-suicide croakers. What are they going to do about it? Are they willing to eliminate distinctions between legitimacy and illegitimacy, distinctions inherited from a culture in which this conception of childbearing was undreamed of? Are they willing to reform many other social conditions, economic and non-economic, which at present make childbearing impossible or possible only at great sacrifice for the women they consider desirable mothers?

We have here, I think, a measure of their insight and a touchstone of their sincerity. At present, they are, they must admit, in an *impasse*. Do they not see girls brought up to conceptions of themselves and of life, of life's duties and privileges, to conceptions which in very many cases the girls find, when they meet life, they are expected to forego or refute, a surrender likely to make of them the colorless, untemperamental, unsexed women Europeans consider the American type? In brief, do they not see that the woman of whom they approve has been educated for a life she is not allowed to live, taught to seek self-expression and then denied it because of the narrow limits within which love and maternity are open to her, limits incompatible with her education? Instead of criticising her because she hasn't fallen in love with the "right" man or because she hasn't borne more children, her critics ought in fairness to be satisfied with having the population maintained by immigration, or by the birth-rate among those immigrants whose peasant education is consistent with the conditions for mating and childbearing obtaining in America—or in that part of America, shall we say, represented by the Board of Education that excludes the teacher-mother or by the State Legislature that makes the control of conception illegal.   —June 1915

A Letter to *The Masses* from a Distinguished Citizen

It is the duty of all patriotic citizens with red blood in their veins to denounce as peculiarly base and criminal the movement toward birth limitation, that is not only condoned, but actively and wilfully defended by THE MASSES.

I, myself, and all men who are not moral cowards or mollycoddles, are heartily in favor of childbearing, because it is right. I favor as genuinely all things that are right, as I oppose all things that are wrong. And to deny that what is right is right is simply a case of conscious and infamous wrong-doing.

Let me repeat, any one who is opposed to the bearing of children by women is guilty of outrageous and flagrant conduct, which is precisely as evil for the man of great wealth as for the wage-earner or small business man.

I heartily favor the law limiting the period of gestation to three months. If this were done, there is no adequate reason why any woman with a single spark of patriotism should not bear at least four children a year. It is literally incomprehensible how any man of average intelligence can tolerate the limitation of progeny or permit his wife to have less than four healthy and vigorous babies annually. To do so is to act with wanton and indefensible baseness.

It is common knowledge that the prevalence of such standards in American society is due to the criminal failure of Messrs. Wilson and Bryan to protect the American flag in Mexico. The utterly preposterous action of President Wilson, who has knowingly chosen to remain at ease in Washington, rather than shoulder a gun and knapsack and die for his country in Mexico, has jeopardized the political future of the United States and reduced the morale of the government to the level of Dahomey.   —May 1915

Emma Goldman's Defense

[On April 20th, Emma Goldman was sentenced to fifteen days' imprisonment for delivering a lecture on Birth Control. She conducted her own defense, and we print her speech below.]

Your Honor: My presence before you this afternoon proves conclusively that there is no free speech in the city or county of New York. I hope that there is free speech in your court.

I have delivered the lecture which caused my arrest in at least fifty cities throughout the country, always in the presence of detectives. I have never been arrested. I delivered the same address in New York City seven times, prior to my arrest, always in the presence of detectives, because in my case, your honor, "the police never cease out of the land." Yet for some reason unknown to me I have never been molested until February 11th, nor would I have been then, if free speech were a living factor, and not a dead letter to be celebrated only on the 4th of July.

Your Honor, I am charged with the crime of having given information to men and women as to how to prevent conception. For the last three weeks, every night before packed houses, a stirring social indictment is being played at the Candler Theatre. I refer to "Justice" by John Galsworthy. The council for the Defense in summing up the charge against the defendant says among other things: "Your Honor: back of the commission of every crime, is life, palpitating life."

Now what is the palpitating life back of my crime? I will tell you, Your Honor. According to the bulletin of the Department of Health, 30,000,000 people in America are underfed. They are always in a state of semi-starvation. Not only because their average income is too small to sustain them properly—the bulletin states that eight hundred dollars a year is the minimum income necessary for every family—but because there are too many members in each family to be sustained on a meagre income. Hence 30,000,000 people in this land go through life underfed and overworked.

Your Honor: what kind of children do you suppose these parents can bring into the world? I will tell you: children so poor and anemic that they take their leave from this, our kind world, before their first year of life. In that way, 300,000 babies, according to the baby welfare association, are sacrificed in the United States every year. This, Your Honor, is the palpitating life which has confronted me for many years, and which is back of the commission of my crime. I have been part of the great social struggle of this country for twenty-six years, as nurse, as lecturer, as publisher. During this time I have gone up and down the land in the large industrial centres, in the mining region, in the slums of our large cities. I have seen conditions appalling and heart-rending, which no creative genius could adequately describe. I do not intend to take up the time of the court to go into many of these cases, but I must mention a few.

A woman, married to a consumptive husband has eight children, six are in the tuberculosis hospital. She is on the way with the ninth child.

A woman whose husband earns $12 per week has six children, on the way with the seventh child.

A woman with twelve children living in three squalid rooms, dies in confinement with the 13th child, the oldest, now the mainstay of the 12 orphans, is 14 years of age.

These are but very few of the victims of our economic grinding mill, which sets a premium upon poverty, and our puritanic law which maintains a conspiracy of silence.

Your Honor: if giving one's life for the purpose of awakening race consciousness in the masses, a consciousness which will impel them to bring quality and not quantity into society, if that be a crime, I am glad to be such a criminal. But I assure you I am in good company. I have as my illustrious colleagues the greatest men and women of our time; scientists, political economists, artists, men of letters in Europe and America. And what is even more important, I have the working class, and women in every walk of life, to back me. No isolated individuals here and there, but thousands of them.

After all, the question of birth control is largely a workingman's question, above all a working-woman's question. She it is who risks her health, her youth, her very life in giving out of herself the units of the race. She it is who ought to have the means and the knowledge to say how many children she shall give, and to what purpose she shall give them, and under what conditions she shall bring forth life.

Statesmen, politicians, men of the cloth, men, who own the wealth of the world, need a large race, no matter how poor in quality. Who else would do their work, and fight their wars? But the people who toil and drudge and create, and receive a mere pittance in return, what reason have they to bring hapless children into the world? They are beginning to realize their debt to the children already in existence, and in order to make good their obligations, they absolutely refuse to go on like cattle breeding more and more.

That which constitutes my crime, Your Honor, is therefore, enabling the mass of humanity to give to the world fewer and better children—birth control, which in the last two years has grown to such gigantic dimensions that no amount of laws can possibly stop the ever-increasing tide.

And this is true, not only because of what I may or may not say, or of how many propagandists may or may not be sent to jail; there is a much profounder reason for the tremendous growth and importance of birth control. That reason is conditioned in the great modern social conflict, or rather social war, I should say. A war not for military conquest or material supremacy, a war of the oppressed and disinherited of the earth against their enemies, capitalism and the

Drawn by K. R. Chamberlain, May 1915

Family Limitation—Old Style

state, a war for a seat at the table of life, a war for well-being, for beauty, for liberty. Above all, this war is for a free motherhood and a joyous playful, glorious childhood.

Birth control, Your Honor, is only one of the ways which leads to the victory in that war, and I am glad and proud to be able to indicate that way.

—June 1916

Christ and the Churches

Drawn by K. R. Chamberlain, May 1914

"You can arrest me but you can't arrest my contempt."

[*The Tanenbaum case depicted in this drawing seemed to illustrate perfectly* The Masses' *thesis on the un-Christian nature of the Christian Church. Consequently, it lavished attention upon every phase of Tanenbaum's experiences from the time he began leading the unemployed into the churches until he was released from jail after serving a one-year term.*]

FRANK TANENBAUM

Transcript of Address to His Judge

We quote from the court record:

THE CLERK: "Frank Tanenbaum, what have you now to say why judgment should not be pronounced against you according to law?"

THE DEFENDANT: "I would like to make a statement, I think."

THE COURT: "You are at liberty to make any statement you desire."

THE DEFENDANT: "I suppose, if I make a statement, that the press somehow will say, I wanted to make myself out a hero or a martyr. I don't know who it was who said—some well-known preacher—that society would forgive a man for murder, theft, rape, or almost any crime, except that of preaching a new gospel. That is my crime. There are in reality, three distinct things I am accused of.

"One is unlawful assembly. I don't know of any circumstances in the world's history where the struggles of the slave class have appeared either legal, or respectable, or religious in the eyes of the master class. I am a member of the slave class. I am a member of the working class, and I know that our struggles to overcome our present condition are illegal in the eyes of the master class and its representatives. Of course it was unlawful. I don't doubt that.

"Another very serious objection against me was that I answered 'Yes' to the statement about bloodshed. Why make all this nonsense about bloodshed? Capital sheds more blood in one year than we would in five. We are being killed every day. We are being killed in the mines, in the buildings, killed everywhere, killed in the battlefield fighting the wars of the capital class. No wars in recent times have been fought in the interests of the workers, and yet everywhere it was the workers who died. We don't fear bloodshed. We have nothing to lose except our miserable lives.

"That district attorney hasn't got heart enough to be a dog catcher. He said I took graft, twenty-five dollars. That isn't true. I did not take twenty-five dollars. It wasn't turned over to me. I didn't want it. It was given to Mr. Martin, the sexton of the Old Presbyterian Church, Eleventh Street and Fifth Avenue. He came along with us. It was a very miserable, windy night, the snow blowing and sleet, and we took the men, eighty-three in number, homeless, shelterless, naked and starving men, took them to a restaurant on the Bowery and fed them.

"How about religion and praying to God? Why, there is no more religious thing I have ever witnessed than that lot of homeless, half-fed, half-dressed, ill-clad men sitting over a long table enjoying a clean, warm meal, laughing and talking. That is the most religious thing I ever saw. And this man, Mr. Martin, paid for that out of his own pocket, out of the twenty-five dollars which he, and not I, held. Then we took these men to Bowery hotel on Third Avenue and put them to bed, and there was ten cents left after the men were put to bed, which I will turn over to the district attorney if he wants it.

"Another far more serious act upon my part, unlawful, illegal, unrespectable, was my attitude towards the priests. Now, I don't know of anyone I was ever impolite to. I am polite to everybody, even to my enemies, because I can afford to be. But I want to tell you that Doctor Schneider is supposed to represent the Gospel of Christ, he is supposed to preach and practice the Gospel of the Man who came down and who died on the cross because the poor, common people listened to Him. One of the indictments against Jesus Christ was that the common people listened to Him gladly. And I want to tell you that if He came down upon earth now, Father Schneider would be the first one to crucify Him..

"There are a few other things I want to say. When I was arrested, that was the first time I had ever been in court, first time I had ever been in the police station or had anything to do with the police. I was so ignorant of these things that when I was called into the magistrates' court I saw the clerk, and I asked the lieutenant if that wasn't the judge. I didn't know, then, anything about courts and judges, which means the law, the present system, and from what I have learned now I have very little respect for them, I must admit, very little respect for them. I feel, after having lived with those boys three weeks in the Tombs prison, every one of them, if they would have been able to go to school, if they had a decent place to live and a decent job, and if they had not been kicked about and driven from place to place as most of them were, they would have been just as good as anybody else, just as good as anybody else, even the district attorney.

"I think now, your Honor, and I am going to say what I think, that when the first man was convicted in this court, justice flew out the window and never returned and never will. You never know, and the law does not take into consideration, anything about human wants or the circumstances impelling a human being to so-called crime. They are not responsible for what they do, their drifting into crimes. You don't know their life. I believe from my impressions and associations with these boys that they are more normal and more spontaneous than others, and that is why they cannot adapt themselves to this rotten society. They feel that as human beings for the sake of a piece of bread it is not worth while to work twelve long hours in a factory.

"There is little more I have to say. This trial for me was arranged by my friends in spite of my protest. I didn't want it. I knew what I was going to get, because I am not one of your class. But they prevailed upon me. They said, 'Give them a chance, they will not find you guilty, because you are not guilty of any crime. There is no damage done, no property destroyed.' There was no property destroyed and no injury, and I knew there was absolutely no violence, and they said, 'You will be freed,' so I agreed to it. But of course I am convicted. It is not a surprise to me. I expected it.

"But I must say that although Lieutenant Gegan treated me very nicely always, during the trial he lied absolutely when he said he didn't call me up the steps. That is an absolute lie. I was on those steps and he told me to come in. He lied. When I took the stand I didn't have to plead my case, just tell the truth exactly as I knew it. I didn't want a trial, but I have got it. I will never, if arrested in labor troubles, submit to a trial again. No more trials for me. The members of the jury, while they may be fair-minded, are not workmen. They don't know the life of a workingman. There is no jury—you could not get a jury of twelve workmen, structural iron workers for instance, to convict me; absolutely no. These gentlemen are members of your class in a way. They are capitalists. They would like to be. They would like to be rich. That's all right, but they are capitalists. Now that is all I have to say. I consider my conviction absolutely unjust. You have tried to question the right of hungry men to get their bread. That is the crime, and I am willing to take the consequences, whatever they may be."   —May 1914

MAX EASTMAN
The Tanenbaum Crime

This is the story of a crime that I saw committed, and by crime I do not mean what is ordinarily meant—an act, whether moral or immoral, which is contrary to law. I mean something unquestionably immoral, an arbitrary assault upon a young man's liberty and his right to live.

I am in a position of advantage in relating this crime, because I sat an observer through the whole proceeding.

I refer, as you have surmised, to the trial of Frank Tanenbaum. Through grace of his attorneys I was present at this trial, although the public —perhaps because of its habit to express contempt when contempt is called for—was not admitted.

It was the first jury trial I ever saw. And I liked the look of the judge, and I liked the look of the jury, and I guessed the boy would be understood and have a good chance. I knew little of his story, and so I interested myself in personating a juror. I banished from my mind every feeling of prejudice or excessive sympathy, put myself in that quite vacuous condition expected of a jury, and gathered from the testimony and arguments the following very simple story. And of the truth of this story, and that it is the whole truth so far as bears upon the indictment, I am quite dispassionately convinced.

On the night of March 4th, Frank Tanenbaum addressed a crowd of the unemployed on Rutgers Square, telling them in the usual language of socialist economics why they had no chance to get work, or even if they got work to get good wages. telling them that not only the interests of capital are against them, but the police and the courts and the military also, who are the servants of capital.

In the midst of this speech he was interrupted once by a woman who said something like this:

"In France the people had to use force to win their Independence. In Paris the streets ran with blood."

"Yes," said Tanenbaum, "and it will take force to overthrow capitalism here, too. And the I. W. W. is organizing the force that will do it when the time comes."

And then later in his speech some one interrupted him to ask why he led the men to the churches and not to the Fifth Avenue clubs.

He said that it was "because the church seemed to him a natural place for a hungry and homeless man to go to ask for food and shelter."

About ten or fifteen minutes after that first interruption concerning the people in France had occurred and been answered, he told the men to line up in twos and threes on the sidewalk and they would all march to a church to get food. If they failed to get it in a church, they would go to a bakery. Some three hundred men must have formed in line to march. But when they arrived at the church of Alphonsius, two police detectives, who had been present, told Tanenbaum that he could not enter the church unless he got permission from the rector.

He said, "All right." And turning to the men —"his army," as the press called them—he told them to wait there until he got permission to enter the church.

He then entered alone with the two detectives, and being told by the assistant that the rector was in the rectory next door he returned, and again telling the men to wait where they were, he ascended the steps of the rectory. When Father Schneider came to the door, one of the detectives said:

"Father, this is Frank Tanenbaum, who wishes to speak to you."

Tanenbaum said: "I have three hundred men here who want food and shelter. If you will give it to us, we'll clean everything up all right in the morning."

"No, I cannot do that," said Father Schneider.

"Will you give us food?"

"No."

"Will you give us money?"

"No."

"Do you call that the spirit of Christ, to turn hungry and homeless men away?"

"I will not let you talk to me like that."

"All right, no harm done, Cap." Here Tanenbaum offered to shake hands and the priest refused.

Tanenbaum and the detectives then descended the steps to return to the army, but the army meanwhile, of their own volition, had entered the church. They had entered in an orderly way in spite of their numbers, and most of them had taken seats near the altar. This caused surprise and some consternation to the occupants of the pews, as you may imagine, and a crowd of newspaper men and detectives coming in at the same time, and talking rather loudly at the back of the church, considerably increased the excitement.

The image of a saint, a little altar, stood close beside one of the entries, and in coming in by that

'HE STIRRETH UP THE PEOPLE'

JESUS CHRIST

THE WORKINGMAN OF NAZARETH
WILL SPEAK
AT BROTHERHOOD HALL
— SUBJECT —
— THE RIGHTS OF LABOR —

Drawn by Art Young, December 1913

[The Masses' *Christmas* issue in *1913* was entirely devoted to an attack on the churches. *As this cover* demonstrates, The Masses *was inclined to feel that the worst crime of the churches was their having* suppressed Christ's essential role as a popular leader.]

door it had been necessary for some of the men to step over the legs of an old man who was kneeling there. His legs projected into the doorway, but they were not stepped upon, nor was the worshipper pushed against nor molested.

One of the congregation testified that some of the men demanded sitting room in the pew he occupied, and that he rose and moved to another part of the church. Another testified that the men kept their hats on, but a photograph taken by a reporter reveals only three men with their hats on, one a detective and another a newspaper man.

Apparently the men had been there only a little while and were almost all seated, when the assistant rector stepped up on a pew at the rear of the church, with his arm around a pillar, and called in a loud voice:

"All those who do not belong to this church will please leave."

This announcement evoked subdued groans, or expressions of disapproval from some of the men. I say subdued, for of the few disinterested witnesses called, a majority testified that they heard nothing of that kind at all. The testimony upon the conduct of the men suggested indeed that they were a little awed, they were timorous. They must have been, for three hundred men entering a room at once in an ordinary way would of itself constitute a tumult. And the prosecution had genuine difficulty in establishing any proof of loud noise or disorder.

Now, Frank Tanenbaum returned from the rectory in time to hear the assistant rector make that announcement from the rear pew. He did not enter the church. He merely stood at the door of the church and called: "Come on, boys, we're not wanted here. Let's go somewhere else."

He and another young man then held a door open for the "army" to file out. He was interrupted after about fifty were outside by a detective, who told him to step inside and close the door, until the reserves should be summoned.

Tanenbaum said: "You needn't summon the reserves. There'll be no trouble here if you'll just let me get these men quietly out of the church." But the detective insisted upon his coming inside, and as he came Tanenbaum turned to the reporters and said:

"I call you to witness that if any trouble, any violence occurs, it is on the heads of the police."

The detective then closed the doors, and placed a uniformed policeman at each of them to prevent further egress.

"You're not under arrest now, Tanenbaum," he said, "but stay inside here until I telephone for instructions from the commissioner."

Tanenbaum then made the announcement to his men: "Sit down, boys. Keep your seats."

After that some time elapsed, during which pictures were taken by the reporters, but one of the congregation testified that she prayed and continued her devotions. The detective finally returned from telephoning the commissioner, and placed Tanenbaum and all the men in the church under arrest.

This is the story of what happened exactly as I think an unprejudiced mind would have received it from the witnesses, arguments of counsel, and interpolations of judge. It is what I myself believe, after listening there impersonally for the most of three days.

At the conclusion of the arguments of counsel there ensued from the bench a long reading of laws and opinions as to the profound and peculiar liberties of American citizens. And it was here that I began to doubt the chances of liberty for Tanenbaum. To be sure Judge Wadhams only delivered himself of the old maxims of popular government—re-asserted the purely political interpretation of the ideals of equality and democracy. But to re-assert those old maxims just there and just then—in the face of that forlorn uprising of hungry and homeless men who wanted only a chance to sweat in this free land of ours—Oh, I gave up before he had traveled very far on that judicial preachment, any hope of a clear and candid confronting of the facts.

My mind returned as he spoke of the liberty and equality of American citizens to the picture of one of the witnesses, a tragic, dark, tattered and half-clad Jewish boy, with the face of a suffering Christ, hunting and hunted to his very death as any man could see, and any man with a heart under his coat could *feel*. He had sat there in the witness stand only a few hours before, telling through an interpreter the frightened story of his destitution, and his hope that this youthful prophet could find him a mouthful of food. I remembered, too, another witness, a fine old, strong, genially wrinkled American mechanic, a Catholic—he had kneeled to the altar when he entered the church—and his testimony that he had been out of work for three months, and that he had gone there because he believed he would be fed, and he was hungry. And I remembered besides a little thing that I should hardly tell. I remembered that the chief personage in the criminal courts building had once said to my friend—"If the people really knew what goes on in this building, they would come here and tear it down." But that was a private communication, as those truths always are, and I will ask you to forget it. I only wanted to observe how these things came to my mind, and others—the whole pith and setting of the story that had been related before us, a story of starvation in an age of wealth.

But let us pass over the charge to the jury. Suffice it to say that Frank Tanenbaum, in spite of all the testimony as to what deference he showed to the police, to the priest, to the laws and customs of things, how carefully he tried to keep his men out of the church until he had permission to take them in, and to get them out after they got in; in spite of the fact that he had gone to other churches on other nights *with intent to ask for bread and shelter,* and in two cases at least had received them and sought nothing else; in spite of all this, and his too evident high motive, and the fact that he was *compelled* to attend the "unlawful assembly" by the policeman who arrested him— still he was found guilty of "assembling with intent to disturb the peace of society."

And the jury did their duty—twelve men "called from their *business* life," as the judge himself casually observed, to pass judgment upon a wage-worker. They did their duty so well that they found the defendant guilty, not only of unlawful assembly, but also of *refusal to disperse when told to do so by an officer.* And the judge had to send them back, telling them that they could find him guilty upon one count only, or else not guilty—it didn't matter which count. And they found him guilty of unlawful assembly.

And so standing there with poise and with the strength of self-restraint, but with no lack of scorn, pointing an eloquent finger at the judge, or jury, or district attorney as he spoke, Frank Tanenbaum uttered a few truths that made the whole solemn-farcical proceeding worth while.

. . . .

So far one might, in retrospect at least, view calmly this whole case as a conflict of ideals. The old political ideal set forth in the rhetoric of the last century by the magistrate, and the new economic ideal voiced in the greater eloquence of the living present by the defendant. One might even smile and rejoice at the evident preponderance of material truth in the words of the defendant. But for what followed there was no smiling.

THE COURT: "Frank Tanenbaum, there is no place in the world where a workingman has such an opportunity for advancement as in the United States of America. One glimpse at the piers where our ocean steamers dock is sufficient to convince any man of that fact. . . .

"It is most commendable to work, to strive, to use every endeavor of heart and mind to better the condition of our fellow men. In that I am sure you have the heartfelt sympathy of all the community, that you should be trying so to do. . . . Your offense is not in seeking to ameliorate the condition of the suffering, but your offense consists in doing it in such a way that you violated one of the rights which all enjoy, including yourself, namely, the right to worship in the manner that you see fit. . . .

"My sympathy goes out to you on account of your failure to appreciate the great opportunities that are here before you in this country, because you have failed to understand the spirit of our institutions. . . .

"It is the judgment of this Court that the extreme penalty which may be imposed in such a case is yours, that you be committed to the Penitentiary for one year and that you pay a fine of five hundred dollars and remain there committed until each dollar is paid, one day for each dollar."

There is, perhaps, some humor in dwelling upon the "opportunities for advancement" afforded by this country to workingmen who are starving because they cannot find a job. There is humor in trying to prove the existence of these opportunities by a glimpse at *incoming* steamers. There is humor too, in convicting a man of "unlawful assembly," upon the ground that he violated the constitutional right "to worship in the manner that we see fit." From a legal standpoint perhaps that is the most humorous of all. It suggests that even technically it was a little difficult to piece together a misdemeanor out of the evidence offered. But that is all merely amusing.

What must outrage the moral sense of every man is that after acknowledging the high motive under which Tanenbaum had acted, confessing that there was no selfish purpose, no desire to injure anyone or gain anything for himself, that he was seeking only "to better the condition of his fellow men," Judge Wadhams inflicted upon that boy who had never been in a law court before, what is by the decent customs of the courts reserved for habitual criminals charged with serious offenses against persons or property, the extreme penalty of the law. Frank Tanenbaum, for his courage and idealism, will lie for two years four and one-half months in a place that by the testimony of its own supervisors is not fit for pigs to live in, unless the indignation of the friends of liberty and justice is made effective.   —May 1914

H. G. ALSBERG
Was It Something Like This?

Extracts From the Daily Press of Rome, toward the End of March, a. u. c., 783.

[*Tribuna Diurnalis, March 26.*]
RIOTS OF UNEMPLOYED IN JUDEA CONTINUE
JESUS OF NAZARETH LEADS HOBO
ARMY ON JERUSALEM.

Missa Impressa Associata.

JERUSALEM, March 26.—Yesterday the army of the unemployed, under the leadership of Jesus of Nazareth, reached the outskirts of this city, camping in Mt. Olive Park. The army is composed of a miscellaneous assortment of hoboes, ragamuffins and weak-minded enthusiasts, who have left devastation in their wake among the olive plantations of the country-side. Their leader has himself set the example by destroying fig trees.

This afternoon a crowd of loiterers, tramps, hoodlums and idle-curious, together with a few worthy unemployed of this city, streamed out of town, along the upper boulevard, to Mt. Olive Park, where the hobo general made a highly incendiary address, urging his followers not to work for a living, to despise the virtues of frugality and thrift, and to look to the king, the property owners and capitalists for sustenance in ease and idleness. The police did not interfere, but detectives were among the listeners, taking notes and ready to quell any disorders that might arise.

[*Editorial in the Tribuna Diurnalis, March 26.*]

With regard to the labor troubles in Judea, and this applies with equal truth to similar troubles throughout the empire, one can only remark on the inefficiency of the local police departments. Unemployment is, of course, a serious and pressing problem. Those who honestly desire work should be provided for by the state. But on the other hand, rioting, destruction of property, inciting mobs to violence and lawlessness should be sternly repressed. Order is the *sine qua non* of any form of government. Softhearted sympathy is misplaced, especially in the present case, as we are informed from reliable sources that the Judean rioters belong chiefly to the class of professional unemployed and habitual roustabouts; that their leader himself has been a persistent, if talented vagrant for years, his only employment having been in his youth, as apprentice in a furniture factory where his persistent idleness earned him an early discharge. We suggest to the authorities of Judea that a few good applications of the constabular rods *now* will save a great many casualties later on.

[*Tempora Romana, March 27.*]
RIOTERS MARCH INTO JERUSALEM, LOOT TEMPLE,
EXPELLING LICENSED STALLHOLDERS AND
PRIESTS WITH VIOLENCE.
JESUS STILL AT LARGE.

Missa Impressa Associata.

JERUSALEM, March 27.—Yesterday, after a night of haranguing and incendiary oratory in Mt. Olive Park, Jesus of Nazareth led his army of hoodlums into the city. After marching through the heart of the town without police interference, they broke into the Jewish temple, and, under the guidance of their leader, who took the most active part in the proceedings, upset all the licensed stalls, drove their owners out, destroyed whatever property they could lay hands on, entered the sanctum itself, expelled the officiating clergy, and even threatened the life of the Rt. Reverend Simon Caiaphas, High Priest, who happened to be in attendance.

Jesus of Nazareth threatened to wreck the temple completely, the priests with death and the complete destruction of the building. His almost insane ravings were replete with vile vituperation of all those in authority and of the hard-working citizens of the empire, and exalted to the skies, as usual, the thriftless and the improvident.

[*Orlis Noctalis, March 27. Gladiatorial Extra.*]
JESUS ARRESTED, ARRAIGNED BEFORE FEDERAL
AUTHORITIES, REFUSES TO GIVE BAIL.

Missa Impressa Associata.

JERUSALEM, Wednesday, March 27.—This evening Jesus of Nazareth was arrested on a warrant issued by Hon. Pontius Pilate, Judge of the Federal District Court, charged with inciting to riot and burglarious entry. He was taken on information lodged by a Mr. Iscariot, a former adherent of the hobo king, but who had become alienated by the latter's lawless conduct.

It is said Jesus was found carousing with his boon companions in a local tavern; wine was flowing like water and the self-styled prophet was enjoying all the delicacies of the season while his dupes were encamped in the rain, without food or shelter, in the public parks.

The prisoner will be held for trial tomorrow. He refused to furnish bail.

Drawn by Maurice Becker, December 1913

Their Last Supper

The crowning ceremony of the Episcopal Convention at New York was a banquet tendered
to the clerical deputies by the Church Club. It cost $10,680—about $20 a plate.

[*This drawing attracted more than the usual criticism. Apparently attacks upon the churches in general
were bad enough, but attacks on particular churches were unbearable.*]

[*Tribuna Diurnalis, March 27.*]
JESUS RELEASED BY FEDERAL JUDGE REARRESTED
BY LOCAL AUTHORITIES, CONVICTION SURE.
Missa Impressa Associata.

JERUSALEM, March 28.—In the federal court, to-day, Jesus of Nazareth was discharged by Hon. Pontius Pilate, who held that the federal authorities had no jurisdiction in the premises. The Rt. Rev. Simon Caiaphas was one of the chief witnesses. Jesus refused aid of counsel.

Judge Pilate ordered the prisoner's release on the ground that he had not been guilty of a breach of the federal law, and that the case was one for action by the local authorities.

Immediately after his release, Jesus, with some of the ring-leaders of the mob, was rearrested by the local authorities and committed to jail pending his trial in the state courts.

[*Editorial from the Tempora Romana, March 29.*]

We are shocked by the cowardly evasion of his plain duty in the premises on the part of Judge Pilate. He should under no circumstances have allowed legal technicalities to prevent him from carrying out his clear duty to the public. Jesus of Nazareth, the leader of the disgraceful Jerusalem riots, should have been summarily punished.

At any rate, we are glad to see that the local authorities of Judea were so prompt to act. When the history of the present wave of lawlessness, crime and hysteria which is sweeping across the empire, comes to be written, theirs will be the credit for the first brave stand in the face of a dangerous manifestation of public sentimentality.

[*Editorial from the Sol Matutinali, March 31.*]
A CLOSED INCIDENT.

A final period has been put to the activities of the Judean Agitator. Had the government taken the riots in hand earlier, the climax might have been less tragic than eventually proved to be the case. But what else could we have expected from the present, vacillating administration? It is to be hoped that the vigorous action of the Judean authorities will do much to check lawlessness and mob rule throughout the country, leaving the sober, hard-working part of our population to pursue their occupations in peace and soon, we hope, in prosperity once more.

As for the problem of the unemployed, which still persists, although to a less degree than we have been led to believe, that should be made a subject of immediate inquiry by a federal commission. —April 1914

SARAH N. CLEGHORN
Comrade Jesus

Thanks to Saint Matthew, who had been
At mass-meetings in Palestine,
We know whose side was spoken for
When Comrade Jesus had the floor.

"Where sore they toil and hard they lie,
Among the great unwashed, dwell I.
The tramp, the convict, I am he;
Cold-shoulder him, cold-shoulder me."

By Dives' door, with thoughtful eye,
He did to-morrow prophesy:—
"The Kingdom's gate is low and small;
The rich can scarce wedge through at all."

"A dangerous man," said Caiaphas;
"An ignorant demagogue, alas,
Friend of low women, it is he
Slanders the upright Pharisee."

For law and order, it was plain,
For holy Church, he must be slain.
The troops were there to awe the crowd,
And violence was not allowed.

Their foolish force with force to foil,
His strong, clean hands he would not soil.
He saw their childishness quite plain
Between the lightnings of his pain.

Between the twilights of his end
He made his fellow-felon friend;
With swollen tongue and blinding eyes,
Invited him to Paradise.

Ah, let no Local him refuse;
Comrade Jesus hath paid his dues.
Whatever other be debarred,
Comrade Jesus hath his red card.
—April 1914

SHERWOOD ANDERSON
The Strength of God

The Reverend Curtis Hartman was pastor of the Presbyterian Church at Winesburg, Ohio, and had been in that position ten years. He was forty years old, and by his nature very silent and reticent. To preach, standing in the pulpit before the people, was always a hardship for him, and from Wednesday morning until Saturday evening he thought of nothing but the two sermons that must be preached on Sunday. Early on Sunday morning he went into a little room, called a study, in the bell tower of the church, and prayed. In his prayers there was one note that always predominated, "Give me strength and courage for Thy work, Oh Lord," he pleaded, kneeling on the bare floor and bowing his head in the presence of the task that lay before him.

The Reverend Hartman was a tall man with a brown beard. His wife, a stout nervous woman, was the daughter of a manufacturer of underwear at Cleveland, Ohio. The minister himself was rather a favorite in the town. The elders of the church liked him because he was quiet and unpretentious, and Mrs. White, the banker's wife, thought him scholarly and refined.

The Presbyterian Church held itself somewhat aloof from the other churches of Winesburg. It was larger and more imposing and its minister was better paid. He even owned a carriage of his own and on summer evenings sometimes drove about town with his wife. Through Main Street and up and down Buckeye Street he went bowing gravely to the people while his wife, afire with secret pride, looked at him out of the corners of her eyes and worried lest the horse become frightened and run away.

For a good many years after he came to Winesburg things went well with Curtis Hartman. He was not one to arouse keen enthusiasm among the worshippers in his church, but on the other hand he made no enemies. In reality he was much in earnest and sometimes suffered prolonged periods of remorse because he could not go crying the word of God in the highways and byways of the town. He wondered if the flame of the spirit really burned in him and dreamed of a day when a strong sweet new current of power should come, like a great wind, into his voice and his soul and the people should tremble before the spirit of God made manifest in him. "I am a poor stick and that will never really happen to me," he mused dejectedly and then a patient smile lit up his features. "Oh well, I suppose I'm doing well enough," he added philosophically.

The room in the bell tower of the church where on Sunday mornings the minister prayed for an increase in him of the power of God, had but one window. It was long and narrow and swung outward on a hinge like a door. On the window, made of little leaded panes, was a design showing the Christ laying his hand upon the head of a child. On a Sunday morning in the summer as he sat by his desk in the room with a large Bible open before him and the sheets of his sermon scattered about, the minister was shocked to see, in the upper room of the house next door, a woman lying in her bed and smoking a cigarette while she read a book. Curtis Hartman went on tiptoe to the window and closed it softly. He was horror-stricken at the thought of a woman smoking, and trembled also to think that his eyes, just raised from the pages of the book of God, had looked upon the bare shoulders and white throat of a woman. With his brain in a whirl he went down into the pulpit and preached a long sermon without once thinking of his gestures or his voice. The sermon attracted unusual attention because of its power and clearness. "I wonder if she is listening, if my voice is carrying any message into her soul," he thought, and began to hope that on future Sunday mornings he might be able to say words that would touch and awaken the woman, apparently far gone in secret sin.

The house next door to the Presbyterian Church, through the windows of which the minister had seen the sight that had so upset him, was occupied by two women. Aunt Elizabeth Swift, a gray, competent looking widow with money in the Winesburg National Bank, lived there with her daughter Kate Swift, a school teacher. The school teacher was thirty years old and had a neat, trim looking figure. She had few friends and bore a reputation of having a sharp tongue. When he began to think about her, Curtis Hartman remembered that she had been to Europe and had lived for two years in New York City. "Perhaps after all her smoking in secret means nothing," he thought. He began to remember that when he was a student in college, and occasionally read novels, good, although somewhat worldly women, had smoked through the pages of a book that had once fallen into his hands. With a rush of new determination he worked on his sermons all through the week, and forgot, in his zeal to reach the ears and the soul of this new listener, both his embarrassment in the pulpit and the necessity of prayer in the study on Sunday mornings.

Reverend Hartman's experience with women had been somewhat limited. He was the son of a wagon-maker from Muncie, Ind., and had worked his way through college. The daughter of the underwear manufacturer had boarded in a house where he lived during his school days and he had married her after a formal and prolonged courtship, carried on, for the most part, by the girl her-

Drawn by Art Young, December 1913

Nearer My God to Thee

self. On his marriage day the underwear manufacturer had given his daughter five thousand dollars and he promised to leave her at least twice that amount in his will. The minister had thought himself fortunate in marriage, and had never permitted himself to think of other women. He didn't want to think of other women. What he wanted was to do the work of God quietly and earnestly.

In the soul of the minister a struggle awoke. From wanting to reach the ear of Kate Swift and through his sermons to delve into her soul, he began to want also to look again at the figure lying white and quiet in the bed. On a Sunday morning, when he could not sleep because of his thoughts, he arose and went to walk in the streets. When he had gone along Main Street almost to the old Richmond place, he stopped and picking up a stone rushed off to the room in the bell tower. With the stone he broke out a corner of the window and then locking the door sat down at the desk before

the open Bible and waited. When the shade of the window of Kate Swift s room was raised, he could see, through the hole, directly into her bed, but she was not there. She also had arisen and gone for a walk, and the hand that raised the shade was the hand of Aunt Elizabeth Swift.

The minister almost wept with joy at this deliverance from the carnal desire to "peek," and went back to his own house praising God. In an ill moment he forgot, however, to stop the hole in the window. The piece of glass broken out at the corner just nipped the bare heel of the boy standing motionless and looking with rapt eyes into the master's face.

Curtis Hartman forgot his sermon on that Sunday morning. He talked to his congregation, and in his talk said that it was a mistake for people to think of their minister as a man set aside and intended by nature to lead a blameless life. "Out of my own experience I know that we, who are the ministers of God's word, are beset by the same temptations that assail you," he declared. "I have been tempted and have surrendered to temptation. It is only the hand of God, placed beneath my head, that has raised me up. As he has raised me so also will he raise you. Do not despair. In your hour of sin raise your eyes to the skies, and you will be again and again saved."

Resolutely the minister put the thought of the woman in the bed out of his mind, and began to be something like a lover in the presence of his wife. On an evening when they drove out together he turned the horse out of Buckeye Street and, in the darkness on Gospel Hill above Waterworks Pond, put his arm about Sarah Hartman's waist. When he had eaten breakfast in the morning and was ready to retire to his study at the back of his house, he went around the table and kissed his wife on the cheek. When thoughts of Kate Swift came into his head, he smiled and raised his eyes to the skies. "Intercede for me, Master," he muttered; "keep me in the narrow path intent on Thy work."

And now began the real struggle in the soul of the brown-bearded minister. By chance he discovered that Kate Swift was in the habit of lying in her bed in the evening and reading a book. A lamp stood on a table by the side of the bed and the light streamed down upon her white shoulders and bare throat. On the evening when he made the discovery, the minister sat at the desk in the study from nine until after eleven, and when her light was put out stumbled out of the church to spend two more hours walking and praying in the streets. He did not want to kiss the shoulders and the throat of Kate Swift, and had not allowed his mind to dwell on such thoughts. He did not know what he wanted. "I am God's child and He must save me from myself," he cried in the darkness under the trees as he wandered in the streets. By a tree he stood and looked at the sky that was covered with hurrying clouds. He began to talk to God intimately and closely. "Please, Father, do not forget me. Give me power to go tomorrow and repair the hole in the window. Lift my eyes again to the skies. Stay with me, Thy servant, in his hour of need."

Up and down through the silent streets walked the minister, and for days and weeks his soul was troubled. He could not understand the temptation that had come to him nor could he fathom the reason of its coming. In a way he began to blame God, saying to himself that he had tried to keep his feet in the true path and had not run about seeking sin. "Through my days as a young man and all through my life here I have gone quietly about my work," he declared. "Why now should I be tempted? What have I done that this burden should be laid on me?"

Three times during the early fall and winter of that year Curtis Hartman crept out of his house to the room in the bell tower, and sat in the darkness looking at the figure of Kate Swift lying in her bed, and later went to walk and pray in the streets. He could not understand himself. For weeks he would go along scarcely thinking of the school teacher, and telling himself that he had conquered the carnal desire to look. And then something would happen. As he sat in the study of his own house hard at work on a sermon, he would become nervous and begin to walk up and down the room. "I will go out into the streets," he told himself, and even as he let himself in at the church door he persistently denied to himself the cause of his being there. "I will not repair the hole in the window, and I will train myself to come here at night and sit in the presence of this woman without raising my eyes. I will not be defeated in this thing. The Lord has devised this temptation as a test of my soul, and I will grope my way out of darkness into the light of righteousness."

One night in January when it was bitter cold and snow lay deep on the streets of Winesburg, Curtis Hartman paid his last visit to the room in the bell tower of the church. It was past nine o'clock when he left his own house, and he set out so hurriedly that he forgot to put on overshoes. In Main Street no one was abroad but Hop Higgins, the night-watchman and in the whole town no one was awake but the watchman and young George Willard, the town reporter, who sat in the office of the Winesburg *Eagle,* trying to write a story. Along the street to the church went the minister, plowing through the drifts and thinking that this time he would utterly give way to sin. "I want to look at the woman and to think of kissing her, and I am going to let myself think what I choose," he declared bitterly, and tears came into his eyes. He began to think that he would get out of the ministry and try some other way of life. "I shall go to some city and get into business," he declared. "If my nature is such that I cannot resist sin I shall give myself over to sin. At least I shall not be a hypocrite, preaching the word of God with my mind thinking of the shoulders and the neck of a woman who does not belong to me."

It was cold in the room of the bell tower of the church on that January night, and almost as soon as he came into the room Curtis Hartman knew that if he stayed he would be ill. His feet were wet from tramping in the snow, and there was no fire. In the room in the house next door Kate Swift had not yet appeared. With grim determination the man sat down to wait. Sitting in the chair and gripping the edge of the desk on which lay the Bible he stared into the darkness thinking the blackest thoughts of his life. He thought of his wife, and for the moment almost hated her. "She has always been ashamed of passion and has cheated me," he thought. "Man has a right to expect living passion and beauty in a woman. He has no right to forget that he is an animal, and in me there is something that is Greek. I will throw off the woman of my bosom and seek other women. I will besiege this school teacher. I will fly in the face of all men, and if I am a creature of carnal lusts I will live then for my lusts."

The distracted man trembled from head to foot, partly from cold, partly from the struggle in which he was engaged. Hours passed and a fever assailed his body. His throat began to hurt and his teeth chattered. His feet, lying on the study floor, felt like two cakes of ice. Still he would not give up. "I will see this woman and will think the thoughts I have never dared to think," he told himself, gripping the edge of the desk and waiting.

Curtis Hartman came near to dying from that night of waiting in the church, and also he found in the thing that happened what he took to be the way of life for him. On the other evenings he had not been able to see, through the little hole in the glass, any part of the school teacher's room except that occupied by her bed. In the darkness he would sit waiting, and then the woman would appear, slipping into the bed in her white night-robe. When the light was turned up she propped herself up among the pillows and read a book. Sometimes she smoked one of the cigarettes. Only her bare shoulders and throat were visible.

On this January night, after he had come near to dying with cold and after his mind had, two or three times, actually slipped away into an odd land of fantasy, so that he had, by an exercise of will power, to force himself back into consciousness, Kate Swift suddenly appeared. In the room next door a lamp was lighted and the waiting man stared into an empty bed. Then upon the bed before his eyes the woman threw herself. Lying face downward she wept and beat with her fists upon the pillow. With a final outburst of weeping she half arose and, in the presence of the man who had waited to look and to think thoughts, the woman of sin began to pray. In the lamplight her figure, slim and strong, looked like the figure of the boy pictured facing the Christ on the leaded window.

Curtis Hartman never remembered how he got out of the church. With a cry he arose, dragging the heavy desk along the floor. The Bible fell, making a great clatter in the silence. When the light in the house next door went out he stumbled down the stairway and into the street. Along the street he went and ran in at the door of the Winesburg *Eagle*. To George Willard, who was tramping up and down in the office trying to work out the point of his story, he began to talk half-incoherently. "The ways of God are beyond human understanding," he cried, running in quickly and closing the door. He began to advance upon the young man, his eyes glowing and his voice ringing with fervor. "I have found the light," he cried. "After ten years in this town God has manifested himself to me in the body of another." His voice dropped and he began to whisper. "I did not understand," he said. "What I took to be a trial of my soul was only a preparation for a new and beautiful fervor of the spirit. God has appeared to me in the person of Kate Swift, the school teacher, kneeling on a bed. Do you know Kate Swift? Although she may not be aware of it she is an instrument of God, bearing the message of truth."

Reverend Curtis Hartman turned and ran out

of the *Eagle* office. At the door he stopped and, after looking up and down the deserted street, turned again to George Willard. "I am delivered. Have no fear." He held up a bleeding fist for the young man to see. "I smashed the glass of the window," he cried. "Now it will have to be wholly replaced. The strength of God was in me and I broke it with my fist." —August 1916

CARL SANDBURG
To Billy Sunday

You come along . . . tearing your shirt . . . yelling
    about Jesus.
        I want to know . . . what the hell . . . you
        know about Jesus.

Jesus had a way of talking soft and everybody except a few bankers and higher-ups among the con men of Jerusalem liked to have this Jesus around because he never made any fake passes and everything he said went and he helped the sick and gave the people hope.

You come along squirting words at us, shaking your fist and calling us damn fools so fierce the froth of your own spit slobbers over your lips—always blabbing we're all going to hell straight off and you know all about it.

I've read Jesus' words. I know what he said. You don't throw any scare into me. I've got your number. I know how much you know about Jesus.

He never came near clean people or dirty people but they felt cleaner because he came along. It was your crowd of bankers and business men and lawyers that hired the sluggers and murderers who put Jesus out of the running.

I say it was the same bunch that's backing you that nailed the nails into the hands of this Jesus of Nazareth. He had lined up against him the same crooks and strong-arm men now lined up with you paying your way.

This Jesus guy was good to look at, smelled good, listened good. He threw out something fresh and beautiful from the skin of his body and the touch of his hands wherever he passed along.

You, Billy Sunday, put a smut on every human blossom that comes in reach of your rotten breath belching about hell-fire and hiccuping about this man who lived a clean life in Galilee.

When are you going to quit making the carpenters build emergency hospitals for women and girls driven crazy with wrecked nerves from your goddam gibberish about Jesus—I put it to you again: What the hell do you know about Jesus?

Go ahead and bust all the chairs you want to. Smash a whole wagon load of furniture at every performance. Turn sixty somersaults and stand on your nutty head. If it wasn't for the way you scare women and kids, I'd feel sorry for you and pass the hat.

I like to watch a good four-flusher work but not when he starts people to puking and calling for the doctors.

I like a man that's got guts and can pull off a great, original performance, but you—hell, you're only a bughouse peddler of second-hand gospel—you're only shoving out a phoney imitation of the goods this Jesus guy told us ought to be free as air and sunlight.

Sometimes I wonder what sort of pups born from mongrel bitches there are in the world less heroic than you.

You tell people living in shanties Jesus is going to fix it up all right with them by giving them mansions in the skies after they're dead and the worms have eaten 'em.

You tell $6 a week department store girls all they need is Jesus; you take a steel trust wop, dead without having lived, gray and shrunken at forty years of age, and you tell him to look at Jesus on the cross and he'll be all right.

You tell poor people they don't need any more money on pay day and even if it's fierce to be out of a job, Jesus'll fix that all right, all right—all they gotta do is take Jesus the way you say.

I'm telling you this Jesus guy wouldn't stand for the stuff you're handing out. Jesus played it different. The bankers and corporation lawyers of Jerusalem got their sluggers and murderers to go after Jesus just because Jesus wouldn't play their game. He didn't sit in with the big thieves.

I don't want a lot of gab from the bunkshooter in my religion.

I won't take my religion from a man who never works except with his mouth and never cherishes a memory except the face of the woman on the American silver dollar.

I ask you to come through and show me where you're pouring out the blood of your life.

I've been in this suburb of Jerusalem they call Golgotha, where they nailed Him, and I know if the story is straight it was real blood ran from his hand and the nail-holes, and it was real blood spurted out where the spear of the Roman soldier rammed in between the ribs of this Jesus of Nazareth.

—September 1915

IRWIN GRANICH
God Is Love

[*Granich, who became better known under the name Mike Gold, was later editor of the* Liberator *and then of the* New Masses. *His early writings, of which this is a good example, required, Max Eastman recalls, considerable editing, but they demonstrate his bright promise as a writer—a promise which remained unfulfilled when he became a communist functionary.*]

Poverty had imprisoned nine old men in a shaky loft downtown and had sentenced them to addressing envelopes forever. Endless, sickening envelopes they were, white and flat and inane, to be addressed with squeaky pens in the fierce and gloomy silence which attends all piece work.

A perpetual grimy twilight hung to the old loft. Brownish air and light came from a mouldering air-shaft; the walls were once white; spider-webs floated like banners of evil from the dusty rafters. Sometimes it rained or snowed in the strange world outside, and then the stale-green old ceiling ran with great, blistery drops.

The pens squealed, often one of the old men broke into a fit of spitting, the spiders wove and plotted their malicious snares in the caverns of the room. And this is all that ever happened in the old loft. It was a horrible cell for innocent "lifers."

Seven of the old men had adapted themselves to this trap poverty had set for their old age. They had always been meek, and so now they found nothing new to revolt against. But the other two old men possessed what are commonly termed souls, and therefore they were unhappy.

One of these two was a fine, red-cheeked old oak of a man, who had once been a sailor. Rheumatism had cheated him out of an honorable death on the waves, and here he was now, diddling with pen and ink for a livelihood.

He was huge and strong, with great tattooed fists and arms, and a head like one of those giant crags that are lifted in defence by the land against avaricious surfs. His mass of hair was white and wild as spray, and he had blue, far-seeing eyes, colored deep by the skies and seas they had known.

He was a heavy drinker, because he needed something in which to plunge the hate he had for the loft and its fungus atmosphere. For he had been fashioned for heroism and deeds, for the open air. He grew sick for the swing of a deck under his feet, for the sharp kiss of brine on his face, for the free winds, tremendous skies, all the drama and strife of the great seas.

Sundays he would sit on a bench at the Battery and look out to the Atlantic with the eyes of a lover, his heart big with loneliness for the deep, broken waters. In the loft he never spoke to the others, but dreamed as he scribbled of strange ports lying in exotic sunshine, of gales and the rank songs of sailormen, of women and fierce moonlight, of the creaking perfumed cordage of a tops'l schooner. . . . He hated the loft and the city with the consuming hate of a caged lion. He was drunk every night, and some of the days. . . .

The other old man dreamed of God. . . . At one time he had been a minister, and what is more, a minister who truly sought God. He had been unfrocked many years back after a lascivious woman of his congregation had snared him into "sin," he never knew how. He had been glad to find a refuge in the bleak fog of New York's underworld after the scandal. The shameful lot of dish-washing and porter-jobs and begging he had regarded as a penance and cross, and he had hugged his sorrows to him in an ecstasy of atonement.

But latterly he was beginning to doubt. The exaltation was leaving him, and the chill of reality was settling down. He sometimes dared to imagine that he had long since expiated his crime, and he wondered why God demanded more of him.

Some nights he would wake and sweat with terror to think that perhaps there was no God of justice. He would reach out as if to catch something that was slipping from him. . . .

"My God, my God, why art Thou forsaking me?" he would weep into his hard, lousy pillow at the lodging house. And there would be only the nauseous smell of the bed-bugs and the swinish snores of the men in the silence. . . .

Yet all things are finally answered, and it was through the other old man with a soul that the minister got his own terrible reply and sigh from the heavens. He was going home in the enfolding gloom and scarlet of an October twilight, a little, round-shouldered old man in a flappy old suit, an umbrella and reading matter in his embarrassed clutch. . . . One knew him for the typical failure of the cities, the amiable, unmilitant kind of a man who has love for man and beast in his watery blue eyes, and is so social that there is no place for him in society. . . .

The other old man with a soul, the sailor, had not come to work that day. . . . He was probably on another spree, and the minister got to thinking wistfully of him. He also thought of God, and this with the dim, cool mystic autumn winds in the twilight conspired to make him very melancholy. . . . It was all so sad, the huge, cryptic sky, the winds out of nowhere, the dying summer and the purposeless throngs of workers. The great tenements hung black and solemn against the last silver stains of light, and somebody was singing in a window. . . .

And then the old minister suddenly befell his fellow-toiler at the loft. The sailor was staggering out of a glaring, hiving saloon, his head lolling and his brave old eyes blurred with drink. He was very drunk and very helpless, and the old minister grew tender for him, and came up and touched him.

"Good evening, brother," he said, taking the other's loose hand in his own. The sailor looked at him stupidly and muttered, "Hello."

"I missed you at the loft to-day," the minister said, gradually edging the other away from the saloon door.

"Yeh, I wasn't feeling so good," the sailor mumbled out of his confused mind. He swayed a little, and hiccoughed. "Come an' have a drink," he stammered thickly.

The minister did not answer, but took a bolder grip on the other's arm, and insinuated him down the street. The old sailor had lost his hat, and his beautiful pure white head was like a kingly plume against the sombre night. His clothes were dusty, and he had also been stripped of his collar and tie. All the fools of the city turned and looked after the two old men as they trod a complicated way through the traffic. The fools wagged their heads sagely, and clacked their tongues.

A hurdy-gurdy shot the night through with music, and the old sailor broke into a few flinging bars

Drawn by Boardman Robinson, January 1917

The Last Supper

Then Judas, which betrayed him, answered and said, Master, is it I? He said unto him, Thou hast said. —*Matthew, 26:25*

"Our Lord Jesus Christ does not stand for peace at any price . . . Every true American would rather see this land face war than see her flag lowered in dishonor . . . I wish to say that, not only from the standpoint of a citizen, but from the standpoint of a minister of religion . . . I believe there is nothing that would be of such great practical benefit to us as universal military training for the men of our land." —REV. DR. WILLIAM T. MANNING, RECTOR OF TRINITY PARISH, NEW YORK CITY.

[The Reverend Manning, whose remarks inspired this drawing, later became the Episcopal Bishop of New York and a leading figure in his denomination.]

of the hornpipe, moving with that mechanical gaiety which is so pitiful in old drunkards. He meekly stopped when the minister begged him to, and was meek until the two came to the next corner, where another teeming saloon gave off a great glitter.

Here he balked flatly, and would go no farther. He wormed himself stubbornly out of the clutch of the frail little minister, and dragged to the door.

"Must have a drink," he repeated again and again in a sullen passion. He shook the minister's appealing grasp off him, and stumbled violently through the saloon door. There was a hum of raucous voices, the swift, hot breath of whiskey, sour beer and tobacco, the bluff welcome of the bartender.

Then the little minister was alone. He grew very sad again, for he had dreamed of rescuing the other from a night of degradation. He wandered vaguely down Ninth Avenue, wondering whether he ought to go home now and leave the sailor to his chances. And the life of the city night smote in on his thoughts and submerged them in its great surf of movement.

The sound and fury of the city night! The elevated roared like an aroused monster overhead; the people stirred and sifted in black masses on the sidewalks; peddlers barked, pianos jangled, light flowed in golden sheets from gaudy store windows; three young girls fled with locked arms down the street, laughing and screaming with joy as three lads pursued them. Chatter, gabble, laughter, hardness, fluidity, on and on the hosts poured, as if this were all of life, raising their complex and titanic anthem of nothingness to the sky!

The old minister looked at the sky and fell to thinking of God again, and so grew sadder and sadder. He thought how alien the sky was over this brick and mortar, how intrusive the stars in the lives of these pushing, screaming people. There was no God of justice, for there was no justice. There was only pain and futility. The sky was a pitiless, needless mystery. There was a void behind its curtain, but no God. What sign was there of a God in the world?

The old man moved in the city night, his soul falling endlessly in bottomless gulfs of negation. And then, fevered and overwrought, he almost fainted when there came to his simple imagination what seemed to him a miraculous answer to his questions.

Sitting on the garbage-laden step of a tenement he beheld a slum mother nursing her infant. There was a light on her face from a nearby store window, but to the old minister it was divinity. His heart melted for love of them both—the famished, ground-down mother, the helpless, trusting child. . . .

"Love," murmured the old minister ecstatically. "God is Love!"

He stood and looked at them long and long, his eyes great and shining. He thought of the life of the mother—how her days were a cycle of woes, and her moments breathed in constant pain. She lived in a pit of despair, and yet she loved. She loved and sacrificed because something moved in her that was divine—something that was God.

It was God. In the life of man God had ever been, even as He was here now on this ash-heap of poverty. God was wherever men died for an ideal, wherever mothers hovered over the babes for whom they had paid in blood and agony.

God was strong. He lived where all else seemed to have died. He stirred men to deeds that were superhuman; he gave weak women a power that was above empires. Yes, God was in the world! He was a flame that lit up the dark marshes of poverty, oppression, pain. God was love!

It was clear now. And one must love in order to know God.

So the old minister searched his heart, and found that he had not loved the world and his fellow-men for many a month. He had almost come to hate, and that was why God had seemed to fail him. He must love again! He must love his fellow-men at the lodging house, the bestial, rum-soaked men who swore so terribly! He must love the silent and soulless men who worked with him at the addressing loft! He must love the fate which had thrust him into these sordid, foul-smelling scenes, for this was his cross, and he must learn to love even his cross!

Love! He would go back to the old sailor and rescue that other drifting life by the power of love. He would go back to the saloon and convince the men there of God, convince them by the love overflowing from his heart and eyes.

So he went back under the bellowing elevated to the saloon. Squalling with light, it was the brightest, most beckoning spot in the dark wilderness of the streets. But its confident hard glare brought all his ingrained shyness up to defeat him.

He walked timidly up to the doors and peeped into the noisy stew of the saloon. Dim in a bank of tobacco smoke he could see the great white head of his sailor friend, also the rough, cruel faces of a rout of other men. Suddenly he knew that he could not go in there and speak of love and so he went back to the sidewalk and waited for the sailor to come out.

The city night closed in and owned him again. It moved fitfully about him with its turmoil, with its cats and babies and sweaty, hard-bitten men and women. He studied a fly-specked whiskey advertisement in the saloon window for more than fifteen minutes. It pictured in poisonous green-and-blue "The Old Kentucky Home." The old man thought it beautiful, and it made him homesick for the soft fields of Ohio from whence he had been exiled.

A foul old woman came up and talked to him. She was dirty and leering, and she proposed a horrible thing to him. But he could almost kiss her for love, for as he noted her smirched dress and repulsive, smutty face there came to him the thought of his dear, new-found God of love. . . . How beautiful He made everything. . . .

Then the old man grew lonely for a while. He read a newspaper by the saloon's brilliant glow. An hour passed, and the old sailor did not appear. . . . The old man paced the street in front of the saloon restlessly, almost impatiently, but could not bring himself to the point of going away. . . . Something stronger than himself held him there. . . . God. . . .

And then finally the old sailor did come. The saloon doors opened outward with a crash, and through them lurched the impotent hulk of the befuddled old sailor. He could hardly stand, and a mean, city-faced bartender stood behind him and pushed the big, unyielding form with contempt and righteous exasperation.

"Out of here, you old bum," he sneered, shoving. "Out before I clip ye one. . . . Ye've made enough gab tonight for such an old son-of-a-bitch. We run a decent, respectable saloon, we do, and I'll have ye know it. . . . Out!"

The sailor looked at him glazy-eyed and unknowing. He resisted automatically, only because he was stubborn of temperament. Dully he would try again and again to push back into the barroom, and every time he did the bartender would kick him in the stomach and send him sodden to the sidewalk. Four times this happened, the old man muttering stupidly all the while. Once in the four times he hit the side of his cheek on the pavement, and it burst open, bleeding copiously.

The minister wrung his hands and tried to interfere, but the sailor thrust him aside. A group of people gathered, but none of them tried to stop the spectacle. Then at last the old sailor was too weak to get up, and lay writhing in the street.

The bartender cast a last withering look at him, and spat with slow scorn at the twisted form.

"It's guys like you what gives a black eye to the saloon business," he said bitterly as he went inside.

Then the old minister elbowed forward and bent over his friend. With difficulty he lifted the heavy body to its feet, while everyone eyed him curiously and even cynically. His meagre muscles strained as he supported the old sailor, but his heart was torn even more for the other's humiliation. . . . The old sailor went with him feebly, like a sick child, mumbling weak complaints. . . .

He would take him to his room, and let him sleep there while he himself walked the streets for the night. . . . In the morning he would come back and talk to him, and help him. . . . The old minister went out in a great flood of pity to the other. . . . The sailor must be given Love . . . he must be taught of God.

They walked a few blocks in this nightmare fashion, in the hum of the avenue. Then the old sailor drew a little out of his stupor, and all the evil of the alcohol in him began to speak. He stopped flat in his tracks before a garish window in which candies and fruits were displayed, and made as if to punch the glass in with his hand, shouting.

The old minister pulled him insistently away, saying gentle, soothing things all the while. But the old sailor was half-crazy now and he tried to shake himself free of the other again and again. He grew impatient and querulous with the minister.

"Who in hell are you anyway?" he demanded. "I don't know you. Lemme go."

"I am your brother," the old minister would say gently. "I want to take you to my room where you can be safe and sleep till morning."

And over and over again with sickening insistency the old sailor would answer, "You ain't my brother. You're a thief, that's what you are. You want to rob me."

He had fallen upon this crazy suspicion in his ramblings, and it gave him a peculiar delight to repeat it over and over. He leered shrewdly and cruelly as he said it, and the minister's heart broke within him. But his kindness did not leave him,

nor his great love for the other helpless old man. . . .

The old sailor particularly delighted in shouting his insane charges when he felt people staring at him. . . . They would invariably cast suspicious eyes at the minister . . . and one or two strangers spoke reprovingly to him, and looking for a policeman, could not find him, and so did not interfere. . . .

And then the two old men, in their difficult passage of the rushing, noisy avenue, came again within the bold illumination of a saloon. Hordes moved before and around it, and its hot, strong breath came out in an assault upon the sweetness of the October wind. The old sailor's eyes kindled as he saw it, and he shook himself like a big dog in the grip of the other.

"I'm going in there," he muttered, struggling to be free. "Lemme alone."

"Brother—" the minister pleaded, holding as tightly as his strength let him.

"Lemme go. I want to go in there."

"Brother, there is nothing in there for you," the old minister said.

"Lemme go, I tell ye. I want to go in and lick that bartender."

"That's not the place," the minister cried. "Don't go in. Come home with me."

"Lemme alone, you thief, you. I'm not going with you, you thief."

The old sailor tried to wrench himself from the other's grasp and was too successful, for he toppled into a bleary heap on the pavement. The minister bent over him sadly, and lifted him to his feet again. A little stunned, the sailor walked a few steps in a docile daze. Then the alcohol madness fell upon him again, and he began his muttering and struggle.

"Lemme go, you thief!" he said more violently than before. "LEMME GO!"

He gave a sudden shout, and made a great muscular twist which almost threw the minister to the ground.

"Thief, thief," the old sailor shouted rabidly in his huge voice. One of his big whirling fists caught the feeble little minister square on the mouth, and the blood spat out. Sick and dizzy, the old minister clung to the other still, with the hope in his mind that the sailor would soon tire.

But the old sailor lashed himself into a greater fury, as the blind fighting devils in him woke in his brain.

"Thief! thief!" and he mauled the other with

great vicious blows, leaving marks wherever he struck. The two wrestled to the pavement, and black flowing waves of people turned aside from their usual channels along the avenue and foamed about as about the center of a whirlpool. There were wits in the crowd. One cried out above the dinning of the street noises, "Go it, you old roosters!" Another shouted, "My bet on the big guy," after the sailor had pounded his iron fist into the other's eye with a distinct crash. Everybody laughed at these witticisms; everyone in the crowd was in fine humor. The crowd spread and grew constantly, grew to sudden feverish immensity with curious men and boys, and pale, pitying and amused women. The antics and ridiculous contortions of the old men brought forth gales of laughter, cheers and hootings.

The little minister yielded to it all with a sick sorrow, taking the beating as he lay in the dirt without an ounce of resistance. He was too broken-hearted to fight, but shut his eyes and suffered each blow in silence, only groaning a little and weeping weakly through it all. . . . It was as if he did not care any more. . . .

The elevators stormed overhead, the street-cars clanked by, wagon wheels rattled, the peddlers barked hoarsely, the young girls still screamed joyously as they ran from pursuant lovers. Beyond the hanging dark, the sky watched as stonily as before. . . .

And—a hurdy-gurdy rang out. The two old men thrashed about in the swill of the street, bruising themselves terribly. And the crowd stood about and sucked Olympian bliss out of the farce. Then a wide form in blue battered through the crowd and loomed over the two old men.

"A cop, a cop," rustled the crowd with respect. It hushed before authority, and in the silence could be heard the repeated cracks of the policeman's loaded club on the poor sides of the old men. . . . He began hitting instantly. . . .

And soon the sailor collapsed, and lay limp on the limper form of the other. The policeman lifted both of them by the scruff of the neck and held their swaying forms steady with each of his big hands.

"You bastards, you!" he spat with loathing, as he regained his breath. . . . He hated them, for they had given him work to do. . . .

"You bastards!" . . . He hauled them to a telephone, and the old minister heard through a red daze the patrol wagon clattering up a few minutes later. . . . He wondered what they would do with him, and did not care. . . . He felt hollow and dark within, and his body was a hammer that beat endlessly against itself. . . . He wept. . . .

And then they threw the two old men with souls into the depths of the van. And the crowd ebbed away grinning, chewing the happy cud of reminiscence.

The hardy old sailor slept as the wagon bounced over the cobblestones, snoring away all his aches and pains. But the old minister could do nothing but weep, holding his shredded face in his hands and weeping sorely.

One of the policemen pulled away his hands and asked, "What's the idea?" not unkindly.

But the old man did not answer, for he really did not know why he wept so terribly. He could only feel his agonized, welted body, and more terribly he could feel a quivering void within him, from whence something had become uprooted. . . .

There was a recurring, overmastering, soul-shaking sense of desolation which came over him like a darkness, the feeling that Someone or Something had tricked him. . . . He wept and wept. . . .

He wept as the sergeant at the desk took his name and charged him on the books with having been drunk and disorderly. He wept as he was led into the dark basement of the station house where the cells were.

In the sickly gaslight a keeper came forward rattling great keys. He had a bristling, round head, and narrow, cold eyes, and he stared at the two old men with hard and blasé impersonality.

"We're all filled up to-night, John," he said to the officer. "I guess we'll have to put these two in with crazy Billy-Sunday nigger."

A cell was unlocked, and the old minister felt himself jammed into it by a single positive push of the keeper's hand. The sailor fell into a grotesque heap on the boards of the cell, and sprawled there, snoring almost immediately. But the other man leaned against the bars, his face in his hands, weeping.

He could do nothing but weep. There was no light in his brain; and he had lost all he had ever owned. He was all alone at the bottom of a black sea of pain; alone. He sobbed and sobbed. And then through his pain he heard a singing and a muttering from the obscure part of the cell. He put his hands away and looked there, and saw strange, burning eyes. And in a shrill, inhuman and piercing strange voice he heard sung a hymn he had loved—

"Abide with me, fast falls the eventide,
  The darkness deepens, Lord with me abide—"

The minister shuddered. He sobbed. He felt he could not suffer much more. "Hallelujah praise the Lord" burst out from the corner of the cell. Then the insane negro sang again the hymn with its burden of trust and yearning and love of God:

"When other helpers fail, and comforts flee,
  O Thou who changest not, abide with me."

He sang it again with hysterical fervency. Chaos, despair, inextinguishable loneliness fell upon the old minister. . . . The disastrous, whirling sense of having been betrayed returned to him . . . the stifling voice . . . the sense of having been betrayed by One he had loved.

"Abide with me, fast fall . . ."

The words twisted like inquisitorial screws into the brain of the old man. Their significance made him writhe. He could not bear this hurt any longer. It was as if the whole night had conspired to torture him. Something must snap. It was his soul which suddenly broke with a great shudder and spilled like poison through his blood. At the fifth time the negro sang his hymn the old minister gave out a great cry of madness. He flung himself fully and madly at the face and chest of the insane negro.

"Don't, don't, don't, don't," he sobbed fiercely. But the negro gave a queer scream like that of some night-prowling carnivore. He turned on the old minister and tore at him with teeth, claws and feet . . . hungrily. . . . Blood spurted on the dark cell air. . . . And nobody heard or came to rescue the gentle old man who had sought God all his days. . . .
                                                    —August 1917

The Masses and the Negro

MAX EASTMAN
Niggers and Night Riders

[*Lynchings and race riots outraged Eastman, as this fiery and passionate editorial demonstrates. His remarks on the problem of violence are especially pertinent.today, but they were not inconsistent with the general apathy toward the Negro previously ascribed to* The Masses. *All men of good will reacted indignantly to lynchings, though few if any could contemplate an equally violent Negro reaction with Eastman's equanimity. The real problem was that few people in the North were alert—or chose to be alert—to the attitudes and practices which daily robbed the Negro of his dignity.*]

White men of Northern Georgia have banded together in a conspiracy to drive out the negroes. They slink out at night and paste threats of death on the doors of black families—death, if they aren't out of the county in twenty-four hours. There have been enough lynchings in that vicinity to prove they mean business, and the negroes are leaving by the hundreds. Many of them are deserting property—real estate and chattels that were the savings of a lifetime. This is what you call "Race War."

There is no more awful thing in this country than the problem here revealed. It is the only problem of democracy that nobody offers an ultimate solution of. I am going to offer one now. It is not so much "ultimate," perhaps, as immediate—for the question where we shall finally arrive is small compared to the question in what direction we shall go. We ought to go in the direction of equality and liberty. And the first step in that direction, when the whites combine against the negroes and call it a race war, is for the negroes to combine against the whites and make it a race war.

There are forces enough in the conditions of industry and politics in the South, to make a Negroes' Protective Association with a militant spirit a great weapon of democracy. A Toussaint L'Ouverture is what the South needs—a fighting liberator, a negro with power, pride of ancestry, and eternal rebellion in his soul. Unless you look to the awakening of such a man, or a thousand such men and women among the negroes, your institutions of charitable education will not amount to the land they are built on. For you cannot edu-

Drawn by George Bellows, May 1914

"But if you have never cooked or done housework—what have you done?"

"Well, Mam, Ah—Ah's been a sort of p'fessional."

"A professional what?"

"Well, Mam—Ah takes yo' fo' a broad-minded lady—Ah don't mind tellin' you Ah been one of them white slaves."

[*This cartoon, although funnier than most, was typical of* The Masses' *acceptance of the universal tendency to see the Negro as an object of humor. The use of comic stereotypes was especially marked in the magazine's early years.*]

cate a suppressed spirit. Not one child in ten million can achieve his full stature against the inhibitions of a humiliated or contemptuous environment. The possibilities of the black man have never been tested, and they never will be tested until after the wine of liberty and independence is instilled into his veins.

We view the possibility of some concentrated horrors in the South with calmness, because we believe there will be less innocent blood and less misery spread over the history of the next century, if the black citizens arise and demand respect in the name of power, than there will be if they continue to be niggers, and accept the counsels of those of their own race who advise them to be niggers. When we speak for militant resistance against tyranny, we speak for democracy and justice. Ev-

erybody grants this as to the past, but few are bold enough to see it in the present.

As for the "ultimate solution," we are not greatly concerned. Nothing is ultimate when you get to it. But if the negroes were to drive the white men out of Northern Georgia, or some other section of the country, it would go far nearer to a solving of the race problem than this homeless and destitute migration of good citizens from one unwelcome to another which inaugurates the year 1913.

They need not your pity. They need not your ethnological interest, your uplift endowments. They wait for their heroes—for them who shall put life and the reality of action into the cry of Paul Laurence Dunbar:

"Be proud my Race in mind and soul;
Thy name is writ on Glory's scroll,
In characters of fire!"

—January 1913

The Masses and the Negro

[*As the letter reproduced here suggests, not everyone on the Left was as unsophisticated about the race problem as* The Masses. *But more interesting than the letter was Eastman's response. Clearly the charge was unexpected, and Eastman's rebuttal lacked his usual crisp assurance. Significantly, it wasn't long after this letter that* The Masses *published other materials which, if not especially sensitive in their treatment of the Negro's situation, clarified the magazine's position.*]

A CRITICISM AND A REPLY

My dear Mr. Eastman:

There is one thing about THE MASSES that strikes me as totally inconsistent with its general policy: it is the way in which the negro race is portrayed in its cartoons. If I understand THE MASSES rightly, its general policy is to inspire the weak and unfortunate with courage and self-respect and to bring home to the oppressors the injustice of their ways. Your pictures of colored people would have, I should think, exactly the opposite effect. They would depress the negroes themselves and confirm the whites in their contemptuous and scornful attitude.

Believe me,   Very sincerely yours,
CARLOTTA RUSSELL LOWELL.

Miss Lowell makes the most serious charge against *The Masses* we have heard. We have been accused of bringing the human race as a whole into disrepute often enough, and our love of realism has borne us up under the charge. But if that same realism when engaged in representations of the negro, seems to align us upon the side of the self-conceited white in the race-conflict that afflicts the world, it is indeed tragic.

One of the pictures we published with greatest enthusiasm was a drawing by Art Young, in which a band of dignified colored people, under a banner of their own organization, were driving one of these same white race-maniacs off the corner of the page in terror.

Another picture was a protest against the Supreme Court's prejudiced decision on the Jim-Crow Law.

But doubtless it is not what we say under the pictures, it is the actual character of the drawing, that leads to Miss Lowell's complaint against us. Stuart Davis portrays the colored people he sees with exactly the same cruelty of truth, with which he portrays the whites. He is so far removed from any motive in the matter but that of art, that he cannot understand such a protest as Miss Lowell's at all.

Some of the rest of us, however, realize that because the colored people are an oppressed minority, a special care ought to be taken not to publish *anything* which their race-sensitiveness, or the race-arrogance of the whites, would misinterpret. We differ from Miss Lowell only in the degree to which a motive of art rather than of propaganda may control us. And, of course, her letter will have its effect upon our minds in that particular.

As illustrating this conflict between the aims of propaganda and the aims of art which is ever present to our editorial board, it is interesting to contrast Miss Lowell's letter with a remark of John Sloan's in regard to Stuart Davis's work:

"Davis is absolutely the first artist," he said, "who ever did justice to the American negro!"

This may be an unsatisfying answer to your letter, Miss Lowell, but at least it gives you a near view of the scrimmage line in all the battles that occur within the editorial board of *The Masses!*
—May 1915

MARY WHITE OVINGTON
The White Brute

[*Miss Ovington was a social worker of good family who wrote one of the first factual studies of the American Negro,* Half a Man: The Status of the Negro in New York (*1911*). *She was one of the founders of the NAACP and enjoyed a long and distinguished career in the civil rights movement.*]

It was a very hot day, and the jim crow car was the hottest spot in the State of Mississipi. At least so Sam and Melinda thought as they got out at the railroad station to change cars to go to their home.

"Come out of the sun into the shade, Linda," he said, when, a heavy bag in each hand, they started to move down the platform.

"I ain't minding the heat," she answered, smiling up at him.

He looked down at her, his dark eyes gleaming from his black face. He was a large, powerfully built man, with big muscles under his newly-pressed coat, and strong hands that showed years of heavy work in the fields. He swung the two bags into one hand and with the free one drew the girl to his side.

"You's the sweetest thing," he whispered.

Again she smiled up at him and her eyes were very soft and dark. Her new straw hat, with its blue ribbon, rested for a second on his shoulder. Then with a little laugh she started down the platform.

"We'll come inside," she said.

They entered the small, ill-ventilated room marked "Colored." It was a dingy place, for the stove in the center still held the winter's ashes, and the floors were thick with many weeks' dust. At one end was a window where the ticket seller would come a little before train-time to serve, first, the whites from their window in the adjoining room, and last, the blacks from theirs. But no one was about now, and the two settled themselves upon the dusty bench. The girl, with a little yawn, leaned back against the wall.

"Reckon you is feel sleepy, honey," the man said tenderly. "You was up all night mos'. We sure had the finest weddin' in the country. Your folks ain't spare nothin'. I never see so many good things to eat nur so many pretty dresses befo' in all my bawn life."

His bride slipped her hand in his. "We wanted to give you a good time."

"You sure did. It was the grandes' time I ever knowed. Dancin' and ice cream and the people a-laughin' and the preacher a-hollerin' with the res'. And all the while my li'l gal by me and me knowin' she was mine furever an' ever, furever an' ever, ter have an' ter hol'."

He pressed the hand that she had given him. "I can't see why you took me, Linda. Tom Jenkins is a preacher and learned in books, and I ain't nothin' but a black han' from de cotton fields."

She pulled his necktie into place, and then, glancing at the door and seeing that there was no one in sight, she drew his black face close to hers and kissed him.

"Tom wasn't much," she answered. "You're so big and strong. You make me feel safe."

He gazed at her and still wondered that she had chosen him. He knew himself to be uncouth, uneducated, scarcely able to read the sign over the doorway, while she had been to school for two years, had worked for white folks and knew their dainty ways. She had lived in a town with many streets and could not only read the newspaper, but could sing hymns out of a book. Then she was slender, with a soft brown skin, wavy hair, and small hands and feet. When she smiled and spoke to him he felt as he did when the mocking-bird told him that winter was gone and he caught the first scent of the jasmine bloom. How could he ever show her his great love?

He longed to perform some service and noticing a tank in the corner of the room walked over to get her some water. But as he turned the spigot nothing flowed into the dirty glass. The tank was empty.

"That's mighty mean," he objected. "Looks like they ain't know a sweet little gal lak you was comin' hyar. Jes' wait a minit an' I'll git you a drink."

Leaving her for a few seconds, he returned, an anxious look on his face.

"De train am late," he declared.

"Of course it's late," she answered a little petulantly. "I've lived near a station all my life and I never knew a train to be on time. Sometimes it's an hour late, sometimes twenty-four."

"Dis ain't so bad as all that. Dis train am two hours late. De ticket man done tole me so."

"That means nearly three hours here. Well, cheer up, Sam. We'll get home some time, and then you can show me our house with the roses growing over the po'ch——"

"And da clock——"

"And the work-table that you made——

"And de turkeys——"

"And the cooking-stove——"

"Yes, ma'am, don't you forget de new cook-stove!"

She laughed and rose to her feet. "Let's go outside," she suggested, "perhaps there's a breeze there."

They left the dirty room and walked out upon the platform. Up the track was the freight depot where were piled bales of last year's cotton crop, not yet moved. A negro lay on a truck fast asleep. Across the track was a group of tumble-down shanties, the beginnings of the straggling little town with its unpainted houses and fences in ill repair. Only the church, raising its slender spire back of the houses, gave an impressive touch to the village. To the right the platform belonged to the whites and two men lounged against the wall. They were young fellows with coarse, somewhat bloated faces that betokened too much eating of fried pork and too much drinking of crude whiskey. Both were chewing tobacco and expectorating freely upon the floor. One of the men carried a gun.

"Suppose we cross the track," Melinda suggested, "and see if we can't get some sasparilla. It would taste good."

"I reckon I wouldn't go 'bout hyar much, Linda. Dis ain't no place fur you and me. De whites is mighty mean and de bes' of the cullud folks is lef' town after de lynchin' hyar twenty years ago."

"A lynching, Sam?"

"Yes, they got him outen one o' dem houses right over yander and tied him to a pos' down de road a bit. He war'n't a *bad* feller, but he done sassed de sheriff—wouldn't let him 'rest him widout a fight—and dey is burn' him alive."

"No, no," the girl cried, and turned a frightened face toward her husband. "Sam, it won't be like that where you live?"

"Dont' you be 'fraid, honey. De white folks is fine down my way if you treats 'em right. I know; I worked fer 'em fer years 'til I bought my lan'. Now I pays my taxes reg'lar, and when I comes along, dey says, 'Howdy, Sam,' jes' as pleasant lak. I neber put on no airs, jes' alys pertend as deir cotton am a heap better's mine, dough it ain't near so heaby, an' we gets along fine. I can't never fergit dat lynching dough," he went on reminiscently. "Pop brung me to see it, hel' me high in his arms. It warn't much of a sight fur a little boy though, de roarin' flames an' de man screaming—how he is scream—and the flesh smelling lak a burn' hog."

"Stop!" the girl cried, "don't tell me any more, it's too horrible."

"I won't, honey. In co'se it ain't for a li'l gal lak you to hear. So you sees I ain't lak dis hyar town much. But we'll go on over dat-a-way and take a walk. It can't do no harm."

"We won't go far, Sam, and you must talk about something pleasant. About the new cooking-stove, eh? You haven't once told me about the new cooking-stove, have you?"

"Don't you be makin' game of me!"

"Get the bags, dear. We don't want to leave them lying about."

"In course we don'. Somebody mought open 'em an' steal dat white weddin'-dress. But 'twouldn' be much widouten you in it. You was shinin' lak a li'l white cloud lyin' close down to be black yearth dat's me."

"Oh, go along," and she gave him a shove.

He was gone a few moments and when he returned he saw that the two white men had walked over to where she stood. She hurried swiftly toward him and he noticed that she was breathing fast.

"That's a right pretty nigger," the taller of the two men said to Sam, "belongs to you, does she?"

"Yes, sir," Sam answered. "She's my wife. Jes' married las' night," he added in a burst of confidence and pride.

"Don't look like it," the white man answered. "She ain't black enough for you, nigger. What are you doing courting a white girl like that?"

Sam threw back his head and laughed. "You sho' is funny," he said.

"Let us go, Sam," Melinda whispered, tugging at his arm. Her face showed both anger and fear and she tried to walk with him across the tracks.

"But the men stood directly in her way. The first one went on: "Don't you all be in a hurry. You don't live here, I know that. Reckon we know every nigger in town, don't we, Jim?"

He turned to his friend who nodded assent.

"Enjoying your trip?" He addressed the bridegroom, but his eyes traveled, as they had traveled before, to Melinda's slender figure and soft, oval face.

"Yas, sah, we's enjoyin' it all right. We's waitin' fur de train now ter take us home."

"What train?"

"De train from the South, sah. Ought to be hyar by two o'clock, but it ain't comin' til fo'. Pretty po' train, to keep a bride waitin'." He showed his white teeth again in a broad smile, but his eyes were fixed anxiously on the white man's face.

"That's a right smart time to wait, ain't it, Jim?" The man with the gun nodded. "Reckon we ought to do something for your amusement. Give your girl a good time, now?"

Sam laughed again to show his delight at the man's facetiousness. "You's mighty good, sir, to think about my girl and me. But we don't need no amusement. We ain't been married long enough to be tired of one another, has we, honey?" and he looked down into Melinda's face.

She was terrified, he could see that clearly. Pulling at his arm she drew him back toward the waiting room. "Come in here, I want to sit down," she said.

Sam led her into the room only to find the white men following him. Standing at her husband's side, the girl turned and for the first time spoke to the men.

"This room is for colored," she said.

The man with the gun spat upon the floor, but did not move. The other, an ugly look coming into his thin, unhealthy face, answered:

"There's plenty of places where a nigger can't go, my girl, but there ain't a place where a nigger can keep a white man out, leastways in this county of Mississippi, ain't that so, Jim?"

"That's so," was the other's answer.

"So listen to what I'm saying. Your train leaves at four?" Turning to Sam.

"Yas, Sah," was the answer.

"Don't you worry, then. I'll bring the girl to you all right. Won't let you miss connection. We wouldn't part husband and wife, but I mean to have my time before you go."

Sam felt the girl's hands about his arm in a grip of terror. Her hot breath was upon his cheek. Patting her two hands with his big one, he whispered, "Don't you worry, honey."

Then he looked at the men and laughed a harsh, scared laugh. "I knows white folks," he exclaimed, speaking to her and to them. "I knows dey don't want to do us no harm. "They jes likes to play wid us, dat's all. Niggers kin always understan' a joke, can't dey, boss?"

"This ain't a joke," the white man retorted sharply. "We-all mean what we say. We ain't jawing at you all this time for nothing. Give us the girl right quick or we'll hang you to the nearest pole and shoot at you till you're thicker'n holes than a rotten tree full of woodpeckers."

"A nigger ain't much account here," the man with the gun added, shifting his weapon in his hand. "We shoot 'em when we feel like it. There's a law in this State for shooting game, but there ain't no law for shooting coons. We burned a nigger here twenty years ago. Got a souvenir of him. Want to see it?" And he thrust a hand into his pocket.

"Sam!" the girl cried.

He looked into the face that had smiled upon him a few minutes before to see her sweet mouth drawn with fear and her eyes starting with terror. His fists clenched and his body stiffened ready for the battle. He measured the man with the gun. He would strike him first, and then, the weapon secured, he could easily shoot his companion. Or he would squeeze those lean necks, one in each hand, and see the eyes start out from the bloated, ugly faces. He would kill them before her, his mate, who had chosen him as her protector.

And after that, what?

As he stood there, alert, tense, ready to strike, before his eyes there flashed the picture of a man tied to a post, writhing amid flames, while to his nostrils came the smell of burning flesh.

His hands unclenched. Pushing his wife behind him, with a dramatic gesture he threw out his arms and appealed to the two men.

"I know de white folks is master hyar," he cried. "I ain't never said a word agin it. I's worked for the white boss, I's ploughed and sowed and picked for him. I's been a good nigger. Now I asks you, masters, to play fair. I asks you to leave me alone wid what's mine. Don't touch my wife!"

For answer the man with the gun struck him down while the other seized the woman. Reeling against the wall, he saw them drag her to the platform and when he had stumbled from the room he watched them disappear among the shanties across the track.

"Got your girl, eh?" a jeering voice said.

The question came from the negro who had been asleep upon the truck, and who now sauntered over to where Sam stood. The outraged husband fell upon him in a blind fury, and beat him with his big fists until the other cried for mercy.

"Get out, then," Sam bellowed, flinging the bleeding man from him. "Get out, if you don't want me to kill you."

The man muttered a curse and slunk away.

"I'm sorry for you," a voice said at Sam's elbow.

The negro turned again with raised fist, but dropped his arm and stood in sullen silence as he saw a white man at his side. The newcomer had emerged from the waiting room, and was looking at Sam in friendly sympathy. He was an elderly man with white hair and beard and kindly blue eyes.

"I'm right sorry," he went on. "I saw 'em just now and it was a dirty trick. I'd liked to have done something for you, but Lord, you can't stop those boys. They own the town. Everyone's afraid of them. Jim there, he's shot and killed two, white men I mean, not counting colored, and Jeff's his equal. They ought to swing for it, but Jeff, he's the sheriff's son."

"You done just right," the man continued, "if you'd a struck either of 'em you'd be a dead man by now,—or worse. They won't stand for nothing from a nigger, those boys. I's right sorry," he said over again, and seeing that he could be of no service he went on his way.

The black man in his strength and his helplessness waited on the platform through the interminable hours. The train-men looked at him curiously as they went about their work, and occasionally a colored passenger spoke to him, but he seemed unconscious of their scrutiny or their words. His frenzy had left him and he stood, keeping silent watch of the cluster of shanties in front of the church spire. Once, when a train stopped and shut the town from his view, his eyes dropped and he stooped and picked up the bags at his feet, but there was no bright presence at his side, and as the cars moved out, he put the bags down again and resumed his patient watchfulness. And while his eyes rested upon the dingy outline of the unkept town, his vision through all the hot, gasping minutes was of a dark-faced, slender girl in the clutches of a white brute.

The men kept their word. As the train from the South drew up they hurried her on to the platform and pushed her and her husband into the jim crow car: "Good-bye" they called and then with lagging steps walked to the village street.

It was late afternoon when the bride and bridegroom reached their home. The western clouds were turning from glowing gold to crimson and all sweet odors were rising from the earth. Violets grew in the grass and honeysuckle clambered over the cabin side. At the porch was a rose bush covered with innumerable pink blossoms. And as though he had waited there to greet them a red bird chirped a welcome from the window sill.

A moment's glow of happiness shone in the man's face and he turned to his wife. Vaguely he felt that the warm earth and the gentle, sweet-scented breeze might heal the misery that gripped their hearts. They had been like two dumb, beaten creatures on the train, bowed and helpless. But now they had quitted the world of harsh sounds and brutal faces and were at home. The man drew a deep breath and stood erect as he opened the door for her, but the woman crossed the threshold with shrinking step and bent head.

It was such a homelike place. All winter he had worked for her, fashioning a table for her use, placing a chair here and a stool there, saving the brightest pictures from the papers to pin against the wall. The dresser was filled with blue and white china bought with money that he had taken from his own needs. Many a time he had gone hungry that they might have something beautiful on which to serve their first meal together.

"Sit down, Lindy, lamb," he said. His deep, rich voice had never been so tender. "Rest yo' hat and coat. I'll git the supper to-night."

He set about his task, lighting the lamp, kindling the fire in the new stove, and cooking the evening meal. But she ate nothing. She would startle violently at the fall of a log in the stove, at the leaf tapping on the window pane, at the cry of a bird.

"That ain't nothin' but the tu'keys, honey," once he said soothingly as he saw her tremble, "they's goin' to roost. They'll be right glad to see you to-morrer."

Presently she rose and in a hoarse voice told him that she would go to bed. He led her into the little chamber that he had built for their bedroom. Setting the lamp that he had carried on the table, he looked up at her, his eyes asking wistfully for a caress. But she turned away and he went out to keep his watch alone.

Sitting in the room which he loved and had fashioned for her sake, the clock ticking upon the shelf told him with every second of the happiness that he had lost. "Looks like I's 'bleeged ter bear it," he whispered to himself, "but it ain't right. It ain't right. No man had oughter treat anudder man lak dat. Seem lak dey think a black skin ain't cover a human heart. Oh God, it ain't right! It ain't right!"

When he crept into the bed beside her he found her shaking with sobs.

"Honey," he whispered, "I's glad you kin cry. Let the tears come. Dey'll help you ter furget."

He would have laid her head upon his breast, but she drew away.

"Lindy," he cried passionately, "I was nigh crazy to keep you, don't you know dat? I could hav' kill dem wid my two han's. But it wouldn't have been no use! It wouldn't have been no use! Can't you see dat? If you jes' thinks you'll understan'. I'd seen dem burn a nigger as had struck a white man. Dat's what dey'd have done to me. Can't you see?' You wouldn't have wanted to have seen me lak dat?

"And what good would it have done? It wouldn't have made no difference. You'd have had to suffer jes' de same. Listen, honey, I couldn't help you, it'd been jes' de same, only you'd have been lef' all alone."

"But you ain't alone now, Melindy, honey-lamb, you's got me, and I'll toil for you while I lives. I'll help you to furgit. I'll love you and I'll work for you from morn till night. I'll tend you if you're sick lak's if you was my baby chil'. There ain't nothin' I kin do fur you as I'll leave undid. Oh, Melindy, I'm here *alive,* don't you want me? I'm alive. You wouldn't rather have a dead man than a live one, would you?"

He stopped panting and listened for her answer.

At length it came in whispered gasps: "I don't know, Sam, I'm afraid. Every minute I'm afraid."

"Don't be afraid," he cried impetuously, throwing his arm about her. "I'm hyar."

And then he stopped. She had not turned to him, but snuggled close to the wall as if seeking protection there.

Outside were the soft night sounds, the vines rustling against the window, the insects' drowsy chirps. Far off, by some distant cabin, came the howl of a dog.

"A dead man or a live cur," he said to himself; and turned upon his face with a sob.

—October-November 1915

MARY WHITE OVINGTON
Letter to the Editor

"THE WHITE BRUTE"

To the Editor:

A number of people have written questioning the truth of my story "The White Brute," printed in the last issue of THE MASSES, and of my right as a Northerner to attempt to portray Southern conditions.

It is eight years since a Southern white woman of the Gulf States told me the story. It was evening, we were in her home, and she was nervous because her husband was out. He had recently, in his little newspaper, espoused the cause of a colored man against a white man of the town. I have forgotten the details, but he aroused the wrath of a dangerous element, and one night two rowdies assaulted him and so beat him that when he was brought home, his wife thought him dead. Hence her concern. She had not felt any especial sympathy for the Negro but perhaps because I was sympathetic she began to talk freely, and to tell me of the difficulties the colored girl met with who tried to live a virtuous life. And then, in just a sentence, she gave me my tale.

What is impossible in it? The lynching? Last summer they lynched a colored man in Mississippi, making a holiday of it. The crowd was very large and by special arrangement many women and children were present to witness the sight. The fact that a colored woman was raped by a white man? Can any honest and intelligent person suppose that it is only the white girl who is in danger in the South? But the husband standing by? If I did not make the reader feel his inevitable helplessness, I shall never try to write again. I hope there are few brutes such as I have portrayed, but strip a race of its rights, make it a subject people, and sometimes, when the decent elements in the community are slumbering, the brute gets his chance.

Perhaps I made a mistake in putting my story in Mississippi, for that is one of the few Southern States that I have never visited, but I said Mississippi because the incident occurred there. Since 1904 I have given the major part of my time to a study of Negro conditions in the United States and to work for Negro betterment. I began with the Negro in my own home, New York City, spending eight months in residence in a Negro tenement in a congested quarter, and visiting hundreds of neighboring homes. In the past ten years I have frequently visited the South. I have seen the Negro on the farm, as a farmer in his own right, or more often as a share tenant. I have entered his cabin, followed his children to school, and talked with him as he worked upon his crop. I know some of the Southern cities well. There is no Negro quarter which I have not visited in Atlanta and I happened to be in that city just before the riots of 1906. I went back a month after the rioting and wrote articles descriptive of the courts and of the exodus of the sober class of artisans as a result of the massacre of the Negroes by the whites.

But, my Southern friends say, you cannot know the Southern Negro and Southern race conditions unless you have lived in the South all your life. But in this they are wrong. I lived in the city of Brooklyn for twenty-eight years when I was offered the position of Head Worker at a settlement in Greenpoint, the city's northernmost ward. I took a car, which I had never before entered, rode through the sugar refining district, which I had never before seen, and reached a perfectly new and unfamiliar section of my native town. There I found a young woman from Michigan who had been in residence in the settlement neighborhood for two months, and in half an hour she showed me her knowledge and my ignorance of a part of my city's life.

Such ignorance of the life of the workers among the employing class is common everywhere, and in the South, added to this, you have a fixed principle that the whites shall not mingle with the blacks. So your Southern woman may know where her cook lives, and as mistress may go into her cook's home, but she never enters the Negro section to take any part in its life. She never visits the schools, never goes to a colored church, and especially never meets on any terms whatever, the educated, well-to-do Negroes who are becoming a fairly numerous body. The ambitions, the strivings of the growing Negro youth who is two generations removed from slavery she does not understand, she even refuses to believe they exist. To her the good Negro is still the faithful servant, and her chief refrain is that the black youth of to-day is disrespectful and trifling and will not work with the old time devotion to the white race.

MARY WHITE OVINGTON, Brooklyn, N. Y.
—January 1916

JANE BURR
Tilly's Apology

[*A poem like this if submitted to almost any journal today would doubtless provoke a moral crisis. But the editors of* The Masses, *untroubled by our concern with what is damaging and insulting to Negroes and what is not, were able to publish it without a qualm, simply because they liked it and that was all that mattered.*]

"*I's down-right bad, Miss Rosie,
But the good Gawd know'd I'd be,
When he gone squanderin' pashion
Like he done done in me!*

She raised us all
Then hung about without any usefulness,
A dark, expected spot on the landscape,
Something with its roots driven deep into the
    memory of things—
Ignored
Like a weather-beaten hitching-post
After the family is driving a six-cylinder.
One day there was a new look in her eye—
The white shot with red,
The black stretched and greedy.

She threaded the handle of her dish pan with a
    ribband
And marching 'round and 'round the house
Thundered upon the tin with an iron bar
Chanting:—

> *"My poker am my fife,*
> *An' my pan am my drum;*
> *Gawd damn de niggers—*
> *An' a* BUM! BUM!! BUM!!!

They came—those officers—
And chased Nigger Tilly;
Ten million years back she went,
Clawing her way up into an acorn tree,
And there on a branch she chittered and jibbered,

> *"My poker am my fife,*
> *An' my pan am my drum;*
> *Gawd damn de niggers—*
> *An' a* BUM! BUM!! BUM!!!

Down she fell
And lumped
Like the sack of carrots in the cellar.
They shoved her onto a board and hurried away,
All that mangled goodness still murmuring—

> *"My poker am my fife,*
> *An' my pan am my drum;*
> *Gawd damn de niggers—*
> *An' a* BUM!!—*bum!—bu—"*

                           —April 1916

J. BLANDING SLOAN
Lee Crystal

(My negro cellmate for a night at Harrison St. Station, Chicago.)

Bronze young leopard
Of radium lighted
Blackest opal eyes,
Animalism in its completion,
Delicate fibre and bone
Knit to be wounded
By all emotions.
Do they think cruelly
That you'll be tamed at all?
And (if at all)
By these police obscenities?

You who were born to strike
If struck at.

Bronze young leopard
Of radium lighted
Blackest opal eyes;

Of night hair dipped in
Nature's richest, livest pitch vat;
Patriot,
(If love of liberty is that)
A few like you
Would make a nation
If allowed to know.

                         —October 1917

An American Holiday

The United States was recently on the point of going to war on account of the killing of some negro soldiers in Texas. But, as if to keep anybody receiving from this an erroneous impression about the American attitude toward the negro, the citizens of Waco, Texas, at about the same time conducted a lynching. A friend of THE MASSES, a woman of the highest integrity and courage, who went to Waco the day after the lynching and who investigated the case, gives the following account of it:

A white woman, the wife of a farmer living near the town of Robinson, near Waco, was assaulted and murdered; suspicion pointed to the hired hand, a negro boy of seventeen, named Jesse Washington, who seems to have been mentally deficient. He was arrested, and a confession was obtained from him—not in his writing, for he could not read or write. Before the confession was had, a mob, loaded into thirty automobiles, came from Robinson to Waco, where the boy had been put in jail, intending to lynch him. He had been taken to the county seat, so the mob went there, only to find that he had been taken to Dallas. Some people from Waco then went to Robinson and urged that the law be allowed to take its course; and on the promise that the negro boy would waive his legal right to appeal for a new trial, and that the execution would take place at once, the Robinson people agreed not to interfere with the course of justice. The boy waived his rights, was indicted, and taken to Waco, where he was to be tried the next day— May 15.

The trial was hurried through, and the jury— one member of which was a convicted murderer under suspended sentence—brought in a verdict of guilty. The little courtroom, which holds 500 people, was packed with 1,500 and there was a crowd of two thousand outside. The judge, a machine politician, began writing in his docket. The sheriff, who had sworn in fifty deputies—who were

Drawn by Stuart Davis, November 1913

Sure of a Wide Berth Now

A Recent Decision of the Supreme Court Opens the Waterways of the United States to "Jim-Crow" Discrimination on Steam-boats.

[Readers who know Stuart Davis as a leading abstract expressionist may find this sample of his early work surprising. Davis caricatured the Negro more often than any other artist on the staff. He was at the far end of the spectrum that began with William English Walling who helped found the NAACP.]

not present—slipped out of the courtroom; he is running for re-election.

A tall man in the back of the room yelled "Get the nigger!" The mob surged forward and seized the boy. The judge, who had a revolver in his desk, made no move to stop them. A door, which locked by a peculiar device, had been fixed so that it would open; the boy was dragged through that door and down a narrow circular stairway.

These details were given me by people present at the trial. What follows is according to other eye-witnesses, backed up by photographs of the event, sold as souvenirs.*

They put a chain around the boy's body, and hitched it to an automobile. The chain broke. Shrieking and struggling, the boy was stripped of his clothes and slashed with knives. Some one cut his ear off; someone else unsexed him. A girl in a law office which looks down on the yard behind the Court House, told me of seeing this done.

They dragged him half a mile to a bridge, where one faction of the mob wanted to lynch him; but another part of the mob insisted on taking him to the City Hall, where a fire was already going. So they dragged him back. One of the photographs shows the waiting mob gathered about the tree, under which the fire is blazing. The mob had got a little boy to light the fire, because a minor could not be indicted.

While the fire was being fed with boxes, the naked negro boy was beaten with clubs, bricks, shovels, and stabbed and cut until, according to the Waco *Times-Herald*, "his body was a solid color of red, the blood of the many wounds inflicted covered him from head to foot." The chain was thrown over a limb of the tree, and he was strung up; when he tried to take hold of the chain, they cut off his fingers. Then they lowered him, by the chain about his neck into the fire. . . . I have a photograph showing the roasted body hanging to the tree—and showing also the joyous, laughing, holiday faces of the mob. Women and children also saw the lynching. One man held up his little boy above the heads of the crowd so that he could see; a little boy was in the top of the tree, where he stayed till the fire became too hot.

Then the body was torn to pieces, and divided as souvenirs among the mob. People went about the next day when I was there, showing fingers and toes. Some one fastened a rope about the torso,

*These photographs, together with a more detailed account of the lynching, may be seen in the supplement to the *Crisis* of July.

dragged it through the streets of Waco. The head was put on the stoop of a disreputable woman's house in Waco's segregated district. Some little boys pulled out the teeth and sold them for five dollars apiece. The torso was taken to Robinson, exhibited, brought back to Waco, and put on the fire again.

The Mayor of Waco was among those who looked on, from his chambers in the City Hall—cursing, it is said, because the tree was being destroyed! The photographs were taken from the City Hall, the photographic apparatus having been brought there in readiness for the event.

Waco is a city of 30,000 inhabitants, with 39 white churches and four white colleges.

Only one of the newspapers commented editorially on the lynching.

The sheriff, it is freely predicted, will succeed in being re-elected.

In the course of my investigation, I asked many people if the same treatment would have been meted out if the woman as well as the boy had been a negro. They said: "We would not have stopped the niggers doing anything they wanted to." I asked, if the woman had been colored and the boy white, what would have happened? "Nothing." If they had both been white? "Oh, white people don't do things like that." I said: "Yes, they do. They do worse things. There is a white man in Texas who cut his wife into little pieces with a knife and took a day to do it. And he is still at large."

I was told: "You don't know the niggers." Well, I went about in the colored quarter of Waco for days, and talked to colored men, and never once was there a gesture or a glance or a tone that could possibly have been thought objectionable; while during that same period I was subjected by more than one white man to disagreeable attentions; in some cases I had to *fight* with them. An official of the Waco jail tried to lock me into a bedroom when I went there to visit the prisoners; and when I came back that same day with some tobacco for them, he shut the white prisoners in their cells, put me in a corridor that ran 'round the building, with all the colored men in the jail for company, locked the door and left the jail for two hours. I did not realize the significance of this at the time; I talked with them for an hour, and was treated with the greatest courtesy; and when I was ready to go I rattled the door and called for the official. A prisoner who was in the warden's office waiting for his release papers, with whom I had been talking, dashed up the stairs, his face pale, and asked if I was all right! He told me the official had gone away for the afternoon. When he finally returned and let me out, he grinned, and asked if I had had a pleasant time. I said I had. "Well," said this Southern gentleman, "I thought if a decent white man wouldn't suit you, maybe the niggers would."

I went to a colored church, and asked if I might speak after the services; and I apologized from the pulpit on behalf of my own race for their treatment of the negro. I took this story to the newspapers the next day. "Do you really expect us to print that?" one editor asked. "Why not?" I said. "There would be another lynching," he told me. I said I had heard that sort of thing, and I wanted to see what would really happen. I was willing, I said, to take the chance. Not one paper dared print the story.

During my stay in Waco my room in the hotel was broken into and searched, my mail opened, and I was followed by detectives; and I was warned to leave the town.

* * *

That lynching in Waco was one of 31 lynchings of negroes in the United States since Jan. 1. Not one year has passed, since 1885, when they began to collect statistics on the subject, with less than sixty lynchings of negroes; some years the number has been as high as 155. In the last 30 years there have been over 2,800 negroes put to death in this manner in the United States.

The National Association for the Advancement of Colored People proposes to raise immediately a fund of at least $10,000 to start a crusade againt this modern barbarism. Already $2,000 has been promised, conditional upon the whole amount being raised. Those interested in this movement should write to Roy Nash, secretary, 70 Fifth avenue, New York City.

This would be a better action on behalf of civilization than merely giving relief to your feelings by denouncing atrocities which happen to be German or advocating that we send an army into Mexico to avenge the incidental killing of a few American citizens during a Mexican war for liberty.   —September 1916

Drawn by John Sloan, June 1913

Race Superiority

V
Wars in General and the War in Particular

NEXT to its treatment of religion, *The Masses* on war is likely to be of greatest interest today. The magazine's view of the origins of warfare was conventionally Marxist: modern war was rooted in an imperialist competitive system from which only capitalists benefited. The editors were not pacifists by any means. They accepted the necessity of revolutionary violence and were elated by the Bolshevik Revolution, but they were not prepared to admit that the international proletariat had any stake in the victory of one imperial system over another. This conviction was reinforced by the outbreak of hostilities in 1914 which, they thought, fully vindicated the Marxist theory of war. However simple this view may seem today, however much it ignored the complex origins of great wars, it had the singular virtue of being much closer to reality than the official explanations of the Allies. To see the war as a struggle between autocracy and democracy made very little sense in 1914, and become only slightly more plausible after the Russian Revolution. The Bolshevik revelation of the secret treaties, and the Versailles settlement thoroughly discredited this rationale, but too late to benefit the anti-war party in the United States.

One need not be a Marxist, therefore, to recognize that *The Masses'* war material has held up so well because Marxism gave some of the editors a stable and essentially adequate platform from which to operate. There were, of course, a great many differences of opinion among the editors on the origins and meaning of the war. The art work, especially that of men like Art Young, was most responsible for the vaguely Marxist position which I take to be the overall impression conveyed by the magazine. But many of the group had quite different views. Max Eastman was an early supporter of the League of Nations, and both he and Floyd Dell were impressed by the irrational, unconscious aspects of the war psychology. Since the staff did not argue with each other in the pages of its own magazine, it contained a range of uncontradicted opinions. In calling them Marxist I mean only to say that there was a substantial agreement that economic causes and imperialist policies bore some relation, however distant, to the war. Whatever confusion may have obtained on these matters, in later years the editors, whether they continued to be socialists or not, never had to apologize for their stand on American intervention as so many liberals were to do. One may argue (as Daniel M. Smith has done recently in his book *The Great Departure*) that America had legitimate security interests in the European war, but this was not a point at issue in the contemporary debate over intervention which raged for the most part at a very low level of sophistication. Anyone who compares what *The Masses* had to say on the war with what was being written in most other journals of opinion will find it hard not to conclude that *The Masses* had the best of it.

A further point which helps account for the timeliness of *The Masses* on war is that conditions today more closely resemble in some respects the world of 1914 than the world of 1939. It may be that the historical lessons of neither period are especially relevant to contemporary foreign policy, but the fact is that the presumed lessons of 1939 are constantly being invoked while those of 1914 get little attention. This is because men are always more impressed by their own personal experience than they are by the cumulative experience of the race. Policy-makers have, as Lewis Mumford puts it, a one-generational frame of reference. Hence, statesmen in the 1930's bent all their efforts to the prevention of another World War I, and since 1945 a new set of leaders, whose emotional reflexes were conditioned by the struggle against fascism, have labored valiantly to avert another World War II. If nothing else, *The Masses* is helpful because it reminds us that the American experience in world affairs goes further back than a mere twenty or thirty years, and that the record is a good deal more complex and far less easily reduced to convenient slogans than a reading of our daily newspaper suggests.

At the same time the magazine was attempting to prevent the socialist movement in America from grinding itself to bits over the war issue, it was also trying to demonstrate that the war was not so unique as the democratic interventionists were prepared to believe. The first task was virtually hopeless. The Socialist parties in Europe saved themselves by going along, however reluctantly, with the war policies of their respective governments. Such an expedient was not available to the American Socialist party—the strong German element in the party would not endorse a war against the homeland and the SP could accede to intervention only by alienating its most important constituency. Moreover, there were positive reasons for resisting an intervention that was opposed by a substantial number of native Americans who were not otherwise attracted to socialism. To some extent American entry gave the party a chance to build for the future by undergoing a repression which could only be temporary.

If such calculations did enter into the decision to oppose intervention all the way, they erred on two important counts. The repression was much more severe than expected. Thousands were jailed including Eugene Debs, Victor Berger, and other key leaders. The party's headquarters were raided and the whole movement successfully tarred with the brush of pro-Germanism. Moreover, the middle-class elements in the party, which included many native Americans and perhaps a majority of its intellectuals, were especially susceptible to the Wilsonian propaganda that accompanied intervention. William English Walling, John Spargo, Charles Edward Russell, and others enlisted in the crusade to make the world safe for democracy and were soon echoing the most strident and vulgar attacks of the popular press on their former colleagues. The efforts of a handful of men like Max Eastman and Upton Sinclair to moderate the passions on both sides were ineffectual. The Socialist party never recovered from this experience and never again played an important role in American life.

The Masses was deeply involved in this partisan struggle. Until it was suppressed it continued to ridicule and expose the exalted claims of the combatants without alienating any more than necessary the well-meaning men and women who accepted the official apologetics. This was not so much a deliberate editorial policy, coolly arrived at, as an instinctive response to the crisis. From the outset the group was determined not only to spell out the costs of war but to puncture the inflated claims which each side advanced to justify its policies. Inevitably Allied pretensions received special attention because American opinion had been outraged by the invasion of Belgium, and the Allies were skillfully exploiting this sentiment. German propaganda was so crude and ineffective that it persuaded no one. If America intervened it would be on the side of the Allies, and those who were determined to prevent this sometimes gave the impression that they were in sympathy with the German position. This was decidedly not true of *The Masses*. Max Eastman made clear in an early editorial that if forced to choose between the Allies and the Central Powers, he would unhesitatingly join the Allies. The point was that *The Masses* did not believe such a choice was necessary.

The need, therefore, of showing that America had no stake in the war impelled *The Masses* to demonstrate that the war resulted from the same causes, had the same effects, and pointed toward the same ends as previous conflicts. This approach could hardly have been improved on, and while it obviously had little effect on world events, it did lead to the creation of a permanently valuable body of material.

Thus, month after month, *The Masses* banged away at the "War of Lies" which each side waged. When the Preparedness campaign was launched, the magazine recognized immediately that its real purpose was psychologically to prepare the American people for intervention. Training camps on the Plattsburg model were of dubious military value, but the publicity they gained, and the great parades which Preparedness enthusiasts staged, helped erode the American resistance to big armaments which had been so conspicuous at the beginning of the war. *The Masses'* anti-Preparedness campaign reached its peak in July 1916, when the entire issue for that month was devoted to Preparedness and featured a long attack by John Reed on the commercial motivations of the War party.

The last months of *The Masses'* life found it trying to stay alive while at the same time recording the suppression of freedom and the rise of the war spirit at home. Again, it was John Reed who struck the hardest blows, notably in his memorable "One Solid Month of Liberty." But Wilsonian democracy permitted no one to go AWOL. Sentiment in the country was too divided when war was declared to allow even as small a band as *The Masses* group to march to a different drummer. The loss of its mailing privileges forced the editors to suspend publication, and before long they were brought before the bar of justice to account for their disgraceful lack of respect for the war effort.

The last days of *The Masses* are difficult to assess. Some felt that the editors' decision to nail their flag to the mast and fight it out to the bitter end was quixotic. Eastman himself shared this feeling to some extent, and in founding the *Liberator* made it clear that he proposed to have no more ships shot out from under him. But in another sense *The Masses'* end was dramatically correct. It died as it had lived, telling the truth as it saw it, rejecting dogmatisms and extravagant gestures of every kind, and maintaining its unique spirit of rebellious affirmation to the very end. To have done otherwise would have been a betrayal of everything the magazine stood for. *The Masses* could not, in any case, have survived the destruction of the world that gave it birth; why then tarnish its memory by trimming sail in the last days? The *Liberator* was to do splendidly what *The Masses* could have done only by violating its essential self. Surely it was better that way.

Wars in General

Drawn by Fred Zumwalt, March 1914

The Dove of Peace

Drawn by K. R. Chamberlain, January 1914

"It checks the growth of the undesirable classes, don't you know."

LOUIS UNTERMEYER
Battle Hymn

Yes, Jim hez gone—ye didn't know?
    He's fightin' at the front.
It's him as bears "his country's hopes,"
    An' me as bears the brunt.

W'en war bruk out Jim 'lowed he'd go—
    He allus loved a scrap—
Ye see, the home warn't jest the place
    Fer sech a lively chap.

O' course, the work seems ruther hard;
    The kids is ruther small—
It ain't that I am sore at Jim,
    I envy him—that's all.

It makes him glad and drunken-like,
    The music an' the smoke;
An' w'en they shout, the whole thing seems
    A picnic an' a joke.

Oh, yellin' puts a heart in ye,
    An' stren'th into yer blows—
I wisht that I could hear them cheers
    Washin' the neighbors' clo'es.

It's funny how some things work out—
    Life is so strange, Lord love us—
Here I am, workin' night an' day
    To keep a roof above us;

An' Jim is somewhere in the south,
    An' Jim ain't really bad,
A-runnin' round an' raisin' Cain,
    An' stabbin' some kid's dad.

He doesn't know what he's about
    An' cares still less, does Jim.
With all his loose an' roarin' ways
    I wisht that I was him.

—January 1914

HARRY KEMP
The War They Never Fought

The Millionaire went forth to fight in The War
   They Never Fought,
The Broker and the Banker, each a place in the
   vanguard sought,
The Preacher left the church behind to march,
   and shoulder a gun,
The Senator tied on his sword, the Magnate sent
   his son,
Then, finding war so fine a thing, he put by all
   his pelf,
And took a rifle in his hand, and went to war him-
   self;
The King served on the battleship, he fought as
   gunner there,

The Emperor went forth on foot the lot of war
   to share,
And none of them on horses rode, but side by side
   they went,
And carried knapsacks, slept in rain, and ate hard
   fare, content . . .
The Poor, the Poor, they stayed at home while all
   these bore the brunt,
Charging, and breasting cannon balls, and starv-
   ing, at the front:
Yes, all the Workers stayed at home and knew a
   lot—
The Ruling Classes were so brave in The War
   They Never Fought!

                           —September 1913

Socialism and the War

[*The World War had a disastrous effect on the
socialist movement generally, but it was particularly hard on the American Socialist party. While
in Europe the labor and Socialist parties in the
belligerent countries proved more responsive to
national than to class loyalties, in America the reverse was true. Consequently, the socialist movement survived the war in Europe, while in America
it was destroyed.*]

WILLIAM ENGLISH WALLING
Socialists and the War Scare

[*The role of the European socialists in the prewar
arms race early attracted Walling's attention, and
he was especially critical of the German Socialist
party which, because of its size and organization,
was regarded as the pace-setter of the world-wide
socialist movement. Walling's remarks were particularly interesting in view of his own response
to American entry into the World War, when he
broke with the American Socialist party and became one of the most prominent left intellectuals
to support the war effort.*]

Carl Liebknecht has made a sensational exposure in the Reichstag of the corruption of the
French and German press by the German manu-

facturers of arms. He showed that these manufacturers were promoting a war-scare for the sake
of business. He also showed that they were in
close and corrupt relations with the German bureaucracy. This exposure has made clear the
purely capitalistic character of the present military
agitation in Europe. But in so doing it has distracted the attention of critics from another extremely important feature of the situation.

For the Socialist members of Parliament have
decided, *for the first time in the history of the
Party,* to make it possible for the government to
obtain the money it needs for its warlike purposes.
The ground on which they do this is, of course,
plausible; namely, that the government proposes
by means of what amounts to a heavy and steeply
graduated income tax, to put a considerable though
still a *minor part* of the burden of armaments on
the wealthy classes, and that this measure deserves
Socialist support.

It cannot be denied that a tax which takes *nearly
all* of this year's income of the multi-millionaires
(although with the apology that it is only to be
levied *once*) must appeal to all Socialists as being
an approach to ideal or confiscatory taxation. Yet
can we consider the *form* of the tax without considering the *purpose* for which it is raised?

This is the question asked by the revolutionists

[249]

of the German Party. But they are now in a minority in the Reichstag group, and the anti-revolutionary majority has decided on the following course —which is a decided moderation of the older militant tactics:

They will vote *against* the military, but they will vote *for* these taxes which are intended exclusively for military purposes.

As the Paris *Temps* says:

"They will not vote for the military law. Of course not. But they will vote the government the hundreds of millions that are the basis of the military law."

The chief supporters of the new policy, David Fischer and Sudekum, have been voted down again and again at Socialist Congresses by majorities of four and five to one. But they now dominate, having been joined by Bebel on this question four years ago at the Leipzig Congress. A long degeneration, indeed, from the revolutionary position of the early German Congresses over which Bebel presided.

The Congress of 1876, for example, declared in favor of the nationalization of railways, but *against* their acquisition by the German Empire, because, as Bebel says in his "Memoirs," such acquisition would serve only the interests of the aristocratic and *militarist State;* the revenue would be wasted on unproductive expenditure whereby the Empire would acquire further power—a power hostile to democracy.

The Berlin *Vorwaerts* explains the new tactics by saying that the military expenditures were certain to be approved by a majority of the Reichstag in any event, and that the only question remaining was whether the money should be raised by still further increasing the heavy burden of indirect taxes that now rests on the people, or by taxing directly the wealthy and well-to-do.

But there was another alternative. The Socialists have been conducting a tremendous agitation for the *decrease* of indirect taxes. They could now say that they would not vote the new taxes on the rich except if accompanied by a *corresponding* decrease of indirect taxes, thus making all additional expenditures on armaments impossible. By their failure to do this, the majority of the Reichstag group has not only abandoned its campaign for lower taxes, but it has taken a position on militarism less advanced than that of many non-Socialist advocates of peace.　　　—June 1913

MEYER LONDON
There Must Be an End

[As a Socialist Congressman, London occupied a key position in the movement. His remarks here were typical of the response of virtually all American radicals in the early days of the war to the collapse of the socialist opposition in Europe.]

The world is disappointed at the failure of the International Socialist Movement to prevent the war.

There is a compliment in this disappointment. There is some consolation in the thought that mankind expected the Socialists to overcome national prejudice, and national hatred, to defeat the secret plans of cabinets, to overpower the gigantic physical forces at the disposal of the rulers of the world.

It is true that in almost all of the Parliaments of the world, the Socialists have vigorously opposed militarism and cheerfully accepted insult and ridicule from patriots and saviors of the nations.

Some went to prison for opposing militarism, others bravely faced the charge of high treason.

As an international force, sad though it may be to confess, Internationalism has so far failed to assert itself.

One of the charming religious ceremonies of the orthodox Jew ends with "Jerusalem next year." But next year finds us still in New York. We put off Jerusalem till next year again.

In a way, International Socialism has had the same fate.

No serious attempt has ever been made to practise it, and no sentiment has any value in life until it is practised.

The advocacy of the general strike as a means of preventing a European war, did not find favor with the leaders of the movement.

It must be assumed that the leaders knew their armies, and that they doubted the readiness of the masses to bring sacrifices for a remote ideal.

Be it as it may, the general strike idea did not prevail at the International Socialist Congresses.

Jean Jaures, who was to renew his fight for the general strike at the Congress which was to be held in Vienna on the 1st day of August, 1914, was assassinated by a madman, just as he strained every effort to prevent the conflagration which is now destroying Europe.

The assassination of Jaures was a fit prelude to

the long drama of madness which has seized the nations.

For many years the Socialists have been warning the ruling powers that it was dangerous to accumulate explosives, and to permit the incubus of militarism to settle itself upon the peoples of Europe.

But when the explosion came, and the universe itself shook to its very foundation, and reason, and science, and the International law of the "upper classes" and the International solidarity of the "lower classes" were blown into atoms and scattered to the winds, the Socialists, together with the rest of their co-nationals, were drawn into the maelstrom of confusion.

The hallucination was complete. The nightmare had full sway.

The proletarians of the world have been at each other's throats ever since.

But if some excuse or explanation can be found for the Socialists of the belligerent nations, what can be said in defense of the attitude of the Socialists in the neutral countries?

Of course, even for them it could be said that the calamity has overwhelmed the minds of men by its very magnitude.

But we have had plenty of time to look around. We, as Socialists, cannot take seriously the accusation of barbarity brought against any of the belligerents by any of the others, nor can we accept the narrow view that it was one ruler and one nation that brought about this cataclysm.

To us, German militarism is no more attractive than British navalism, nor has the prospect of the Cossacks' rule any particular charm for us.

But while we are neutral, we must not and cannot remain indifferent.

It is not true that nothing can be done by the neutrals to help terminate the war.

There is in each of the belligerent countries a large number of men who are opposed to the war.

Karl Liebknecht is leading the revolt in Germany.

The Independent Labor Party of England has voiced its protest against the intrigues of diplomacy and the machinations of cabinets.

We must lend courage and strength to the struggling minorities.

Had the neutral countries been mere innocent onlookers, the situation would not be so grave, but the neutral countries have not remained neutral. They have been adding fuel to the fire. They have been sending food and ammunition to the belligerents, and the greatest sinner in this respect has been the United States of America.

I say food and ammunition. It is just as wrong to send food to Germany as it is to send ammunition to the Allies.

We have been preaching against war. We have been advocating internationalism. We have taught the world to look upon the United States as the champion of peace.

Does not history offer a great opportunity to the American people? Cannot the working class of America refuse to make arms and ammunition? Is it not our duty to refuse to export any article which may be used by either of the belligerents?

How can the Socialist movement remain indifferent? How can the American Federation of Labor permit its members to directly aid in the work of destruction?

One can hardly blame the Government of the United States for refusing to put an embargo on food and ammunition. After all, the Government is a mere agent. The people have not spoken. Every group of the community is absorbed in its own little group interests. All that the Government can do is to maneuver skillfully between the rocks of conflicting interests.

It is up to the working people to act.

A general strike of the workers engaged in the manufacturing of ammunition, and in the exporting of articles of food, would undoubtedly bring a great deal of distress; would upset industry and involve great sacrifice.

But is not the entire history of labor a story of martyrdom? Has not labor been compelled to undergo deprivation and inflict injury upon itself in its struggle upward?

Has there ever been a decrease of hours of labor, or an improvement of any condition, without sacrifice?

The workers have struck for wages. They have struck for the ballot. Can they be made to strike for International Peace?

Can labor rise to its mission and its opportunity in this great crisis of the world?   —May 1915

MAX EASTMAN
The Pro-War Socialists

[*This judicious essay, written at a time when socialists were hysterically attacking one another, was far from representative of the emotional climate on the left. Eastman's appeal for tolerance was futile. Even had the anti-war socialists been capable of dispassion, the hatred generated by the conflict had led pro-war socialists to speak and act as if the American Socialist party, and not Germany, were the main enemy. Yet Eastman's ability to adopt an "above-the-battle" posture constituted an extraordinary personal achievement.]*

If this magazine has contributed anything to social revolutionary philosophy in America, its contribution has been a resolute opposition to bigotry and dogmatic thinking of all kinds. It has insisted upon the recognition of variety and change in the facts, and the need for pliancy in the theories of the revolution. It has insisted that the world can no more be saved by a single ism—syndicalism, socialism, single-taxism, anarchism or whatever—than it was saved by a single God. Along with theology, we have urged the dumping of theological methods of thought. We have asked our readers to use all general ideas as working hypotheses, and not as havens of rest. We have foresworn the absolute and the abstract and the predetermined, and tried to meet each fresh and developing situation with a fresh and developing mind.

The reason for rehearsing this matter just now is that we wish to bespeak a respectful hearing for those socialists who have resigned from the party in the sincere belief that this war must be fought to a finish for the liberation of the world. We think they are entirely, and somewhat pathetically, wrong. But we also think that there was no antecedent, *prima facie, overhead* certainty that they would be wrong. It was, and is, altogether possible that a situation should arise in which a national war must be fought to a finish for the liberation of the world. Time holds more various wonders in her womb than our intellects can ever prepare for in advance. And in these days above all, we ought to know it. We can not merely lie back upon an orthodox throne of grace and laugh at these men and women as faint-hearts and apostates. That is too easy. In a world like this—headstrong and changeful and challenging thought—the burden of proof really lies with the man who sticks by his opinions. We ought to be a little ashamed, offhand, that we have the same attitude to war that we had before so much happened. We ought to be liberal-minded toward these enterprising deserters, and a little concerned to defend our own less flexibility.

A liberal mind is a mind that is able and willing to imagine itself believing anything. It is the only mind that is capable of judging beliefs, or that can hold strongly without bigotry to a belief of

its own. I have been practicing my liberality a little on Upton Sinclair's address to the Socialist Party. I quote the parts that seem to contain the essence of his pro-war position, and I urge those Socialists who are so afflicted with certitude, that they did not even read it in their party organ, to join me in this wholesome exercise.

SINCLAIR'S RESIGNATION

"The adoption by a 12 to 1 vote by the membership of the Socialist party of the so-called 'majority report' on the subject of the war brings us to a painful decision. Except for two or three periods of continued residence abroad, I have been a member of the party for 16 years, and during that time have given practically all my energies to the task of helping to build it up; but now I find myself so far out of agreement with the membership on the most important of all immediate issues that for me to remain in the party would be to misrepresent both the party and myself.

"I cannot but believe, Comrades, that the difference between our opinions comes from the fact that I have lived in Germany and know its language and literature, and the spirit and ideals of its rulers. Having given many years to a study of American capitalism, as it exists in the domain of the beef trust, the steel trust, and the coal trust, I am not apt to be blind to the defects of my own country; but, in spite of these defects, I assert that the difference between the ruling class of Germany and that of America is the difference between the seventeenth century and the twentieth.

"I find those with whom I talk here in the West utterly unable to conceive what the Prussian ruling class is. They cite its modernness, its use of science, failing to realize that this is precisely the thing which makes it dangerous—a beast with the brains of an engineer. They cite the good care it takes of its workers, failing to realize that every farmer who fattens animals for the slaughter house does the same thing, and from the same motive.

"But this question of autocracy versus democracy cannot be settled by force, you tell me; no question can be settled by force, my pacifist friends all say. And this in a country in which a civil war was fought and the question of slavery and secession settled! I can speak with especial certainty of this question, because all my ancestors were Southerners and fought on the rebel side; I myself am living testimony to the fact that force can and does settle questions—when it is used with intelligence.

"If the civil war had not been fought out, if Horace Greeley and the other pacifists had been able to call a truce, the chances are a hundred to one that I today should be a slave-owner and a pro-slavery propagandist. It is certain that there would be standing armies of several million men on each side of the Mason Dixon line, European empires in Mexico and South America, European intrigues and alliances in this country and Canada, and participation of the North and South on opposite sides in the present war.

"In the same way I say that if Germany be allowed to win this war—and by her ruling caste it is clearly understood that 'to win' means to escape from their predicament with their hold upon Germany, Austria, Bulgaria and Turkey unbroken—then we in America shall have to drop every other activity and devote the next 20 or 30 years to preparing for a last-ditch defense of the democratic principle. This is what I foresee; and how, when I see it, can I fail to warn the American working class?

"I say that this war must be fought until there has been a thorough and complete democratization of the governments of Germany and Austria, and I say that any agitation for peace which does not include this demand is, whether it realizes it or not, a pro-German agitation. The argument that we have no right to say under what institution the German people shall live seems to me without force. The Germans did not scruple to make war on the French and to set up a republic in that country. They did this because they believed that a republic would be less formidable from a military standpoint; and it is now on the cards that the world shall do the same thing for the Germans, and to the same purpose.

"For these reasons, Comrades, I cannot follow you in your declaration that this is 'the most unjustifiable war in history,' or in your policy of mass opposition to the draft. But I would not have you think that I have gone over bag and baggage to the capitalist system. I believe that there is a work of enormous importance to be done by the forces of radicalism in the present crisis.

"We have to compel a clear statement of peace terms by the allies, and to see that those terms contain no trace of the imperialist programs of the aristocracies of England, Italy and France. We have to fight the efforts of our own exploiters to saddle the costs of the war upon the working classes of the next generation by means of an enormous bond issue. We have to keep up the fight for decent terms for labor. In this and a thousand other matters we are needed—and we are rendering ourselves impotent by taking the anarchist attitude that all governments are equally bad, and must be opposed without discrimination.

"I have done what I could within the party. I pleaded against the majority report, but I could not even be heard. The Appeal to Reason, a paper to which I have been a continual contributor for 16 years, refused to allow me to put my ideas before its readers.

"And now comes the news that the Appeal has been suppressed; and along with it the American Socialist, THE MASSES, the International Socialist Review.

"The whole party press has been practically wiped out—just as the party organization will be wiped out if it endeavors to carry into effect its formally declared policy of mass opposition to conscription. Once before in American history there was mass opposition to conscription—in the streets of New York; all students of our history know how it was dealt with by that arch despot and destroyer of human liberty, Abraham Lincoln.

"I intend to go on working for Socialism as hard as I can, and when this crisis is past, when the breakdown of the Prussian caste system seems to me to have progressed far enough, I may come back and ask you to take me in again. You will then decide whether or not you care to do so. Yours for social revolution,

—UPTON SINCLAIR."

When I let go and imagine myself believing all this that Sinclair so earnestly sets forth, I find that doubt assails me at three points inexorably. I doubt in the first place, his judgment of fact—that the ruling classes of Germany have a sufficient hold upon the people ever to perpetrate an overt policy of conquest over the democratic nations—and such a policy must needs become overt, before it could involve us in the "last ditch defense" which Sinclair foresees. I know that the habit of loyalty to a dynasty is difficult to eradicate, and it has become thoroughly "jelled" in the nervous systems of the German people. But I see in every paper that comes to my hand indications that it is breaking up under the tragedies of war and under the uses of industrial civilization. I believe that the revolutionary democrats in Germany have, if they could be gathered together, millions of followers now, and that there is a mass of contrary passion and understanding in that country strong enough to prevent any emperor-soldier that ever may come, from launching such a feudal gesture over the modern world. I still believe in the economic determinants of democracy, and I know that these determinants obtain in Germany as elsewhere, only they came late to that empire.

The most learned and brilliant man in America, and the man best able to write a proof—if proof could be written—that the German dynasty must be conquered from the outside before the world will be free, is Thorstein Veblen. And I have read every page of Veblen's book* with studious zeal to discover such proof, only to be convinced again by the failure of his ingenious mind to find it, that it does not exist. He has never written a book in which that magniloquent scientific satire, his unique contribution to the world's literature, is so well sustained, and he has never written a book so clearly and confidently reasoned. But the main points that you would ask him to prove, namely: (1) that "it is in the nature of a dynastic state [such as Germany] to seek dominion, *that being the whole of its nature,*" and (2) that the habits in the German people of loyalty and subjection to the dynastic state, cannot be supplanted (or confused) in time to avert an attempt of the German empire at world conquest *unless the Allies conquer now*—these points are in no wise established. There is no more a hint of real proof for either one of them in Veblen's learned volume than there is in Sinclair's clear-spoken letter. Both Sinclair and Veblen seem merely to have accepted the war myth, not only neglecting to advance any points in its favor, but ignoring all the indications to the contrary.

Sinclair speaks of a "last-ditch defense" for America in the future. If America expended the wealth which she will throw into the war upon coast defenses, there is no power in the possible future of Europe that could ever approach her.

For the military fact most absolutely established by this war is the impregnability of coast defenses against attacks from the sea. Germany's submarine bases on the coast of Belgium are not ninety miles away from the exclusive dominion of the greatest sea-power in the world. They are the points at which it would be supremely desirable for that power to attack and weaken her enemy. The fortifications of these bases moreover were not long prepared in advance, but have been for the most part improvised since the German occupation during the war. And yet the great British fleet of ships built for the sole purpose of outdoing Germany, and now riding just out of range, is powerless and puny as a cockleshell before these fortifica-

*An Inquiry into the Nature of Peace and the Terms of Its Perpetuation. Macmillan & Co., 1917.

[254]

tions. What would be the strength of a German naval attack conducted on the other side of two thousand miles of ocean? This is one of the questions that arise even after we grant, for the argument's sake, that the German people might allow a German emperor to *try* to conquer the world.

I suspect that within a few months Sinclair will begin to seek for reasons why it will not be so altogether hopeless for democracy if the Allies fail to conquer Germany. And the reason he will seek them is that it will gradually dawn upon his mind that perhaps the Allies *cannot conquer* Germany. That, at least, is the second point at which doubt assails me when I imagine myself in Sinclair's attitude. He writes all these urgent sentences, directing that we pour out our blood to defeat Germany, without ever asking whether we can defeat Germany or not, and if we cannot, whether we would not better save a little blood for some other enterprise.

I do not think the Allies can win a decisive victory over the Central Empires. I suppose I will be locked up in jail by some crime-clerk in the United States Post Office if I am caught saying this. It is considered unpatriotic or cowardly, or treasonable, to consider the chances of failure in undertaking a war-like national enterprise. But it is obviously more important to consider this than to consider anything else under the sun, and I cannot help letting it creep into my mind occasionally.

We can make a peace with Germany which will give her a sphere of considerable influence toward the East, and also restore her colonies. But I doubt if we can do more than that, now that Russia has lost her interest in imperialistic war. They are so happy in Russia that they have a hard time hating anybody; and that has greatly, and I believe permanently, weakened the arms of the Allies. This is all a technical question, however, and I have no more information than Sinclair has. I only wonder— since he never mentions it—whether he ever thought of this question in making up his mind to the war.

Assuming that he has thought of it, and that to him victory over Germany seems as possible as it does desirable—and agreeing with him in my imagination—I find a third doubt assailing me. What shadow of assurance have we, I ask myself, that the outcome of this nationalistic victory will be "a thorough and complete democratization" of the Central Empires? I see no disposition on the part of the English ruling classes—who boss the Allies —to write this laudable plan of Sinclair's into their peace terms. Has Sinclair any guarantee that England will go on fighting for "democratization" after she has gained a territorial victory, and has he any guarantee that she will stop fighting for a territorial victory in case the "democratization" comes first?

Sinclair and Walling have gone over to this war with a kind of enthusiasm, as though they were going to direct it. Sinclair says that "any agitation for peace which does not include this demand [for democratization of Germany and Austria] is pro-German." Well, that shows that Sinclair himself is perfectly sincere and thoroughgoing in supporting the war as a war for democracy. But it does not show that it is a war for democracy, or that capitalistic political governments are going to adopt this idealistic basis of judgment. Sinclair writes his own terms of peace and goes to war along with the Allies; but I read the terms of peace that were written by the governments of the Allies, and I stay at home. That seems to be a final great difference between us.

I doubt his judgment of the facts about Germany. I doubt his judgment of the possibility of conquering her, and even when I grant his facts and his possibility, I doubt the result which he seems to be so sure—because he wants it—will come. So I am about as far away from him as I can be. And after reading his document sympathetically, I come back to the purpose of the Socialist majority, and the Syndicalists, and the I. W. W., to fight the militarization of this country at the hands of our industrial feudalism, as one comes back to the dry, hard, disreputable fact, after reading a grand romance about a struggle for liberty that was honorific and stylish and popular with the press.

Nevertheless I want to assert that it is possible to read his document sympathetically. It is possible to imagine oneself seeing these facts and potentialities exactly as Sinclair does, and as all those others do who have resigned with sincerity and intellectual courage from the group whose sympathy and support they have had so long. It is possible and important for us to do this. We are not—thank God—a church. And disagreement is not heresy and resignation is not apostasy. And I, for my part, have faith enough in the underlying motives of the pro-war Socialists, and the anti-war Socialists, to believe they will most of them be working together along the main highway of industrial liberation as soon as this present extreme turmoil of passions and opinions is past.

—September 1917

"From Upton Sinclair"

[*Sinclair was one pro-war socialist who kept his temper and his common sense.*]

DEAR MAX EASTMAN:

Our too-patriotic government is responsible for the fact that I have only just read your September issue with the answer to my letter of resignation from the Socialist party. I suppose you will give me space to reply. I will try to be brief, and also to emulate the courtesy and fine temper of your article.

First you "doubt if the German rulers have enough control over their people to perpetrate an overt policy of conquest over the democratic nations." Well, my dear Max, if this war hasn't taught you about *that*, you are one of a very small minority! The German rulers had control enough to get a vote of credit to raid Belgium, to overrun Serbia; would you have thought that possible? Of course, these were not "democratic nations"—but then what are the "democratic nations," from your present point of view? I ask in all sincerity, for in other columns you laugh at the idea that England and America have any right to call themselves democratic nations. Is Russia a democratic nation now? Only the other day the Berlin *Vorwaerts*, crying defiance to the world, boasted of Germany's sustained prowess as proven by the newly initiated march into Russia—democratic Russia, trying to hold her national elections! You say you "see indications that the German habit of loyalty is breaking up under the tragedies of war." Of course, Max! But whose argument is that? Really, that is naive of you. I have been asking to have the screws of war put on the Germans; you have been asking, month after month in THE MASSES, to have them taken off; and now *you* claim the results which my policy is producing!

Second, you say that America's proper policy is coast defenses. I won't say much about that, because you will have already read Joe Wanhope's answer in the New York *Call*. For the sake of those who missed it, I will say briefly: Germany has but a few miles of seacoast to fortify, all the rest is too shallow for ships. We have 13,500 miles to fortify, and it would cost more than all the military establishments of all the nations of the world. And what about the men to man all these forts perpetually? Will you stand for that militarism? With the resources of present science, Germany could land an army in any one of a hundred Atlantic harbors, entrench undisturbed, and begin

[255]

a march of conquest. With ten years more of Prussian preparing, the aeroplane would be able to cross the ocean and destroy cities at leisure—because our easy-going democratic government, our innate, humane pacifism, would have been asleep while such preparations were being made. I know just how it would be, because many years ago I read Blatchford's efforts to wake up England, and I know what I myself did. Instead of advising England to arm, I went over and appealed to the moral sense of the German Socialists! That is the stage at which you are to-day, Max; you are just a few years younger than I.

You ask can the allies win a military victory over Germany? And your answer is No. You add: "This is all a technical question, however, and I have no more information than Sinclair has. I wonder—since he never mentions it—whether he ever thought of the question in making up his mind to the war." I answer: Yes, I have thought of it. I have thought of nothing so much. I have made investigations, and I believe I possess knowledge. I am surprised to know that you admit possessing none, and appear to think that nobody else possesses any. Do you believe, Max, that the German High Command does not know to a dot its own losses, temporary and permanent? Do you believe that the allied commands do not know the German losses? Do you not know that the obtaining of this information, the analyzing of it and the plotting of the curves, day by day, is the sole task of an important military department in every nation? And don't you suppose that the results become known to neutral students and get published in technical journals?

It is a question of German man-power, and without going into details I will tell the figures as I think I know them at the present moment. Germany has about 3,500,000 men on the firing line. She has about 500,000 effective reserves, plus some 300,000 of the class of 1919—eighteen-year-old boys who will become available this fall. This will last her over the winter—though it would not have lasted had the Russians fought. Assuming that the Russians do as they are doing now, falling back step by step but not collapsing completely, I believe that the German line will crack early next summer. I think I know this in the same way that I would have known in the fall of 1864 that the Confederate line would crack in the spring of 1865, assuming that Grant kept on his hammering. I spent two years studying the Civil War for my novel, "Manassas;" I studied it from the inside, through

Drawn by Maurice Becker, September 1914

Whom the Gods Would Destroy They First Make Mad

the documents of the time, and so I know how it feels to live through a long war, a war of attrition. I know what peace commissions Horace Greeley would have been forming had he been alive to-day, and I know what editorials Max Eastman would have written had he been alive in 1864.

Finally, you ask have I any guarantee that England will stand by the program of "democratization" in Germany—that she will stop fighting when the "democratization" has come. Why, Max, we both know England; we know that it consists, just like America, of Tories fighting Liberals for the control of the country. We know that it differs from Germany in that the Liberals do sometimes win, and are always able to a certain extent to influence the foreign policy of the government. I don't have to be a prophet to tell just what will happen in England when the great change comes in German public life, assuming that it does come. The English Tories will want to go right on conquesting; the Liberals will want to stop; Labor will threaten a general strike, and we, the United States, will have the final say, because we are paying the bills. And that is why I want us to devote our Socialist energies in this crisis to organizing a clear and enlightened determination to force a stop the moment the German people have achieved a revolt. I say we should give them the guarantee that we will help them to that extent, but we should not weaken that position by indicating the slightest extenuation of the crime they have committed in standing by their barbarian government. I say that if our Socialist press and party had taken that position it would not be so largely discredited and so impotent as it is to-day.

Apropos of this, let me answer your note to the effect that the party has grown so fast since the adoption of the St. Louis resolutions, my answer is that the party once appealed to Socialists, and to Socialists alone; there were a vast number of pacifists and a vast number of Germans to whom it made no appeal, and from whom therefore it received no support. It has now adopted a program which appeals to these large elements of our population. I am not in position to assert that its sudden new growth has come from those elements, but I would like to see a census made and the results published. I will wager you a Red Cross button, Max, that there are more German names among the last four months' recruits than there are among the last four months' desertions! Also I will venture the guess that these new recruits will be of slight service to the party and will prove inadequate compensation for the party's enormous loss of influence with the mass of every-day Americans.

UPTON SINCLAIR.
—November-December 1917

Christianity and the War

[*The tendency of the Christian belligerents, which included almost all the major combatants, to claim divine sanction for their efforts predictably attracted* The Masses' *attention.*]

Drawn by Boardman Robinson, July 1916

The Deserter

Drawn by Harry Osborn, April 1915

"Christian Patriot, will you call on your God to help you when your country goes to war?"

Drawn by George Bellows, July 1917

THIS man subjected himself to imprisonment and probably to being shot or hanged

THE prisoner used language tending to discourage men from enlisting in the United States Army

IT is proven and indeed admitted that among his incendiary statements were—

THOU shalt not kill
        and
BLESSED are the peacemakers

[258]

The War in Europe

[*The extensive attention paid by* The Masses *to the European war from the very beginning produced a body of material combining analysis and indictment that constitutes one of the most remarkable attacks ever delivered against any war.*]

The War of Lies

Food is as important to armies as ammunition—but more important than either is an unfailing supply of lies. You simply cannot murder your enemy in the most efficient manner if you know he is in every essential the same kind of a man as yourself.

Governments have tried to lay up a sufficient stock of lies before wars start, but always in vain. The progress of popular intelligence scraps such lies almost as fast as they are manufactured. The only safe way is to produce an entirely new stock in the panic days immediately before the war, when the people have no time or inclination to think, and are cut off from all communication with the other side. After the war starts, of course, the industry may be indefinitely continued.

This should be borne in mind in reading tales of the barbarous atrocity of soldiers, now on one side and now on the other.   —October 1914

JOHN REED
The Worst Thing in Europe

In a city of Northern France occupied by the Germans, we were met at the train by several officers and the Royal automobiles. The officers, genial, pleasant, rather formal young fellows in the smart Prussian uniform, were to be our guides and hosts in that part of the German front. They spoke English well, as so many of them do; and we were charmed by their friendliness and affability. As we left the station and got into the machines, a group of private soldiers off duty loitered about, looking at us with lazy curiosity. Suddenly one of the officers sprang at them, striking at their throats with his little "swagger stick."

"*Schweinhunde!*" he shouted with sudden ferocity. "Be off about your business and don't stare at us!"

They fell back silently, docilely, before the blows and the curses, and dispersed. . . .

Another time a photographer of our party was interrupted, while taking moving pictures, by a sentry with a rifle.

"My orders are that no photographs shall be taken here!" said the soldier.

The photographer appealed to the Staff Lieutenant who accompanied us.

"It's all right," said the officer. "I am Lieutenant Herrmann of the General Staff in Berlin. He has my permission to photograph."

The sentry saluted, looked at Herrmann's papers, and withdrew. And I asked the Lieutenant by what right he could countermand a soldier's orders from his own superior.

"Because I am that soldier's commanding officer. The fact that I have a Lieutenant's shoulder-straps makes me the superior of every soldier in the army. A German soldier must obey every officer's orders, no matter what they may be."

"So that if a soldier were doing sentry duty on an important fort in time of war, and you came along and told him to go and get you a drink, he would have to obey?"

He nodded. "He would have to obey me unquestioningly, no matter what I ordered, no matter how it conflicted with his previous orders, no matter whether I even belonged to his regiment. But of course I should be held responsible."

That is an Army. That is what it means to be a soldier. Plenty of people have pointed to the indisputable fact that the Germany army is the most perfect military machine in the world. But there are also other armies in the present war.

Consider the French army, rent with politics, badly clothed, badly provisioned, and with an inadequate ambulance service; opposed always to militarism, and long since sickened with fighting. The French army has not been fighting well. But it has been fighting, and the slaughter is appalling. There remains no effective reserve in France; and the available youth of the nation down to seventeen years of age is under arms. For my part, all other considerations aside, I should not care to live half-frozen in a trench, up to my middle in water, for three or four months, because someone in authority said I ought to shoot Germans. But if I were a Frenchman, I should do it, because I would have been accustomed to the idea by my compulsory military service.

The Russian army, inexhaustible hordes of simple peasants torn from their farms, blessed by a priest, and knouted into battle for a cause they never heard of, appeals to me even less. Of all the armies in this war, I might make a secondary choice between the Belgians, doing England's dirty work, and the Servians, doing Russia's; but I hesitate at the sight of two hundred thousand Belgians who made a fierce, short resistance at Liege, Namur and Brussels, practically wiped off the face of the earth. "The Belgian army does not exist!" All that remains of that drilled and disciplined flower of Belgium are a few regiments restoring their shattered nerves in barracks, and quarreling with

their Allies. The Servian army is still making heroic last stands, but that is no fun.

And crossing over to the Austrian side, I call to mind that hideous persistent story about the first days of the war, when Austria sent her unequipped regiments against the Russians. Only the first ranks had rifles and ammunition; the ranks behind were instructed to pick up the guns when the first ranks were killed—and so on.

But I could fill pages with the super-Mexican horrors that civilized Europe is inflicting upon itself. I could describe to you the quiet, dark, saddened streets of Paris, where every ten feet you are confronted with some miserable wreck of a human being, or a madman who lost his reason in the trenches, being led around by his wife. I could

BELGIUM

IRELAND

Drawn by K. R. Chamberlain, July 1916

Protecting the Rights of Small Nations

tell you of the big hospital in Berlin full of German soldiers who went crazy from merely hearing the cries of the thirty thousand Russians drowning in the swamps of East Prussia after the battle of Tannenburg. Or of Galician peasants dropping out of their regiments to die along the roads of cholera. Or of the numbness and incalculable demoralization among men in the trenches. Or of holes torn in bodies with jagged pieces of melanite shells, of sounds that make deaf, of gases that destroy eye-sight, of wounded men dying day by day and hour by hour within forty yards of twenty thousand human beings, who won't stop killing each other long enough to gather them up. . . .

But that is not my purpose in this brief article. I want to try and indicate the effect of military obedience and discipline upon human beings. Disease, death, wounds on the battle-field, Philosophical Anarchism, and International Socialism, seem to be futile as incentives to Peace. Why? As for the bloody side of war, that shocks people less than they think; we're so accustomed to half a million a year maimed and killed in mines and factories. As for Socialism, Anarchism, any democratic or individualist faith—I don't speak of Christianity, which is completely bankrupt—the Socialists, Anarchists, et al. *were all trained soldiers!*

I seem to hear shouts of "England! Look at England! England has no conscript army!" Well, if England has no conscript army now, England is going soon to have one. The Englishman has been prepared for this war by adroit press alarms for years. Hardly one ordinary Briton—of the class that fills the ranks of her far-flung regiments—who did not admit that war with Germany was coming, and that he would have to fight. I could digress here for pages to tell you the terrible means by which England filled her "volunteer" army; how workingmen of enlistable age were fired from their jobs, and relief refused their wives and children until the men joined; how others were intimidated, bullied, shamed into fighting for a cause they had no interest in, nor affection for; how Harrods' great department-store loaded a truck with young clerks and sent them to the recruiting-office, with a big sign on the side, "Harrods' Gift to the Empire."

You have perhaps said to yourself, "In the English army an officer is not allowed to strike an enlisted man." That is perfectly true. When an English soldier gets impudent to his superior, the latter orders the nearest non-commissioned officer to "Hit him." But the English soldier is seldom insubordinate. *He knows his place.* The officer

caste is a caste above him, to which he can never attain. There are *rankers* in the British army— men who rise from the ranks—but they are not accepted by the army aristocracy, nor respected by the men. They float, like Mohammed's coffin, between heaven and earth. I bring to your notice the advertisement which appeared lately in the London *Times*: "Wanted—Two thousand young *Gentlemen* for Officers in Kitchener's Army." I have seen the English army in the field in France; I have noticed the apparent democracy of intercourse between men and officers—it is the kind of thing that takes place between a gentleman and his butler. Yes, the English soldier knows his place, and there's no Revolution in him. In Germany there is a little hope from the people—they do not think for themselves, but they are corrupted and coerced; in England, the people do not have to be coerced—they obey of their own free will.

And if you want to see those whom the Germans themselves call "an army of non-commissioned officers"—the best soldiers in the world—look at the first British Expeditionary Force, two hundred and fifty thousand men who have served seven years or more from India to Bermuda, and around the world again. These are the real Tommy Atkinses that Kipling sung. They are usually undersized, debauched, diseased little men, with a moral sense fertilized by years of slaughtering yellow, brown and black men with dum-dum bullets. Their reward consists of bronze medals and colored strips of ribbon—and their ruined lives, after they are mustered out, if they are not maimed and useless, are spent opening and shutting carriage-doors in front of theatres and hotels.

No, I'm afraid we must leave England out of this discussion. England breeds men that know their place, that become obedient soldiers whenever their social superiors order them to. The harm does not lie in joining Kitchener's army; it lies in being an Englishman. In no other self-governing nation in the world would the people acquiesce in the complete suppression of representative government at the order of a military dictator like Kitchener.

At the begining of this article I gave two instances of what a German must become to be a good soldier. But since Germany has for more than forty years armed and trained her entire manhood, the consequences of the system must appear in her national life. They do. The Germans are politically cowed. They do what they are told. They learn by rote, and their "Kultur" has become a mechanical incubator for sterile Doctors of Philosophy, whose pedantry is the despair of all youth except German youth. Nietzsche is the last German genius, and 1848 the last date in their vain struggle for political self-expression. Then comes Bismarck, and the German spirit is chained with comfortable chains, fed with uniforms, decorations, and the outworn claptrap of military glory, so that today small business men and fat peasants think like Joachim Murat and talk like General Bernhardi. Allow me to point out that the party of "Revolution," the German Social-Democrats, is as autocratic as the Kaiser's government; and that the crime for which a member is expelled from the Party is "insubordination to the Party leaders." I was informed proudly by a Social-Democratic Deputy in the Reichstag that the Party was now *collecting Party dues in the trenches;* and that, when requested, the *Government deducts the dues from the men's pay and hands it over to the Party organization!*

The German people—*Cannonen-futter* ("Cannon-food") they are jocularly called—went to war almost without a protest. And today, from top to bottom of Germany, the investigator must seek hard before he finds a single dissenting voice. Germany is practically solid; when the Government has an official opinion, the street-cleaners have that same opinion in three days. That is the logical result of universal military service in a country where the classes are not inalterably fixed, as they are in England. And that, let me insist, is what is absolutely required for an efficient army. There is no choice. Thorough efficiency can only be attained at this time by an Autocracy, and so only can an army be attained; in a Democracy, neither efficiency in government, nor an efficient army is possible.

I hate soldiers. I hate to see a man with a bayonet fixed on his rifle, who can order me off the street. I hate to belong to an organization that is proud of obeying a caste of superior beings, that is proud of killing free ideas, so that it may the more efficiently kill human beings in cold blood. They will tell you that a conscript army is Democratic, because everybody has to serve; but they won't tell you that military service plants in your blood the germ of blind obedience, of blind irresponsibility, that it produces one class of Commanders in your state and your industries, and accustoms you to do what they tell you even in time of peace.

Here in America we have our chance to construct someday a Democracy, unhampered by the stupid docility of a people who run to salute when the band plays. They are talking now about building up an immense standing army, to combat the Japs, or the Germans, or the Mexicans. I, for one, refuse to join. You ask me how I am going to combat a whole world thirsting for our blood? And I reply, not by creating a counter-thirst for the blood of the Japs, Germans, or Mexicans. There is no such thing as a "moderate army" or an "army of defense." Once we begin that, Japan, Germany, or Mexico, whichever it is, will begin to build up a defense against us. We will raise them one, and so on. And the logical end of all that is Germany; and the logical end of Germany is, and always will be, War. And you, gentle reader, you will be the first to get shot.
—March 1915

JAMES HOPPER
Soldiers of France

Through a village full of troops resting in houses half or three-quarters destroyed by artillery, we came to a road which we crossed, then a field, and went down two steps made of earth. Our feet were in what seemed at first a furrow. But as we walked it deepened; its sides rose to our knees, to our waists, to our shoulders, higher than our eyes; we sank gradually till we were filing through the plain with our heads beneath its level.

Under our feet was a little walk made of round pieces of wood laid across and held together by longitudinal strips. To the right and the left—so close to each other that they left not much more room than needed for broad shoulders—the sides of the trench rose vertical, freshly re-cut, yellow and gleaming.

We began to come to cross-galleries, and to widened spaces where several of these would meet. At the intersections, signposts were stuck, bearing jocular names, such as Boulevard des Italiens, or Place de la Concorde. We met a general coming out after his tour of inspection. His shoes were caked with mud, his plain old greatcoat was plastered with it. He stopped to chat a moment amiably. "I've just been on my little morning walk," he said.

Meanwhile we had been getting deeper into the zone of fire. To the right and the left, ahead and behind, rifle shots were crackling, sometimes several together or in quick succession, sometimes a lone shot between two silences, some far, some near, some seemingly almost at our elbows. But the impression, somehow, was not of war, but

Drawn by Henry J. Glintenkamp, October 1914

The Girl He Left Behind Him

rather a festive one. We could not see those who shot. And blind in the depths of our narrow gut, with the cool gray morn overhead, we got out of that irregular and brick crackling a vision of a hunt passing above us along the surface of the plain, of guests in corduroy shooting partridges courteously.

We had been passing now and then fatigue parties of soldiers, with picks and shovels, with objects being brought out or in, once with a mitrailleuse in need of repair; always these men had stepped off the walk for us and had stood in the mud of the little channel dug to carry off the water, their backs against the wet trench-wall, their stomachs sucked in. But now we came to a party which did not make way, at the first disturbing sight of which it was we, this time, who went into the ooze of the gutter, with our backs against the wall. First came two men bearing a stretcher between them. A gray cloth had been thrown over the stretcher; its folds blurred, but left still eloquent, a rigid outline. A second stretcher passed, also covered, also of significant and immobile silhouette. But the third was not covered, and some difficulty in rounding a sharp corner ahead of the first stretcher stopped this one for a full minute against me, beneath my eyes.

On the stretcher lay a little dead *piou-piou* in red pants. His head was covered with a blue sweater which recalled to me the days of coming winter when all the women of France had been knitting. He lay on his stomach, his knees brought up slightly beneath him, as if he had been struck while vigorously butting forward, and because of this position, which shortened him, and because of the gay red pants, he looked like a child.

He lay so that the soles of his shoes were turned up toward me. These shoes were too large for him. And the way the toes were curled up, the way the big hobnails were worn down and the sole between them corroded, the way the mud still caked them and the way the red pantaloons were turned up above them—all this told so strikingly how well and with what innocent alacrity the little *piou-piou* had tramped and toiled and charged for France!

For a moment the finger of reality lay on our shoulders, then again was gone. The haze above, the ghostly sun, the great silence which, heavily, muffled all sounds and filled all the interstices between sounds, all this placed us in a sensation of dream. We were in a second-line trench now; we were told to speak only in whispers because of the

Others watching so near. Already, as a matter of fact, we had been speaking in whispers; but it was not because of the Others; we could not believe in the Others. Once I sprang up to a step cut into the earth and looked over the parapet. All I saw was the ground sloping gently into a wall of fog. A hand seized my elbow, pulled me down. "You're going to get your head broken," the captain growled.

Every once in a while we came to a little gut opening in the trench, and if we entered it, we came in a few steps to the mouth of a cave, and, sticking our heads within, saw four, or five, or six soldiers sleeping in there, bedded in straw, their sacks beneath their heads, their guns and bayonets along their flanks. They did not stir at our presence; they slept, without a movement, without a sound; as if they had slept thus a hundred years. A little farther we would come to another such cave, with its five or six sleeping soldiers. And at length we gained from this a vision of the plain with its intricacy of trenches and galleries (two hundred and fifty miles of trenches and galleries to each fifteen miles of front) and its innumerable little caverns filled with sleeping soldiers armed and equipped. We saw the great plain, bare and dead above, murmuring with life within, the great hollow plain with its legions waiting under enchantment for the stamp of the foot and the call of the Voice.

Suddenly, on the ground above, so near that we could not tell where, a tremendous explosion cracked the air. I saw the captain just ahead of me flatten himself against the wall of the trench, and then, as if by magic, flowers of mud crystallized on his kepi and his coat like an instantaneous mushroom growth. "*Ça y est,*" said the captain. He looked at his watch. "Ten o'clock. That is their regular time here." A second explosion followed, not so near this time, but with that same crackling abruptness which seemed to split one's bones. Then there was a third, five or six more, and we saw that the shells were dropping in front of our trench. "They are short," someone said. And, as if in denial, a shell now passed overhead. It passed with a soft, blurry sound and a small musical creaking like that of a pigeon's wing, and seemingly so slowly that we had time to look all upward and search the fog instinctively for the silhouette of some great bird.

We were now in a gut between the second and the first line trench, not more than a few feet from the latter which, in turn, was only seventy-five yards from the first line German trench. But the officers stopped now, gathered and consulted. I guessed that they were worried about our precious persons and wavering in their promise to let us into the first-line trench, and so, very quietly, I slid along the last necessary few feet.

I obtained just one good look before I was called back, but what I had seen was enough. I had seen the soldier of France of this war. The soldier of France in the last of the kaleidoscopic guises which through the centuries he had assumed, each time supremely. The same fighter who stopped Attila, who, cuirassed and casqued, led in the mystic surge of the Crusades, who, in the Hundred Years' War fought the longest and most stubborn defensive in history, in the sixteenth century the most gallantly futile skirmishes; the same man with the chameleon exterior and the eternal soul whose War of the Revolution is the type and model and ideal of all revolutionary wars, and whose Napoleonic period, only a few years after, presents the arch example of the War of Conquest.

He stood on a step cut out of the earth, his belly against the oozing trench-wall. His feet were in a tub full of straw, and because of the many woolens he had piled on beneath his capote, his silhouette was cubic. He had wrapped a scarf over his soggy kepi, past his ears and under his chin, and within that, his face was a bramble of wild beard. And his whole bulk, the scarf, the beard, the dark blue uniform with its blackened buttons, all of him was enveloped in an armor of mud which held him stiff, and seemed a part of his vigilance.

He stood there, absolutely motionless; out of the bramble of his beard I could see against the light his eyelashes, level and steady toward the German trenches; his gun lay on the parapet before him, and his hands lay also on the parapet, one on each side of the gun, flat, easy and very patient; you could imagine with what an oily, sure gesture he would take up that gun. Thus silent and immobile, he waited; wrapped in the soil of France as if in the folds of a flag.   —August 1915

MAX EASTMAN
War for War's Sake

It is not only the waste of blood but the waste of heroism that appalls us, and makes all emotion inadequate. If we could only dip up that continentful of self-sacrifice and pour it to some useful end!

Probably no one will actually be the victor in this gambler's war—for we may as well call it a gamblers' war. Only so can we indicate its underlying commercial causes, its futility, and yet also the tall spirit in which it is carried off. A better informed pen than mine has indicated some of its causes on another page. And I will only add a protest, on the one hand against those prophets of praise-and-blame who think they have fulfilled the function of intelligence in such a crisis by pointing a finger of reprehension against something they call "Germany," and on the other hand against those German wiseacres who reply by sighing, "Ah, you do not understand—it is the conflict of racial cultures—of the Teuton against the Slav for the destinies of civilization."

But we dare to assert that racial animosity the world over is animosity against an economic rival. There is, of course, in us a survived impulse of suspicion against a man of alien traits, but the common qualities of human nature can very quickly smooth that over, as they have done a thousand times in history, when it is not rubbed up by a real or imagined clash of interests. The father of the "Pan-Slavic" idea was, I am told, an Armenian, Loris Melikoff, who became premier of Russia, and recognized a good business idea as soon as he saw it. And the fathers of the "Teutonic Civilization" idea are those fighting barbarians, the ruling classes of Germany, the least civilized people in Europe.

So let us drop the race rant forever, and let us not confuse the pleasant-hearted people of the Rhine, who love a sweet song and a quiet thought just as much or as little as any of us, with their archaic rulers and all the retinue of physical and intellectual lackeys that come with them out of the past. It is not a national trait but a class trait that has given to Germany the position of grandiose aggressor in this inevitable outbreak of commercial war. Her rulers have preserved a kind of pugnacious ego-mania that may once have accorded well with their station in life, and they are ready to undertake with a flourish of swords matters which the modern bourgeois rulers of France and England would go about both more hesitantly and with a more cultivated cunning.

There is reason to hope that this undertaking will be their last—that Germany in defeat will become a republic. It seems at least as though one more harvest of death and devastation, with the Kaiser in command, might disillusion a few eyes.

But is there not even a greater and more novel hope? Will not the progress of industrial and true liberty in all the nations be furthered by this final experience of imperial carnage? The progress of liberty itself is a fight, and we need have no fear that it will faint on the battlefield. The spirit of benevolent reform may faint on the battlefield, but the fighting spirit of liberty will flourish. That is the great hope.

I do not believe a devastating war in Europe will stop the labor struggle. I believe it will hasten the days of its triumph. It will shake people together like dice in a box, and how they will fall out nobody knows. But they will fall out *shaken;* that everybody knows. Nothing will be solid as it was before, no title, no privilege, no property. Discontent among the poor will be enormous. And the ideal of industrial democracy is now strong enough and clear enough to control that discontent, and fashion it to a great end.

Indeed, if this tragic gamble, once begun, is carried to the point of devastating Europe, the gamblers will find themselves facing a most unexpected power. For with untold labors of reconstruction to be done, and inadequate numbers of workers to do them, it will be time to bow down and beg from what workmen there are. It is the ever-waiting army of the unemployed that makes it so easy to exploit labor. And when they have made labor scarce, they will find labor proud.

It was only thirty-one years after the Black Death had decimated the population of the British Islands that Wat Tyler marched into London with thirty thousand kings at his back, and told the crown and court of England just what he wanted, and where, and when, and not why. And the crown, and the court, and the church, and the bench, and all the elegant elaborate props of feudal exploitation, bowed down to a man whose name had been unknown in the kingdom eight days before. Things can happen, you see!

So the spirit of industrial liberty will not die with the death of soldiers. It will burn right through the ranks of the armies that fight. We will hear little of it. We have not heard much of the anti-military demonstrations of Socialist and Labor bodies through France and Italy, and of the martial despotism that breaks them up in Germany and Austria and Russia. We have heard little of the noble mutinies and patriotic treasons that are the glories of this war. The best news will not come to us, because of the censorship of the press. But we can imagine it.

The assassination of Jaurès, the great political leader of the working people of France, was a significant prelude to a general European war, for he was a leading spirit of the world in the working-class struggle against war. He had declared in a convention of the International Socialist party that at the first threat of hostilities the workers of France and Germany ought to lay down their tools in a general strike, for they have no interest in shooting each other to serve the commercial interests of their masters. And do not think, because you hear nothing to the contrary, that the message of Jaurès and thousands of agitators like him, is being forgotten by all the workers of Europe. It will be spoken by soldiers in the camps, and it will be spoken by the wives of soldiers, the waiting mothers of their children—"Workers of the world —you have no quarrel with each other—your quarrel is with your masters—unite!" And it will be remembered by them all in the long run, because it is true.   —September 1914

The Trader's War

[*Although unsigned, this article was written by John Reed.*]

[This article is written by a well-known American author and war correspondent who is compelled by arrangements with another publication to withhold his name.]

The Austro-Servian conflict is a mere bagatelle— as if Hoboken should declare war on Coney Island —but all the Civilization of Europe is drawn in.

The real War, of which this sudden outburst of death and destruction is only an incident, began long ago. It has been raging for tens of years, but its battles have been so little advertised that they have been hardly noted. It is a clash of Traders.

It is well to remember that the German empire began as a business agreement. Bismarck's first victory was the *"Zollverein,"* a tariff agreement between a score of petty German principalities. This Commercial League was solidified into a powerful State by military victories. It is small wonder that German business men believe that their trade development depends on force.

"Ohne Armee, kein Deutschland" is not only the motto of the Kaiser and the military caste. The success of the Militarist propaganda of the Navy League and other such jingo organizations depends on the fact that nine Germans out of ten read history that way. There never was any Germany worth talking about except when, under the Great Elector, Frederick the Great, and Bismarck, the Army was strong.

It is this belief, that the power and prosperity of Germany depends on its Army, which explains the

Drawn by K. R. Chamberlain, December 1914

Teuton Against Slav

surprising fact that one of the most progressive, cultured and intellectually free nations on earth allows the Kaiser to kaise.

The progressive burghers of Germany would have put an end to "personal government" and military domination long ago if they had not believed that they were threatened by their neighbors, that their very existence hinged on the strength of their Army. They have grumbled under their grievous taxes, but in the end they have paid, because they believed they were menaced.

And they were menaced.

After the Franco-Prussian war of 1870 came the *"grunderzeit"*—the "foundation period." Everything German leaped forward in a stupendous impulse of growth.

The withdrawal of the German mercantile marine from the sea has reminded us of the world-wide importance of their transportation services. All these great German fleets of ocean liners and merchantmen have sprung into being since 1870. In steel manufacture, in textile work, in mining and trading, in every branch of modern industrial and commercial life, and also in population, German development has been equally amazing.

But geographically all fields for development were closed.

In the days when there had been no army and no united Germany, the English and French had grabbed all the earth and the fulness thereof.

No colonial markets—on which her rivals subsist—were left open to Germany except some scattered tribes of African Negroes, who will buy nothing but calico and rum.

England and France met German development with distrust and false sentiments of Peace. "We do not intend to grab any more territory. The Peace of Europe demands the maintenance of the Status Quo."

With these words scarcely cold on her lips, Great Britain took South Africa. And pretended to endless surprise and grief that the Germans did not applaud this closing of another market.

In 1909, King Edward—a great friend of Peace —after long secret conferences, announced the *Entente Cordiale,* whereby France promised to back up England in absorbing Egypt, and England pledged itself to support France in her Morocco adventure.

The news of this underhand "gentleman's agreement" caused a storm. The Kaiser, in wild indignation, shouted that "Nothing can happen in Europe without my consent."

The Peace-lovers of London and Paris agreed that this threat of war was very rude. But they were getting what they wanted without dirtying their hands in blood, so they consented to a Diplomatic Conference at Algeciras. France solemnly promised *not* to annex Morocco, and above all pledged herself to maintain "the Open Door." Every one was to have an equal commercial chance. The storm blew over.

The unbiased observer must admit that the Kaiser had made a rude noise. But after all, why should anything happen in Europe without Germany being consulted? There are half a hundred million Teutons in Central Europe. They certainly have a stake in the fate of the Continent.

It was bad form for the War Lord to let off bombastic epigrams and to "rattle his sword." But it was *bad faith* for pretended advocates of Peace to conspire in secret conclave to back each other up in repudiating their engagements to preserve the Status Quo.

One example out of a thousand of how the French observed their pledge to maintain an Open Door in Morocco is furnished by the method of buying cloth to uniform the Moorish army.

In accordance with the "Act of Algeciras," which required that all contracts should be put up at international auction, it was announced that the Sultan had decided on a large order of khaki to make uniforms for his soldiers. "Specifications" would be published on a certain day—in accordance to the law—and the cloth manufacturers of the world were invited to be present.

The "Specifications" demanded that the cloth should be delivered in three months and that it should be of a certain width—three yards, as I remember. "But," protested the representative of a German firm, "there are no looms in the world of that width. It would take months to build them." But it developed that a far-seeing—or fore-warned—manufacturer of Lyons had installed the necessary machines a few months before. He got the contract.

The Ambassador at Tangier has had to hire extra clerks to forward to Berlin the complaints of German merchants, protesting against the impossibleness of France's "Open Door."

For a couple of decades the Germans have felt that their normal industrial development was being checked on every hand—not by the forces of nature, nor their own shortcomings, but by wilful, hostile, organized opposition.

Perhaps the most exasperating thing of all has been the row over the Bagdad Railroad. A group of German capitalists secured a franchise for a railroad to open up Asia Minor by way of Bagdad and the Persian Gulf. It was an undeveloped country which offered just the kind of commercial outlet they needed. The scheme was blocked by England on the pretext that such a railroad might be used by the Kaiser to send his army half way round the world to steal India.

But the Germans understood very well that the English merchants and ship owners did not want to have their monopoly of Indian trade threatened.

Even when they scored this big commercial victory—the blocking of the Bagdad Railroad—the English diplomats protested their love of Peace and their purehearted desire to preserve the Status Quo. It was at this juncture that a Deputy in the Reichstag said, "The Status Quo is an aggression."

The situation in short is this. German Capitalists want more profits. English and French Capitalists want it all. This War of Commerce has gone on for years, and Germany has felt herself worsted. Every year she has suffered some new setback. The commercial "smothering" of Germany is a fact of current history.

This effort to crowd out Germany is frankly admitted by the economic and financial writers of England and France. It comes out in a petty and childish way in the popular attempts to boycott things "Made in Germany." On a larger scale it is embodied in *"ententes"* and secret treaties. Those who treat of the subject in philosophical phraseology justify it by referring to the much abused "Struggle for Existence." But at any time in the last few years sincerely liberal ministries in Paris and London could easily have made friends with Germany—and the Kaiser would have crumbled into dust.

There can be nothing surer than that the Germans as a whole are not bellicose, that they support the Kaiser and all the heavy charge of militarism because they know they are menaced.

Instead of granting the few concessions called for by their young and aspiring rival, England and France tighten their strangling grasp. Posing as Apostles of Peace, the smotherers say "Don't struggle" to their victim. "Above all, don't draw the sword—that isn't Christ-like."

There is no reason to doubt that in this sudden crisis the statesmen of London and Paris sincerely desired "Peace." War is a gamble. The "peaceful," bloodless process of smothering is surer—and safer.

"Every year of peace," another leader of German public opinion exclaims, "is for us a defeat!" And every German business man believed him. And every German workingman, who thinks that his own welfare depends on the prosperity of his employer, believed it, too.

No wonder that the industrial classes of Germany—although they are better educated than their English competitors, more alive and progressive than their French rivals—support the military tyranny of the Kaiser. Peace means gradual ruin. In the appeal to arms there is at least a chance of victory.

No one can have a more utter abhorrence of Militarism than I. No one can wish more heartily that the shame of it may be erased from our century. "It is neither by parliamentary oratory nor the votes of majorities that the great questions of the day can be solved but by blood and iron"—"durch Eisen und Blut"—these words of Bismarck's are the motto of the Reaction. Nothing stands more squarely in the path of democratic progress.

And no recent words have seemed to me so ludicrously condescending as the Kaiser's speech to "his" people when he said that in this supreme crisis he freely forgave all those who had ever opposed him. I am ashamed that in this day in a civilized country any one can speak such archaic nonsense as that speech contained.

But worse than the "personal government" of the Kaiser, worse even than the brutalizing ideals he boasts of standing for, is the raw hypocrisy of his armed foes, who shout for a Peace which their greed has rendered impossible.

More nauseating than the crack-brained bombast of the Kaiser is the editorial chorus in America which pretends to believe—would have us believe—that the White and Spotless Knight of Modern Democracy is marching against the Unspeakably Vile Monster of Medieval Militarism.

What has democracy to do in alliance with Nicholas, the Tsar? Is it Liberalism which is marching from the Petersburg of Father Gapon, from the Odessa of Pogroms? Are our editors naive enough to believe this?

No. There is a falling out among commercial rivals. One side has observed the polite forms of Diplomacy and has talked of "Peace"—relying the while on the eminently pacific Navy of Great Britain and the Army of France and on the millions of semi-serfs whom they have bribed the Tsar of All the Russias (and The Hague) to scourge forward against the Germans. On the other side there has been rudeness—and the hideous Gospel of Blood and Iron.

We, who are Socialists, must hope—we may even expect—that out of this horror of bloodshed and dire destruction will come far-reaching social changes—and a long step forward towards our goal of Peace among Men.

But we must not be duped by this editorial buncombe about Liberalism going forth to Holy War against Tyranny.

This is not Our War.   —September 1914

HOWARD BRUBAKER
Silver Linings

[*Brubaker contributed a monthly column of items like this to both* The Masses *and the* Liberator, *and later continued the feature in the* New Yorker.]

Nicholas Murray Butler is stranded in Europe.

We no longer have to read humorous sayings by Vice President Marshall.

A deluge of pictures of Sir Thomas Lipton wreathed in smiles has been averted.

Lieutenant Porte has stopped postponing the date on which he will not sail across the Atlantic in an airship.

People no longer say: "Preparation for war is the surest guarantee of peace."

S. S. McClure on his return to America declared that Ireland would never accept home rule and that the Kaiser would never carry out his war bluff. Home rule fans, take renewed courage.

"DEMOCRACY ON BOARD"

The headline is furnished by the New York *Tribune;* the story by an American refugee, Perry Tiffany. Do your own laughing.

"One humorous side of the situation was the fact that the butler and the maid from the yacht sat with us at the same table on the tramp ship."

The New York *Times* in an editorial six inches long joshes Ford, the automobile man, because his latest publicity venture ran foul of the war news.

Drawn by Art Young, October 1914

Britannia in Righteous Wrath Resolves to Crush Out German Militarism

[*The idea for this cartoon was suggested by William English Walling.*]

As usual with the *Times*, this editorial carried its refutation with it.

At the hour of going to press Beloochistan was greatly depressed and humiliated because it had not received any kind of ultimatum from the Kaiser.

The Kaiser, besides being all the officers of the German army and navy, is an admiral in the British and Russian fleets as well as those of Norway, Sweden, Denmark and Greece. He also holds odd jobs in Austria and Spain. Why not let the Kaiser put on all the uniforms he is entitled to and fight himself to a finish?   —September 1914

CARL SANDBURG
Buttons

I have been watching the war map slammed up for
    advertising in front of the newspaper office.
Buttons—red and yellow buttons—blue and black
    buttons—are shoved back and forth across the
    map.

A laughing young man, sunny with freckles,
Climbs a ladder, yells a joke to somebody in the
    crowd,
And then fixes a yellow button one inch west
And follows the yellow button with a black button
    one inch west.

(Ten thousand men and boys twist on their bodies
    in a red soak along a river edge,
Gasping of wounds, calling for water, some rattling
    death in their throats.)
Who by Christ would guess what it cost to move
    two buttons one inch on the war map here in
    front of the newspaper office where the freckle-
    faced young man is laughing to us?
                                    —February 1915

MABEL DODGE
The Secret of War

[*Although not the most perceptive analysis of the causes of war ever published, this article was interesting if only because it was one of Mabel Dodge's rare appearances in print before the publication of her three-volume autobiography,* Intimate Memoires, *in the 1930's. She was known primarily for the salon she maintained for several years which brought together, at one time or another, most of the radicals, intellectuals, and artists in New York City.*]

THE LOOK ON THE FACES OF MEN WHO HAVE BEEN KILLING—AND WHAT WOMEN THINK ABOUT IT.

We knew that if we could get to Paris, where we could see something, we would understand it all better. And we knew that we *had* to understand it—that we could never get away from it until we did.

We *had* to know the hidden reason—the principle behind that overwhelming fact that all the nations of Europe and some of Asia and Africa were at war with each other in the Twentieth Century.

So as soon as trains began to pass people through from one country to another, we went away from Florence, glad to leave the trifling incoherencies of that August in Italy.

In Paris it was still difficult to believe that there was war. Beyond the fact that everyone talked of it—that the papers spoke of nothing else—that the streets seemed full of the paraphernalia and preparation for war, we nowhere saw signs of war itself. I am sure I don't know what we expected. Perhaps no one ever sees war as he expects to see it. Perhaps "Tommy" in the trench shooting away monotonously, under orders, at a clump of trees in the distance, says to himself in surprise: "So this is war!"

With flags flying from every door and window, Paris never looked more gallant. The Germans, we heard, were only a few miles away. Yet Paris in the sunshine seemed smiling, like a great lady going to the guillotine *en grande toilette;* exquisitely French.

The streets were empty of all, save motors carrying soldiers and officers, and every variety of cart and truck bearing the Red Cross Flag and pressed into the service of the army for provisioning and for transporting the wounded.

With the officers of the Government at Bordeaux, Paris under the Military Governor was a model of order and precision. From one day to the next France adopted the strict discipline of militarism and everything proceeded as though by machinery. There were no signs of discontent. All the families of soldiers were provided for within the organization—women thrown out of work received a franc and a few sous over, a day. Soup kitchens were established everywhere. Some of them were organized by the Syndicalists, who were acting for the Government. They had stopped all their own propaganda to urge their men to the front. Almost a great humanitarian movement, seemed the war to these Frenchmen, and they unhesitatingly sent all the workers to "the war which is to kill war."

The two busiest spots in Paris were the square in front of the Invalides and the Rue Royale, near the Madeleine.

All day long men came and went in the Place des Invalides bearing messages—getting orders—and twice a day they pulled up at the Taverne Royale to rush in and eat, and out again. There officers in wonderful uniforms sat down for a bite with their brothers and cousins dressed in the red trousers and blue coat of the volunteer soldier, and there all day there came and went a stream of color and a stream of electric excitement.

Up and down on the sidewalk flowed the idle and the curious—looking for news—for incident—the eternal Parisian spectator whose life is passed, in wartime or in peace, in watching others act.

Sometimes a pair of Highlanders would motor up and take a couple of seats at a table outside—those neat bare knees were loved in the Rue Royale! And the air men with the wings of Mercury embroidered on their sleeves, came and went. Their eyes seemed full of light.

All that we saw done was done for war. Everyone was going about on the business of war, and always of war itself we saw no sign, yet these men had all seen it—they had been in it—they were it. There is some difference between the men who are in it and those who are not, and the difference isn't in the uniform. *It is in the man himself.* Some chemicalization has taken place. He is transformed by it. He is perhaps not more alive, but he is differently alive than he was before. Somehow he is quickened in the way that nothing else has ever quickened him. This is true of all the men that I saw.

And so always seeing the signs of this unseen thing called war—this lure that has drawn all these millions of men together on to strange soil to kill each other—we asked ourselves more and more: What is it?

Does anyone know? It is called by so many names.

Some are calling it patriotism. A great many are calling it that. The Socialists and Syndicalists in France are calling it a humanitarian movement. They say that they have gone to war to destroy militarism. In Germany some of them are fighting because they have been ordered out and they call it "an officer's war"; others are fighting with an intellectual motive, to increase the opportunity for expansion and growth, and they call it a war against Czarism and the British death grip.

The German Socialists have told us that they go to war against their French brothers with sorrow in their hearts, but that they go to bring greater life to the future of Socialism by destroying the oppressive enemy.

And yet one English "Tommy" told me on the street one afternoon—he and his chum had escaped from some Germans and had wandered into Paris for a day and a night before looking for their battalion—

"We don't want to kill those German chaps," he said, "and they don't want to kill us. It's all just a dirty mess—it's war."

But he had been killing—he had the look; and he had just escaped with his life from the Germans by a fluke—but his eyes were full of light.

A French soldier told me that after the battle on the Marne he and his chums would go out to the battlefield in the evening after fighting all day and they would help the wounded German soldiers all they could and give them cigarettes.

"Ils nous appelaient Kamarads!" he said; and he, too, had the look of having been quickened by war.

And think of this. A soldier hardly ever knows where he is. Even in his own country he cannot tell because the names on the sign posts along the road are painted out. He is simply moved about by orders which are just comprehensible enough to obey at that moment. When he isn't on the move, it is mostly summed up in the command:

"One! Two! Three! Fire!"

At the battle of the Oise these terrible words were flung at the French and English soldiers for three days and three nights without stopping.

That is war.

The motive for it the soldier calls by a poor or by a glorious name—according to his temperament.

I think that in France and England only the politicians say that they are fighting to destroy German militarism. Ask the soldiers why they are fighting. A good many of them only know that they are there because they *have* to be, a good many others because they heard the bugle call. And now that they are there, most of them like it. Some of the mystics have been saying that some great natural force behind men and governments precipitated this war and is pushing it on beyond the will of humanity.

"Nothing less than a miracle can stop its fearful momentum now," they say.

Drawn by K. R. Chamberlain, January 1915

At Petrograd

RUSSIAN OFFICER: "Why these fortifications, your majesty? Surely the Germans will not get this far!"
THE CZAR: "But when our own army returns . . .?"

[273]

But men like fighting. That is the force behind the war. That they will stop liking it—will be the miracle.

Of course, if they can find a principle to fight for, they fight and like it still better, but what war is for the main part is the inconceivable, the inevitable love of—fighting itself. There is no deeper meaning than that to be found in it, and there never has been any other.

If there were any other stronger reason than that, there might be some chance of peace in disarmament.

We have been saying for so long that war isn't civilized. We should have realized perhaps that civilization isn't human. Perhaps peace isn't human. Not in the same way that men are human.

It has just been laid over the human qualities and we live to see its most finished products proving their efficacy in the service of the most primeval instinct!

I believe that even the gods and Mr. Chesterton must be dazzled at the spectacle of the great aeroplanes soaring like divine birds over cities and men, dropping upon them their bombs full of deadly gases and dynamite, at the command of Government!

Is that what is meant by the phrase "civilized warfare"? Warfare brought to its highest degree of deadliness and cruelty through machinery?

In Paris we learned that they are calling it "The war of machines."

Of his own machine guns, a wounded French officer said to me:

"I don't believe men could stand mowing each other down like that if they met in a hand to hand conflict. But with the machine gun—you just go on turning the handle. The narrow streets of the town of Soissons where we had been fighting all day were piled high on each side with men, where the machine gun had been playing all the afternoon."

In London one saw even less of war, but more than ever the illusion of it. The motor cars were all bearing signs: "To arms!" "Your King and country need you!" "The duty of every man is to his country!"—and all the music halls were full of "artists" singing of war and its most gallant aspects.

The cinematographs showed pictures of the "brave boys" at the front and of the unbelievably inhuman enemy.

All these incentives were brought to a degree of art that was hard to analyze, which seemed to be a

mingling of the simple and sincere poetic feeling of the people and the self-conscious control of diplomacy. It was very real.

All things seemed to flow together in London, for one end.

Since there is no conscription in England, social pressure supplies the necessary force when there is any hanging back. The ruling class needs the whole nation for an army in order to prevail, and men love war.

"Simon says thumbs up? Thumbs up!"

But this organized unspoken pressure made it seem, as one keen observer said:

"A fashionable war!"

In Florence we had thought that through the effect of Emperor William's "Superbia," it was a religious war—and in Paris we could not help seeing that behind its imperturbable military order and its smiling mask, it was, for all that, a defensive war to save France from German manners —so in London it resolved itself for us into a war of "Rule Britannia."

To this Moloch they are sacrificing the first born—and all the others. To maintain the illusion of Empire, women are urging their men into the field, and fathers are sending their sons—up to the last.

The day after the Earl of Plymouth lost his second son at the front, he sat behind Asquith to support him as he made his great recruiting speech; and this typifies, I think, not only the attitude of Englishmen, but of all men of the ruling class.

And all these men that are urged to go, go out joyfully with death in their hearts. Hardly a man but whose heart leaps at the sound of a bugle! It was in Paris that this truth came upon me. I had come up to see war, and I had expected to find the terror—the horror of war—and I didn't find it anywhere. I was going about with a sober face, full of sympathy, and I found the whole nation of men, soldiers and officers, happy.

They were somehow happy and excited.

Paris was serious and intensely concentrated, but it wasn't unhappy. One saw nothing very sad.

The women all stayed in their houses.

Only a few miles away men were falling by hundreds, but by some process that takes place in human nature those who saw it were spared from feeling it.

It has been said that a sight of terrible human suffering produces its ineradicable effect upon the human mind, but perhaps much horror prevents its own realization because sensibility gets dulled by repetition.

At the same time that I found out the deep universal principle behind war, I found out something else about it that is just as deep and just as universal. Women don't like war.

A poor woman with seven children down in Whitechapel, whose husband had been away at the front for six weeks and no word from him, said to me:

"Wot I'm awskin' yeh is what it's all *for?* That's what *I* want to know. Wot's it all abaout?"

Not enough other women have asked this question and found out the answer, but their instinct against war—aroused and conscious—is the only force that can ever meet and overcome the other force of its appeal to men.

The only hope of permanent peace lies in a woman's war against war.   —November 1914

Preparedness

[*The Preparedness campaign which was initiated early in the war by General Leonard Wood and other advocates of American entry—and which included parades, recruitment for voluntary military-training camps, and extensive publicity—was a regular target of* The Masses.]

WALTER G. FULLER
The Battle Cry of Peace

That mysterious title, "The Battle Cry of Peace," has intrigued my curiosity ever since I first saw it. Variants, just as elusive, have been running through my mind, such as "The War Cry of Friendship," "The Death Rattle of Life," "The Love Song of Hate," until at last I have been obliged to see the motion-picture play itself in the hope that I should thus solve the problem. The educational value of this rare and refreshing entertainment has been so highly praised by the National Security League, and the Army League, and the American Legion, that I feel that I ought to testify publicly to the several important facts which I myself have learned from this film, as follows:

That Mr. Hiram Maxim, like Noah of old (to whom I imagine Mr. Maxim bears a close physical resemblance), is a wonderful old gentleman, whose prophecies of impending doom are shockingly disregarded by his light and frivolous fellow-countrymen and women, with the exception of a choice little group of about a score of patriots, who, like all audiences shown in moving-pictures make up in enthusiasm and unanimity what they lack in numbers.

That the pacifists, most of whom appear to be very unpleasant-looking foreign spies, are in full control of the destinies of this unhappy country.

That the invading army, when it comes, will spend most of its time smashing the furniture (most of it very ugly stuff) in our homes, and making very violent and disagreeable love to young American ladies, whose abhorrence of the enemy is doubtless greatly increased by the hideous uniform he wears. It is also very clear—and here is a crumb of comfort for poor Mr. Maxim—that the enemy's soldiers are very bad marksmen, for they completely fail to hit the hero, even when shooting at him with a machine-gun at a distance of about ten yards.

That according to some ingenious diagrams which are presented on the screen during the progress of the play, like the powder in the jam, the population of America may be represented by a great figure of a man about as tall as the Statue of Liberty, but alas, the army and navy of this miserable country are seen to be represented by a little figure about the size of a baby kewpie. This distressing fact, and others equally gloomy from the point-of-view of the author, Commodore Blackton, were received with roars of laughter by the audience, which it may be supposed is what usually happens, for there quickly appeared on the screen a reproachful message from the gallant commodore himself, saying, more in sorrow than in anger, "Ah, but this is no laughing matter."

Washington, Napoleon, Lincoln, Grant, and Lee, when they appear on the screen to give their hearty support to Gen. Leonard Wood, Col. Roosevelt, Capt. Jack Crawford (the Poet Scout), and the Rev. Dr. Lyman Abbott, in their plea for preparedness and a billion-dollar loan, are seen to be very pleasant and friendly, not to say familiar gentlemen, obviously of like passions with ourselves.

That it is clearly the Commodore's opinion that here as in Europe war is an old man's game, for all the chief supporters of this plea for "preparedness" are either septuagenarians or octogenarians beginning with the fiery old Irishman, a Veteran of the Civil War, who begins the play, exciting our admiration by his vigor and enthusiasm rather than by what he says. Then various pictures show us Mr. Maxim, Dr. Lyman Abbott, and a group of hoary admirals including apparently a twin brother of von Tirpitz (to whose appeals for a bigger navy nobody listens but the hero), and lastly eight hundred members of the G. A. R. all waving little American flags and looking very self-conscious and uncomfortable.

At this very improving entertainment even the programme is not without its lessons. It begins with an earnest and pathetic, not to say maudlin, address by the gallant Commodore to the "Mothers of America" to whom the play is dedicated "with respect, reverence, and admiration." Though not a mother myself, I could not refrain from reading this soul-stirring appeal, so full of simple home truths like, "the hand that rocks the cradle rules the world," and "let us have peace," and "we must be the champions of the laws of humanity." But it is surely a somewhat doubtful compliment that the Commodore pays to his naval and military friends when he tells the mothers of America that "no body of men are half so anxious for peace as are the army and navy!"

On the second page of the programme is set out prominently a quotation from the writings of the Prophet Ezekiel (doubtless the Rev. Lyman Abbott discovered this choice morsel for the Commodore, . . . "what damned error but some sober brow will bless it and approve it with a text"). On the same page the Fire Notice caught my eye. I imagine we do not have to thank the Commodore for this warning, though indeed the note of preparedness is struck here also—but in another key. This fire notice ends with these words which seem to me to have a deeper significance than is intended: "In case of disturbance of any kind, to avoid the dangers of panic, *walk,* do not run." . . . Here, I think, Fire Commissioner Adamson gives us better advice than does either the Prophet Ezekiel or the Commodore Blackton.

—December 1915

[276]

AMOS PINCHOT
The Courage of the Cripple

Colonel Roosevelt has supreme confidence in war. Billy Sunday, Lloyd George and the bishops of England have a steadfast faith in it; so apparently have most Christian clergymen in America. But can those of us who are without faith believe that going on fighting until Germany is brought to her knees will free the world from the threat of Prussian militarism?

Nations and individual men follow the same psychological progressions. For instance, the history of the nation Germany is paralleled with amazing faithfulness by that of the man William the Second; and indeed by the lives of many men, who, like William, began life handicapped, and yet had the vitality and will-power to overcome or compensate for early disabilities. Not only do such men and nations often succeed in compensating; they frequently end in over-compensating to a point where to all outward appearances, they are stronger and more aggressive than they would have been, if at the outset they had started on even terms with the rest of the world.

1. The boy William was born with a physical inferiority. He was a delicate child with a withered arm. When he came to manhood and the throne his sense of disability was increased; for Bismarck was master of Germany and William was permitted to be Emperor only in name. Then William's compensatory process began. In the Austrian controversy, he made Bismarck's position untenable; and the Chancellor resigned, leaving him supreme. As for the withered arm, if William could not make it sound, he has at least developed a great right arm, and with it lifted so terrible a sword that the world has forgotten about the other one.

2. In early life, Theodore Roosevelt was shelved by bad health. With a determination we now speak of as characteristic, but which may not have been so then, he went West, lived for years the life of the open and built up a constitution more than ordinarily robust. He came back, went to the legislature, was police commissioner, governor, a great president, a recipient of the Nobel prize and a writer of sorts. But these accomplishments were not enough; they did not slake Mr. Roosevelt's thirst for the purely physical qualities he once lacked and set up as his model. They did not literally enough assure him that he had compensated successfully. Consequently, Mr. Roosevelt selects

Portrait of American Citizen Agonizing over His Inability to Participate in a War Providentially Close at Hand

other lines of action that emphasize possession of physical strength. He goes in for the strenuous life, and becomes our main apostle of virility. When occasion offers, he naturally assumes the rôle of the cowboy, because the cowboy is highly symbolic of the vital type he once fell short of. Next, in the Spanish War, he appears as a rough-rider; a distinct promotion in the scale of virility, the rough-rider being in essence the cowboy plus the added feature of participation in the virile game of war. Later on, as an explorer, plunging into jungles and living among wild men and beasts, he approaches still nearer to the primitive male; until finally, in the recent Mexican crisis, Colonel Roosevelt reaches his apotheosis, for, lo! he stands before us proposing to raise a whole division of cowboys, rough-riders and explorers and to be su-

preme over this entire congress of virilities in the capacity of Major-General.

3. Page, the American high-jumper of a generation ago, began life a cripple. His problem was to walk as other men. But this accomplished, he wanted to run, to jump, to jump higher than any man ever jumped, and he succeeded. Why? Because a constant vision of the thing beyond, soundness of limb, created in his years of invalidity impulses so durable as to still urge him forward after their mission of bringing him to equality with other men had long been accomplished.

4. In his maturity, Nietzsche was Germany's most distinguished preacher of aggression; to him is attributed, rightly or wrongly, much of the ruthless power-worship of intellectual Germany of to-day. But Nietzsche as a child was a weakling. Af-

ter his father, the pastor of Röcken, died, the boy was brought up mainly by grand-parents and female relatives; by them, as well as by the parochial conventions of a provincial village, he was kindly, but none-the-less cruelly repressed. Soon in this restless, non-conforming spirit the compensatory process commenced. His will to power philosophy, calling upon mankind to join him in repudiating all cultural restraint, expresses the swing of the pendulum from early impotence to mastery. Like the Kaiser, Roosevelt and Page, Nietzsche's aggression was rooted in weakness, not in strength; like theirs, his insistence on power is reminiscent of a time when, in spite of natural capacity, he was shut off from it by very positive inhibitions. Like them, too, he sought to be the superman, because he once fell so short of the average man in power and opportunity to function. Nietzsche died insane, believing he was God.

5. Why is Germany aggressive? Why is she militarist? Why have people who understood Germany little hope of ending her militarism through war? And, why are those who want a lasting peace and yet protest against an early one—why are these well meaning believers in war working against the end they have in view?

Germany has had only a few years of nationality. In '71 Bismarck, Moltke and the old Emperor made a unification of unsympathetic, half-hostile states. The unification was not a natural growth, not a popular movement, but a feat of strength performed by a handful of men who said, "Let there be a nation." But if the foundations of the German nation are insecure, the soil in which they were laid is still more so; from the Ninth Century to the unification, the German story is one of attempted empire that rose, towered and crashed into disorganized fragments. In 843, the Treaty of Verdun made Charlemagne's son ruler of a loosely joined empire. By the Tenth Century it had grown to include what is now Germany and also Holland, Belgium, and a part of Poland and Italy. Though not a nation in the modern sense, still there was distinct consciousness of nationalism. Then came disintegration, which continued for several centuries until, in the Thirty Years War, Germany lost all semblance of nationality; her population went from twenty to six million; her people starved and wallowed in ignorance; her princes fled and lived abroad in more civilized courts. The project of German nationalism was over for the time being.

By Frederick the Great's time, reconstruction had begun, but it had not gone far. Though he was a Prussian and a Brandenburger, no one more frankly than Frederick admitted this; he said that the Germans were still barbarians and the rear-guard of civilization. And, on the whole, Germany seems to have agreed with him; she was unsure of herself, tender of her past, without confidence in the future, and aggressive in proportion to her lack of self-confidence.

Next came the Napoleonic period of humiliation. Bonaparte crushed Prussia, made his headquarters in the palaces of the Hohenzollerns; said of the latter and the Prussian aristocracy in general: "I will make this noblesse beg bread in the street," and forced a division of German troops to fight in the French army. That success in the Franco-Prussian War did not remove from the German soul the humiliation of 1806 is shown a hundred years later, when, through the mouth of William the Second, Germany is still talking revanche, still proposing to wipe out with blood the score chalked up against her honor by Bonaparte.

The psychology of modern Germany has been profoundly influenced by her history. A picture of continuing failure, amounting, in fact, to a racial tragedy, has entered deeply into German subconsciousness and become a sort of permanent background, against which are judged the phenomena of recent times. And Germany's geographical position has powerfully reinforced the fear element aroused by her history. Germany grew up, like a lonely imaginative child, surrounded by menacing giants and ogres. There was Russia to the north, huge, slow moving, drowsy, of unmeasured strength; some day Russia was sure to wake up and move across Europe like a tide. France to the west and south, tempered, flexible and at home with ideas—the despair of raw, unformed Germany. Also, to Germany, France has been a country of infinite possibilities, first because she had her diseases of militarism and French kultur experiences under Louis XIV and Napoleon, and reacted into democracy; and second because popular revolution, a thing that Germany has almost wholly lacked, has unified the French people and made them sure of themselves. But more important than either Russia or France, there was England, with mastery of the oceans, success in colonization and a long established supremacy in trade. England most of all has given Germany a compelling sense of impotence, loneliness, newness and comparative poverty.

Starting from a history that rang the changes of

calamity, and a geographical position that stimulated the fear complex formed by such a history, Germany has unrestingly carried on her fierce compensatory struggle; and it has been a successful one, at least in a material sense. From Bismarck's time up to the present war, there is a pulling together of the states, not a spiritual union, but, at all events, a strong political one. Nationalism, driven on by a consciousness of past failure and present superficiality, has been cultivated in a subservient people by the government, by school and university, until it has become a religion and finally a fanaticism. There has also been an industrial renaissance; a perfectioned, smooth-functioning state absolute has arisen; and in the last ten years, Germany has become the first military power of the world.

But all this is not enough. As in the case of the Kaiser, Roosevelt, Page and Nietzsche, arrival at the point of equality with others has only been a signal for departure for goals beyond. Those vital compensatory forces, created through centuries of fear and disability, still hold Germany and drive her on—to supremacy in arms because she was humbled in arms; to supremacy in nationalism because she had none; to supremacy in culture because, while Europe was semi-civilized, she was savage; to world conquest, because she had been taught to see herself ringed by hostile nations crouching to spring.

The writer is not pro-German; he is what is called pro-Ally. He loathes the German state, because it forces the individual into a rigid government-made mould; he thinks that authority, especially military authority, has made Germany a poor place for the average man to live in. He believes that the German government has been the main, though not the only, aggressor; that it prepared for and forced war; that the enslavement of the Belgians and the Zeppelin raids are atrocities, although, in fact, mere fringes of the huge fabric of cruelty woven by the super atrocity of war. Above all, he sees in German militarism a sword over peace—a worse menace even than England's navalism or American militarism as promoted here by our own absolutists and commercial buccaneers. And, for these very reasons, he looks with dismay at the futility of the plan of crushing militarism by prolonging the war.

Even if it were possible to annihilate the German armies, it is wholly impossible to crush German militarism. For generations, German militarism has flourished, like a weed in a barnyard, upon crushing. Only Germany's own liberal thought and democracy can put an end to it; and, as long as the fear complex lasts, and the bulk of the people are convinced, as they now are, that they are fighting a desperate defensive war, there will be no liberal thought or democracy, no effective reaction against militarism. Extreme pressure from without, fear, humiliation and a virtual repetition of old disasters will only strengthen militarism, justify it, harden it, and make the crust of official absolutism, that now covers Germany, so metallic that democratic impulses will be unable to germinate and break through. And, above all, these things will set the stage on which the old progressions from inferiority to compensation, from compensation to over-compensation and from over-compensation to aggression will be re-enacted in another tragedy for Germany and the world.

But yet our apostles of violence are undismayed. They continue to assure us serenely that the smashing prescription will do the trick. Especially they advise that the war must proceed, so that the Kaiser, the military class, etc., may be thoroughly punished. They want Germany to repent, confess her sin and acknowledge the saving grace of countries with more guns of heavier calibre. They cannot see that the Kaiser and the military class are effects not causes, only a superficial expression of something that is going on in the German soul. They confidently insist also that a nation of seventy million people can be permanently broken and incapacitated for war, as simply and as satisfactorily as we permanently break men and boys in our prisons and incapacitate them for rebellion against society. They do not take into account the fact that fifteen years from now, Germany, left with a grudge, will have practically as many men of fighting age as she would have had, if the war had never been fought, and probably a good many more than she has today. They fail to consider that Germany's material resources will not stay crippled, because her lands and her industries cannot be destroyed and her children will continue to grow into men and women. Early peace, they say, would also be a calamity, because Germany has not suffered enough. The loss of seven thousand young men a day, more or less, for two years and a half, mourning in almost every home in the empire, hunger, bankruptcy and the rest of it—apparently in the eyes of our Christian friends faithful to war, these do not add up to enough misery to put the fear of God into Germany as completely as our friends desire.

Drawn by Boardman Robinson, September 1916

Logic

PREPAREDNESS ADVOCATE: "If we don't prepare
as they did, it'll happen to us."

We do not question the sincerity of those who have faith in war and believe in the efficacy of force. The world is filled with men who believe in it; it is part of an inheritance coming to us from the time when we ate our food alive. Our economic system is deeply rooted in it. We thoroughly believe they believe in force, honor it, trust it, and gladly accept this opportunity of recommending it. But whether these good people are not really a good deal more deeply interested in justifying and exalting force than they are in ending militarism or bringing about a lasting peace is something that we, and perhaps they themselves, cannot answer. Nevertheless we cannot help seeing *that* these men who are most tireless in telling us that the war must go on, so that militarism will be destroyed in Germany, happen to be the same men who are most tireless in booming the spirit of militarism in America, and in urging the United States to get into the war, or, at least, to take a position that would mean war. They are sowing, here, the same narrow nationalism, the same fear of other nations, the same spirit of aggression that, for a generation before the war, was sown in Germany by its militarists, its clergy, its politicians and power-preaching professors. But here, they tell us, it is not for aggression, but all purely in the interest of national defense. So it was in Germany; and no amount of argument, even if carried to the point of reducing Germany as did the Thirty Years' War, will ever persuade the average German that his nation was organized for anything but to repel boarders.

What, then, is the answer to those who, like Colonel Roosevelt (who, by the way, does not seem to have been rendered less aggressive by recent political birchings), who, like our bishops, munition-makers and evangelists tell us that the peace of the world depends upon fighting it out till Germany is whipped?

To them no answer can be made that will carry conviction; for they do not think in terms of history or human psychology, but in those of primal instincts. But to the liberal thought of the world, the answer is simple. No matter how much she may or may not deserve it, Germany cannot be whipped either into impotence or consciousness of her own aggression. The aggression itself must be attacked through a policy that is understanding of its deeper causes. And the first step in this policy is to switch the controversy from the physical into the realm of reason.　　　　—March 1917

MAX EASTMAN
The Masses at the White House

[*The Union Against Militarism which sponsored this meeting had been founded by Crystal Eastman, among others, and was one of the more influential of the smaller American peace groups.*]

President Wilson represents our theoretical popular sovereignty with beautiful distinction. He is a graciously democratic aristocrat. He models his public style upon the pattern of the eloquent Burke. Nobody else in the United States has ever been affected by Burke's eloquence, because Burke's speech on Conciliation was a required reading in our high-schools. But Wilson must have been educated at home. He quotes Burke at length, and, if you can believe it, with real appreciation.

I had seen him and heard him quote Burke before, but not with the dignity of office added to his natural talents in that direction. You can easily see in an hour's conversation what power he wields over our country post-office politicians. It is the power of aristocratic and yet real knowledge. They are treated handsomely, they know that, but they always find themselves a little tongue-tied and unable to answer back on the same level. For Mr. Wilson not only quotes Burke, but he quotes Burke to the point. He has an adroit logic, as well as a technical knowledge and the diction of a king's minister. He is the ablest man that has been in that office for years.

After our call at the White House in the interest of democracy against militarism, we retired to a neighboring hotel, and unanimously agreed that we had been handled beautifully. The President had taken us into his intellectual bosom, told us all about the delicate practical question of *how far* "preparedness" must go in order to be adequate, explained to our minds the difference between an absolute principle and its specific applications which are always relative, patiently and confidingly elucidated the difficulties of anyone but an expert's deciding those relative questions, and throughout the interview always referred to the Union Against Militarism as though he were a member of it. The whole interview became in his hands a friendly and harmonious discussion of how "we" could meet the difficulties of national defense without the risks of militarism.

We all liked him, and we all sincerely believed that he sincerely believes he is anti-militarist. For my part, more yet, I believe that he sincerely hates his preparedness policies, and justifies them to his mind in only one way. He knows that they are in themselves a betrayal of the progress of civilization, and his heart is in that progress as he understands it. But he justifies those policies by dwelling very strongly in his mind upon the idea of world-federation and the international enforcement of peace. He tries to think of our egregious war appropriations merely as a step towards that practical hope. He told us so. And though most of the newspapers failed or refused to see it, that was the big result of our interview.

President Wilson spoke of the establishment of world peace by means of a "family of nations" who should say "we shall not have any war," and back that "shall" up with force, as the natural practical thing to accomplish after the war is done. He characterized it as a "very practical ideal," and alluded to it several times in answering our questions. The close of our interview was characteristic:

Mr. Pinchot: Mr. President, it seems to me that we have got to recognize the fact that we are just like everybody else, and that we are not the least bit less aggressive than any other nation. We are potentially more aggressive, because our economic organizations are more active, more powerful, in reaching out and grasping for the world trade. The organization of the International Corporation is one of the great trade factors of modern history; and it seems to me that if you hitch up this tremendous aggressive grabbing for the trade of the world with a tendency to back up that trade, there is going to be produced an aggressive nationalism.

The President: It might very easily, unless some check was placed upon it by some international arrangement which we hope for. I quite see your point.

This puts President Wilson so far. above and beyond Theodore Roosevelt in sensing the tragedy of the world today, and apprehending a road out into the future, that it ought to be set in plain terms before every citizen.

It is the true issue between the two candidates for nomination. Preparedness is no issue. They are all for that in the ruling class. But whether those who control our society shall see the practical wisdom of international action and understanding, or whether they shall commit us to that insane and bigoted nationalism which has ravaged Europe, is a vital question for us all.

Roosevelt has announced his motto: *Americanism and Preparedness.*

We will announce Wilson's for him: *International Action and Preparedness.*

He will never announce it for himself, because he is too much affected by the fear of Roosevelt's popularity. Roosevelt has already frightened him into imitating those foolish and rabid sayings about the necessity of "intense Americanism" if anything good or noble is to be done. His party advisers, I suppose, think it is good politics for him to go before the press club and imitate that bosh. But it is not good politics.

The common people of this country do not want war. They will vote for the man who holds out a surety that there will be no war. They are divided as to whether "preparedness" brings war or prevents it. But as to whether rabid nationalism brings war or prevents it, they are not divided. They know that rabid nationalism is the one indispensable condition and sure cause of war the world over. That is an article of common sense.

"Intense Americanism in everything"—a more pitiable, small, egotistical and murder-breeding motto at this time of the whole world's tragedy could hardly be devised.

Intense Germanism, intense Britishism—those are the causes of the European war. The people of the United States intuitively know this, and they will reject the man with the jingo motto, and they will accept the man who boldly points the way out of this perennial calamity. I wish that President Wilson might point the way to all as boldly as he did to our committee, for there is no issue so great as that in upper class politics today.   —July 1916

Drawn by John Barber, July 1915

"They ain't to be no swimming at Coney this summer."
"Why not?"
"They say the Germans have poisoned the ocean."

ARTURO GIOVANNITTI

The Day of War:
Madison Square, June 20th

A hawk-faced youth with rapacious eyes, standing
on a shaky chair,
Speaks stridulously in the roar of the crossways,
under the tower that challenges the skies, terrible like a brandished sword.
A thin crowd, idle, yawning, many-hungered, beg-
garly, rich with the inexhaustible treasures of
endless hours of dreaming and scheming.
Imperial ruins of the Mob.
Listens to him, wondering why he speaks and
why they listen.
The fierce incandescence of noon quivers and
drones with the echoes
Of distant clamors, grumbling of voices, blarings
of speed-mad fanfares;
But as the roar reaches the group, it turns and
recoils and deviates, and runs around it,
As a stream runs around a great rock,
And his voice alone is heard in this little island of
silence.
His arms go up as he speaks; his white teeth fight
savagely with his black eyes,
His red tie flows tempestuously in the wind, the
unfurled banner of his heart amidst the musketry
of his young words.
He has been speaking since dawn; he has emerged
from the night, and the night alone shall sub-
merge him.
They listen to him and wonder, and grope blindly
in the maze of his words,
They fear his youth and they pity it,
But the sunlight is strong on his head,
And his shadow is heavy and hard upon their
faces.

Suddenly, like a flash of yellow flame
The blast of a trumpet shoots by, its notes ram-
ming like bullets against the white tower.
The soldiers march up the Avenue. The crowd
breaks, scatters, and runs away, and only six
listeners remain:

A girl, a newsboy, a drunken man, a Greek who
sells rugs, an old man, and the stranger I know.
But he speaks on, louder, with the certainty of the
thunder that only speaks after the bolt.
"Workers of America, we alone can rehabilitate
this generation before history. We must and
shall stop this war."
The Greek vendor moves on; wearily the old man
turns towards a seat, far away.
But he speaks on.
"The great voice of Labor shall rise fearlessly to-
day, and the world shall listen, and eternity
shall record its words."
The drunken man grumbles, stares at his open
hands and lurches away towards the approaching tramway.
But he speaks on.
"Our protest and our anger shall be like a cloud-
burst, and the masters shall tremble. Brothers,
don't you see it? The Revolution is at the
threshold."
The newsboy swings his bag over his shoulder and
dashes away through the park.
But he speaks on.
"As sure as this sun shall set, so will injustice and
tyranny go down. Men and women of America,
I know that this is the great day."
The stranger I know shrinks in the hollow places
of himself; he fades; and vanishes, molten in
the white heat of that young faith.
But the girl stands still and immobile, her up-
turned face glowing before the brazier of his
soul,
As from the tower one by one drop at his feet the
twelve tolls of the clock that marks time, the
time that knows and flows on until his day
comes.
And the girl, and the tower, and he
Are the only three things that stand straight and
rigid and inexpugnable
Amidst the red omens of war,
In the fulness of the day,
In the whiteness of the moonlight,
In the city of dread and uproar.

—August 1916

The War at Home

[During the months between American entry into the war and the magazine's own suppression, The Masses *documented the consequences of America's new role.]*

MAX EASTMAN
Revolutionary Progress

In these days the title Revolutionary Progress expresses only a resolute desire. No measure in politics and no movement in industry is having the least success in increasing the proportion of wealth or leisure or liberty which falls to the working-class. Their small liberty is, in fact, cut down steadily by the growth of militarism under the menace of national war. Caste and class-rule are in the ascendant; democracy is marking time.

On the other hand all the reforms which do not touch the system of caste are proceeding with a velocity the world has never seen. The acceleration of the rate of progress is continual, and it is due to the fact that more and more people every day are reading the news. Any idea which will serve the interests of people in both classes catches around the world like fire. And many of these ideas, though they are not revolutionary in motive, do indirectly and ultimately contribute to the chances of the working-class struggle. They improve the field on which it must be fought.

Chief among them, of course, is the idea of eliminating war by international union. Patriotic war has always meant death to liberty and the struggle for human rights. The old republics provided for a dictator in war-times, and those who loved dictators needed only to keep a war coming. England has her dictator now. She has long ago suspended the better part of her Magna Carta. A French senator announced the other day amid applause that he thought the statues of liberty ought to be veiled, that civil rights should no longer be recognized. "There is but one right left," he said, "and that is the right of war." In the effort to conquer Prussia these countries are becoming prussianized. And our country, always imitative of European vices, is following along.

Nevertheless, in the midst of this, there has arisen and gone abroad with the highest prestige the idea of eliminating war altogether through a super-national union. Perhaps the greatest power possessed by chief executives in our time is their advertising power, and President Wilson has used this power dramatically. He had made international union a subject of consideration to every serious mind in the world. And that is all that was needed. The biggest of big business, and the most intelligent, is interested in this idea. It wants to eliminate war; it was even wondering how. Now it has been told how, and, speaking in decades, the thing is done.

I believe that the histories of all the nations of the world will hold a venerated record of President Wilson's address to the Senate. For I know that with communication growing fluent and rapid all over the earth, people all over the earth learning to read and translate each other's news over-night, with scientific and social and vast commercial combinations overspreading all tongues and peoples, the political union of the nations for the adjustment and defense of their common interests is inevitable. Peter the Hermit was its prophet. President Wilson will have been its initiator. It is the most momentous event conceivable in the evolution of a capitalistic civilization. And it is also the one hope of preserving that struggle for a new civilization which we call Socialism, or Syndicalism, or the Social Revolution, or the Labor Struggle, from the continual corruption of militarism, and the ravaging set-back of patriotic war.

It was not surprising that a genial evangelical Americanistic Sunday School peace preacher like Bryan should oppose this plan. He thinks that Peace and the Herald Angels will abolish war, and all that politics has to do is to keep clear of foreign entanglements. So he cheerfully identifies the President's proposal of a world-congress with Taft's "League to Enforce Peace," and denounces the international policy with the same smiling fortitude with which he supports the cause that it alone can win.

The President has carefully avoided the expression "League to Enforce Peace," knowing, I believe, that it is utopian to hope that nations will go to war in remote parts of the earth because they have promised to—knowing also, perhaps, that it is utopian to expect the American nation to promise to. He has proposed an international union "to

Drawn by Robert Minor, July 1916

ARMY MEDICAL EXAMINER: "At last a perfect soldier!"

ensure peace." It is the proposal of a conference or congress of the nations after the war, a congress which would presumably undertake and arrange the reduction of national armaments, as provided in the Hensley paragraphs of our Naval Appropriation Bill, and might become a government of the seas with police power adequate for the elimination of minor war causes. This supra-national government, once it exists with eminence, will inevitably attract a part of the loyalty of all peoples. It will swing a vast body of sentiment to itself, and make nationalistic quarrels less agreeable to men's emotions at the same time that it furnishes a mechanism for their settlement. That is not a League to Enforce Peace. It is an application in grand scale of the tested principle of union for the elimination of patriotic quarrels. It is the only way that wars will ever be made generally unlikely and unnatural.

It is a pity that Bryan is too full of the Herald Angels to add his emotions to the weight of this policy.

It is a pity that Benson is too full of the doctrinaire "dope." Benson used to have a strong vein of political common-sense. I remember his article in THE MASSES on a previous presidential election —it outraged our Marxian subscribers. But a year's campaign as the official candidate of a body of doctrine seems to have turned him into the regular party theologian, and his attitude in the *Appeal to Reason* toward the President's message is even more ancient and undiscriminating than Bryan's.

There are two great impediments to practical judgment—sentimentality and dogma.

—April 1917

MAX EASTMAN
A Passionate Magazine

The editors of *The New Republic* seem to have been seized with a highly intellectualized lust for bloody combat. I was shocked by their mobilization order. They had the submarines out and the guns firing before the subscribers had time to realize the magazine had gone to war. I had often predicted they would go to war, these liberal intellects, in the front rank—ahead, in fact, of the republic. But I was really shocked at the joyful unction with which they did it.

Those bold letters on the front cover:

WITHOUT DELAY DIPLOMATIC RELATIONS MUST BE BROKEN. THE NAVY SHOULD BE MOBILIZED. STEPS SHOULD BE TAKEN TO ARM ALL MERCHANT SHIPS. THE TERMS AND CONDITIONS OF OUR ENTRANCE INTO THE WAR SHOULD BE DISCUSSED AND ANNOUNCED.

Where now is the suave and judicial externalism of the "journal of opinion"?

The New Republic has given expression to a great many radical ideas—birth control education, freedom of speech, the right to strike, government ownership of railroads. Its editors have a great liberality of view, and we have to thank them for many deliberative and careful pronouncements in favor of radical progress. But they never put their heart in their pens before. It was never:

WITHOUT DELAY THIS KNOWLEDGE THAT IS VITAL TO LIFE MUST BE MADE ACCESSIBLE TO THE PEOPLE. SPEECH MUST BE FREE. STEPS SHOULD BE TAKEN TO GUARANTEE TO THESE WORKMEN THE RIGHT TO STRIKE. THE TERMS AND CONDITIONS OF TRANSFER OF THE RAILROADS TO THE REPUBLIC MUST BE DISCUSSED AND ANNOUNCED.

No—they always managed to hold in on those topics, these young men, maintaining that infinite equilibrium and freedom from the propaganda note which bespeaks a finished intellectuality. But now the miracle is broken. An emotion is acknowledged. *The New Republic* has a mission. And its mission, as well as I can gather from the first two numbers, is War on Germany and Anglo-American Imperialism—Victory without Peace.

—April 1917

JOHN REED
Whose War?

"The current ebullition of patriotism is wonderful."
—Rev. Dr. Parkhurst.

By the time this goes to press the United States may be at war. The day the German note arrived, Wall Street flung the American flag to the breeze, the brokers on the floor of the Stock Exchange sang "The Star Spangled Banner" with tears rolling down their cheeks, and the stock market went up. In the theaters they are singing "patriotic" ballads of the George M. Cohan-Irving Berlin variety, playing the national anthem, and flashing the flag and the portrait of long-suffering Lincoln —while the tired suburbanite who has just been scalped by a ticket-speculator goes into hysterics. Exclusive ladies whose husbands own banks are rolling bandages for the wounded, just like they do in Europe; a million-dollar fund for ice in field-hospitals has been started; and the Boston Budget for Conveying Virgins Inland has grown enormously. The directors of the British, French and Belgian Permanent Blind Relief Fund have added "American" to the name of the organization, in gruesome anticipation. Our soldier boys, guarding the aqueducts and bridges, are shooting each other by mistake for Teutonic spies. There is talk of "conscription," "war-brides," and "On to Berlin. . . ."

I know what war means. I have been with the armies of all the belligerents except one, and I have seen men die, and go mad, and lie in hospitals suffering hell; but there is a worse thing than that. War means an ugly mob-madness, crucifying the truth-tellers, choking the artists, side-tracking reforms, revolutions, and the working of social forces. Already in America those citizens who oppose the entrance of their country into the European melée are called "traitors," and those who protest against the curtailing of our meagre rights of free speech are spoken of as "dangerous lunatics." We have had a forecast of the censorship—when the naval authorities in charge of the Sayville wireless cut off American news from Germany, and only the wildest fictions reached Berlin via London, creating a perilous situation. . . . The press is howling for war. The church is howling for war. Lawyers, politicians, stock-brokers, social leaders are all howling for war. Roosevelt is again recruiting his thrice-thwarted family regiment.

But whether it comes to actual hostilities or not, some damage has been done. The militarists have proved their point. I know of at least two valuable social movements that have suspended functioning because no one cares. For many years this country is going to be a worse place for free men to live in; less tolerant, less hospitable. Maybe it is too late, but I want to put down what I think about it all.

Whose war is this? Not mine. I know that hundreds of thousands of American workingmen employed by our great financial "patriots" are not paid a living wage. I have seen poor men sent to jail for long terms without trial, and even without any charge. Peaceful strikers, and their wives and children, have been shot to death, burned to death, by private detectives and militiamen. The rich have steadily become richer, and the cost of living higher, and the workers proportionally poorer. These toilers don't want war—not even civil war. But the speculators, the employers, the plutocracy —they want it, just as they did in Germany and in England; and with lies and sophistries they will whip up our blood until we are savage—and then we'll fight and die for them.

I am one of a vast number of ordinary people who read the daily papers, and occasionally *The New Republic,* and want to be fair. We don't know much about international politics; but we want our country to keep off the necks of little nations, to refuse to back up American beasts of prey who invest abroad and get their fingers burned, and to stay out of quarrels not our own. We've got an idea that international law is the crystallized common-sense of nations, distilled from their experiences with each other, and that it holds good for all of them, and can be understood by anybody.

We are simple folk. Prussian militarism seemed to us insufferable; we thought the invasion of Belgium a crime; German atrocities horrified us, and also the idea of German submarines exploding ships full of peaceful people without warning. But then we began to hear about England and France jailing, fining, exiling and even shooting men who refused to go out and kill; the Allied armies invaded and seized a part of neutral Greece, and a French admiral forced upon her an ultimatum as shameful as Austria's to Serbia; Russian atrocities were shown to be more dreadful than German; and hidden mines sown by England in the open sea exploded ships full of peaceful people without warning.

Other things disturbed us. For instance, why was it a violation of international law for the Germans to establish a "war-zone" around the British Isles, and perfectly legal for England to close the North Sea? Why is it we submitted to the British order forbidding the shipment of non-contraband to Germany, and insisted upon our right to ship contraband to the Allies? If our "national honor" was smirched by Germany's refusal to allow war materials to be shipped to the Allies, what happened to our national honor when England refused to let us ship non-contraband food and even *Red Cross hospital supplies* to Germany? Why is England allowed to attempt the avowed starvation of German civilians, in violation of international law, when the Germans cannot attempt the same thing without our horrified protest? How is it that the British can arbitrarily regulate our commerce with neutral nations, while we raise a howl whenever the Germans "threaten to restrict our merchant ships going about their business?" Why does our

Drawn by Henry J. Glintenkamp, August 1917

Conscription

Government insist that Americans should not be molested while traveling on Allied ships armed against submarines?

We have shipped and are shipping vast quantities of war materials to the Allies, we have floated the Allied loans. We have been strictly neutral toward the Teutonic powers only. Hence the inevitable desperation of the last German note. Hence this war we are on the brink of.

Those of us who voted for Woodrow Wilson did so because we felt his mind and his eyes were open, because he had kept us out of the mad-dog-fight of Europe, and because the plutocracy opposed him. We had learned enough about the war to lose some of our illusions, and we wanted to be neutral. We grant that the President, considering the position he'd got himself into, couldn't do anything else but answer the German note as he did—but if we had been neutral, that note wouldn't have been sent. The President didn't ask us; he won't ask us if we want war or not. The fault is not ours. It is not our war.   —April 1917

MAX EASTMAN
The Religion of Patriotism

Nothing could be more calamitous than for patriotism to become the established religion of this country. I do not know exactly what religion is. Every psychologist has a different theory of its origin and nature. Some say it originates in fear, others in wonder, others in the filial affection, others in gregarious instinct—a desire for infinite companionship. But I doubt if the religious emotion is any of these single things, the same in different cases. I think that any object or any idea which appeals to *a considerable number* of our instincts, and offers them a *combined satisfaction,* may become the focus of an attachment so controlling, and so *fixé,* as to gain that uncanny and unreasonable priority among our feelings which we call religious. The religious object *binds* us (as the Latin original of the word implies), not by a single tie, but by gathering into itself so many threads of our impulsive nature that no one motive whatever can break its hold. God is indeed a refuge to our fear, a temple to our wonder, a parent for the little child that lives in our heart. He is an infinite companion. He satisfies so many of those native cravings which the terms of life leave thwarted, that His hold upon us becomes supernormal and sovereign, and our whole being is transfixed by His name as though we were maniacs and He our obsession.

In order for this to happen, however, it is necessary that we have the gift of making God seem real. In past ages, with a Christ or a Virgin Mary giving the warmth of flesh to the picture, and a general consensus of mankind supporting the opinion that God *is* real, it was not difficult to acquire this gift. Perhaps almost a majority of mankind possessed it, and the religion of God was one of the determining forces in history. In this day, however, for many reasons, it is growing difficult to make God seem real. The money and machine character of our civilization leaves little room for miracles. A belief in supernatural causes is dangerous in a factory and impractical in a bank. And, moreover, Jesus Christ expressed so many principles of conduct wholly out of accord with our industrial life, that the ministers of his gospel are forced to deny him and betray his ideals continually while asserting his godhead, and this makes them seem weak and queer, and his godhead dubious. Deity is identified with the church, and the church is hypocritical and alien to everyday life, and so deity grows slippery and unpleasant to our minds. God is a long way off. There is no sovereign motive in our lives.

That is good—It allows us to be intelligent and agile in various kinds of enjoyment and enterprise. It lets us love truth more whole-heartedly, and become acquainted with liberty. It is so lofty a state, in fact, that most people have not the strength of stem to endure it; they think they must find something to lean on and bind themselves around. And so our godless age has been characterized by a wistful hunger and search after religions. It is the age of "isms." And some of these isms have been able to bind together a number of native impulses, and hold men almost as strongly as God did. Socialism with its doctrine of Universal Brotherhood to be attained by the method of Class War, offers almost infinite indulgence of two otherwise unreconciled impulses—pugnacity and social love. With its system of revealed economics, it offers, too, an Absolute in which mental curiosity can rest. It has its gospel according to Marx. Socialism is no mean religion. But it is not a religion that binds or blesses the rich and powerful, and so it could hardly become established in a country like ours. For an established religion we needed something a little more like God—a little vaguer and more elegant and better adapted to bind in among other motives the economic self-interest of those who rule. We needed something that would give us the same emotional crystallization without greatly disturbing the profits on capital.

Quite consciously a great many good people were searching for a thing of this kind, for a new and vigorous religion. And now, through the lucky accidents of history, they have found it. For there is nothing more copiously able to bind into its bosom the multiple threads of human impulse, and establish that fixed and absolute glorious tyranny among our purposes, than military patriotism. You will see how everything that was erect in this country bows down to that sentiment. The love of liberty, the assertion of the rights of man, what little of the ethics of Jesus we had—these things must obviously yield. And not only these, either, but the common principles of morality and truth. We shall see men devoting their utmost energy to an endeavor which they declare to be evil.

"Gladly would I have given my life to save my country from war," says William J. Bryan, "but now that my country has gone to war, gladly will I give my life to aid it." This Christian gentleman, whose morality was perhaps the most rigid thing we had in the country, thus boasts that he will devote his declining years to a cause which he considers wicked. Like Abraham who would slaughter his son at the bidding of God, Bryan is ready to do murder—he has called it murder—for the sake of his country. And this seems entirely right and noble to his countrymen. To me it seems utterly ignoble.

Not only morality, either, but the ideal of intelligence itself, of truthful seeing, will be abandoned. Men will glory in the ignorance and celebrate the stupidity of what they are doing. "I shall vote," said Senator Stone, against "the greatest national blunder of history," but after that "my eyes will be blind to everything but the flag of my country."

When ordinary alert perception has been renounced, it is needless to say that the extreme ethical visions of Jesus must go, and that God—long suffering God—will be denounced from the pulpits that were his last refuge. I suppose the pew-holders of Henry Ward Beecher's church are satisfied with Newell Dwight Hillis, for they have stood a good deal from him besides his preaching, and here is his creed of patriotism:

"All God's teachings about forgiveness should be re-

scinded for Germany. I am willing to forgive the Germans for their atrocities just as soon as they are all shot. If you would give me happiness, just give me the sight of the Kaiser, von Hindenburg and von Tirpitz hanging by the rope. If we forgive Germany after the war, I shall think the whole universe has gone wrong."

When God is thus enthusiastically ejected from the rostrum of the most famous church in the country, to make way for the patriotic emotion, I think we are justified in the fear that patriotism may become our religion.

Patriotism indulges that craving for a sense of union with a solidary herd, which is an inheritance of all gregarious animals. It is a craving which our modern sophisticated, citified, and diverse civilization leaves unfed in normal times. There is a great swing towards war on this account even among the most pacific people. They are flocking for a drink of this emotion. Men are willing to be dead, if they can only be dead in a pile.

This quite organic and almost animal craving is what makes us talk so much about the "great spiritual blessing" that war will bring to our unregenerate characters. When a desire springs so deeply from our ancient inheritance as this gregarious hunger does, we always feel it as mystic and inscrutable, we attribute a divine beneficence to the satisfaction of it. As a matter of fact, it would be better for the progress of society, in science and art and morality and happiness, if this terrible solidarity could be mitigated instead of enlarged. For it inhibits individual experiment, and it falsifies the facts of life, always pretending the nation is more socially and brotherly organized than it is. The "great spiritual blessing" is in fact a distraction of men's minds from the pursuit of truth and from realistic progress. It is the temporary indulgence of a facile emotion.

"I pray God," said President Wilson at the dedication of a Red Cross Memorial, "that the outcome of this struggle may be that every element of difference amongst us will be obliterated. . . . The spirit of this people is already united and when effort and suffering and sacrifice have completed this union, men will no longer speak of any lines either of race or association cutting athwart the great body of this nation."

To the instinctive man, the altogether righteousness of this aspiration, and the entire beneficence of the condition outlined, is as much taken for granted as the goodness of virtue. And yet, if seriously considered, such a state of affairs would be aesthetically monotonous and morally stagnant.

Drawn by R. Kempf, June 1917

Come on in, America, the Blood's Fine!

Aside from the mere satisfaction of the old instinct for herd-union itself, there would be no health, no beauty, no life in it.

"Liberty and Union, One and Inseparable, Now and Forever," is the watchword that adorns the statue of Daniel Webster in Central Park. And that too seems obvious—it has become a proverb. And yet if it has any meaning whatever, the meaning is false. It has become proverbial merely because it celebrates, with some show of regard for individual freedom, this gregarious instinct of mankind which is the central armature of the religion of patriotism.

According to my idea, however, the satisfaction of a single instinct, even though so arbitrary and ancient-rooted as this, cannot acquire that peculiar hypnotizing force upon us which makes us name it religious. We might love union and the monotony of the herd very much, and still continue to act morally, and exercise intelligent judgment, and perhaps love God and walk humbly with our neighbor. But it happens that the moment we declare for the herd, and let loose our enthusiasm into that vent, especially at war time, a half dozen other starved monsters of passionate desire that our lawful and cultivated life has caged and thwarted rush to this outlet and find satisfaction.

One of them is angry hate. Men are full of it, and they get small chance to exercise it in these days of legality and respectable convention. The war liberates them. They can rage and revile and spit upon the enemy with the sanction of all contiguous society, and without immediate personal danger. I think this is what makes a declaration of war especially palatable to ministers of Christ. They have repressed so much more personal spleen, as a matter of professional necessity, than the rest of us, that they let go all the more violently into the national spout. Nobody will demand that they apply the ethics of Jesus to the relations between nations; they can go on preaching forgiveness as a personal matter, while enjoying in this national festival the emotions of implacable hate.

Here is a conversation overheard in a restaurant conducted by two innocent and colorless Germans, man and wife. The talkers are American patriots.

"Did you read what Ambassador Gerard said about the German boys torturing foreigners in Germany?"

"Yes, and it's true too. They're cruel. They're savages, the Germans. They wouldn't stop at anything."

"You bet, look at these people. I bet they're spies. We'll be over there and string them up one of these days."

The sudden and copious flow of malice which follows a declaration of war suggests that a really dire condition of the natural organs has been relieved just in the nick of time. Another and even more bursting reservoir that ordinary moral conduct never half relieves is rivalrous egotism. Society suppresses the braggart, for the reason that if bragging is to be done, each member of society feels fully entitled to do it, and there is no other solution short of bedlam. In consequence every individual is full as a bladder with inexpressible self-esteem. And by a quickly articulated emotional device, this passion too is sluiced into the channel of patriotism. A man identifies himself with his country, and then he brags about his country to his heart's desire, and nobody observes that he is bragging about himself. Only sensitive people know that patriotic loyalty is so much less flame-like and beautiful than loyalty to a friend or an idea—they feel this cold vein of complacence in it.

The patriotic religion has a hold here that God never had. God wanted people to be humble. A religion that lets us brag without knowing that is what we are doing is far more gratefully adjusted to our constitutions. We can love our country and make sacrifices for it, we can have all those altruistic satisfactions, and yet not suffer the self-abasement that is inevitable in loving a Supreme Being. It is our country; it is not simply Country, abstract and awful.

Our country comforts us too, even as God's fatherhood did. Our filial affection is gathered up into the bosom of the fatherland. We were conceived and born in its bosom; it is our native place, the place that sheltered us long ago when we were happy; it will still care for us (especially while we are fighting for it), and give us that sense of the Everlasting Arms without which perhaps no religion would retain its extreme dominion among our feelings.

Yes, patriotism binds us by as many ties as God. We need not be surprised at those Methodist conventioners, who denounced for treason the lowly delegate who wished to put God before his country. In the very nature of the case, if our theory of religion is true, there can be no two religions. If God will not fall in step with the United States army, God must go. That has been made plain in every pulpit in this vicinity, with the noble exception of the Church of the Messiah, where John Haynes Holmes spoke not only for the sovereignty of God, but even for the ethics of Jesus, on the eve of War.

Patriotism has, like other religions whose object of worship is a little open to question, its extreme sensitiveness, its fanatical intolerance. The ceremonial observances are enforced with zealotry, and those who blaspheme with unassenting presence are likely to be thrown out bodily or confined in jail. At one of the meeting-places of patriots on Broadway, known as Rector's, one night at two A. M. the ceremonial of the national anthem was being enacted, and while all the devotees were rising or being assisted to their feet, Mr. Fred Boyd and two companions—heretics of this religion—endeavored quietly to remain in their seats. Chairs, tables and salad bowls were employed by the orthodox to enforce the tenets of their creed, and these failing, a policeman was summoned in the name of the fatherland, and Mr. Boyd and his companions arrived at the night court. Here they were severely reprimanded by a judge, who acknowledged, however, that they had disobeyed no law, not even the law of God, which is usually invoked upon such unfortunates as wish to act upon their own judgment in public.

To me patriotism, in practically all of its forms, is distasteful. And I confess to a feeling of strange solitude in these days of its divinity that no other revolutionary opinions have brought me. Much of the time I wonder what it is that separates a handful of us from the concourse of mankind. We are so motley a handful: Christians, Atheists, Quakers, Anarchists, Artists, Socialists, and a few who just have a fervent pleasure in using their brains about truth. You could bring us together, and we would not agree upon anything else under the sun—but we agree in disliking the religion of patriotism. We can not stand up when the national anthem is played, not because we have any theory about it, but because the quality of the emotion expressed is alien and false to us. We cannot partake of the communion and be true to ourselves. And so many of us do not go to these meeting-places at all, or we come in late, or otherwise we try to avoid the acute discomfort of sitting quiescent under the scowling malice and ignorant suspicion of a mob indulging its fixed and habitual emotion.

As I count over the little group that I know who feel this way about committing themselves to the new religion, I find two or three traits that seem somewhat to explain it. Some of the group are platonic in their temperament—given, that is, to falling in love with ideas. And so many beautiful ideas, like justice and proportion and mercy and truth, have to be renounced and reviled in abandoning oneself to this religion, that they find it absolutely impossible. They can not tear themselves away from their loves.

Others are temperamentally solitary. They are actually lacking in gregarious impulse, or have an opposite impulse to kick out and desert whenever the herd agrees upon something. They cannot even understand patriotism, and these modern days make them not only sad, but bitter and contemptuous of men.

Others are rationalistic, and have a theory about patriotism, and their emotions are controlled by a theory. But there are not many whose emotions are controlled by a theory.

The character that is most common to those who cannot commit themselves to this religion, is the character of having already really committed themselves to something else. And this too is rare enough. Most of the people in our days of nervous modernity—busy with labor, or busy with entertainment—never heartily abandon themselves to anything. Such people welcome the orgy of nation-worship merely as a chance to feel.

I think of Mayor Mitchel, for example, as a little fox-like political man, who has stepped very carefully here and there, taking a bit, giving a bit, to this and to that—church, politics, business, society, dress. He shows very plainly that he never abandoned his soul to any purpose or any experience. But now he has—and it is doing him good. One cannot but smile in sympathy with the Mayor's boyish extravagance in this the first experience of his life. One cannot but wish him the good luck of other experiences before he dies. And he is typical of the average man and man-of-affairs. They go in for this facile religion of the fatherland, or at least they show no resistance against it, because they not only are not committed to anything else, but they never have been committed to anything. Other religions always seemed to require courage, or faith, or loneliness, or energy-of-intent; this requires only the most social and joyful abandonment of intelligent judgment and moral restraint. It is the easiest religion under the sun to feel and feel deeply, for it gives the highest quantity of satisfactions, requires no imaginative faith, and demands only at the most that physical crowd-courage which is our common heritage.

I do not believe many people will ever be led to feel unpatriotic. To argue against these tribal and egoistic instincts is like arguing against gravitation. But I do hope that a fair proportion of the intelligent may be persuaded to resist the establishment, in their own minds or in American society, of patriotism as a religion. Let them understand that to indulge and satisfy some one or two of the emotions that enter into this compound, is a very different thing from binding all these satisfactions into a fixed and rigid and monumental sentiment which will exercise absolute dictatorship in their minds. Strong minds do not need any religion. They are able to bear the responsibility and the labor of thinking and choosing among the values of life anew every morning. But even for those who must have a religion, an exposure of the extreme easiness of patriotic enthusiasm, its quality of general indulgence, might make them wish to bind themselves, if they must be bound, to some god that is more arduous and demanding of personal character. —July 1917

The Censor

One of our most esteemed contributors, George Creel, has been appointed chairman of the Board of Censorship for the war. Once George Creel wrote an article on "Rockefeller Law," which was censored by all his employers, including the most radical popular magazine in the United States. He brought it to us. We passed it. Our readers will remember. So will George Creel, we hope.

—June 1917

JOHN REED
One Solid Month of Liberty

In America the month just past has been the blackest month for free men our generation has known. With a sort of hideous apathy the country has acquiesced in a regime of judicial tyranny, bureaucratic suppression and industrial barbarism, which followed inevitably the first fine careless rapture of militarism.

Who that heard it will ever forget the feeling of despair he experienced when Judge Mayer charged the jury in the Berkman-Goldman trial:

"This is not a question of free speech," he said, "for *free speech is guaranteed under the Constitution*. No American worthy of the name believes in anything else than free speech, *but free speech*

does not mean license. . . . Free speech means that frank, free, clear and orderly expression in which every man and woman in the land, citizen or alien, may engage in *lawful and orderly fashion.* . . ."

The italics are ours. The definition is the new American definition of freedom—the freedom for which countless millions have died in the long uphill pull of civilization—which is, in effect, "freedom is the right to do what nobody in power can possibly object to."

Emma Goldman and Alexander Berkman were not convicted of the charges upon which they were ostensibly tried; they were convicted by the Assistant District Attorney's constant stress of the term "Anarchist," and by the careful definition of that term, brought out by both Judge and Prosecutor, as one who wishes wantonly to overthrow society by violence.

After conviction the prisoners were brutally hustled from the court to the trains which whirled them to their prisons, without even the customary respite granted to prisoners to settle their affairs. Moreover, not only was their bank account seized, including money belonging to other persons, but part of their bail was held up *while its sources were investigated*—ostensibly to find out if any of it belonged to the defendants, but actually with the effect of intimidating those who put up the bail. And last outrage of all, the clerk of the court claimed and took out of the amount of bail some $500 as his rightful fee!

Next in order is the wholesale suppression of the radical press by the Post Office, some eighteen periodicals, among them THE MASSES, being denounced as "unmailable" under the Espionage Act, without any specific grounds being specified.

"Because," Solicitor Lamar is reported to have said to the representative of one paper, "if I told you what we objected to, you'd manage to get around the law some way."

Now I happen to have been one of those who lost a good many pounds fighting the original censorship provision of the Espionage Bill in Washington. And we licked it, finally, in the face of the whole Administration. But what did the Administration care? It does what it pleases, and finds a law to back it up. If the entire Espionage Act had been defeated, some obscure statute passed in 1796 would have been exhumed, and the radical press suppressed just the same.

All of which goes to prove that in America law is merely the instrument for good or evil of the most powerful interest, and there are no Consti-

Drawn by Henry J. Glintenkamp, October 1917

[*This drawing was the basis for Glintenkamp's indictment under the Espionage Act. Although the editors accepted responsibility for its appearance, Floyd Dell recalls that Glintenkamp had arranged for it to be published without either his or Eastman's knowledge. Glintenkamp then fled to Mexico, leaving the other editors to face the consequences.*]

tutional safeguards worth the powder to blow them to hell.

The attack of soldiers and sailors in Boston upon the July first parade and the Socialist headquarters, which sent a thrill of rage through the heart of every lover of liberty in this country, was followed by two horrors more sinisterly suggestive.

The first was the race riot in East Saint Louis, where the large negro town was sacked and burned, and more than thirty black people, men and women, were butchered. Eye-witnesses tell how innocent negro passers-by were pursued by white men with smoking guns, who shot them down in the streets and then kicked their dead faces to jelly; how white women with streaming hair and foaming lips dragged negresses from street cars and cut them mortally in the breasts with knives.

All this of course outdoes the feeble German atrocities. It rivals the abominations of Putumayo and the Congo. The "war of civilization" begins to lose its drawing power. And the spirit of our own American soldiers in battle is beginning to appal those who know it. Read Arthur Guy Empey's *Over the Top* if you want to know how barbarians revel in sheer butchery. I met a friend who had served in the British army. I have killed eight Huns with my own hands," he boasted, "and I want to kill ten more. Greatest sport in the world." Killing niggers is, of course, also great sport.

Anent this matter, Colonel Roosevelt and Colonel Samuel Gompers had a tiff upon the platform at Carnegie Hall, where both were patronizing the Russian revolutionary mission from the standpoint of our superior democracy. Colonel Roosevelt thought that the workingmen who killed the negroes that were brought in to take away their jobs ought to be hung. Colonel Gompers seemed to think that the negroes were to blame for allowing themselves to be brought in to take the jobs. Neither of the Colonels referred to the gentlemen who had brought the negroes north in order to smash trades-unionism forever.

The second mile-stone in the history of the New Freedom was the wholesale deportation, at the point of a gun, of some hundreds of striking workingmen from the mines in Bisbee, Arizona, into the American desert. These strikers were loudly heralded as "I. W. W.'s" in an attempt to bemuse the truth; but it is slowly leaking out that the mining company deported from Bisbee all the men who were striking in an orderly fashion for decent living wages and conditions, whether I. W. W.'s or not. And not only that, but all sympathizers with the strikers, *and even the strikers' attorney!* Many of these men lived in Bisbee, owned property there; some of them were torn from the arms of their wives and children. They were loaded on cattle-cars and sent to Columbus, N. M., whose outraged citizens promptly shipped them back north, until they halted in the middle of the desert—foodless, waterless, homeless.

At the present writing the United States Army is feeding these dangerous characters, and there is talk of interning them for the balance of the war—on the ground that they have been subsidized by German gold. And in the meanwhile, the Phelps-Dodge corporation, which owns the mines—and Bisbee—is not allowing any one to enter the town without a passport!

Samuel Gompers protested to the German trades-unions against the deportation of Belgian workingmen. But even the Germans didn't deport Belgians into the middle of a desert, without food or water, as Bisbee did—and yet Gompers hasn't uttered a single peep about Bisbee.

Out in San Francisco, the bomb trials go merrily on. In spite of the exposure of Oxman, the utter contradiction and discrediting of the state's witnesses, Mooney is still going to die. Mrs. Mooney has only with the greatest difficulty been acquitted, and District Attorney Fickert asserts that the other prisoners will be vigorously prosecuted. Alexander Berkman has been indicted in the same case, and Bob Minor is threatened with indictment.

District Attorney Fickert no longer relies upon the evidence. Like Prosecutor Content, he cries, "This woman is an anarchist. Either you must destroy anarchy, or the anarchists will destroy the state!" And so the most patent frame-up ever conceived by a Chamber of Commerce to extirpate union labor goes on, and indictments rain upon all who have dared to defend the Mooneys.

This country-wide movement to wipe out organized labor, which was launched a year ago in Wall Street with such a flourish of trumpets, and which Mr. Gompers defied at Baltimore with quotations from Shakespeare, is developing quietly but powerfully. An investigation recently made in Omaha, Nebraska, by Carl Sandburg, shows the businessmen of that community organizing along the lines of San Francisco, sending out invitations to scabs everywhere, and evidently framing up something on which a union man can be railroaded to the electric chair, as they railroaded Tom Mooney on the coast.

Meanwhile, organized labor lies down and takes it—nay, in San Francisco, connives at it. Gompers is so busy running the war that he has time for nothing except to appoint upon his committees labor's bitterest enemies. I suppose that as soon as Tom Mooney and his wife are executed, Gompers will invite District Attorney Fickert to serve upon the Committee on Labor.

The suffrage pickets in front of the White House, set upon by mobs of government clerks, then by the police, arrested time and time again upon no charge, and finally committed to the workhouse for sixty days, were, as the world knows, hurriedly pardoned by the President as soon as it was evident how prominent they and their husbands were. But at the same time that he pardoned them for their "crime," he intimated that he was too busy over his "War for Democracy" to give any attention to their petition—which was a petition for the fundamental rights of citizens.

It is the blackest month for freemen our generation has known. —September 1917

The End of *The Masses*

What Happened to the August *Masses?*

1. August issue presented for mailing at New York post office, July 3d.

2. Copies of August issue forwarded to Washington for "examination." The Solicitor of the Post Office Department, the Attorney General, and Judge Advocate General Crowder, of the United States Army, conferred about excluding it from the mails and decided that this should be done.*

3. Letter received July 5th from T. G. Patten, postmaster of New York City, informing us that:

"according to advices received from the Solicitor of the Post Office Department, the August issue of The Masses is unmailable under the Act of June 15th, 1917."

4. The business manager of THE MASSES interviewed in Washington Solicitor Lamar, who refused to state what provisions of the Espionage Act the August MASSES violated, or what particular parts of the magazine violated the law. (July 6th.)

5. THE MASSES retained as counsel Gilbert E. Roe. Bill in equity to federal court, to enjoin postmaster from excluding the magazine from the mails, filed July 12th. Motion made returnable before Judge Learned Hand on July 16.

6. Hearing postponed till July 21st, the Post Office Department being unprepared.

7. Argument lasting all day, July 21st, on motion for injunction.

The Post Office Department was represented by Asst. U. S. District Attorney Barnes. He explained that the Department construed the Espionage Act as giving it power to exclude from the mails anything which might interfere with the successful conduct of the war.

Four cartoons and four pieces of text in the August issue were specified as violations of the law. The cartoons were Boardman Robinson's "Making the World Safe for Democracy," H. J. Glintenkamp's Liberty Bell and Conscription cartoons, and one by Art Young on Congress and Big Business. The Conscription cartoon was considered by the Department "the worst thing in the magazine." The text objected to was: "A Question," an editorial by Max Eastman; "A Tribute," a poem by Josephine Bell; a paragraph in an article on "Conscientious Objectors"; and an editorial, "Friends of American Freedom."

Gilbert E. Roe, on behalf of THE MASSES, urged that the Espionage Act was not intended to prohibit political criticism or discussion, and that to permit the Post Office Department to use it as cover for arbitrary acts of suppression, would be to recognize a censorship set up without warrant of law.

8. Preliminary injunction against postmaster granted by Judge Hand.

Judge Hand, in an extended decision, sustained THE MASSES' contention at all points. The construction placed by the postal authorities on the Espionage Act was shown to be invalid. The specific provisions of the law, he points out, are not violated by the magazine. Its cartoons and editorials "fall within the scope of that right to criticise, either by temperate reasoning or by immoderate

*Date of conference unknown; rumor that the Generals, in spite of pressure of war business, celebrated Independence Day by deciding to suppress *The Masses,* cannot be verified.

and indecent invective, which is normally the privilege of the individual in countries dependent upon the free expression of opinion as the ultimate source of authority." The expression of such opinion may militate against the success of the war, but Congress has not seen fit to exclude it from the mails, and only Congress has the power to do so. The pictures and text may tend to promote disaffection with the war, but they cannot be thought to counsel insubordination in the military or naval forces "without a violation of their meaning quite beyond any tolerance of understanding." The Conscription cartoon may "breed such animosity toward the Draft as will promote resistance and strengthen the determination of those disposed to be recalcitrant," but it does not tell people that it is their duty or to their interest to resist the law. The text expresses "high admiration for those who have held and are holding out for their convictions even to the extent of resisting the law." But the expression of such admiration is not a violation of the Espionage Act.

9. Formal order, requiring postmaster to transmit the August MASSES through the mails, served on District Attorney, July 25th, with notice that it would be presented to Judge Hand for signature, under the rule, the following day.

10. *United States Circuit Judge C. M. Hough signed at Windsor, Vt., an order staying execution of Judge Hand's order, and requiring parties to appear before him at Windsor, Vt., Aug. 2, to show cause why stay should not be made permanent pending an appeal which had been taken the same day by Postmaster Patten and which cannot be heard for several months.* Some one must have been waiting before Judge Hough to get his order for a stay at the very time Judge Hand had his order before him for signature. For the orders were signed the same day, and the judges were hundreds of miles apart.

That is the history of the case—so far. Our attorney will oppose the staying of Judge Hand's order. If he succeeds, you will get your August issue through the mails—unless the Department thinks of some other way to stop it. If our attorney doesn't succeed, we will have to adopt other ways and means.

We will do our best to reach you. We publish THE MASSES because you want it. THE MASSES is your property. This is your fight as much as it is ours. We are not going to quit. We do not believe you are, either. We need money to help pay expenses. We need subscriptions. We need bundle orders for the magazine for sale or distribution. You know the facts. The way in which you will help us is up to you.   —September 1917

[298]

MERRILL ROGERS
The Insolence of Office and the Law's Delay

[*Rogers was business manager of* The Masses.]

The September issue contained a chronological history of THE MASSES' fight against the Post Office up to the time of going to press. Roughly, what happened was this: The August number was presented for mailing and declared unmailable by Solicitor Lamar of the Post Office Department on the ground of violation of the Espionage Act of June 15th, 1917. Failing to get a declaration from Lamar as to the specific article or cartoon which he considered in violation of the law, injunction proceedings were entered against the Postmaster by Gilbert E. Roe, our attorney, to force the Post Office to transmit the number through the mails.

Judge Hand, who heard the case, decided the case in our favor and upheld THE MASSES on every point for which it contended. Directly, the Post Office obtained an order for a hearing on a stay of execution of the injunction, returnable before Judge Charles M. Hough, at Windsor, Vermont, several hundred miles from New York.

About that time we went to press.

The course of events since then has been so amazing as to astonish even those who are most skeptical as to justice in law and the value of constitutional rights.

In the first place, the hearing on the stay was purposely brought before one of the most reactionary and Tory judges on the bench. That was part of the game, of course. But the fact that a stay was asked indicates more clearly than anything else the tactics the Department resorted to in order to win.

A stay of execution on an injunction, it would seem, is a procedure that has long been in disuse among lawyers. Technically, it is perfectly legal, but the bar generally and the bench have recognized the immense amount of confusion that would result if one judge got into the habit of staying an injunction granted by another and have consistently refused to make use of it. Judge Hough himself admitted that in his thirty years' experience he had never known of a similar case.

In spite of this, the order for the stay was granted. This meant that our first victory was nullified; that the August MASSES could not pass through the mails until after the regular appeal on Judge Hand's decision which the Post Office will bring some time in October. For all practical purposes the Post Office had won.

In granting the stay, Judge Hough said that the only damage resulting to THE MASSES would be that connected with the August issue, and should THE MASSES win ultimately suit could easily be entered to recover what monetary loss had been sustained. In fairness to Hough it is, perhaps, right to say that he was not cognizant of the full plan which the Department had worked out to destroy us.

What came later left no doubt how ruthless was the intention of the Post Office to "get" us.

The September issue was presented for mailing in the usual way and word was sent that it would not be allowed to go through the mails until advice was received from the Solicitor at Washington. For about ten days we were unable to get any word. Gilbert Roe was in Washington and demanded of Lamar that he render a decision. Lamar told him the Department hadn't made up its mind; apparently it would take as long a time as it pleased.

Almost coincidentally, came a letter from the Department requiring us to appear in Washington, August 14th, to show cause why our second-class mailing privileges should not be taken away. The reason advanced was that we were irregular in publication and therefore not entitled to the privileges. The reasoning was simple. The August issue had not gone through the mails. Therefore, by reason of such irregularity THE MASSES had ceased to be a "newspaper or periodical within the meaning of the law." The fact that the August issue had been presented for mailing and refused; the fact that we had standing in our favor a court decision requiring the Post Office to allow the issue to go through the mails was of no consequence. The privileges were taken away.

Just previously to this, we had applied to Judge Hough to revoke his stay of Hand's injunction. We contended that the Department was making a use of the order which was never intended. Hough said that the new facts were technically immaterial and the order could not be vacated. But he remarked that the Postmaster's assigning as a reason for his second-class mailing action an omission on our part for which he was solely responsible sounded like a poor joke.

And the Post Office is going to realize some day just how poor a joke it is. We have no intention of letting up on this fight. We are absolutely confident that ultimately we are going to win—and in the process we are going to show the people the essential viciousness of bureaucracy. For the present we must ask subscribers to have patience and make use of our newsstand distribution.

—October 1917

Bunches of Justice

Here is a clipping from the Buffalo Express of July 26th:

"A United States court has decided that THE MASSES cannot legally be barred from the mails. This ought to be good, convincing evidence to Max Eastman and his kind that we have a much juster government in this country than they supposed—much juster, in fact, than they deserve."

This convincing evidence of the justice of our country lasted about six minutes. For no sooner was Judge Hand's order to the Post Office signed, than the United States District Attorney appeared with his order from a superior judge compelling us to show cause why he should not stay the execution of Judge Hand's order, pending an appeal to be argued in October. We did "show cause," namely the injustice of holding up a magazine until its monthly value was lost in order to find out whether it should be held up or not. The stay was granted, nevertheless, and Judge Hough in granting it, began his decision with the following statement:

"After considerable experience in appellate practice, and such recent inquiry as I have been able to make, no other instance (under Sec. 129, Jud. Code) of application to a Judge of the Appellate Court to stay an appealed order of this nature, is known to me."

The judicial temper of the mind of this judge, who set a precedent heretofore unheard of in our laws, is exemplified in this sentence, also quoted from his decision:

"It is at least arguable whether any constitutional government can be judicially compelled to assist in the dissemination and distribution of something which proclaims itself 'revolutionary,' which exists not to reform but to destroy the rule of any party, clique or faction that could give even lip service to the Constitution of the United States."

This sounds more to us like editorial denunciation than judicial decision. It comes as a surprise, too, because our impression was that the constitution is no longer mentioned among gentlemen. We thought THE MASSES was about the only magazine left that did care to risk its reputation by supporting that revolutionary document.

Following this "stay of execution" we received

a note from Mr. Burleson inviting us to come to Washington and show cause why our second-class mailing privilege should not be revoked because we have not mailed the magazine regularly. We went to Washington and "showed cause"—namely, that we have not mailed it regularly because the Post Office itself secured this stay of execution which privileged them to refuse to allow us to mail it, pending an appeal to a higher court, which shall determine whether they have to allow us to mail it or not.

This did not seem to Mr. Burleson a sufficient cause for acting with justice, or even with the courtesy of a gentleman in a controversy, and although he had studied the September issue and evidently decided that he could not lawfully exclude that from the mails, he has revoked our whole mailing privilege because the August issue, by order of the Court upon request of the Post Office, was *temporarily* excluded *pending an appeal*.

I commend these facts to the Buffalo Express for further comment. —October 1917

The Policy of *The Masses*

An Editor's Reflections
by Max Eastman

WHEN I was asked to write an "afterword" for this anthology I said "Sure!" with gay confidence. I hadn't a doubt that all sorts of comments and anecdotes of the old *Masses* days would occur to me when I sat down to write. And indeed they have. But it turns out that all of them, every single one that has contemporary interest, have already been written and published in one or the other of my two volumes of memoirs. In *Enjoyment of Living* I described how *The Masses* got started, and in *Love and Revolution* how it got stopped. In the by-going I gave a life-sketch of all the editors and contributing editors who are still renowned—or ought to be. There is little I can add. But there is a chapter in *Enjoyment of Living* called "The Policy of *The Masses*," which I think will interest people who share in any degree the generous opinions William O'Neill has expressed about the magazine. It will only add a footnote to his excellent introductions, for he has an expert knowledge of the history of the period and a trained gift for reliving history. But a footnote by one who actually lived this bit of history is perhaps just what he meant by an "afterword."

Here, at any rate (with the permission of Harper and Row), are a few of my reflections on the policy of *The Masses*, written thirty years after the government arrested us and put us out of business:

For me the magazine had one plainly evident superiority, a clean and clear make-up. My contempt for the crazy clutter of type and pictures that is considered "popular" by American magazine editors was enthusiastically shared by *The Masses*' artists. We all liked plenty of space. We wanted each object, whether art or literature, presented as a unit, in adequate isolation, unpecked at by editorial sales talk. We wanted the text to read consecutively as a work of art should, not be chopped up and employed as a lure to jump the reader over into advertising pages at the back. The only clash between me and those artists, and that a brief one, concerned the importance of size in reproducing pictures. The generous dimensions of the drawings in *The Masses*, a notable innovation in American magazinedom, was due entirely to them. I merely yielded to their arguments—and raised the extra money required.

Another feature I can not take credit for was the dominantly realist note in text and pictures. *The Masses* marked, I have been told, the first appearance of "realism" in an American magazine. But I was ignorant of, and indifferent to, schools of art and literature. Of the new movement in art represented by Sloan, Bellows, and the other pupils of Robert Henri, I had never heard. My theories of poetry did, to be sure, assert the kinship of its defining values with those of real experience, but rather as a scientific fact than a contemporary enthusiasm. They fitted me to preside with sympathy over an outburst of dirt and dreariness in realms before consecrated to sweetness and light. But I can not say that I had any tendency of my own to disparage reality as a means of demonstrating my interest in it. Indeed, I think I exercised a moderating influence upon this not wholly rational factor in the realist enthusiasm. I tried to qualify with an occasional happy color that triumphal flaunting of the sordid for which *The Masses* became rapidly and quite justly famous.

The long-time result of our pictorial revolt, it seems to me, was to introduce into commercial journalism some of the subtler values of creative art. This change, at least, did take place, and *The Masses* led the way. Norman Hapgood saw it coming and when he took over the editorship of *Harper's Weekly* deliberately set out to imitate our pictures, employing our artists to produce them. The public was not ready, and he himself lacked experience or the instinct for it. We used to smile at him because he would pay big fees for photographs of paintings which the artists were only too eager to give away. America was then still provincial in these matters. But in 1925 *The New Yorker* found it natural to do what Norman Hapgood had awkwardly strained after, and the pictorial revolution for which *The Masses* artists worked without pay turned out to be one of the most profitable innovations in the history of journalism. At least that is my view, and I take no credit for this innovation except as a willing pupil. The central force in putting it through was John Sloan, and I consider my aesthetic development under his guidance one of the lucky turns in my very accidental education.

In ideological matters I was rather automatically in control, and I don't remember any disputes about my changing the policy from extreme right to extreme left socialism. In the number of June 1913 —to take a typical example—we endorsed the general strike in Belgium, supported the I.W.W. strike which we called "the war in Paterson," backed Karl Liebknecht's fight against the social democratic majority in the German Reichstag, affirmed that the so-called "bandits of Mexico" were the real patriots of the country, satirized the "fifty-seven varieties of national religion," ridiculed an Old Testament story, and featured a lyric by a striking Paint Creek miner longing, in anything but pure poetry, for the coming of the spring:

> I will not watch the floating clouds that hover
> Above the birds that warble on the wing;
> I want to use this GUN from under cover—
> Oh Buddy, how I'm longing for the spring.

At the same time, in the brief fourteen pages of that number, there were five jokes without social significance, two merely humorous drawings, a piece of fanciful fiction, a lithograph by George Bellows of happy children playing in Central Park, and an unsigned lyric by the editor entitled "June Morning":

> De sun am shinin' bright,
> Am fillin' me full ob light;
> Ah done git up ea'ly,
> An' wash mahse'f mo' thor'ly.

It is this catholicity of *The Masses,* its freedom from the one-track mental habit of the rabid devotee of a cause, for which I as editor was most responsible. I never could see why people with a zeal for improving life should be indifferent to the living of it. Why cannot one be young-hearted, gay, laughing, audacious, full of animal spirits, and yet also use his brains? The everlasting cerebral attitude of such papers as *The Nation* and *The New Republic,* the steady, unbillowy, unjoy-disturbed throbbing of grey matter in their pages, makes me, after some months, a little dogsick. And yet on the other hand I hate and always did hate smart-alecky and irresponsible leftism. This posture of mind was, I think, my chief contribution to *The Masses.*

My theory that art is in general essence, whatever practical functions it may take on, a technique for arresting the onward stream of action and damming up a deeper pool of consciousness, was already made clear in *Enjoyment of Poetry*. I was reading the proofs of that book while we were starting *The Masses*. Naturally then, as editor, I did not harp incessantly on propaganda. I tried to have plenty of things in every number which had nothing to do with socialism, and some whose values were wholly comprised in themselves—some items, if you will, of art for art's sake.

Aside from enhancing life, that seems to me the wisest way to conduct propaganda. The cherished idea is there, and it is there in clear and honest form. But it is not so drummed upon that only those already interested will listen. Loyalty to principle takes the place of zealotry, and enlightenment that of indoctrination.

Another thing that gave *The Masses* a special flavor was my steady objection to dogma and insistence on experimental thinking. In our second number John Sloan and I took a stand (in editorial and cartoon) on the chief issue then agitating the socialist movement, that between "political action" and "direct action."

"Now one and now the other is more important," I insisted. "All these questions of method are to be answered differently at different times, at different places, in different circumstances. . . . The one thing continually important is that we keep our judgment free. Tie up to no dogma whatever."

Later Art Young drew a picture of a complacent cherub carrying a tiny pail of water dipped from the "Ocean of Truth." The pail was marked "Dogma," and my editorial read:

"I publish this little picture in answer to numberless correspondents who 'want to know just what this magazine is trying to do.' It is trying *not* to try to empty the ocean, for one thing. And in a propaganda paper that alone is a task."

This freedom from dogma enabled us to join independently in the struggle for racial equality and woman's rights, for intelligent sex relations, above all (and beneath all) for birth and population control. Socialist dogma declared that all these problems would be solved when the economy of capitalism was replaced by a cooperative commonwealth. I was convinced to the contrary.

"Some future age looking back will be horrified at our unconscious subjection to a money power, and those looking back will be unconscious under the tyranny of some other power," I wrote in my notebook.

A basic political trait of *The Masses* was its emphasis on liberty as the goal of the class struggle. The socialist doctrine appeals to three major motives: the love of liberty, the yearning for brotherhood or human solidarity, and the wish to plan and organize things in a rational manner. There is also the religious motive, the desire of God's orphans to believe in something beyond reality. Socialists differ profoundly according as one or the other of these passions stands in the center of their motive-pattern, and all four were doubtless represented in the old "*Masses* crowd." But I think most of the contributing editors shared my dominant interest in human freedom. So far, at any rate, as I shaped its policy, the guiding ideal of the magazine was that every individual should be made free to live and grow in his own chosen way. That was what I hoped might be achieved with all this distasteful palaver about politics and economics. Even if it cannot be achieved, I would say to myself, the good life consists in striving towards it. As my notebook of those days declares: "I can bear the prospect that the world may never be free, but I can not bear the prospect of my living in it and not taking part in the fight for freedom."

William L. O'Neill is Professor of History at Rutgers University. His books include *Divorce in the Progressive Era; Everyone Was Brave: The Rise and Fall of Feminism in America; Coming Apart: An Informal History of America in the 1960s; The Last Romantic: A Life of Max Eastman; A Better World: The Great Schism—Stalinism and the American Intellectuals;* and *American High: The Years of Confidence, 1945–1960.*